Caldwell's Homestead

Havoc in Wyoming

Part 1: Caldwell's Homestead

Millie Copper

This is a work of fiction. All characters, places, and incidents are products of the author's imagination or are used fictitiously. Any resemblance to actual people, places, or events is entirely coincidental.

Technical information in the book is included to convey realism. The author shall assume no liability or responsibility to any person or entity with respond to any loss or damage caused, or allegedly caused, directly or indirectly by information contained in this book of fiction. Any reference to registered or trademarked brands is used simply to convey familiarity. This manuscript is in no way sponsored or endorsed by any brand mentioned.

ISBN-13: 978-1-7327482-3-1

Written by Millie Copper

Edited by Ameryn Tucker

Proofread by Light Hand Proofreading

Cover design by Dauntless Cover Design

Original cover design by Kesandra Adams

Also by Millie Copper

Now Available

Havoc in Wyoming: Part 2, Katie's Journey

Havoc in Wyoming: Part 3, Mollie's Quest

Havoc Begins: A Havoc in Wyoming Story (Part 3.5)

Havoc in Wyoming: Part 4, Shields and Ramparts

Havoc in Wyoming: Part 5, Fowler's Snare

Havoc Rises: A Havoc in Wyoming Story (Part 5.5)

Havoc in Wyoming: Part 6, Pestilence in the Darkness

Havoc in Wyoming: Part 6, Pestilence in the Darkness

Christmas on the Mountain: A Havoc in Wyoming Novella

Havoc in Wyoming: Part 7, My Refuge and Fortress

Stretchy Beans: Nutritious, Economical Meals the Easy Ways

Stock the Real Food Pantry: A Handbook for Making the Most of Your Pantry

Design a Dish: Save Your Food Dollars

Real Food Hits the Road: Budget Friendly Tips, Ideas, and Recipes for Enjoying Real Food Away from Home

Join My Reader's Club!

Receive a complimentary copy of Wyoming Refuge: A Havoc in Wyoming Prequel. As part of my reader's club, you'll be the first to know about new releases and specials. I also share info on books I'm reading, preparedness tips, and more. Please sign up on my website: MillieCopper.com

Who's Who

Jake Caldwell: A bachelor until age thirty-seven, he married Mollie and suddenly became a dad to four girls. A couple of years later they added a son. Jake juggles work, a farm, and family life—sometimes it's a struggle.

Mollie Caldwell: Wife to Jake and mom to Sarah, Angela, Calley, Katie, and Malcolm. With a full-time work-from-home job, homeschooling, and their small farm, she keeps busy. A few times a year she works out of state for a week. This is one of those weeks.

Malcolm Caldwell: Jake and Mollie's youngest child. He's *almost* eleven and is Jake's right-hand man. He's the only child still living at home.

Doris and Evan Snyder: Neighbors and good friends of the Caldwells. Evan is a retired deputy sheriff, having been part of the county's Specialized Services Division. Doris is retired from both the Navy and a government job. She insists she wasn't a spy or anything, but she doesn't talk about the work she used to do.

Tate Garrett: Husband to Sarah, Mollie and Jake's oldest daughter. They used to live in Oregon but have recently moved only two hours away, practically neighbors by Wyoming standards. Tate's parents, Keith and Lois, and his sister, Karen, are visiting from out of state.

Alvin and Dodie Caldwell: Jake's parents. They are both in their seventies and fiercely independent. They live in the nearby town of Prospect.

Robert, Theresa, Michelle, and Ashley Caldwell: Jake's brother and his family living in California. Michelle and Ashley are the same age as Calley and Katie.

David, Betty, Noah, and Andrew Hammer: Neighbors and friends of the Caldwells. The Hammers are Texas natives recently transplanted to Wyoming. They love the cooler weather and wide-open spaces. David and Betty are both retired. Noah is sixteen and Andrew is in his early twenties. Two more adult children live in Texas with their spouses and a grandbaby. Their oldest son lives back east.

The MacIntyre Family: Alex and Natalie, along with their children, teach permaculture and homesteading immersion classes. Their classes are a great way to learn the ins and outs of farm life. They have many skills and abilities for living off the land.

Dan Morse: The community bully. He tends to make a show of knowing it all. Evan calls Dan "an imbecile who lacks a shred of common sense."

Chapter 1

Jake
Thursday, Day 1

"Hold her leg," Malcolm says in a calm, steely voice.

I adjust my grip to keep her from pulling away. She fights back. Her left leg almost slips out of my hand as she gives a powerful kick. She lets out a shriek as if we're killing her.

"Enough of that, now," Malcolm smoothly tells her. "You're going to be just fine. It's not like this is your first time."

She doesn't believe him and, as if to make a point, folds up her legs and completely collapses. I lift her back up so Malcolm can finish the task at hand.

Man, am I glad my wife will be home tomorrow; she's getting a talking to about this crazy goat. Milking usually falls to Mollie.

At least she trained our son how to take care of it before she went on her work trip—all I have to do is help. With my big clumsy hands, Nigerian Dwarf goats are way too small for me to milk. At ten years old, Malcolm still has small hands, making it fairly easy for him.

With my job as a school custodian, I always have the summer off but usually pick up a summer-only, temporary job with the school district. This year, thanks to budget cuts, the temp jobs are gone.

So Malcolm and I are holding down the fort—well, the farm anyway. In addition to goats, we have a good-sized garden, which seems to get larger every year, as well as assorted small livestock, trees, and vines. The thirty-acre parcel was bare ground when we bought it, just a few years ago, lacking everything except sagebrush, cactus, wild rabbits, and the occasional rattlesnake.

It has definitely been a labor of love bringing it to the place it is today, with a whole lot more love needed to get it where we want it.

Unfortunately, my love for our land has been waning. Not the land, necessarily, but all the work that goes along with having a farm. Lately, I find myself wanting to throw in the towel on the whole mess, sell all the animals, let the weeds take over the garden, and allow the vines and trees to wither and die. Working full time, farming, and trying to keep my marriage together has been a challenge.

Since I'm not working a paid job this summer, we agreed I'd spend my time focusing on the half-done projects looming on the farm, repairing things needing repaired, and playing full-time farmer. Essentially, the traditional honey-do list. Yeah, I participated in putting this list together, but most of the items on it were at Mollie's suggestion.

While the day-to-day essential items to keep our farmstead going take some time—feeding the goats, chickens, ducks, sheep, and pigs plus watering the gardens and orchards—they are easy to do. It's the other things that fall by the wayside.

It wasn't always like this. But then, with a phone call, everything changed.

"Dad, I'm done with her. You can let go." Malcolm's voice, carrying a hint of annoyance, brings me back to the present.

I let go of the crazy goat's leg, and, as if by magic, the goat's disposition immediately changes. She looks around, and I swear she winks at me as if to say, *Take that.*

Mollie has names for all the goats. I can't remember most of them, but I'm thinking of several names for this one right now, none of which would impress Mollie. Did I mention how much I'm looking forward to my wife returning home?

I take a deep breath. Even though the job of a farmer may not be for me, I do love living here. The views are breathtaking. The neighbors are fantastic. And it's peaceful. Tucked away on the edge of the wilderness, it's the kind of place a person can really get away. The lazy river, in view from our milking shed—well, not the water but the trees lining the river—provides a great place to spend an afternoon, with a fishing pole in hand.

Bakerville, Wyoming. Peaceful. Quiet. Safe.

Chapter 2

Malcolm

Milking goats isn't my idea of fun. They're very cute, especially the babies. But they smell bad, and I don't really like having to get so close to them. Most of the time, Mom works from home and is the one in charge of the goats. When she first "suggested" I be in charge of the milking while she worked in Oregon, I wasn't happy about it. Even though she presented it as a question— "Malcolm, how do you feel about helping with the milking this summer?" —I knew it wasn't an *actual* question.

"Hmmm. I think I feel . . . neutral. I don't want to get kicked or head butted, but . . . maybe. I'm really a quarter below neutral. I'd rather not have to milk, but I'll do it. Do you think it's time I learn to milk? I guess it's fair. Since I drink so much of it, I should have to get it out of the old girls."

Mom gave me a weird look, then started laughing. "You definitely have a way with words, Malcolm. A quarter below neutral, huh? When I'm in Oregon next month, it'd be great if you could be in charge of the milking. Your hands are a better fit than your dad's. He'll help by holding their legs so you don't get kicked, just like you help me with the wilder ones. And you can't get head butted while they're in the milk stand since the head is secured."

"Oh, yeah. I guess that's a good point. I've only been butted by the babies before anyway, and only because we were playing. I guess I'm not really worried about the head butting. You think Dad will hold on good? I know sometimes they kick pretty hard and I can't hold on very good."

"Well."

"What?"

"You can't hold on very well. Yes, I think he'll do fine."

"Oh . . . yeah. I can't hold on very *well.* I forgot about using well and not good. Even though good makes more sense to me. Okay, I'll learn how to milk." I did a good job not sighing when I said that. Or did I do a well job? I'm not sure. Good sounds better, but—anyway, I didn't *really* want to learn how to milk.

"Thank you, Malcolm. That'll be a big help. We'll start tomorrow morning with teaching on what to do. You'll be a master before I have to leave."

"Only Sheba, right? She's the only goat we're milking?"

"Right now. On Friday, Miss Priss will be ready. Her babies will be two weeks old and ready to share."

"You think she'll be better this year than she was last year? Remember, Mom? She's the one I kept having to hold on to for you. Still, she'd kick over the milk container."

"Yep, I do remember. I'm not sure how she'll be. She's kind of a wild thing but is super easy to milk. You'll see. The milk comes out fast, so you just have to hang on for the ride. Now we need to get started with schoolwork. What do you think? Math first?"

"I'm about 50 percent neutral on math. No, make that 0 percent. How about we skip math and listen to a story while playing with a LEGO set?"

"Nice try, Malcolm. How about we do math, read aloud, spelling, science, and finish up our unit study on Ancient Egypt. Then we can talk about a story and LEGO blocks."

"I guess . . . "

So that's how I became the milker man.

This morning, we started the chores early so we could pick up baby chicks from the post office—another bunch to add to those we're already raising.

It's a pretty long drive to Wesley, over half an hour, and I slept all the way there. I wanted to sleep on the way back, but all those chicks were very noisy and made too much racket for me to sleep. When we got back home, we put the chicks in their brooder, finished the chores, and did the milking.

After breakfast, Dad starts washing the dishes. "Hey, Malcolm, will you go let the old goats out? Then meet me in the yard so we can get a few things done there."

"Sure, Dad, be right back." I run to the goat pens.

"C'mon, mama goats. You guys eat some weeds or something. And stay away from the hay bales. Oh no, no you don't, little guys." I throw up my knee and keep the baby goats from escaping. "Your moms get to go out because they know to come back when I shake the food container. You guys aren't that smart yet. I'll end up chasing and tackling you guys. I've done that before, and it wasn't very fun. Well . . . it was kind of fun, but I don't want to do it again."

Our two little dogs are in the yard with Dad. Scooter is running all around trying to get Penny to play with him. Penny is a pretty old dog and doesn't really like to play. One of our cats, King Triton, is sitting on top of the fence giving the dogs a funny look.

"Hey, Dad, the goats are out. That little brown boy goat tried to get past me, but I didn't let him. Did you hear him cry when he couldn't go with his mom?"

"I didn't hear him, but it's good you kept him from getting out. I can tell by looking at him he's trouble, just like his mom."

"You need help with the watering?"

"Nope. I've got it going, Buddy."

Dad calls me *Buddy* a lot. Mom usually calls me by my real name, Malcolm. I'm not sure which name I like better. I know Dad calls me Buddy because I'm his Little Buddy. I'm glad he dropped the little part. I'm almost eleven and not so little. Anyway, I'll be eleven in December—which is pretty soon.

When I was just a kid, I thought maybe we could change my name to Lloyd after my favorite character from LEGO NINJAGO. Lloyd was the Green Ninja before he became the Golden Ninja, also called the Elemental Master of Energy. Green is my favorite color, and I really like Lloyd's hair. I wish my hair could look like his, golden and smooth.

But nooo. My hair is dirty dishwater blond—I learned about that color on a video, and it definitely fits my hair. Mom says it's dark blond and will probably turn full brown as I get older, just like hers.

While I have Mom's hair color and the same green eyes she has, I got my dad's hair texture. It's kind of rough, not smooth like Lloyd's. I'd like to have my hair longer, but as soon as it starts growing longer, it poofs out funny. Mom says it grows like the hair on a buffalo. Dad calls it a wool cap. When I'm older, I'm going to not cut it and just let it grow and see what it looks like. Maybe it'd be smooth like Lloyd's if it was longer.

One thing Lloyd and I do have in common: we're both kind of short. Of course, he's made of LEGO bricks, so that's probably why he's so short. My mom is short, so maybe that's why I'm short. Dad says I'll probably spurt up—that's the word he used—when I'm around fourteen. He says that's when he got so tall. My uncle Robert, Dad's brother, is even taller than Dad. I'd like to be as tall as he is.

My sister Calley taught me about Lloyd and NINJAGO. She and I are a lot alike. We both like cartoons and video games. She loves NINJAGO, Pokémon, Avatar, and Disney movies—just like me.

Calley is old and married now. She married Mike last year. For the third time, I was the ring bearer. My first ring bearer job was when my oldest sister, Sarah, married Tate. The wedding was kind of nice. I don't really remember much . . . I was pretty young, maybe six?

Angela, another one of my sisters, got married too. Her husband is Tim. They were married during the summer at a lake. I wore shorts and flip-flops. I don't think that's the right clothes for a ring bearer to wear, but Tim and my dad were also wearing shorts and flip-flops, so I guess it was okay.

I wore pants, a tie, and a vest to the other weddings. Mom wore a dress to each of the weddings, and all of my sisters wore dresses too. I think girls just like to get dressed up. Angela and Tim have been married awhile now, and I even have a nephew, Gavin.

I have one more sister, Katie. She's not married. And by the time she gets married, I'll be too old to carry the rings. I think ten should be the cutoff age. Hmmm . . . maybe I'll ask her to hurry up and get married. I think she has a boyfriend. I heard Mom and Dad talking about him. His name is Leo, but we haven't met him. Katie lives very far away while she's in college. Mom made me find where she lives on a map once, but I can't remember where it is now. Somewhere in the middle. We're kind of in the middle, too, but she's more in the middle.

"You ready to get a move on it?" Dad asks.

"What are we doing first today?"

"I'm going to fix the door on the brooder coop. I noticed it was hanging a little weird this morning when we put the chicks in. That won't take long. Then I need to repair a spot the boy goats opened up on their house. After that, we'll go get wood. Sound like a plan?"

"More wood? Jeez, Dad. We've got so much wood this week. Where are we going today?"

"To the national forest."

"Bummer. I was hoping we'd just go to the reservoir. We were just up in the forest on Sunday. Going there takes *allllll* day. And Mom isn't here to help. Don't you think it'd be best if we waited for her to come home so she can stack the wood in the truck? That'd be better."

"Nice try, Buddy. Nope, I want to get as much wood as we can this week. You and I can handle it. We'll take the small utility trailer with us today."

"*Daaaad,* that really will take all day. We have to fill the truck *and* the trailer?"

"Yep, just like Sunday. And it didn't take all day, only a few hours. I'll bring us lunch. Today's load, and probably two more, will give us most of what we need for winter."

"Okay, so I guess we have to go to the forest today?"

"That's the plan."

"Fine, but I'm not excited about it."

"It won't be too bad," Dad says, tweaking my nose. "We'll get our wood gathering done, then we can have time to do fun things later in the summer."

"Okay, Dad. I guess we can go get wood today."

"I'm glad you approve," he says with a laugh. "Let's go work on the brooder coop."

"Okay. Mom will be home tomorrow night?"

"Yep. It's going to be a late night for you. She's not in until almost midnight."

"So . . . I guess I'll have to start doing school again?"

"Probably on Monday."

I'm glad Mom is coming home soon, but I'm really not looking forward to starting school again.

Chapter 3

Jake

It's getting to be about that time again—haircut time. Mollie does this for me with the hair clippers. Before we were married, I paid for haircuts. Partly because of the lady who did the cuts. Yeah, she was something. Always super friendly and not bad to look at. Not bad at all.

Now, I'm way too cheap to pay the fifteen to twenty bucks. Besides, Mollie's cuts turn out just as good, and she's even better looking than the other lady. I take a gander in the mirror and notice my hair is grayer than the last time I checked. With it longer, it almost looks like a gray halo. Yikes.

At fifty-one, I suppose a little gray is to be expected. Should I use one of those hair color for men things? Nah . . . can't quite bring myself to do it.

While I try hard to keep myself fit and not looking fifty-one, hair dye just seems like more than I want to deal with. I'll stick with keeping my body in shape. Not always an easy task.

I suck in my gut. Have I put on a few pounds? I need to go for a jog. There's a 5K over the Fourth of July, and I have a goal to come in under thirty-five minutes. Yeah, a slow jog for most, but it works well for me.

This week, with the busyness of our days, jogging has slipped by the wayside. Malcolm and I went to our Yongmudo class, a Korean martial art practice we started taking as a family last fall, but other than that and chopping wood . . . I sigh. I need to get in a good run. I'll do it tomorrow morning.

Just one more night. One more night of sleeping alone. A few months ago, I would've been happy to sleep alone every night. Now, not so much.

A short while later, I finish tidying up the kitchen while Malcolm is listening to the radio and working on an art project in the loft.

"Overnight tonight, around or before midnight, we will see areas of scattered thunderstorms impacting the northern counties of the state."

Scattered thunderstorms are pretty common this time of year. Scattered is the key word; we never know if the storms will reach us or not. Many times, there will be rain a mile or less away, and we'll remain dry as a bone. That said, we have had a decent amount of moisture this spring. With the limited amount of annual precipitation, we're always happy for rain, and I'm hopeful it will reach us tonight. But not so much I can't jog in the morning.

Earlier, I checked all the rain barrels and drained some of the fuller ones into a portable barrel kept on a small trailer. The Quadrunner makes moving the barrel wherever the water is needed a breeze. In the high desert, water is a precious commodity, so we try to get the most use out of it as we can.

"It's just about bedtime."

"Five more minutes, Dad? I'm finishing up a drawing I'm working on. And we're going to read tonight, right?"

"Of course, don't we read every night?"

"Yeah, I was just making sure. I really want to find out what happens with the kid in the story. You think we'll finish the book tonight?"

"Nah, don't think so. There's still several chapters. Maybe, one of these nights, you should read a little to me, then I won't get so tired reading."

"No way. Mom makes me read out loud during school. When you read to me, it's not schooltime."

I have to laugh at his logic. Since he was a baby, I've read to him almost every night at bedtime. It's a tradition both of us love.

The music on the radio stops midsong.

"We have just received reports of three plane crashes. Planes landing at JFK in New York, Los Angeles International, and Chicago O'Hare have all crashed while trying to land. It is unknown if there are any survivors. It is unknown if these crashes are related, but considering they've happened within minutes of each other, there's suspicion of terrorism. We'll interrupt again as we have more information."

The music starts up again. I run upstairs to our loft and turn on the TV. Connected only to rabbit ears, we get a whopping three channels.

NBC is talking about the crash. Malcolm has turned off the radio and is beside me.

"Dad, what does this mean?"

"I'm not sure yet, Buddy. Let's watch for a minute and see."

"At this moment, we know three airplanes crashed at three different airports while attempting to land. There is speculation these are related events, but we do not yet have confirmation of this. Again, planes landing at JFK, LAX, and O'Hare have crashed while attempting to land."

The newscaster suddenly has an odd, panicked look to his face as he puts his hand up to his ear.

"Folks, we're receiving reports of a fourth crash at Dallas/Fort Worth. Repeat, we have unconfirmed reports of a fourth plane crash while attempting to land at DFW."

Need to call Mollie. Straight to voicemail. No surprise. When she's in Oregon for work, she stays at her boss's house, in their guest room, and the reception is terrible.

I send her a text. Several minutes later, she texts back—she's trying to call, but it won't connect. Is this our usual reception problem, or is everyone else in America trying to call at the same time?

We text back and forth about the crashes. It seems we know about the same amount: the planes appear to have been shot down while attempting to land, likely with some type of surface-to-air missile.

"At this time, all flights are being grounded. Those in the air are being diverted to the nearest smaller airport. They are trying to avoid larger airports since the four affected are some of the busiest in the US. There may be a relation, and these large, busy airports might be targeted."

Ya think? Seems pretty likely. The grounding is too late; they announce a fifth crash in Miami.

Malcolm and I are now wide awake. He asks questions I can't really answer: How many people have died? Will more planes crash? Who did this? When will Mom be home?

A new message from Mollie. She's going to her bedroom and will try to call again once she's up in the room, the best place for reception. I really wish Ben and Clarice had a landline so I could reach her. We have a landline . . . will it get through? If she texts again saying she can't get through, I'm going to try it.

The news comes back abruptly from a commercial. Looking at the announcer's face, I assume there has been another crash. Nope.

"We have received reports of numerous explosions going off in New York near JFK. I repeat, multiple bombs have just gone off near JFK Airport."

Malcolm hears about the explosions. I can see by his face he's trying not to cry. I wonder if my face looks the same, and I suspect it does. I feel like crying too. Part of me wants to turn off the TV and go to bed, assuming all will be well in the morning. I remember having this feeling all those years ago, when the second plane hit the World Trade Center.

"We expect the president to speak in a few minutes. We'll cut to him at that time."

I try to call Mollie. What? It's actually ringing? Almost a miracle. I'm so happy to hear her voice. She knows about the bombs and the president preparing to speak.

"With my plane canceled, I wonder how long they'll remain grounded if it's missiles being shot. How can you defend against that?"

"I have no idea. I think you should keep the rental car and drive home tomorrow. I don't like you being there with all of this going on. I'm glad you took the suitcase, the get-home bag, with you before. You may need it. I'm calling Doris after we hang up to see if Malcolm can stay with her while I run into town. I'm going with *Plan A*."

"It's a good idea," Mollie stammers. "What about the children? Katie is so far from home."

"I think we should encourage them to do their own *Plan A*. I feel like these are simply terrorist attacks as opposed to our country being under attack, you know? What do you think?"

"That's how I feel. But with Katie being so far away, she'd have a super hard time getting home if things get bad quick. That scares me. I'm so glad Sarah and Tate live nearby now. Angela, Tim, and Gavin would have a long trip if they had to walk, but they could do it. I know Calley says she'll stay at her home and band together with Mike's family. You know how I feel about that . . . I just wish she was still a little girl and I could tell her what to do. Suggest they enact *Plan A*, yeah . . . I guess that's all we can do."

Plan A is an alert we've devised when discussing possible scenarios to things which could happen. We use this alert for times when our paranoia takes over and we think there could be an "event" in the near future. Several years ago, when we were still living on the West Coast, a large storm knocked out our power, downed many trees, and generally made a mess of our area. Gas stations and businesses were closed, the grocery store was barely operating, and even the bank was shut tight. The storm was an eye opener for us.

Mollie started researching things to better prepare us if there was a similar storm in the future. One thing led to another, and we soon realized the United States, as well as the rest of the world, had some seriously scary issues going on. That's when we really started paying attention. We became what people commonly, and not always kindly, refer to as "preppers."

Over the past few years, we've put provisions in place—relocating, starting a small homestead, adding guest housing, stockpiling, and much more—to provide a safe place, a retreat, for our family and extended family.

We've decided, if we can, we'll use our *Plan A* alert for any last-minute preps we feel are needed. It's a little dangerous because, if we have concerns something serious is imminent, we don't want to be away from home. On the flip side, if we can get a little more "stuff" which can make a difference, we feel we should. Us preppers like our stuff.

A few months ago, we put bug-out bags together for each of our adult children, their spouses, and our grandson with essentials to help them reach our home. Our procedure for *Plan A* was detailed as part of these bags.

"Yes, uh, can you do the thing where you text them all at the same time? Just suggest to implement *Plan A*. Don't push them too much. Tread easy, Mollie."

"Jake. I'm well aware of the need to tread easy. I think I know them pretty well. And, yes, I know they aren't fully onboard with all our . . . plans . . . especially Calley. I can handle this."

Oops. "Sorry, honey. I know you can handle it. And, honestly, it's better for you to be the one sending the text. Besides, I can never remember how to do that group thing you do." I try to break the tension with a laugh, but it falls short. "I know what you mean about Calley. You raised her to be an independent person. She'll do what she feels is best, with Mike's input. You can't blame Mike for wanting to stay with his folks. He knows they're all welcome here, but this will be a last resort for them."

Mollie says nothing, and I wonder if we've been disconnected. Maybe she hung up on me. "Are you still there?"

"Yes. I'm here. Just thinking. It's just so . . . cliché."

"What is?" I ask, not understanding. "The plane crashes? The explosions?"

"You know, this . . . I can't even tell you how many end-of-the-world books I've read where the husband and wife are apart when the trouble happens. It's such a tired story line."

Oh, not what I was thinking of. "Uh-huh, only this isn't one of those books. This is really happening."

"Uh . . . right. I know that. It's just so beyond my belief it *is* happening. And I know we discussed it could, and we made provisions and plans for it, but . . . I never really thought . . . I mean, seriously, Jake. I'm gone so rarely the odds should've been I'd be at home."

"We can't control things like this. Sure, the timing is terrible, but it has happened."

She's quiet, but there's a slight sniffle. Is she crying?

"Mollie, honey, let's pray." Praying aloud isn't something I'm very comfortable with. I can pray silently, no problem, but once I try to get the words out everything kind of falters. Our marriage counselor gave me lots of guidance on praying out loud and encouragement in leading my family to be strong in Christ. Oh, I know it's not popular in today's circles for the husband to be the head of the house. And believe me, we still struggle with it, but I'm doing my best to take the lead. That said, Mollie is no wallflower. We're a team.

"Yes, let's pray."

I clear my throat and begin, "Our Heavenly Father, we come to You tonight with heavy hearts. We're . . . shocked over these events—the planes, which have been purposefully crashed, and now the explosions. Please be with the families who have experienced loss tonight. Let them feel Your comfort. I ask You to be with Mollie and bring her home to us quickly and safely. And be with our daughters, to keep them away from harm. If it's Your will, Lord, please use this tragedy to fully open their hearts to You. Please give Malcolm and me strength while we wait for Mollie to return. It's hard for me to agree to sit idly by and not rush to her rescue. I'll need Your help with this, Lord. We pray these things in Jesus' holy name, amen."

Mollie and I have an agreement. If one of us is home and the other is gone when a world-altering crisis occurs, the person at home stays home—no going searching for the other one. With Mollie in Oregon, it's up to her to get home. And, of course, right now, it's ridiculous to think she can't just drive home and be here as early as the day after tomorrow. But part of me thinks I need to go and get her—bring her home and make sure she's safe.

Mollie sniffles again. "Thank you. I love you, Jake. I'm going to go watch the news for a bit. Stay in touch as best you can. And kiss Malcolm for me."

Chapter 4

Jake

"Hello?"

"Doris? It's Jake. Have you seen the news?"

"No, I'm working in my craft room. Evan has gone to bed, and the TV's off. What's going on?"

"There have been five plane crashes and now an explosion in New York where one of the crashes happened." Her TV is now in the background.

"Oh no," Doris says with a cry.

"Can you watch Malcolm for me? I want to run into SuperMart and grab a few things. I'd take him with me, but with what's happening . . . ." I let my voice trail off for her to fill in the blanks. We suspect Evan and Doris Snyder, our neighbors, are pretty much on the same wavelength as us. Mollie and her both read the same type of books and discuss them. *One Second After* is one they often reference. I haven't read it but know of it from Mollie. They'll be talking about who knows what and one of them will say, "As long as it's not *One Second After,*" or something like that.

"Of course. Bring him up. You'd best hurry, I think the store closes at midnight."

Malcolm has his boots on and is ready to go. I grab my keys and consider whether I need to take my sidearm. I don't carry in my daily life.

I work at a school, and while Wyoming enacted the School Safety and Security Act in 2017, which allows local school boards to decide if district employees can conceal carry in school buildings, my district has yet to make a determination. We still follow the Gun-Free Zone motto.

A school in Grover, Wyoming, had a shooting in early May. Several adults were killed, but thankfully no children, before the shooters were stopped by a husband and wife visiting their child's classroom. That district had discussed the School Safety and Security Act and decided to remain a Gun-Free Zone for the time being.

I decide against taking a gun tonight, not really seeing a need for it more than any other day. Mollie, who chooses to conceal carry almost every time she leaves the house, is comfortable with her sidearm. Me, not so much.

I'll wear it, especially when hunting or hiking, but it always feels like something extra attached to me instead of the tool it is. Even though I'm not comfortable carrying, I'm very comfortable shooting.

"Malcolm, give me a minute. There's a few things I need to do before we go. Can you grab Mom's shopping lists for me?"

A few minutes later, we're loaded up. Empty gas cans, part of our *Plan A*, in the bed of truck, list in my pocket, keys in my hand.

"I guess that's it," I say. "You ready to go?"

"Dad, I think you forgot something."

"Okay . . . what?"

"You forgot to lock the house."

He's right. I did. Not long ago, we rarely bothered with locking our doors, either to the house or the cars. Over the past few months, things have changed. There have been a rash of burglaries in the surrounding towns, and our community has even been hit two times now. I'm trying to create a habit of locking the doors when we leave.

"Oops. Thanks for reminding me. I still forget sometimes."

He shakes his head at me.

Doris meets us at the door. She's tall, around five foot nine, dressed in jeans and a black polo shirt with the logo for their retirement business—a gun training school. She's retired from the Navy and some sort of government job. I once asked her what exactly she did for the government, and she jokingly said, "If I tell you, I'll have to kill you." At least I think it was a joke . . .

"Hey, Jake," Evan greets me. "Doris told me what's happening. Mind if I ride into town with you? She's thinking of that book she read and thought I should pick up a few things."

"I'd welcome the company. You ready to go?"

"Yep. Let's roll."

Evan is slightly shorter than Doris and has a very solid, sturdy stature—not fat but powerful. While he always offers a warm smile, with the way he moves and carries himself, he portrays a person not to be messed with. There's a slight imprint under his button-up shirt.

A retired deputy sheriff, he's rarely without a sidearm, so it's completely normal for him to be carrying tonight.

Three miles of wash-boarded gravel and we finally hit the pavement. Once there, we turn on the radio. They are talking about the address from the president, with comments from both side of the aisle. One side thinks his talk was too short and didn't inspire confidence. The other side said it was right up there with the Infamy Speech delivered by President Roosevelt after the attack on Pearl Harbor. Evan and I decide it falls somewhere in the middle.

There's more coverage of the plane crashes and affected cities. All of the plane crash cities have now had multiple explosions in or around the airports—JFK, Los Angeles, Miami, Chicago, and Grapevine/Irving, Texas, near DFW. It seems bombs are being detonated near the crashes where all the firefighters, police, and rescue workers are—purposely killing our first responders.

"Those dirty . . . what a cheap shot," Evan sputters. "We always knew . . . you know, when I was still with the sheriff department . . . we drilled for mass disasters. We drilled for the possibility we'd be secondary targets. But what it sounds like here, they were caught unaware." He shakes his head, then turns abruptly to stare out the window.

We're almost to the highway when Katie, my youngest daughter, calls. She's, understandably, shook up. She can't reach Mollie and wonders if she should head home.

She lives in Manhattan, Kansas, while attending college. I want to tell her yes but don't really know the answer. I married her mom when she was only eight, and as far as I'm concerned, she's my little girl. I'd feel much better with her here. I'd feel better with all of our girls here. Katie and I agree; right now, it seems only the five cities are affected. If things change tomorrow, she may want to head home, but she's safe for now. Safe for now . . .

Chapter 5

Malcolm

Miss Doris doesn't look very good. As soon as Dad and Evan left, she started crying. Not just a little bit of crying but sobbing—a word I learned in vocabulary but haven't really seen anyone do before. Mom cries sometimes, but not like Doris is crying. Her face is in her hands, and her body keeps shaking. The noise she's making almost causes me start crying. I don't know what to do to make her feel better.

After what seems like forever, she looks up at me. "I'm so sorry, Malcolm. I'm just so sad. It's just unbelievable. When 9/11 happened, it was bad. And so scary. This seems so much worse. Five planes shot down. Five. And then they set off car bombs or something when the first responders arrived to try and help. It just seems so . . . unfair. So unfair."

I think she's going to start crying again, but she doesn't. Instead, she pulls me into a hug. "How are you? Are you okay?"

I feel my eyes filling up with tears. I try to say I'm okay, but I can't. Now I start crying, not the way Doris was crying but . . . calmer. She continues to hold me for several minutes until I start to pull away.

"I'm scared for my mom," I say. "She's supposed to fly home tomorrow. Dad says she won't be able to and she'll have to drive. It's a long drive, and she gets tired when she drives. I go with her when she drives to Oregon to help her stay awake, but . . . " I start crying again.

"Hey, hey," Doris says softly. "She'll be fine. She'll know to stop and rest if she gets tired. I'm sure she'll miss your company on the trip, but she'll be fine."

"You think so?" I ask between hiccups.

"I do. I know so. She knows when to push herself and when to rest. When she's home and she gets tired, what does she do?"

I try to answer with, "I don't know," but it comes out more like, "Eh-don-nah." I guess Doris knew what I meant because she says,

"She rests, right? When you do your martial arts thing and she's tired afterward, doesn't she rest?"

"Well, yeah. But that's different. It's easy to know you're tired when you're doing something like *Yongmudo*." I stress Yongmudo so she can remember what it's called. "But when you're in a car, getting tired kind of sneaks up on you. It does for me anyway. I won't be tired at all, and then suddenly we're stopping the car and I realize I've fallen asleep. She could do that. She could fall asleep while she's driving."

Doris looks at me with a wobbly looking smile. "Does she usually fall asleep while she's driving?"

"No . . . I don't think she ever has. But she could."

"Sure, I guess," she says while nodding. "There's a first time for everything. But I don't think it's something you need to worry about. Your mom will be able to drive just fine. She'll stay awake, and when she's tired, she'll stop. She'll get a hotel room and relax."

"Jeez, you mean she'll go to a hotel without me? I like hotels. Maybe, when she gets home, we can go to a hotel. I like the ones with swimming pools. There's a great big hotel with a great big swimming pool in Billings. I want to go to that one. We went to another hotel in Billings, but the pool wasn't very big. It had a small slide, but the other one has a big slide. You can even see it on the outside of the hotel it's so big!"

Doris laughs. I think we both feel a little better thinking about the big slide. I wonder if we can go there the day after Mom gets home. She'd probably like it; it would be relaxing for her after the long drive.

"Do you want to rest on the couch until your dad gets back?" Doris asks.

"Maybe in a little bit. I'm not sleepy now. Can we play a game or something?"

"Sure. You want to play Dominoes?"

"Yeah, I like that game. The short one, not the really long kind."

"I only have the one kind. We've played it before."

"Oh. Mom has the long one. We play it sometimes when my sisters visit. It goes on forever. I always have to stop before it ends."

"You remember where I keep my games? You can go ahead and grab it. I'm going to turn up the TV volume a bit, just to check if there's anything new. Will it bother you?"

"No, why would it?"

"Just asking. If you get tired of hearing about the plane crashes, you tell me and we'll turn it back down, deal?"

"Sure. Deal."

I beat Doris at Dominoes. She asks me if I want to play again, but I decide I'd like to draw for a little bit.

While I'm drawing, I listen to the news people. They keep saying the same things over and over. They replay the president talking several times, then they tell us what they think he meant while he was talking. Someone even comes on and talks about the clothes he was wearing. I guess it's a big deal his tie was red. Someone said it should've been blue. I didn't know tie color mattered when planes had been crashed.

"Doris, do you think there's something else we can watch for a little while?"

She jumps up from her chair. "Of course we can. Should I put a movie on? What do you feel like watching?"

"*Pirates of the Caribbean*," I quickly answer.

"Which one? The first?"

"How about number four?"

"Sorry, kid. I don't have that one. Number one or number three is what I have."

"Number three, I guess." Three is fine, but four is much better.

I keep drawing while the movie is going. After a little bit, I decide I might be more comfortable stretched out on the couch. The couch is very comfy . . .

Chapter 6

Jake

The forty-five-minute drive feels considerably longer. I check my phone as soon as we park. A missed call from Mollie and two texts, telling me she's gone to the gas station. I say to Evan, "Hey, I'm right behind you. Just going to call Mollie back."

He lifts one hand in acknowledgment.

"Hey, babe. Where are you?" Mollie asks in way of greeting.

"Just pulled into SuperMart. Did you hear all the cities with plane crashes have now had explosions?"

"Yeah, I heard. I'm going to gather my stuff and leave tonight."

"You think it wouldn't be best to wait until morning? You can get some sleep and leave when you're fresh."

"I'm not sure what morning will bring," she says with a sigh. "Will the attacks stop? Will they escalate overnight? I'm thinking I should at least try to get out of the I-5 corridor area. It seems Seattle and Portland would be good targets if they wanted to stop commerce. Whoever *they* may be. Is Malcolm with Doris? Was she still up?"

"He is. She was. Evan had gone to bed, but Doris woke him up when she found out about what was happening. He's with me. He's stocking up too. After this, we're stopping at the ATMs to get out cash."

"You can also get more cash when you check out. I think they'll let you have a hundred."

"Yep, I'll do that and still go to the ATM. That way I can get money out of both the checking and savings."

"Good thinking. If I leave tonight, I'll stop by one of the bank branches and pull out more money. Did you bring our saved cash with you?"

"No. I left it at home. I figured there'd be no problem using the debit card tonight."

"Perfect. But I think we should use the credit card, then we'll just settle it up when the bill comes in. We have a good amount of cash at home, but I'd like to save it and get more as we can. I have paychecks ready, and I'm going to ask Ben if he's okay with distributing them to everyone tomorrow. I'll have the receptionist drop my check in the bank for me. I think it's best to get as much cash out of the bank as possible tonight and hold on to it. Who knows what the daylight will bring?"

"Yeah. You know, everything will probably be okay, and we'll have egg on our face."

"I'm okay with that— "

"Me too. Still, this is a good idea."

"It is. I bought several things at the mini-mart when I filled up. It just seemed smart."

"Good idea. I grabbed the list you'd started. I thought of a few more things while driving in. Is there anything you want me to make sure and grab?"

"Canning jars, we can always use more of those . . . flats too. Even though we have the reusable ones, I'd like more flats and a few rings. First aid items, dried and canned food . . . gosh, Jake. Everything. I know you know what we usually get, so follow your gut. Even if this turns out to be nothing, we can always use the basic items."

"Uh-huh. Also, I heard from Katie. She must have tried you after she got your text, but it wouldn't connect. She's upset, of course, and following through with *Plan A*."

"I talked with Sarah," Mollie says. "Tate's folks are on their way for their planned visit. They're somewhere in Nebraska tonight and will be at their place tomorrow. It'll be good for Tate to have them there."

"Yeah it will. I'm going to head into the store. Let me know if you decide to leave tonight. I'll trust you to know what feels best to you. I just want you to be safe."

"Okay, I'll make a decision when I get back and check the latest news."

"I love you. Be safe."

I'm already walking in as we disconnect. I don't want Mollie to leave tonight, while at the same time I do. There is some merit to getting past the I-5 corridor.

I glance around the parking lot and am surprised to see several cars. I guess we're not the only ones with a *Plan A*.

I hit the pharmacy section and the toiletry aisles first, tossing everything into the cart which might be useful. We're well stocked on all of these things. But if the stuff hits the fan, I may not be shopping again any time soon.

The garden section is next door. We have plenty of heirloom or open pollinated seeds in, and this year's garden is already in. Even so, they'll keep fine until next year. I toss several seed packets into my cart. A few more can't hurt.

We thought long and hard about putting in a garden this year. We've been having such a tough time with our marriage, taking the season off had some appeal. Mollie made the final decision on sticking with the garden, declaring tending it is a bit like therapy. An actual therapist, our marriage counselor, agreed.

Oh . . . what's this? Bare root berry vines. It's a little late for these, but at a clearance price of $1.50 each for the remaining ten bundles, it's too good to pass up. We have a couple of spots along our fence line that can use filling in. And if the world falls apart, I won't miss the fifteen bucks. I briefly stop to consider our motto for this year: Nothing New. I shake my head. *Plan A* takes precedence. Besides, since we already have vines, these aren't really new.

Electrical, hardware, automotive, housewares—moving through the departments, there's plenty to toss in the cart. Beyond hardware is sporting goods, one of my favorite areas.

Evan's at the ammo counter. He reloads his ammo plus has a considerable amount on hand. We also stock a decent amount of ammo and have reloading equipment and supplies as part of our preps—however, I've not yet learned the art of reloading.

"Jake," Evan says, "those two-way radios there are the same ones we used last year when we were hunting. I'm getting two sets to add to what Doris and I have. I drove over one last year, and we haven't replaced it yet. These aren't quite the quality, but they'll be fine. How many do you and Mollie have?"

I think a minute. We bought them so when the ladies were hunting together, they could call us if they needed help. The only help they ever needed was hauling their deer out after they had them down. We were more than happy to oblige. Mollie originally ordered one pair, then at least one additional pair for our storage shelf.

"Not sure. At least four. I think they could come in handy. If we don't need them, they'll make fine Christmas gifts."

"I like the way you think," Evan says with a goofy smile. He finishes up and says he's heading to the grocery department. I notice his cart's already looking pretty full. I nod and place my ammo order, plus have the clerk retrieve two pairs of radios out of the locked case for me. While he's getting what I need, I make a dash through the section to add more stuff to my cart.

Have I forgot anything? Can I move on to grocery? How about clothing? Nope. Not on the list. Might be smart to pick up a few things anyway.

Finally, at the edge of grocery where the cases of water are, my cart is getting pretty full. With the canning jars on the bottom rack, there's no place to put water.

"Hey, Jake. How's it going?"

"Getting there. Gonna grab another cart. You keep an eye on this one for me?"

"Sure, Jake. No problem. Grab me one, too, will you?"

Back with the carts, we both agree we're about done and just want to make a run through grocery. I continue on through the aisles, adding anything that looks good.

I finally make it to the coffee. Time to really stock up. Sure, we have an insane amount of coffee at home, but really, who wants to run out of coffee? Not me. Six cans of regular ground coffee and a dozen instant. Feeling bad for a minute after practically wiping out the instant, I put three back and grab three boxes of the individual instant packs.

I make a quick stop at the little kiosk thing they have with fancy cheeses and lunch meats for premade sub sandwiches, two ready-made pizzas, and a clamshell of cold chicken, and follow Evan to the registers. Precooked food means no cooking tomorrow. Sounds good to me.

Twenty minutes after midnight. There have been several announcements saying the store is closed. I'm not the only one still milling around. I step behind Evan in line—he chose the tobacco line. Perfect, since I want to buy a few cans of Copenhagen. A nasty habit for sure, but one I've yet to break. There's someone between us who looks like they've also stocked up a bit. The self-checkout area is busy, and two other checkers are trying to get people out.

I've never been a fan of shopping trips, considering them a necessary evil. After leaving the store, we stop at our ATMs for cash. Then we stop at a gas station near the edge of town. I'd like to get a couple of the twenty-pound propane tanks, popular for barbecue grills, that the gas station has in cages near the front entrance, but the store is closed and only the pumps are open. If it wasn't after midnight and the town wasn't shut down, I'd make a stop at the lumber yard and several other places.

How about a greenhouse?

Mollie and I have been talking of building one—well, we were talking of it before we put everything on hold. It's something we should have done early on when setting up our homestead. But we couldn't really commit to a design. Mollie was set on having an oversized dug-out greenhouse since the below ground design would be a nice feature with our cold winters. With the extra work involved with digging out the space, I was in favor of a classic aboveground design. Suddenly, the fact we haven't put in the greenhouse weighs heavily on me.

About five miles out of town, we hit a storm cloud. It's dumping rain. Evan and I talk very little on the drive, both of us lost in our own thoughts. The rain stops several miles before we reach Bakerville. On our gravel road, there are potholes filled with water. Looks like we got a good downpour.

I roll down my window and take a deep breath. The smell after a good rain takes me back to my childhood in Northern California. Our summers would be hot and dry with no rain for the entire season. Just when I'd begin to think the miserable summer would never end, heaven would open up and we'd be blessed with a deluge. My brother and I loved the first rain and would run and play, much to my mom's dismay, trying to catch the raindrops on our tongues. We'd come in soaked to the bone and happy. Mom was sure we'd catch our death from colds.

At Evan's place, I help him unload his purchases.

"Looks like about it," I say. "If anything ended up in my stuff, I'll get it back to you."

"Yeah, sure. Same here."

"I think I'm going to head into town tomorrow. I know it's probably silly, but there's a few projects Mollie and I have been putting off that I suddenly feel the need to work on. Or at least buy the stuff so I can work on them."

"Probably a good idea," Doris says. "While I really think this is nothing more than what we're seeing tonight . . . well, I'd hate to be wrong—for it to be something on an even larger scale."

"I agree with my lovely wife," Evan says, giving her a wink. "When 9/11 happened, I didn't think about the world in the same way I do now. Sure, we were on high alert for weeks afterward, expecting additional attacks, but we expected them to be isolated events. Now . . . I don't know, our society is different. I can envision a scenario where our enemies could want to cause us grievous harm—even more so than they've already done."

"I'm right with you. Doris, thanks so much for keeping Malcolm. Wish I could carry him out to the truck so I don't have to wake him, but he's a little big for that."

"I'm awake, Dad. I'm ready to go."

At home, Scooter and Penny greet us loudly. I let them out in the backyard for a bit while I start carrying stuff in. Malcolm heads straight to bed. Other than the fridge stuff, putting away my purchases can wait until tomorrow.

2:00 am. I check the alarm on my phone; there's a text from Mollie. She's starting for home tonight. She'll go down the Oregon coast and cut across to Eastern Oregon, avoiding the interstates as best as she can. She says she's probably paranoid but is okay with it. She also asked if I could start on the greenhouse. I guess great minds and all that . . .

It sounds like a good plan.

Chapter 7

Jake
Friday, Day 2

Have I even slept? Tossed and turned, sure, but actual sleep . . . I'm not so sure. I finally give up and head for the kitchen. While the sun is still below the horizon, the sky is beginning to change. There's a wash of pale color beginning to peek over the mountain range to the east.

Now is a good time for a short jog. I'll run uphill from here toward the Snyders' house. With our wide-open land, we can easily view the Snyders' place, but by road it's just shy of a mile. The incline makes for a good workout, and it's close enough I don't feel too bad about leaving Malcolm home. Before leaving, I shake him gently awake to let him know. I wear a headlamp with a red light in hopes of preventing me from falling and busting myself open.

I started jogging the year Mollie and I were married. Before, my fitness routine consisted of hiking into a canyon and back out near my Northern California home. That was intense. I'd challenge myself almost daily to beat my time. When Mollie and I were first married, we lived in a Portland suburb, and finding good hiking spots took about an hour's drive. There were many walking and jogging paths in the community, so jogging became my fallback. Katie, only eight at the time, would even go with me on short jogs. She still has a love of jogging and incorporates it in her life.

A mile or two is what I try to do most weekdays, long runs on weekends when I can fit it in. It used to be easy to accomplish this when we lived in Casper, before moving to Bakerville, but with the busyness of our farm, I rarely make these long runs.

The famed "runner's high" is a real thing. When jogging, my mind seems to let go. I can focus on my breathing and the feel of my feet hitting the ground. Then I reach a point where my mind starts to wander. I almost feel as if I can solve the problems of the world. The farm doesn't seem to be such a burden. I remember the love Mollie and I share and how we used to be so full of passion. Whew-wee. We couldn't get enough of each other. Never thought those feelings would change.

Our trouble started with a phone call. My best friend Kenny, his wife, and three children were killed in a car accident. Sharri, Kenny's wife, was a good friend of Mollie's. In fact, Kenny and Sharri were the reason we got together. They introduced us. We were both devastated over their deaths, but we handled our grief separately instead of together.

When we started having trouble, it caught me by surprise. First a little bickering and then it turned into more. During the worst of times, we could barely be in the same room for fifteen minutes without her turning on me for something. And the things she would say . . . they were extremely hurtful. At first, I wouldn't respond at all. I knew Mollie was hurting from losing Sharri. I knew I was hurting from losing Kenny.

While I was sure it would soon get better, instead, our fights turned into multiday events. We were miserable and close to divorce, staying together only because of Malcolm. That, and neither of us really having the energy to even bother with a divorce.

Darkness begins to surrender to light as I turn and start back toward home. Along the creek, a whitetail deer with a small fawn browses the overgrown brush. Neither seem overly concerned with me sharing their space.

~~~~~

"Hey, Dad. Anything new about the plane crashes and explosions?"

"Good morning, Buddy. I haven't checked the news. I finished most of the chores and am ready to milk."

"Can I bring the little radio out to the milk barn with us so we can listen while we milk?"

"Sure. I guess that's fine. It's good to know what's happening, but I don't want you to get totally enveloped in this. We're going to limit how much time we spend with the radio, television, and computer while this . . . *thing* is going on. I remember when 9/11 happened, and people had a hard time just viewing the news coverage."

"Okay, Dad," he says dejectedly.
~~~~~

Together, we check the chicks and freshen up their hot water. They all look very healthy and frisky this morning.

The troublemaking goat hasn't improved her disposition. Malcolm is very good with her and talks in a calm, soothing voice. Thank goodness he's milking her, and not me. We listen to the radio while milking but there's nothing new.

After finishing up with the goats, I take a look at our hay. We have a fair amount of hay on hand. We try to buy a year ahead and have just finished the hay from two years ago in March. We started on last year's hay then. A couple weeks ago, a farmer I often buy hay from offered me some over-wintered hay at a slight discount. It's almost time for first cutting, and he needs the space. With what we already have, we're still a little short of our desired two-year supply. I'd planned to wait until after this year's cutting to buy more. Now, I think I should see if my farmer friend has any additional. I'll give him a call after breakfast.

We've just finished up our breakfast when my phone chirps a new message.

"I'm hitting the road. Bought out part of the local SuperMart. I feel a little silly about it but decided a few things would be a good idea. Those few things turned into an overflowing cart. Among the highlights are a mountain bike with baskets for both the front and rear, a camp stove, backpacking food staples, some first aid things, and a 5 gallon bucket of prepacked emergency meals. Yeah, I may have gone overboard. I'm heading toward Redmond. I'll decide my route home from there. I love you. Tell Malcolm I love him too."

I laugh a little about Mollie buying so much stuff. She's always a very good steward of our finances and really knows how to stretch a buck. That said, when there's something she feels a strong need for, she'll buy it. I know she's very shook up and thinking it may be a long haul to get home. When she says backpacking food, I know she's getting stuff which is very shelf-stable and we'll definitely use if she doesn't need it on her trip home.

Purchasing the bike was a great idea and also something we can use here. We each have a bike, but there aren't any extras for when the older children visit. When Katie was here last summer, she suggested we go on a bike ride. We were one bike short, so the ride didn't happen. We talked about buying another bike then, but never made it to town to do so. I pray Mollie won't need to use the bike for anything other than some fun, future event.

I start to send a reply text to Mollie when my phone rings. It's Tate, our oldest daughter Sarah's husband.

"Hi, Jake. You have a few minutes?"

"Of course, Tate. Just finished up breakfast. Think I'll go into town in a little bit. What's up? You and Sarah holding up okay with everything going on?"

"It's not easy. In so many ways, it feels like 9/11 again, but at the same time, very different. I'm not noticing the comradery from after 9/11. You know, I was a senior in high school then and made my decision to join the Air Force after that day. Before then, I was only toying with the idea. And I'm not the only one from my class who joined up."

"I remember there was a modest rise in enlistments after 9/11—nothing like following Pearl Harbor, but some. I don't think I knew the reason you enlisted."

"Well, not the only reason but definitely the deciding factor. Anyway, it's a terrible thing. Sarah is pretty upset, especially with Mollie not being home. She's very glad we moved so close to you all. Which brings me to why I'm calling . . . "

"Okay?"

"Sarah and I bought a travel trailer this morning. It's a used, For Sale by Owner one I found a few weeks ago in a nearby neighborhood. It's older but very clean. We were wondering if we could park it at your place for now."

"Uh, yeah. Sure. We have plenty of room for it."

"Thanks, Jake. We're thinking, if we needed to stay there for a while, the extra space would be helpful. Especially since my parents are visiting . . . well, they'll be here shortly anyway."

"Oh! Absolutely. Great idea. I remember Mollie said your parents were heading up. They planned to stay here a few days also, to check out Bakerville and the area. Malcolm and I have the studio ready for them."

"Oh, good. Yes, they'd love to visit and get a feel for your community. The lack of state employment tax has a huge appeal to them. With the trailer, we were thinking more along the lines of, if one of those disasters you and Mollie are always planning for happened, we'd live in the trailer.

"Makes sense. We have the bunkhouse and cabin, but a space of your own—I get it."

"We think so too. Besides, we don't have space to park it at our rental."

"Okay, yep. Park it here, no problem."

"I think it's a pretty nice trailer. An '85, so pretty old, but it's good sized at thirty feet. Oh! And two doors—one in the bedroom and one in the living room. It's not exactly what we'd like to have for recreation, which is why we didn't buy it when we first looked at it, but the price was right, and it makes sense."

"Yeah, it sure does. Bring it on down. You know, it would be a good idea to bring some plywood and insulation to skirt around it, just in case you found yourself needing to live in it during the winter."

"During the winter? It's June. Why would we need to think about winter right now?"

"Well . . . probably nothing more will happen, but if it did, we don't know what the trouble could be or how long it would last. I'd sure hope it's minor and solved quickly. What I do know is, living in a camp trailer over the winter is not fun. Skirting the trailer so the wind doesn't blow underneath makes it much warmer. Adding the insulation, even more so. It would also need to be well staked so a big gust didn't move it or topple it. I'm sure you've heard the stories of that happening here and in Casper."

"I guess I have. I'm just having a hard time thinking that far ahead. Sarah thought the camper was a good idea just in case we needed to be there for a few days since Billings is a bigger town and could be a target. But I don't think either of us really think this could be a long-term thing. Do you?"

"Wish I knew. I pray nothing else happens. You know we've always told you and Sarah to come here for any type of emergency situation. And I know you read some of the same type of books Mollie likes. Didn't she give you a book about an EMP for Christmas?"

"She did. I haven't read it yet. I do read those books, but more for entertainment and the gun play in them than anything. I don't think of them as a possible reality. Most of them are way out there."

"I guess they are. I don't read as many as Mollie does, but she sometimes tells me about ones she reads. Truth is, many of the books are very plausible. The scenarios could happen. A man-created event like an EMP could happen. Or a natural event like a CME, which is very similar to an EMP, and it has happened before."

I pause to await a response from Tate, envisioning him rolling his eyes. After a moment, I forge on.

"None of us know what the future holds. This is the reason we prepare. Because of an unknown future. A worldwide disaster doesn't have to happen for us to find a use for our preps. Mollie has a friend whose family lived on their food storage and supplies for a year when her husband lost his job.

"Buying plywood and insulation is a small expense that could make a big difference. Besides, didn't you say your folks are considering living in a camp trailer if they move up here? They'll need the plywood and insulation to skirt their place if they're planning on living in it over the winter."

"I guess you're right," Tate says with what I think is a sigh. "Sarah and I have been filling up our pantry when we find good sales. She reminds me it's like insurance, and since we need food anyway, we're not out anything. I don't really have any projects in mind needing plywood and insulation, but you're right about my parents. They are talking about a camp trailer. I think my mom may want to park it somewhere warmer over the winter, though."

"Well, whatever you think is best, Tate. I just know I'd feel better having what I need on hand when I needed it. Especially if there was a possibility I couldn't get it easily."

"Okay, Jake. Well, I should get things ready and head your way. See you in a few hours?"

"Sure. I'm going to go into town. If I'm not here when you arrive, park it on the north side of the driveway, alongside the garage. I can move it if needed."

"Thanks, Jake. Let us know when Mollie gets home."

"Will do. Talk to you later."

As I hang up, I think about the difference in the way Mollie and I think compared to how Tate and Sarah likely think. It's not like we completely dwell on the terrible things which could happen, but we definitely look at things differently. Setting up the farm, stockpiling goods, building guest housing . . . and the fact I'm planning to drive into town this morning to pick up materials to build a greenhouse *just in case* we don't have the ability to build our planned greenhouse. Not things normal people do.

Tate and Sarah were fortunate to find a nice rental in Billings, even though it's smaller than what they were looking for. It's only about eight hundred square feet and on a small city lot. At least it has a driveway, but Tate's right—no way to park a trailer there. Sarah was able to keep the job she had in Oregon and telecommute; it was a huge blessing that allowed them to move quickly.

Tate, a diesel mechanic, hasn't found permanent work yet, but has several applications out. He's been picking up day labor jobs through a temp agency. His folks plan to spend a few weeks visiting and checking out the sights, so he's not in a big hurry to find work, wanting to spend some time with them.

Thinking of Tate's folks reminds me to call my own parents. Mollie and I have plans to include them, but they are so independent, we doubt they'll join us. My dad, seventy-five and very spry, walks every day, hunts, and fishes. My mom is seventy-three, joins Dad on his walks, and loves fishing even more than he does. She doesn't hunt but goes along most of the time, even if it's simply to sit in the truck and wait for him.

They both love living in Wyoming until winter hits. Then it quickly loses its appeal. Not good, since our winters last half the year.

We don't talk to them about preparedness. Not openly, anyway, like we do with the children. We have broached the subject several times, but they didn't really seem comfortable and steered the conversation in a different direction. They know about our bunkhouses and studio apartment but think it's just for when the kids come up to visit. And they haven't been in our basement since shortly after construction was completed, so don't know it is wall-to-wall stuff and have no idea about the extra features the basement holds. They both love to come out and visit, see our animals, and spend time with Malcolm. Many times, my mom has said if she was twenty years younger, she'd like a place like ours. I can only hope, if it was obvious things were going bad, they'd be willing to stay with us.

Thinking of my parents, my mind automatically shifts to my brother, Robert, and his family living in California. We used to be very close, but after I moved to Wyoming, our contact decreased. He used to say he'd come for a visit but hasn't made it yet. I've been back there a few times but not often enough. Besides my brother, I still have several friends there. Thinking of them all and what could happen is mind boggling. There are so many friends and loved ones we want to protect from harm. My phone rings again. My dad.

"Jake. You been watching the news?"

"I haven't watched any this morning, just last night, but we listened to the updates on the radio. They saying anything new?"

"I'm not sure if it's new. They are saying the planes were shot down with surface-to-air missiles. Then, after the emergency personnel arrived at each airport, a stolen ambulance or something was let in full of explosives—just like the car bombs that happen in other countries. About the same time as the car bombs were detonated, multiple other bombs went off around the airports, in the parking lots and taxi areas; even trains and buses exploded. Anywhere from eight to fifteen explosions at each airport. The death toll is estimated to be somewhere around five hundred to one thousand people per airport, not including the people on the crashed planes. It's pretty much a madhouse right now, trying to sort things out."

"Is anyone claiming responsibility?" I ask.

"Not that I know of. The talking heads have plenty of speculation, but I don't think it's anything except speculation. I wouldn't worry about it, though. I'm sure this will all blow over."

"Yeah, Dad. You're probably right. At least I hope you're right. With all of the flights grounded, Mollie is driving home. She left last night but is taking a roundabout way to avoid Portland and Seattle, just in case."

"Avoiding those is smart all the time. You know I can't drive through Portland."

I chuckle a little. "That's true, Dad. She's heading over Highway 20 to Redmond and will come home from there. I think it was a smart move on her part. You hear anything from Robert?"

"Talked to him early this morning when he was on his way to work. The trouble in LA is plenty far away, but they're still concerned, of course."

While I'm sure my dad is right and the LA trouble is far enough away, my gut doesn't fully agree. No sense worrying him, though. "Sure, I can understand that. Even as far away as we are, I'm concerned. Well, I better get going."

"Okay, Jake. I'll talk to you in a few days."

"Okay. And, Dad?"

"Yeah?"

"You know, if things don't blow over and this turns out to be a big deal with large effects, we have some plans in place for things. Those plans include you and Mom plus Robert and all of them."

"I'm sure it's going to be fine. You'll see. Bye."

Most likely, Dad's right. Everything is going to be fine. This tragic event will be known as another day which lives in infamy. There may be statues or memorials at each of the airports, movies will be made, songs will be written, and we'll say things like "Never Forget." Chances are, many of us will forget. Not the ones who lost loved ones, of course, but the rest of us. It's like Tate was saying—the comradery we saw after 9/11 doesn't seem to be there today like it was then. I pray my dad is right.

Chapter 8

Malcolm

Dad read aloud the text Mom sent. I think he wanted to make me feel better by letting me know what she's doing. I feel worse. Why'd she stop and buy a bunch of stuff? Why doesn't she just drive home, very fast, and not worry about any of that junk? And a bike? Nah . . . I've seen Mom ride a bike. She's not very good at it. I don't think buying a bike was smart at all.

The more I think about it, the more I decide I'm kind of mad at her. Dad says she went down the Oregon coast, actually driving farther away from us. He said she thought it might be safer than driving through the cities. I think she was just scared to drive in Portland. Last time we visited Oregon, she told me she hates driving in Portland. She made a point of taking a highway that kept her out of the actual city. I would've loved to go downtown. We were there when Sarah got married, but I don't really remember it. I know they have skyscrapers, of course, but I didn't get to hang out downtown at all. Yeah, I think she just didn't want to drive in Portland. And she does love the beach. Maybe she wanted to stop for a visit at the beach before coming home.

I wish I could talk to her on the phone. Usually, when she's gone and I stay here, I'm with Grandma and Grandpa. She'll call to talk to me, but I never really want to talk. This week when she called, she asked to talk with me, but I was busy playing Minecraft. Now, I think Dad should get her on the phone right now so I can tell her to come home. She can visit the beach another time, she can drive through the city, and she just needs to get home.

Dad is talking to Grandpa on the phone right now. As soon as he hangs up, we're calling Mom.

Chapter 9

Jake

While I can hope my dad is right and the worst is over, my gut tells me to continue preparing for the unknown. Just in case last night was a precursor with more to come, I have things to do.

"Dad," Malcolm says urgently, "you need to call Mom. She needs to come home fast."

"Yeah, Buddy. She's doing her best. I'll try her now."

The call goes straight to voicemail. "Sorry, Malcolm. I can't get her. We'll send her a text, and she'll receive it when she has service."

Malcolm lets out a combination sigh and growl. It's a common sound he makes when he's angry, irritated, or frustrated.

"Hey, you don't need to do that. Some things are out of my control. Cell service is one of them. I know you're worried about your mom, but behaving that way toward me is not helpful," I say as gently as I can.

"I know, Dad. I'm sorry. Can you send her a text?"

I nod and put the text together. I read it aloud for Malcolm to approve.

"Glad you're on your way home. No new developments overnight. Decided to head to town to pick up materials to build a greenhouse. It won't be exactly what we've been talking about, definitely smaller and not a dug out. I don't think the building cost will be very high. We can add the one we want later. Better safe than sorry. Malcolm is good, he misses you. Tate and Sarah bought a camp trailer, they are going to park it here for now. I tried to call you but phone just went to voicemail. Will try later. We love you."

"I need to make a couple of calls, then we'll get going with stuff," I tell Malcolm as I'm dialing. He nods and stomps up the stairs. My farmer friend answers on the second ring, and I make arrangements to get the rest of his old hay—just shy of two more tons.

First order of business today is putting away last night's purchases. I call to Malcolm so he can help me out.

"You done on the phone? Can we call Mom again? She really needs to stop messing around and get home now," he says, with not only urgency but anger.

"We just sent her a text, remember? What's going on, Buddy?"

"What do you mean? Mom's not here. She has to be here."

"And she wants to be here. She can't help she was gone when this happened. I know she'd have given anything to be right here, home with us. But— "

"Call her, Dad. Tell her to stop visiting the beach and get home."

"Visiting the beach? She's not visiting the beach."

"You said she was driving down the beach. You said she went south instead of east. Wyoming is east of Oregon. Why'd she go south?"

"Ah . . . she thought if she went down the coast highway, instead of going straight to Portland and then up toward Seattle, it would be safer. When she left last night, we thought maybe there'd be more attacks. She wanted to be far away from Portland if another attack happened."

Malcolm seems to calm slightly. "So she's trying to find the safest way home?"

"That's exactly what she's doing. She just wants to keep herself out of harm's way. I'm with you. I wish she would've just gone through Portland last night. Then she'd be closer than she is now. But she did what she thought was right with the information she had. Today, she'll get closer to home. She might even make it home by tomorrow night."

"Really? You think she could be home tomorrow night?"

"It's definitely possible, depending on how far she drives today. If not tomorrow night, the next day."

"Okay, but can we try to call her again?"

"Yes, we can try again."

"Do it, Dad. I think we should talk to her."

Straight to voicemail. I shake my head. "Sorry, Malcolm. We can try again later. How about helping me put away the stuff I bought last night? Then I want to go into town. There are a few more things I'd like to pick up."

"Yeah, I'll help. But we really need to call her."

"I'm with you. We'll call her when we can."

"You know, Dad, I think if you and Mom had smartphones, they'd probably work better."

"Oh, you think so, huh? You don't think our flip phones call and text just as well?"

"I don't think so. I think smartphones use the internet and would work better."

"You might be right, but your mom is in the car driving. I don't think she has internet where she is any more than she has cell service. If she was, say, in a restaurant and hooked into their internet signal then it would definitely work better. But on the road . . . I don't think it matters whether she has a flip phone or smartphone."

"Yeah, well, I think you guys should get smartphones anyway. And we really need to call her."

"We will, Buddy. We will."

With that, he seems to be appeased for the moment. Of course, I thought he was fine after we sent the text. Maybe he started thinking about Mollie being gone and freaked out a bit.

"Malcolm, let's pray together. Let's pray for your mom to have a safe trip home and pray for the families affected by last night's tragedy."

He nods and we join hands. After we're finished, we start putting things away.

The medical items I bought last night belong in a dedicated closet upstairs. The well-stocked closet has over-the-counter medications and healthcare items, plus a variety of antibiotics and other "prescription" medicines. Most are fish or animal antibiotics, but a few are things we were able to order from compound pharmacies over the internet. The internet provides a wealth of medical supplies. We've done an excellent job of stocking up on medical supplies, if I do say so myself.

Everything else will go to the basement. The staircase to access the basement is located off our bedroom. We don't have inside access from the public spaces of the house. We planned this limited access to keep the basement from being a feature, as it's a space we don't show off except to family. Our bedroom has an exterior door with a small, enclosed mudroom. From there, you can either go into our room or into the basement. The staircase ends directly in the recreation room, which is housed under our bedroom and Mollie's office.

The rec room features a foosball table, a large table for games or cards, a chess table—with a game always at the ready—a small kitchenette, a bookshelf full of board and card games, and plenty of seating. The ten-foot ceiling, along with a large egress window, helps it feel spacious.

Besides the rec room, there's a small guest room and our version of a Jack and Jill bath: two powder rooms which share a room with a tub and shower combination. One powder room has direct access from the recreation room. The second powder room is accessed from the storage part of our basement. This long pass-through style of bathroom, with two toilets and two sinks, was an important part of our design.

The storage section is our main answer to storing our mass amounts of acquired goods. It's divided into smaller rooms, all with numerous shelves and storage cabinets. While storage areas in basements are likely very common, ours is probably a little more extensive than most.

"You think we can fit all of this, Dad? The basement is already pretty full."

"I think we can do it. We'll start with the food. Let me unlock the door."

This section, affectionately referred to as the "grocery store," is our main food storage area. Our longer-term food items—housed in three- or five-gallon mylar-lined buckets, vacuumed sealed bags, or purchased in sealed #10 cans—are tucked away in here.

Everyday food items start their Caldwell life in the basement, oftentimes preserved for long-term storage in vacuum-sealed bags or other methods, or in commercial packaging for cans, jars, or something else good for preservation. As we use the food in the upstairs pantry and kitchen, we shop our basement grocery store. Then, when we make new purchases, we restock the grocery store. We have a few additional food storage areas: a custom root cellar and storage under each bed. The combination of everything is a great system, which works well for us.

Ten minutes later, I say, "Whew. It fit nicely. We'll move the rest of these things to the root cellar. We even have some space left so we can buy more stuff today."

"More stuff? Gosh, Dad. We have so much now."

"We do . . . but did I tell you Tate's parents are visiting? They might need to stay here a few days, so having extra food is smart."

Malcolm rolls his eyes at me. I choose to ignore it.

"Let's put the ammo away next."

"Good. The ammo is heavy." He makes a show of moving the bag the necessary few feet to the gun room—also kept locked but with a biometric deadbolt. I open it up for us. The ammo is quick to put away. I take a quick look over what we have. I might pick up a few more of some calibers today. Why not?

Before going to the root cellar, we put all of the miscellaneous items away. Most of these are in the main area, either on open shelves or in locked cabinets. One of the features we added to our storage section was a slightly dropped ceiling. The ten-foot ceiling in the living spaces is dropped to about seven feet in the storage section. We built a sturdy loft-style ceiling and store things like toilet paper, paper towels, and other lightweight personal items in this space. The dropped ceiling has an additional function.

"Dad, can I go up the ladder and put those things away?" He gestures toward a few things I bought specifically for the females last night—not my favorite things to purchase, and I can't imagine Malcolm wants to put them away.

"Uh . . . yes, I guess that'd be fine."

"I'm pretty sure they go in this section here, right next to the baby stuff, right?"

"Yeah, looks like the right place."

"Did you buy any toilet paper or paper towels?"

"Nope. Didn't even think of it. We'll get those today."

"We probably have plenty, but you know Mom likes to make sure we don't run out of those things."

"Yes, I do know." I chuckle. We've had many conversations about things like reusable toilet paper. While she has the materials to make things, it'd be good to not have to use toilet paper that needs to be washed.

"Is that it?" Malcolm asks.

"Uh-huh. The only things left are what I want to put in the root cellar."

"Do you think we can go through the tunnel instead of going out and around? You know, since we're here and everything."

Ah . . . the tunnel to the root cellar. This is something Malcolm loves, but also something that shows just how badly Mollie and I need tinfoil hats.

Chapter 10

Jake

After we have everything put away, I think about our next steps. First up: the greenhouse. I take a few minutes to make a materials list. Up until recently, when new projects were put on hold—part of our Hail Mary to save our marriage—I'd been collecting things for our planned greenhouse, giving me a nice collection of windows, a few doors, and even a couple of skylights I've picked up over the years from secondhand sources. There's some lumber, too, but we'll need to purchase several things in town to round out my plans.

Should I take Malcolm along today? Doris or another neighbor could keep him. It's a risk in case something severe were to happen while we were in town, such as an EMP, and we had to walk home. We have a small get-home bag in each vehicle, but for today, and likely the near future, our large bug-out bags will be riding along.

While we've focused on preparedness for several years, until recently our bug-out bags left a lot to be desired. We put together basic bags several years ago out of school backpacks we found on clearance. When we moved to Bakerville, we bought better-quality hiking backpacks and created decent bags.

We also created a get-home bag for Mollie. She took a large, checked suitcase with her last winter when she went to Oregon. Inside was a trekker's backpack plus basic equipment and supplies to help her get home.

Once our bags were finished, Mollie suggested we build bug-out bags for each of the children and their spouses, modeled after our new bags, so they'd have the essentials they needed and could just toss them in the car and go. If they ended up having to walk, it could be a good start to what they'd need to get here.

Sounded like a good idea, and a few months ago, we moved forward with it. Figuring out everything to put in the bags, it was apparent this was going to be an expensive endeavor. Expensive but worthwhile.

After we sent everyone the backpacks, the conversations really started. We had always been very open with the girls about our concerns. Sometimes, they thought we were just plain weird. Other times, they agreed there may be something to be concerned about. When the economy was really bad in '08 and '09, unemployment kept going up and up. Sarah and Angela were adults and could see what was happening. They were fortunate not to be too affected. Calley and Katie were somewhat shielded from it due to their ages and not being part of the workforce.

People say the economy is just fine now. Is it? With the US debt at over twenty trillion dollars, it's hard to think we're in good shape. How can our country ever pay off this large amount of debt? And the low unemployment rates seem questionable. Are people no longer being counted? Work requirements have lowered the number of people receiving food stamps, and analysts also say the improved economy is reflected in the food stamp recipient drop. I don't know; it all seems like a house of cards to me.

And then there are the other things we see happening: riots, terrible arguments between the political parties, even people talking about a second Civil War. And we have the continual concern of other countries. Not long ago, there was an article about Russia threatening to vaporize some of our cities. It feels like we're on the brink of something big.

When we sent the backpacks, Sarah and Tate were still living in Oregon, and they sent us several hundred dollars and asked us to add it to our prepping efforts. Since they moved to Billings last month, they've brought storage food items over on two different occasions. We visited Angela and Tim over Easter, and they sent us home with several hundred pounds of dry goods. Katie had several shipments of dehydrated meals sent to our place; placed an order through our co-op drop, which Mollie collected with her regular order; and has been utilizing online ordering to have things sent directly to us. Well, officially these are coming from Katie. Mollie and I recently began to suspect Katie's friend Leo is behind the shipments, especially when one of the orders had his name on it.

Calley and Mike thanked us for the packs. They said they completely understood our need to send them, but they plan to stay at their home and band with Mike's folks if anything should happen. They'll consider beefing up their pantry. Mollie had a hard time with this conversation. She has a history of overreacting, and I was fully expecting a big blow up. I was pretty surprised at how calm she remained while on the phone. She reminded Mike and Calley the door would always be open for them and Mike's family. She asked them to keep the packs in their front hall closet where they'd be easily accessible.

After hanging up the phone, Mollie still didn't lose it. She just sighed and said, "I expected the conversation to be like that. Out of all the girls, I know Calley doesn't really get it. I can completely understand Mike wanting to be with his family. I just wish they'd do the preparations needed to actually stay there safely." Then she began to cry.

~~~~~

"Hey, Buddy, let's get cleaned up and head into town."

"Can we try to call Mom first?"

"Definitely. I was thinking maybe I'd try from the home phone. Maybe it would make a difference compared to using my cell phone."

"Good idea, Dad. You know, about those smartphones . . . " His voice trails off while I push the buttons to call Mollie. Again—straight to voicemail.

"Sorry, Buddy. It didn't go through. We'll try again later."

About twenty minutes later, I find Malcolm building something with LEGO blocks and ask if he's ready to go. "Sure, Dad. I'm ready. You think I could get something? I wouldn't mind a new LEGO set."

"We'll see." He doesn't ask for stuff often. I suspect he's feeling the stress of last night's attacks. Is he thinking stockpiling LEGO sets makes sense in the way we stockpile other things? We never hide our preparedness lifestyle from Malcolm, nor do we dwell on it. It's just part of our life. He's never known anything else.

He might think all families have basements full of food, bug-out bags lined up and ready to go, and closets full of clothes and shoes in a variety of sizes. And, yes, we do have LEGO sets in one of those closets, along with games, toys, and small gift items. Mollie loves this closet since it means she usually has presents for any event that comes up.

While I'm doing the few necessary things needed before we leave, I think about Mollie and her skills at organizing our basement, closets,
~~~~~

and other hidey-holes. She keeps track of preparations with spreadsheets and has a master list showing where to find things. Good thing, since I'd be lost without her here. I'll give her my receipts for all these purchases so she can update her spreadsheets. Thinking this gives me pause.

If a catastrophic event happened while Mollie was gone, could I take care of everything on my own? I've thought of this before, in passing, but I'm now faced with the reality of Mollie not being here and a potentially serious threat looming. Now, it's feeling very real. With Mollie in Oregon . . . I hope, again, my dad is right and this will all blow over.

I feel a little guilty being so blasé about it blowing over. How many lives were changed forever last night? How many husbands will never see their wives again? How many children are now orphans?

Time to get ready to go.

Focus, Jake, focus.

Today, I'm towing our larger utility trailer so I can be sure to get everything. Listening to the radio, it doesn't sound like there are any new developments or information on last night's attacks. What did catch my ear is something new.

"In other news, health departments in about a dozen major US cities are reporting an increased number of foodborne illnesses. Most of the cities are seeing both Shiga toxin-producing E. coli and Salmonella Typhi, also known as typhoid fever.

"Limited cases began appearing a few weeks ago. Yesterday, there were an estimated 137 E. coli and 268 typhoid cases. There have been at least six deaths associated with the E. coli outbreak and eight from typhoid.

"While E. coli has made the news many times in recent years, typhoid fever tends to be related to developing countries or people who have recently visited those places. It's closely related to salmonella, which typically causes food poisoning as it can only affect the stomach and digestive tract. S. Typhi, on the other hand, causes a body-wide and life-threatening disease because its toxin can enter all of the body's cells and cause infection.

"There have been recent reports of typhoid fever incidence in homeless camps. The incidences from the last several days are believed to be unrelated to those occurrences.

"Please visit our website for information on symptoms for both E. coli and typhoid fever. Early diagnosis can help with a full recovery. We will update this story as more information becomes available."

What's typhoid fever? Something that happens after disasters, like the hurricane that hit Haiti a few years back, right? Sounds right. And I have a vague recollection of talking with Mollie about the homeless camps the report just mentioned, though I can't remember the details.

I do know what E. coli is. We have a friend who spent a week in the hospital with it, and he had a mild strain. What's going on with these both occurring?

First stop: the bank. Part of our savings plan is keeping cash on hand, stashed in a variety of locations around the house and land. For every dollar we put in savings, we add an equal amount to our on-hand stash. We keep a base cash amount, equal to three to six months of living expenses, then use any over the base for purchases when needed. Yeah, keeping that much cash around sounds nuts, but by dispersing it in various locations, not just tucking it under our mattress, it gives us peace of mind and availability as we need it.

While we've always used the method of keeping half of our savings in cash and half in the bank, the amounts were not always up to where they are now. When Malcolm was younger, Mollie only worked part time. Once he wasn't quite so needy, she started adding hours and responsibilities. Now, part of what she does brings in new business, so she gets a monthly commission on that plus a quarterly sales bonus. For the last couple of years, each of her quarterly bonuses was over five figures.

While we don't let the cash dip below three months of expenses, we do sometimes go over six months' worth. Many of the projects we've done around the homestead were made possible because we had the cash available when the deal came up. We haven't had any high-cost deals come along since last summer, because we're officially on hiatus from projects, so our cash on hand is quite high right now—well over the six-month expense mark.

The money in the bank and credit union works as our investment vehicle. We each have retirement accounts set up through our employers. We try to max these out each year to get the full benefit. Once we reach these deferral limits, we move on to IRAs. Depending on the income phase out and Mollie's bonuses for the year, we either invest in traditional or Roth IRAs. Mollie, the bookkeeper in our family, sorts all of this out and then tries to explain to me what she's done. She's not always successful in helping me understand. I just go with it. Today, I'm emptying our savings.

The teller doesn't want to give me cash, telling me it's not a good idea to walk around with that much. Considering it's really not *that* much, I'm slightly confused. I assure her I'll be fine. She goes and speaks with the manager; he looks me over, gives her a nod, and pastes on a smile before walking my way. I've met him a few times before when we've done business in the bank.

"Hello, Mr. Caldwell. You're comfortable withdrawing a large amount of cash?"

"Hello. Yes, I am. Though, it's not a terribly large amount—only a little over four thousand."

"We'd prefer to offer you a cashier's check made out to wherever you wish to make your purchase."

"No thanks. I'll be making several small purchases. I'll take my cash."

He leans in conspiratorially. "Is this about the attacks last night? Your money shouldn't be affected."

I lean in also. "No, this is about taking my money out of the bank to use how I see fit. Thanks."

He looks at me and pauses, then nods to the teller and says, "Go ahead."

It's interesting I'm questioned for such a small amount. Four thousand isn't much to take out. Maybe I'm not the first person who's been in here this morning withdrawing cash. This thought leads me to a new decision. I'll be heading to the credit union we use next.

The credit union visit goes about the same as my visit at the bank, with hesitation on their end to provide the cash I request. I close out our three CDs. I briefly consider taking money out of the IRAs, but quickly decide the idea is absurd and irrational.

As it is, I'll probably be back at the bank and credit union in a few days with my tail between my legs . . .

Chapter 11

Malcolm

Town is different today. People seem . . . sad. But not just sad—scared. Scared like Doris and I were last night. When we went to the banks, the workers didn't really want Dad to take his money out. They finally gave it to him, but it was almost like they thought he shouldn't have it.

I've learned a little about how banks work and did a unit study on the Great Depression a few months ago. Dad also has a book his great grandma wrote a long time ago, and she talks about what it was like living during the Depression. I know it started when the stock market crashed, and then people went and took all their money out of the bank.

I guess maybe they thought Dad was doing the same thing today. He wasn't the only one in the bank taking cash out. I overheard another lady, and she sounded like she was getting upset when they didn't give her the money she asked for. What I've learned about the Great Depression was scary. I don't think plane crashes would cause something like a depression.

After we finish getting money, we go to the builder's supply store for the greenhouse materials. I've been here a lot with Dad when we need something for a project. Dad has a list of things he wants to get for the greenhouse he's going to build. I know a greenhouse is something Mom has wanted for a while.

"Check it out, Buddy. These windows will work great, and they're on clearance. We'll get all five of these marked-down ones. I'll need a few more, so we'll see what else they have."

"Where are you putting the greenhouse, Dad?"

"Good question. I'm going to add it on as a lean-to on the processing shed. I'll use the building as a back wall, put windows on the front south-facing wall, add a greenhouse roof, have a door on the east end, and close off the west end. How does that sound?"

"Confusing. Do you have a drawing of it?"

"Nope, sorry, Buddy. It's all right here." He motions to his temple with his index finger. "I have a list of what I need but no drawing or plans. I think it'll work out fine."

I shrug. I'm not convinced. "What about this?" I show him a screen door by the cheap windows.

"Great find. We can use it to help with airflow. Well done."

I help Dad load the windows on a flatbed cart. We'll need to come back for the screen door.

"Let's go to the desk. I need to order some lumber and we'll get everything sorted out."

It takes a little bit for Dad to get everything he needs. He ends up buying not just lumber and stuff but a couple of greenhouse-in-a-box things the sales lady said were a good deal. I don't think Mom is going to like them, but I don't say anything about it.

After Dad pays, I stay out of the way while some guys help load the trailer. Today we brought the bigger utility trailer. Not the little one we use for wood, but one we use when we're hauling long boards so they don't hang over the end. With all of the stuff we bought, a lot of the space is used up.

We go to SuperMart next. We buy lots of stuff: toilet paper, food, water, coffee—all kinds of things. Dad finally says we can go to the toy section, and he lets me pick out a LEGO kit while he buys puzzles and games. We like playing cards and games. Then Dad buys a few baby toys.

"Why are you buying those?" I ask. "For Gavin?" Gavin's my nephew. He belongs to Angela and Tim. It's okay to have a nephew, but it'd be better if he wasn't still a baby. He's almost two now, and Angela says I shouldn't call him a baby anymore. He can walk and talk pretty good, but we can't really play yet.

"This one's for Gavin." Dad holds one up. "The others are for Mom's gift closet. You know, it's always good to have gifts."

"I guess so," I say with a shrug.

"So, Malcolm, I'm thinking we should go look at the guns. You've grown quite a lot lately, and I think we can get you a full-sized .22 rifle. How's that sound?"

"Sounds great, Dad! I think you're right. I'm ready for a bigger one. The shotgun you got me is bigger than my .22, and it fits me fine."

"I agree. Let's go see what they have."

We walk toward sporting goods. "Do you think Gavin would like my .22? He might need to grow a little, but it's a good gun. It shoots really straight."

Dad laughs and says, "The gun is good, but the straight shooting is you. You have an amazing aim."

I'm proud to hear Dad say that. We do a lot of shooting on our gun range at home and over at the Snyders' range. My .22 is a single-shot youth model with iron sights. I'm pretty accurate up to a hundred yards.

"So you think Gavin can have it some day?"

"Yes, I think he can. We'll keep it for him."

Dad and I look at the .22s and find one we both like. Dad has a concealed carry permit, so he can carry his handgun; this makes it easy to buy the new rifle. I can't wait to take it home and try it out. Dad even buys a new gravity target so we can practice. We have to leave the gun in sporting goods until we're ready to go—the salesclerk has to walk us out. Dad picks up more stuff in sporting goods.

"Hey, Malcolm, what do you think of buying a bike?"

"I already have a bike. Do I need a new one?"

"I think your bike is fine. And your two backup bikes are fine too."

When we go to the dump, we always check out the free bike section. I've found a couple of extra ones I can use if something happens to my good bike. Dad got me tires that won't puncture and a few extra parts for the good bike, so I think I'm set.

I'm wondering what he's thinking, when he says, "You know, Katie loves to ride bikes, and when she visited last time, we didn't have one for her to ride. Your mom's bringing a bike home with her, but it might be good to have a few more. That way, when your sisters and brothers visit, we can ride." We end up buying two mountain bikes, plus a bike and a baby trailer for Gavin.

After SuperMart, Dad takes us to the feed store—where he buys *even more* stuff—then we go to the auto parts store. He grabs a couple of gas cans, then stops and looks at a really big gas can—the kind that fits in the back of a pickup truck.

"Maybe we should take a look at these fuel tanks. Your mom and I have talked about buying these, but we've always stuck with the smaller cans, just because they're easier for us to use and rotate. I hate the idea of having a tank in the back of the truck all the time."

I'm not sure what he wants me to say. "Sure, Dad. Pretty big. You could probably put all of the fuel we have in the small gas cans in one of those and still have room left over."

"But maybe it wouldn't have to ride in the truck. Let's find a clerk to get us what we need."

Dad talks with a clerk and finds out what they have in the store is limited. We can order pretty much anything, but all they have today is a 110-gallon transfer tank for diesel and a 75-gallon tank for gas. Dad seems shocked when the guy tells him the price. He shakes his head, but still buys one of each, along with a whole bunch of stabilizer stuff.

After we're done at the auto parts store, we stop by one of the sporting goods stores in town. We live in an area with many outdoor adventures and have several sporting goods stores. We shop at all of them, but the one Dad takes us to today is the one he buys hunting stuff at. The others are more for hiking and have skiing stuff in the winter.

I like the ski stuff. During the winter we downhill and cross-country ski. Downhill is fun. Cross-country is a lot of work, but I still like it. I try to ski every day at home during the winter. We also snowshoe, which is Mom's favorite. It's fine but I'd rather ski. I really like winter when the weather isn't too hot. In the summertime we hike and fish. Those are fun too, but I get hot and sweaty. Both winter and summer, we practice martial arts.

We started learning Yongmudo last year. It's pretty fun, and I'm now a yellow belt. We've even taken some extra workshops for Judo and grappling. Grappling is like wrestling, and we get to roll around on the ground. Our instructor says we're learning mixed martial arts so we can defend ourselves. I've heard about kids being kidnapped, and I don't want that to happen to me, so I pay attention when we're training.

Dad buys socks and other stuff, then he says, "Just one more stop before we go home." He mutters something about how it's a miracle his credit card hasn't exploded from overuse.

"Good," I answer, "I'm tired of shopping. I want to go home and put together my new LEGO set."

"We'll find time later. Once we're done in town, I want to unload everything and then pick up some hay and grab some more wood."

"*Daaaad*, I'm tired of getting wood."

Dad gives me a look.

"I mean, we've got a lot of wood this week. We probably have enough," I stutter.

Dad firmly says, "We're going to get more."

I try not to sigh and ask, "What time is it?"

"A little before noon."

"Is that all? It feels like we've been in town forever. Where else are we going?"

"Propane place, I want to buy a few more tanks. Oh, and then to the gas station before we head home."

"What kind of tanks? Like the one on the barbecue grill?"

"Yep, I'd like four of those and two of the larger 100-pound ones like we use for the guest cabin."

Dad is going overboard with the propane tanks. I know we already have several of each of the kind he wants to get. And we have the regular big ones the truck comes and fills up. The one for the house is huge. Dad told me it's a thousand gallons, and it has something called a "wet leg" on it so we can refill the tanks for the barbecue grill and the guest cabin. We also have two 500-gallon tanks, one for the garage and the other for the bunkhouse. They have the wet leg things too. And the propane guy was just at our house a few weeks ago. He filled us up then.

Mom and I were outside watching when he finished, and he told Mom, "You're full up. Didn't take too much. The three tanks seem to be a little overkill for your usage." Mom just smiled and thanked him for coming out.

I don't know . . . maybe it's a good idea to have so much propane. We do use it for lots of things—the furnace, our cooking stove, and hot water heater, for sure. Dad showed me how all of those work and hook up to the propane. I guess keeping those working is good.

As Dad is loading up the propane tanks, his phone rings. Maybe it's Mom!

Chapter 12

Jake

We've just finished cramming the propane tanks into the truck when the phone rings. Malcolm is looking at me expectantly. "Sorry, Buddy. It's not your mom."

He sighs and asks who it is.

"Not sure, how about I answer it and find out," I say with a wink. He rolls his eyes at me.

"Hello?"

"Is this Jake?"

Sounds like a salesman. I'll make quick work of this. "Yep."

"Jake, this is Bubba Larson. You bought a cabin from me last year. Gave you a great deal on it, remember?"

I do remember Bubba. He's the guy we got our second bunkhouse, which we refer to as *the cabin*, through last summer. While our original bunkhouse was stick-built on a slab, this is a prefab unit we found on clearance quite by accident. The cabin was our last big project before we went on hiatus.

"Oh. Yeah. Hello, Bubba. What can I do for you?"

"I was thinking of what I can do for you, Jake. You see, I have a smaller cabin I need to repossess tomorrow. It's just north of where you live, and I was thinking you might need another cabin for when your family visits. I can give you an amazing deal on it."

The deal he gave us last year was a great one. But when I think of all of the money I put on our credit card this morning to buy the greenhouse stuff, plus my crazy shopping trip last night and the additional stuff today, I just shake my head. "That's mighty nice of you, Bubba, but I'm not sure we're in the market for another cabin."

"Well, I can appreciate that, Jake. How about I tell you a little about it and then you decide?"

"Okay, but I only have a few minutes. I'm on a time schedule today."

"Sure, sure. I understand. This was one they ordered from me several months back. They bought it and turned it into one of those tiny houses that are all the rage. They were parking it at a friend's house for now. When I delivered it, instead of putting the cabin on blocks, they had me put it on a gooseneck trailer he'd purchased. The cabin is 8 x 20 feet, and the trailer is about 28-feet long. He said the extra would give them a nice porch."

"Okay. Makes sense."

"Yeah, so they build their tiny house with a sleeping loft and everything. But the Missus, she can't stand living in it. Says it gives her claustrophobia. Like most people, they bought it on credit and have been making the payments to me. They called me a few days ago and want to turn it back in instead of finishing out their contract. Husband says not only does the wife not like the tiny house, she doesn't like it here and wants to move back to Florida or wherever it is they came from. Of course, after last night, they might be rethinking moving to Florida."

"So you're disconnecting the cabin from the trailer and picking it up?"

"Yep. He's already removed the bolts connecting everything together and has taken out the kitchen appliances and things he thought he could sell. The loft is still in place, the plumbing, wiring, and all that. I'm not quite sure what condition I'll find it in, but I suspect you'll be pleased with it and able to make it work for your needs."

"Well, that's just the thing, Bubba. I'm not sure I have a need for it."

"Would you find a need for it if I were to deliver it to your place and only ask two thousand for it?"

Suddenly, I'm thinking I could find a need for it. At 8 x 20 feet, it's about 160 square feet, so not very large, but with a sleeping loft, it could make a very nice cabin for someone. I don't need a project, but this sounds almost too good to pass up. And it could just sit until I have time to work on it. I have enough cash to cover it but decide to make a counteroffer.

"I'm not sure, Bubba. I think I'd find a better need for it at fifteen hundred."

"Eighteen hundred and I'll deliver it tomorrow before noon. I'll even throw in the setup blocks. Of course, it would be the same cash deal we did last time."

"Of course, cash is what I had in mind. I can do seventeen hundred."

"You drive a hard bargain, Jake. But you are, truthfully, doing me a favor, and we have a deal. I'll see you tomorrow. If I get to the cabin and it's not in the quality I expect, I'll give you a call so I don't catch you unaware. If it's better than I expect, our deal holds. If it's worse, we can discuss it."

"You're a fair man, Bubba. I'll see you tomorrow." I hang up. What have I done?

"What'd you buy, Dad? Something that'll make Mom happy or make her shake her head?"

"Good question, Buddy. I'm not really sure. Let's try to call her and we'll find out."

Malcolm gives me a big smile, which quickly turns to a frown when, once again, the call goes to voicemail.

Pulling into our yard, Malcolm says excitedly, "Nice, Dad. I like the trailer house. Is that Tate and Sarah's?"

"Yeah, must be. It looks decent from the outside."

"Can we go in and check it out?"

"Sorry, Buddy. It's Tate and Sarah's place. Next time they come to visit, we can have them show us the inside."

"Okay, I guess that's fine."

"Let's get the stuff unloaded, then we'll grab something to eat."

The SuperMart and sporting good items go in the house to be put away later, while the packaged greenhouses can go in the garage, or as Mollie calls it, "the eye sore," an extremely oversized shop close to the size of our house. Personally, I'm rather fond of it and think it might be a tad too small. The greenhouse construction supplies can be stored in my processing shed for now since I won't need to use the space until hunting season.

My processing shed was one of our earlier projects and is a dream come true for me. It's the perfect place for me to take care of hunted and harvested animals, chickens, and waterfowl. The extra-high roof gives me a great hanging area for skinning. I can then hose down the floor with a pressure washer so everything looks as good as new. The high roof will also be helpful for adding the greenhouse lean-to. I'll be able to easily add on without giving up headspace in the greenhouse.

Malcolm and I get everything unloaded in about fifteen minutes. It all fits but does make for a tight space. I'll definitely have to figure something out before it's time to process chickens. I can barely move and wouldn't be able to have things set up the way we need. Maybe the new cabin from Bubba should become a storage unit? If we keep buying like I'm buying now, we'll need more storage. Should I call a halt to the purchasing? We're over twelve hours from last night's attacks, with nothing new happening. It's likely this was a onetime event, like 9/11, and our lives won't be changing too much.

We head in the house to put away the pile of purchases. After many trips to the basement, the front room no longer looks like a warehouse. The basement, however, does. I did my best to keep things organized, but some shelves and cabinets were already full. I'm feeling pretty silly about my purchases.

A quick glance at my ringing phone and I let out a loud breath. Finally! "Malcolm, it's your mom. I'll talk for a few minutes, then you can say hi."

"Great, Dad!" he says while bouncing up and down.

"Hey, honey! Where are you?" I don't even try to contain my excitement at hearing from her.

"I'm in Redmond, Oregon, eating lunch at a park."

"Good. I'm glad you're farther from Portland. No new stuff happening, but it's good to be in a less populated area. I imagine you're breathing easier."

"I am. What have you been up to today?"

"I'll tell you in a minute, but first, there's a young man standing here who can't wait to talk with you."

"Super! I miss him so much. Put him on."

I hand the phone to Malcolm, who has a big grin on his face. "Hi, Mom. You almost home?"

I can see his disappointment when he realizes she's still in Oregon and it's still a long drive. They talk for a couple minutes and then he says, "Mom, you drive careful. If you get tired, you should stop and rest. You could also have the radio on and sing songs. It might help keep you awake."

He pauses to listen to her response. "Okay, Mom. I'll see you soon. I'll take care of Dad until you get here. Oh, and don't worry about Miss Priss—she and I are starting to understand each other. Bye!"

Malcolm hands me the phone and says, "I'm going to go to my room for a few minutes."

"Sure, Buddy. I'll call you when it's time to go get hay."

He shakes his head as he goes up the staircase.

"Hey, Mollie. He sure misses you."

"I miss him too. I want to be home so bad it hurts."

I feel the same way and swallow hard to control my emotions. I move on to sharing about my greenhouse purchases, SuperMart and sporting good excursions, and the call from Bubba.

"So . . . you agreed to purchase another cabin? Do we need another cabin? And what about our no-new-projects agreement for this year?" Mollie asks, sounding slightly annoyed.

"I'm not sure we need another cabin. But I think the price is amazing, and I could possibly resell it for more than what I paid if we decide we don't need it. Or we could keep it for storage. I filled up the processing shed with the greenhouse materials. I won't take this on as a project right now unless absolutely necessary. It can just sit there and hold our stuff."

Mollie lets out a large exhale. "Hmm. Well, I trust your judgement on this. Do you think we're good now with the purchases you've made and the car full of stuff I have? Should we consider *Plan A* complete?"

"I think *Plan A* is a definite success. Unless something big happens, or should I say, something additional, we should hold off on anything else. You focus on getting home. Keep your gas tank filled and find a place to stop tonight where you can get some good sleep. Leaving so late last night, you must be tired."

"I was doing pretty well, but the longer I sit here, the more I'd welcome closing my eyes. Did you hear about the foodborne illnesses?"

"I did. I'm not sure why people would be getting typhoid. Isn't that something people get when the water is polluted, like after a hurricane?"

"Yes, it can be. And it's also quite common in developing and third world countries. You've heard of Montezuma's Revenge? That's often typhoid and why you shouldn't drink the water, have ice, or eat lettuce when visiting those places. I find it interesting typhoid and E. coli are both being reported in these high numbers and wonder if it could be intentional. Remember hearing about the cult in The Dalles, Oregon, that did the bioattack back in the '80s?"

"Vaguely. They poisoned salad bars or something?"

"Right, with salmonella culture to try to make people sick and decrease voter turnout."

"Okay. And?"

"What if this is something like that? What if these are deliberate attacks causing foodborne illness?"

"Do you really think this is related to the terrorists, Mollie?"

"Maybe? It just seems super suspicious that two different foodborne illnesses are causing widespread outbreaks. Typhoid didn't even used to happen here. It's more of a third world type thing but is cropping up in homeless camps. You remember, we talked about that."

"Vaguely, I remember you mentioning it, but I can't remember the details. Something about unsanitary conditions and people getting sick?"

"Yes, exactly. But the news report said these latest outbreaks are not related to the homeless camps. Sounds like it's very widespread. Feels intentional to me. But you do know, I could be paranoid."

"You could be right. Not about being paranoid . . . well, that too. But about the illnesses. Something like that would definitely cause more terror."

"Exactly. I was going to go to a restaurant for lunch—thought it would be a nice break—but the outbreaks made me think twice about it."

"Makes sense. I think that's often terrorists' goals, to stop us from living our life and to make us live in fear."

"Huh. I thought their goal was to kill everyone who didn't believe the same as they do," she says in jest, at least I think it's in jest.

"Yeah. Maybe so."

Mollie decides to take US 97 to Biggs Junction, cross the Columbia there, and head through Yakima.

"I thought you were going to skip Yakima. Isn't there an Army base or something there?"

"I think there is. I think avoiding big cities is my best bet. Yakima isn't very large. But maybe you're right. I could go to the Tri-Cities instead."

"I think it would be better. From there, it's not too far to I-90. If everything remains quiet, you could hop on there and be home in no time. Tomorrow, even."

"Yes, getting on I-90 would speed it up. It isn't far from Tri-Cities to 90 at all. I think that's what I'll do. Looks like about 250 miles to Tri-Cities. I should be able to make it at least to Spokane tonight and be home tomorrow. I'd better get going. Keep in touch?"

"Of course. Malcolm and I are going to get a load of hay and then a load of wood from the reservoir. Maybe even two loads of wood. I decided against going up in the forest. I don't want to be so far away from home, just in case. Plus, it's already a little late in the day for a trip like that."

"I agree. I'm glad you'll be sticking closer to home. Talk to you soon. I love you."

"Love you too, honey."

Chapter 13

Jake

We've added more hay to our supply, I've talked with each of my girls—all checking in after trying to reach their mom without success—and we're getting ready to gather another load of wood. This time we'll go to a nearby private reservoir, owned by a friend who allows me to take all of the fallen trees to keep his lake cleaned up.

Before heading out for wood, I take some time to do a few other things. Starting with figuring out a spot to put the cabin Bubba is bringing tomorrow. I tinker for what I think is only a few minutes and am surprised when I check and it's getting late. We need to get a move on it. When I start the truck, the radio immediately comes to life.

". . . the Brooklyn Bridge, connecting Manhattan and Brooklyn; the Golden Gate Bridge in San Francisco; Mackinac Bridge, which connects the Lower and Upper Peninsulas of Michigan; Seattle's Lacey V. Murrow Memorial Bridge; and Portland's Marquam Bridge. We believe these are just a few of the bridges that have been attacked. Even as I speak, I'm receiving more information and additional explosions are being reported throughout the US. We expect more information shortly.

"Again, there appear to be widespread incidents of explosions on or near bridges throughout the United States. At this time, we can confirm explosions on the Brooklyn Bridge, Golden Gate Bridge, Mackinac Bridge, Lacey V. Murrow Memorial Bridge, and Marquam Bridge. We're working on getting more information and details on the extent of damages. We have unconfirmed reports of explosions on other bridges and will provide additional details once these reports have been confirmed."

Horror. Shock. Anger. So many emotions rushing through me. Taking out the bridges was a concern after 9/11. Was this on the official radar after last night's attacks? And why weren't provisions made to prevent it?

Mollie would know for sure, but I think the Marquam is the double decker on I-5, right through Portland. Friday afternoon, the bridge was sure to be packed, maybe even bumper to bumper.

"Dad? What's going on?"

I try to remain calm and speak without alarm. Fail. "Sounds like the terrorists have hit again. A few bridges have exploded."

"Bridges exploded? A bomb went off on the bridge?" Malcolm is nearly hysterical.

"I'm . . . I'm not really sure," I stammer. "They're saying there were explosions on or near several bridges. They are still confirming what's happened."

"Where's Mom?" His voice is now full of tears. I turn and face him. The tears in his eyes threaten to brim over.

"She's okay. Your mom's in Central Oregon, around Redmond. Remember what she said when you talked with her? She's not near any of the bridges." *Thank you, God . . .*

"Okay." The relief in his voice and on his face is instant. "You calling her?"

"Yeah, Buddy. I'm going to try her right now. Let me go in the house instead of sitting in the truck. You can play while I take care of this."

"Okay. I don't know how much playing I want to do, but I'll wait out here. Let me know what she says."

I take the kitchen radio into my room and call Mollie from there.

I'm surprised when the phone connects and she answers with a weary, "Hey, babe."

"Honey! Have you heard? They're blowing up bridges now!" I say, with a little more agitation in my voice than I intended.

"I've heard. They said the names of a few. The Marquam in Portland was one of them, the Golden Gate, and the one in Seattle I-90 is on."

"Last night, they took out air travel. Today, they're taking out our bridges. They are also possibly connected to the food poisoning stuff. People are going to be too scared to leave their homes."

"True. I'm not far from Biggs Junction and the bridge over the Columbia. I'm scared to drive over the bridge."

"Oh, jeez! It seems like it may be a good target since they hit the two bridges in Portland going over the Columbia."

"Jake, hold on a second. The radio announcer is back."

Her radio comes through the phone.

"We have confirmed reports, the Sellwood and Fremont Bridges in Portland have been destroyed, along with the double-deck Marquam. The Interstate Bridge and the Glen Jackson Bridge, connecting Portland to Vancouver, Washington, have also both been attacked but are still standing. These bridges are closed until the extent of the damage can be assessed.

"Across the US, there have been over forty-five bridges hit so far. It's believed a truck loaded with explosives drove onto each bridge and then the driver detonated a bomb. This type of attacker is often called a suicide bomber. The results of these attacks vary in degree from minimal damage to total destruction. This attack, on the day after five airplanes were brought down and five of our US cities were affected by weapons of mass destruction, is surely related. We're expecting an address from the president shortly."

"Ah, Mollie. This is bad."

"I know," she says with a sniff.

"Where are you?"

"I don't know. Somewhere on 97, a ways from Grass Valley, pulled over on the side of the road. I stopped when I first heard the report. I was going to take a look at the map and find a new route home without big bridges. Do you think any of my Portland friends were killed today?"

"I don't know, honey. I can't even imagine the number of people who died today and yesterday. I haven't really heard many numbers yet from yesterday. Nothing firm, anyway."

"It's terrible. No, that's not even the right word for it. It's beyond terrible, but I can't think of a better word to use. I want to get home. Do you think I should just stay on this road and get to I-84, then take it to Pendleton? I can go north there, I think, and hit 90."

"Pendleton is past the Gorge, so you wouldn't have to cross the Columbia that way."

"Right. Let me pull out the map and take a look. There's still a bridge I'd have to cross. It looks like it goes over the Snake, and it looks like a good-sized one."

"Maybe you should find somewhere to stay tonight? Let the bridge activity calm down and then we can find you a good route tomorr— "

"Jake, I need to be home."

"I know, and we need you here, want you here. But I feel like you should stay off the interstate for now. Maybe take one of those backroads to get to Pendleton and sleep there tonight. I don't want you too tired to drive."

"I'm fine to drive. I'll stop . . . "

She's crying. Shoot, I feel like crying myself. I want to comfort her, but what can I say?

"Mollie, I'm sorr— "

"It's fine. I'm tired and upset and . . . just . . . I'm just so overwhelmed and sad—so incredibly sad—about all of this. The planes, the bridges, me not being home with Malcolm. With you. You could be right. I might be more tired than I realize."

I take a deep breath. A plan, she needs a plan. "I think you can get from 97 over to the road Condon is on. Can you take a look? Then from there get to 395? I think Pendleton is on 395."

"Jake! *Seriously*? I'm telling you how I'm feeling and you're giving me directions?"

Oops. Guess she didn't need a plan. She wanted me to listen, to commiserate. One of these days I'll get this right. "Sorry, honey. I was just so focused on helping you get home, I . . . I wasn't paying attention to how you may be feeling about all of this."

She's completely quiet.

"Honey?"

"Yeah. I'm here. I know you're trying to help." She takes a deep breath. "Let me see. Condon is on 19. Pendleton's on 395. It looks like it would be a maze to get there, but I can. From Condon, I can take a road to Hepner and then from Hepner to Pilot Rock, which is on 395, and then up to Pendleton. I could stay in Pendleton tonight," she says morosely.

"I think that'd be good." As tired as she sounds, I wonder if she'll be able to drive as far as Pendleton.

"I wish I would've just darted through Portland last night instead of going south. I'd be so much closer to home now if I would've just done it."

"I know, but your instincts to stay out of Portland and Seattle were good. Besides, no use wishing now."

"I guess you're right. I have to admit, I'm so tired I don't know if I can make it to Pendleton."

"You can probably find someplace closer. Maybe Condon or Hepner."

"Maybe. They're pretty small but might have a hotel. And I have my gear, so I can camp. A bed sounds wonderful, though, after sleeping only a few hours in the car last night."

"Don't push yourself or drive when it's not safe. You don't want to risk an accident, which would delay you getting home even more."

"No kidding, Jake. You don't need to state the obvious."

I say nothing, choosing to let her snark slide.

"Sorry, Jake," she says softly. "I shouldn't have said that. I'll start looking for a place and will let you know. Have you talked with the girls?"

"I've talked to all of them. They each said they tried to reach you, but your phone went to voicemail. They know how sketchy connections can be. Hey, it sounds like the president is coming on. Let's listen."

I turn up my radio so I can hear.

"My fellow Americans, it's with a heavy heart I report our nation continues to be the target of terrorist activities. As of yet, we have not identified the culprits but believe we are getting closer to knowing who is responsible. Today, many of our nation's bridges have been attacked. Some were devastated by, what we believe to be, suicide bombers driving panel trucks loaded with explosives. In many cases, these trucks caused severe destruction. Other bridges were targeted by handheld surface-to-surface missiles with devastating results. As of now, we have confirmed reports of forty-eight bridges affected, with varying degrees of damage. We will provide the list of these bridges after I have finished speaking with you.

"Due to today's attacks, we're closing or limiting access to other bridges across the nation which we've determined to be likely targets. Last night, our nation came under attack with the deliberate crash of five airplanes while attempting to land. This was followed by the detonation of multiple explosives at and very near each airport experiencing a crash.

"Today, we continue to see evil with the destruction of our bridges. The loss of innocent life is staggering. Immediately following last night's attacks, I implemented our emergency response plans. Our emergency teams are working at all five cities which were attacked.

These cities are Queens, New York; Miami, Florida; Los Angeles, California; Chicago, Illinois; and DFW Airport in Texas.

"With the bridge disasters, we're distributing teams as we can to all affected areas to assist the local fire and rescue departments. I ask for your cooperation, as citizens, to help where you can and obey all requests from your local government. Let us come together during this time of tragedy and show those who oppose our very way of life we cannot be broken by their cowardly acts. We will find those responsible and bring them to justice. None of us will forget these times, but we will persevere. God bless each of you. God bless America."

"So, they're closing other bridges? That sounds smart but could make it harder for me to get home," Mollie says.

"Yeah, I agree on both accounts."

"And it doesn't sound like they know much more about who's responsible."

"Don't think they do. But, then again, if they did, they might not say anything if they're planning something."

"I guess that's true." We hear a new voice on the radio.

"Please listen closely while we read the list of bridges targeted today and the towns affected. We ask if you are in these towns to please follow the instructions of your local officials. Staying at your home is safest, but please do heed calls to donate blood and requests for any trained first responders or medical personnel."

As she reads the list, there are bridges we knew of and many we didn't. They've hit quite a few in New York, Boston, the one going over the Potomac in DC, and the big bridge connecting the Keys to Florida. While most bridges are on either the east or west coast, there are at least two in the Midwest: The Lewis and Clark Viaduct—connecting Kansas City, Kansas, and Kansas City, Missouri—and the Speer Boulevard Bridge in Denver. There are several more collapsed bridges I don't recognize or can't pull up a geographical picture of where they are located. It does seem the terrorists are doing their best to halt transportation and scare people into staying home.

"Do you think we should see if Katie wants to come home? It might be a challenging trip for her, like it is for me, if she's avoiding bridges," Mollie says.

"I'll call her. You should get on the road and find someplace to rest up. Hopefully, by tomorrow, the bridge destruction will be done and you can make some good time getting home. Let me know when you find a place to stay. I love you."

"I love you, and . . . Jake, I'm sorry I was so snappy."

"This is a hard time, Mollie. You'll be home soon, and you can make it up to me in person," I waggle my eyebrows, even though she can't see them.

"Sure thing, Mister." She gives a small laugh. "Please call all of the girls, just to check in with them. Let me know how they are when we talk again. And hug Malcolm for me."

I suddenly want to hug Malcolm for both of us. I stare out the window and watch the chickens. They are running around looking for bugs or whatever they can find. They have no worries about their families not being at home. They don't need to wonder if any of their friends died today. They don't need to think about how to tell their ten-year-old son terrorists have struck again, and his mom may be further delayed in getting home.

Malcolm. There he is. Sitting in the goat pen playing with the baby goats. They are climbing on him. Is that a laugh? He rubs the smallest goat under the chin, then hugs her tight. *Thank you, Lord, for giving him a small, simple joy in the midst of this pain and chaos.*

Chapter 14

Jake

"Hello?"

"Katie. You have a minute to talk?"

"Of course. Have you talked to Mom? Is she okay?"

"I just hung up with her. She's outside of Redmond, Oregon. She's fine. I guess you've heard about the bridges?"

"I have, Jake. They attacked the bridge connecting Kansas City, Kansas, to Kansas City, Missouri. Can you believe that? And a bridge in Denver. Attacking the bridges is going to make transportation difficult. It makes me not even want to drive for fear of having to go over a bridge."

"I suspect you're not the only one feeling that way. Your mom and I were wondering if you feel like you should stay there or try to make your way here?" There's a rustling sound and some murmuring. She's talking with someone. Probably Leo. She returns back to the phone after a few moments.

"I'm not sure, Jake. While these latest attacks are terrible, it still seems like attacks and not a widespread event, you know what I mean?"

"I do. While these are terrible attacks, they are still not near you— "

"Exactly, Jake."

"—and you're feeling safe in your home, so it's normal to want to stay. The hard thing is knowing when the right time to leave is. I'd prefer you err on the side of caution and leave sooner rather than waiting until the last minute. I know your mom would prefer that too."

"I know," she sighs. "And if I ever feel unsafe, I'll for sure leave."

"Does your friend plan on coming with you? Leo? Will you bring him if you come home?"

She doesn't say anything for several seconds. "Yeah. I'd like to bring him. The things we've been sending were so he wouldn't be a burden if it hit the fan and we needed to come home."

"Your mom thought that might be the case. What are your plans with Leo?"

"What do you mean? I'd like to bring him home with me if I have to bug out."

I laugh a little. I guess my question wasn't as clear as it should have been. And I'm suddenly wondering why I haven't asked Katie this before or why Mollie hasn't. Has she? I'm pretty sure if she did, she'd tell me what Katie said.

"I mean, in general. Are you two serious?"

Katie drops her voice a little. "We're serious."

Why haven't I heard this before? Who is this guy, serious about my daughter, who I've heard so little about? She lives fifteen hundred miles away, but that's no excuse. If he's in love with her and she's in love with him, we should meet him. I don't do well keeping the irritation out of my voice with my next question.

"And were you planning on bringing him up here to meet us under normal circumstances?"

"I am, Jake. We're waiting for school to get done and Mom to come back from her trip. You know, we're planning on coming up over the Fourth of July, to cheer on you and Mom in your 5K. I know I've been kind of quiet about him, and I didn't really mean to be. It was just . . . awkward. I know you and Mom aren't wanting any weddings right now, so I was trying to keep things quiet so you wouldn't start freaking out about another wedding. Well, not *you* freaking out, but Mom. And we're not to that point, so . . . You'll like him. I promise. Don't be mad. I wasn't trying to be sneaky. Not really, anyway."

I barely capture a sigh. "I'm not mad, Katie. I just want the best for you. And it's pretty hard for me to imagine any guy being good enough for you."

She laughs a little. "Well, Leo is pretty amazing. I told Mom some about him. Did she tell you?"

"She told me he went to school with you and graduated last month. She said he's a few years older than you."

"Yes. He's a good guy. You'll like him. He majored in business but works construction during the summer. Before college he was a Marine. We bike and run together and have lots of things in common. He likes to hunt and fish, so you'll have things in common with him too."

"That sounds fine, Katie. So he's doing construction this summer, and then what?"

"He is, he's worked for the same place every summer since he moved to Manhattan. They really like him. He's not . . . I guess, he doesn't really know what he's going to do after summer. The business degree seemed smart, you know, kind of well-rounded and a good option, but he doesn't want to work in an office. I guess you could say he's kind of having 'buyer's remorse' now that he has the degree."

"Okay? So, he's just going to keep doing construction? Is there enough money in that?"

"He does okay, and he's very frugal—another thing you'll like about him—so his money goes a long way. But what I think he's really going to do is see about becoming an EMT. He took a class a few summers ago, at a community college nearby, but didn't take the certification test. He's talking about it now like it's what he wants to do. Might even see if he can do what's needed to move forward with the certification this summer. We'll see."

"All right, Katie. That sounds fine. Hopefully nothing more will happen and you'll be able to come up for a visit. I told your mom I'd call you and see how you're doing and what you're thinking. Her phone service is in and out, as usual, but you could try her later. I know she'd love to hear from you."

"I tried her, but the call went straight to voicemail. What's her plan for getting home?"

"Her plan is fluid at the moment. She's working her way to Pendleton, Oregon, on small highways. She's pretty tired since she slept very little last night. I'm pretty sure she's just looking for a town to stay tonight and will get back on the road tomorrow. We're hopeful things will calm down and she'll feel comfortable driving over bridges to get here."

"Okay. I'll try her later, and I'll text her too. Keep me posted if anything with her changes, please."

"I will, Katie. Take care."

"Bye, Jake."

I'm still a little irritated at Katie for not telling us more about Leo. Her explanation is plausible. Mollie did make it clear she needed a break from weddings. I don't think Katie is saying she's planning to get married, but it sounds like she thinks it's a possibility. She finishes school in January. Until just a few months ago, she talked about going on a half-year mission trip with her Kansas church. Lately, we haven't been hearing about the trip at all. I suspect this thing with Leo is the reason.

I text the rest of the girls. Since I can't remember how to do a group text, I send each an individual text telling them their mom is fine, she's in Oregon and will be home as soon as she can, Katie is staying in Kansas for now, and asking how they are doing.

I leave the bedroom and go into the main part of the house. My text notification goes off before I can get there. It's Sarah.

"Glad Mom is fine. I didn't think she was near Portland but was concerned. I can't believe so many bridges are gone. This is scary. It makes me not want to leave our house. I'm glad we bought the trailer and Tate took it down to you. He's home and his folks are here. I didn't realize his sister was coming along so she's with them. Our little house is full up. We have decided just to stay in Billings and not go up to Bozeman for the weekend like we were planning."

I text back, *"Sounds good."* I know I should say more, but I'm tired of texting and being on the phone.

Chapter 15

Malcolm

I'm trying to be brave and not cry. I've cried too much since last night when the planes crashed and then the airports exploded. Now, the radio says bridges have also exploded. I know Dad and Doris both said things will be fine—everything will be okay—but that was before this newest . . . problem.

At least Mom isn't where the bridges are. I was so mad at her for not driving in Portland, but the radio said some of those bridges were destroyed. What if Mom would've been on it when it blew up? I feel bad I was mad at her for not wanting to go to Portland.

I scrunch my face up to keep tears from popping out of my eyes. I try to force the tears to stop, but they don't and seem to shoot out like lasers from my eyes. I need to go . . . somewhere. I don't even really know why I'm crying.

Maybe I just wish Mom was home. I know planes have crashed and bridges have exploded, but I don't really understand all of it. I think it's bad, very bad. And I know lots of people have died. I also know this is something I'm going to remember for the rest of my life.

I decide to go and visit the goats. I'll let the big mama goats out in the field and then play with the babies. They're always fun to play with. The goats are happy to see me and rub up against my legs, kind of like a cat.

"Hey, little goats, something bad happened today. Something bad happened yesterday, too, but I think maybe what happened today might be worse. I don't know, but I feel like two bad things in a row means . . . something more. Maybe Dad will let us watch the news and see what's happening."

We have a few toys and things for the goats to help keep them from getting bored. I move over to a little obstacle course we've set up for them. It's just a couple of wooden platforms with stairs and ramps so they can climb around. I sit on one of the steps. The little goats decide

I'm part of the obstacle course and start climbing on me. I wish I had some raisins to feed them. Baby goats like raisins.

"Little boy goat, you need to be gentle with the others," I say to the biggest goat, as he tries to push the smaller goats out of the way so he can be in what he thinks is the best spot, the step right above me.

I start thinking about some of the school lessons Mom and I have done. I'm homeschooled. I've always been homeschooled. Sometimes I wish I went to a regular school so I'd have more friends. I do know a few boys who live near us, and they go to regular school. One of them told me they do fun things like recess and eat hot lunch. He also says they have to sit in a desk all day and can't talk. I don't have a school desk, and I can talk any time I want.

My favorite schooltime is when we listen to stories on the internet—what Mom calls books on tape, even though they aren't on a tape but on the computer. I can sit anywhere I want and draw or play with a LEGO set while the story plays.

We do a lot of what Mom calls unit studies. That's where I learned about the Great Depression and the Dust Bowl, which went along with it. I've learned about the solar system, some of the presidents, Christopher Columbus, Cinco de Mayo, the Emancipation Proclamation, and a whole bunch more.

Not too long ago, we had a unit study on 9/11. I hated that one. 9/11 stands for September 11, 2001—the day bad people used airplanes as bombs. They flew the airplanes into the World Trade Center and the Pentagon. There were four airplanes taken over by terrorists. On one of the airplanes, the people fought the terrorists and didn't let the plane get used as a bomb. When I started hearing about it, I thought maybe someone was able to fly the plane and help it land. I was really sad when I found out that plane crashed too.

When Mom was helping me with the lesson, she was really sad. She said, even though she wasn't anywhere near any of the plane crashes, it was still a terrible day. She said, when it happened, she was very upset. Later, she was not only upset but also mad. And then she started to tell me why she was mad but stopped herself and said she'd teach me more about 9/11 at a later time.

I guess, when I'm old like her, I'll think about last night's plane crashes and today's bridge explosions the way she thinks about 9/11. I guess, even then, it will make me sad. I'll probably be mad too.

Chapter 16

Jake

I fill a glass with water. *Pull it together, Jake. Malcolm needs you to be strong. Cowboy up and just do what you need to do.* My pep talk pretty much sucks. Am I crying? What the . . . I am crying. *Help us, Lord. Help us get through this,* I pray silently. It's many minutes before I pull myself together enough to get on with things. Besides, what else could happen? What else could happen . . . I make a snap decision to disconnect our house solar system and our whole-house generator. I think about the consequences of this.

Our solar system is a fully standalone system, not the type which sells power back to the electric company. This type of standalone system continues to work, even if the electric company power is off, via batteries storing the produced energy for later.

We have a few things, including our main freezer and our beverage fridge, always hooked up to this system on dedicated outlets. Our well pump is also hooked to the solar but is set up to only run on demand; I flip a switch when I want to use the well to fill our large underground cistern. Our water enters the house from the cistern and a small pump powered by the electric company, with an option for alternate power. I can top off the cistern now, giving us two thousand gallons of well water, and then disconnect the system. I'll plug the main freezer and small dorm-sized beverage fridge into a regular, connected-to-the-power-company outlet. I'm pleased with the way we've set up our electrical system to take advantage of solar and grid power separately.

We have a whole-house generator as a backup to the solar system; if the sun doesn't shine enough, the generator will automatically come on. I disconnect this also. We have two smaller, portable generators, which can be moved around as needed, plus a backup in the basement still in the box—I bought two when I found a great Black Friday deal. I also have an older generator I broke the pull start on. It's a respectable one, putting out a decent voltage. I bought the parts to fix it; I just haven't got around to doing so.

This is probably overkill, but my gut tells me this isn't over. The scenario in *One Second After* Mollie and Doris are always talking about is on my mind.

Three small, twelve-volt, RV-style solar systems are on hand for backup in the basement in our homemade Faraday cage. We talked about having backups for each system—the bunkhouse, cabin, milking barn, and the processing room—but decided against it. We also don't have a backup for our house solar system.

We chose not to have a backup for the house, other than extra wire, for a couple of reasons. Cost was a factor. Even the small systems are expensive, and our house system is more than double the cost of all the small systems combined.

Another factor, if we were ever in a situation where our main solar systems went out and we couldn't replace them, it might be best not to have these systems. Do we really want to be the only house on the hill with the lights on? Even with blackout shades and practicing light control, the risk could be too high.

With the small systems, we can hook one up to use during the daylight for things needing a power source, such as keeping batteries charged and using some power tools and small kitchen appliances.

But now that we're actually in a situation of such uncertainty, I'm rethinking a backup to our main system. It's feeling pretty real today, and I currently see more benefits to keeping the power going than not, such as keeping the freezers frozen. Maybe I should contact the guy who set up our system and see if he has any returns in stock. I hate the idea of spending the money, but the last twenty-four hours have put me on a spending spree anyway . . . what's several thousand more? I snort at this thought.

Tonight, I'll email our solar guy and see what he has. For now, I'll disconnect our solar system. *Yeah, Jake, you're not at all paranoid* . . .

"Malcolm, time to get some wood," I yell.

He walks around the side of the house. "Okay, Dad."

From the look of his face—smudged with dirt except where the skin has been cleaned by tears; red eyes, with one swollen more than the other; a large brown splotch on his nose, which looks like it may be goat poo; and his bottom lip caught between his teeth—I instantly realize I should've had him inside with me.

I don't say anything as I open my arms up. He practically vaults into my embrace and immediately breaks down.

Trying to speak between gulps, he says, "I don't know why I'm crying, but I'm so sad."

I attempt to keep my own composure. Fail. My tears join his. I don't know how long we stay this way, grieving, and . . . I guess what my grandma would've called caterwauling. By the time we pull ourselves together, I'm exhausted. All I really want to do is have a cold drink and relax.

Instead, I say, "I guess we probably both ought to wash our faces. I think you have a little something on your nose—something the goats left on the ground."

He gives me a funny look and then says, "I don't think it's all on my nose. You have goat poop on your shirt."

Then we both laugh like crazy men.

We wash our faces and hands; I don't bother changing my shirt but do wipe it off. I figure I'll get dirty with the wood anyway. What's a little goat poop? We crawl into the pickup and head the short distance to the wood cutting area.

We're about fifteen minutes into our work when a horn honks. It's David and Noah Hammer, neighbors across the creek.

"Howdy, Jake," David says in his slow Texan drawl.

"Hi, David, Noah. What are you two up to?"

"Saw you guys working when we were driving by and thought we'd help. Might be good to get our minds off of things."

I nod. "Yeah. We won't turn down the help."

"Terrible times we're living in," David says as we're stacking wood in the truck. "Very Biblical, makes me worry what might be next. Of course, Mark tells us, no one will know, '*But of that day and that hour knoweth no man, no, not the angels which are in heaven, neither the Son, but the Father.*' Still . . . I have to wonder."

"Mm-hmm," I grunt as I move a rather large piece. David leads the community Bible study we attend. We've had several discussions on various events and happenings which seem very prophetic. I can't say I disagree with him.

"This is really hard on Betty, you know, with our other children and grandson living so far away. She's almost beside herself and has practically begged them all to come here. Our little community seems like such a safer option than east Texas and Philadelphia."

"Yeah, and no bridges," sixteen-year-old Noah says, "nothing of any size, anyway."

"Are there lots of bridges in Texas where your brother is?" Malcolm asks.

"Yep, some. Lots between here and there. Not just my brother—his wife, my nephew, and my sister and her husband. They are all still in Texas," Noah answers.

Malcolm nods and asks, "And Philadelphia . . . who lives there?"

"My oldest brother."

"Oh . . . I don't think I know him."

"Sure you do. He was here last summer. Looks like me only with a black beard instead of gray, remember?" David says, waggling his eyebrows at Malcolm. "Him and my daughter were both here when we had that barbecue."

Malcolm shrugs. "Maybe. I was only nine then, and it's hard to remember things from when I was so young."

David lets out a hearty chuckle. "Yeah, well, wait until you're sixty-five and then see what you can remember. I'd lose my head if it wasn't for my young son here reminding me to keep it attached."

"I bet you're glad your other brother lives here now," Malcolm says.

"Yep, sure am. Betty and I are very happy he decided to move up. One less offspring to worry about." David turns to me. "Say . . . didn't I hear Mollie was working out of town? She back home now?"

Tears immediately fill Malcolm's eyes. I gently touch his arm and offer him a small smile.

"Not yet. Her flight was due in tonight. She's driving the rental car home. She should be here . . . I don't know . . . maybe late tomorrow night or Sunday. Just depends on . . . things."

"Right. Sorry to hear that, Jake. We'll be praying for her safe travels. Well, let's get this done."

Noah and Malcolm move to a section with several downed limbs and start dragging them over near the truck. The limbs are great for our rocket stoves, a unique heating system we've employed.

Malcolm is chattering away and occasionally laughing. I'm glad his mind is off the disasters, for the moment at least. Noah, always quiet, says little.

I've shut down the saw and am moving cut logs when the sound of an approaching engine catches my attention. Not a car or truck, an ATV of some sort.

Within a few seconds, a side-by-side comes into view. Dan Morse. Most of the people we have living around here are people I enjoy and want to spend time with. Dan Morse isn't one of those people.

"Looks like Morse," David says. "Haven't seen him around for a while. Thought he might have moved. Wonder what he's doing back here?"

I shrug and continue to work. When Dan is close enough, I raise my hand in acknowledgment. The return gesture is a one finger wave . . . of sorts.

"Whoa. Not sure if that was directed at you or me," David says with a small chuckle.

"Huh. I'm not sure. Can't think of any reason. Dan was around a lot when we first started coming up here. He'd stop in when we were camping, before our house was finished."

"Yeah, our builder said the same thing. When he was putting up our house, Dan was there quite a lot asking questions. There's something kind of *off* about him. Even so, I'm always cordial to him. Betty thinks maybe he's just insecure and tries too hard to impress people. I don't know about that."

"Well, I'm not going to worry about it. Maybe he's a little on edge about everything happening. I know I am."

With David and Noah's help, we make quick work of filling up the truck bed and trailer. I invite David to stop at our place for a cold beverage on his way home, but he asks for a raincheck. This is okay by me since we need to get the wood unloaded. I have very little time before needing to do chores. Then, before dark, I'll get the vines planted. I suppose we should fit supper in there somewhere.

I'm dreading digging the holes to plant the vines in our rocky, hard ground. The new plants will be added to an already existing row of vines along the front of the property. These make a great divider from the road and are another part of our security measures, adding difficulty for people getting onto our land. We have an antelope fence—three rows of nonbarbed with a top row of barbed—in place so the vines, many with their own sharp spikes, can use the fence for support.

"Dad? You think we should listen to the radio, just in case, while we do this?"

I think about it for a few moments. I don't want to expose him to too much of this, but don't want him to think I'm keeping information from him either. "Sure, Buddy. Run and get it. We can listen for a few minutes."

Malcolm runs off after the radio while I start getting things together for digging.

Malcolm is back with the radio blaring "Proud to be an American."

"Hey, Dad. Mind if I change the channel?"

Malcolm prefers anything but country and likes a station which plays current music. I can handle it in small doses so agree changing the station will be fine. Malcolm carries the radio and a shovel while I handle the rest of our tools.

"Following today's bridge attacks, we are seeing a mass exodus from the affected cities. Forty-eight bridges across the US were destroyed today. Three of those bridges connected the island of Manhattan to other New York City boroughs. The remaining bridges are practically abandoned, the tunnels are full of traffic, and the ferry system is overwhelmed. We're seeing similar scenarios in other cities, including Seattle, Portland, Baltimore, and the District of Columbia.

"So far, no one has claimed responsibility for the bridge attacks or last night's airport attacks."

Once we reach the line of vines, I say, "Let's hold off on this a minute. I'd like to see how the roads look near where your mom is traveling. Thought maybe we could check them on the computer. You think you could help me with that?"

"Sure, Dad. That'll be easy."

"Yeah, for you, since you're a whiz on the computer. For me . . . not so much."

"True. I get more practice with school and stuff."

"Yep, no doubt. Grab the radio. Go ahead and shut it off for now. We'll listen again later."

Inside, Malcolm pulls out his school laptop. "You know the road name, Dad?"

"Let's start with I-84 in Oregon."

"Hmmm. I found the Oregon Department of Transportation. They have something called TripCheck. Under the alert section, it says, 'I-84: Closure without detour from the origination of I-84 at the I-5 Interchange to Biggs Junction.' Below there, it also shows I-5 South in Portland closed due to the bridge being out. And from Wilsonville to Eugene it's closed. For I-5 North, it says the bridge is out and the

Highway 205 bridge is out. How many bridges did Portland lose?" he asks wide eyed.

"I think there were two or three more besides the three you just read about."

"Wow, Dad. Why so many in Portland?"

"I'm not sure. They hit several in New York also. Maybe because those towns have quite a few bridges with a lot of traffic on them. Some key bridges were definitely hit."

Malcolm shakes his head and goes back to the computer. After a couple of seconds, he says, "Uh-oh. It looks like people didn't pay attention to the road closures. There's a news article saying people fled from Portland and are now stranded on the interstate. From Portland to The Dalles, nothing is moving. From The Dalles east many miles, it's bumper to bumper. Hotels are also full all the way to Pen . . . Pen . . . ton or something.

"Pendleton?" I ask.

"Yeah. I think that's it. P-E-N-D-L-E-T-O-N. It's a hard word."

"It is. It's also over three hours from Portland. I'm kind of surprised a town so far from Portland would be affected by this. Your mom was planning to stay there tonight."

"Do we need to call her?"

"No, before we hung up, she said she was too tired and didn't think she could make it that far. She'll stay somewhere else. You see anything else important?"

"Gas is a problem. This says stations are running out. There's too many cars needing gas. And one station says they don't know how they can even get any more with so many idiots blocking the interstate. That wasn't a very nice thing to say. I'm sure people were just scared and thought leaving Portland would make them safer. Don't you think, Dad? Portland is pretty big. I wouldn't want to be there when bridges were blowing up."

"I think you're probably right."

"The same guy calling people idiots says his town is even running out of food. The . . . 'horde of locusts' . . . have eaten all of the food in the restaurants and are buying up everything in the grocery store. 'Strangers are taking food from his family.' What's he mean? Aren't locusts bugs? Is there a problem with bugs also?"

"I think he's referring to the people fleeing Portland as a horde of locusts. Swarming locusts are known to do lots of damage and can decimate crops. I think he's using an analogy for what he sees happening."

Malcolm gives me a single nod and goes back to reading the internet articles. I have to admit, I'm concerned. The bridge attacks were only four hours ago. If this has happened already, what will tomorrow look like?

"You know, Buddy, I think I'll call your mom."

Where's my phone? It's not on my belt in its case. Did I drop it when we were cutting or unloading wood? Ugh. All I need right now is a broken phone. When was the last time I had it? I had it in the kitchen before going out to do the wood. Sure enough, it's on the counter. And I have three texts awaiting me. I read Mollie's first.

"Tried to call but couldn't get through. I'm at Cottonwood Canyon State Park around 30 miles north of Condon, I think. I'm going to see if I can get a spot here. I'm beat and ready to sleep. There isn't any phone coverage in the park according to the FAQs sign I'm reading. I think I'll take a nap, then I'll come back out here and try to reach you. I love you."

The next are from Calley and Angela, thanking me for letting them know where Mollie is and how Katie is. Both say they are fine.

I try to call Mollie, just in case she's wrong about the service. Straight to voicemail. I send a text instead of leaving a message, telling her what's happening and suggesting she fill up her gas tank as soon as she can.

I don't know if people might get off the freeway and head toward Condon. I'm trying to think what town the turn off is at from I-84. We've taken the route before when going hunting near Prairie City. It's just after Biggs Junction . . . Arlington. Yes, that's what it is. It's a small town with one gas station I can remember. Nothing else sticks out to me about that town, other than it doesn't seem like it was too far from Arlington to Condon. I have no memory of any state park along the route but can't imagine it's that far off the freeway if it's before Condon.

Then I remember Mollie wasn't going to Condon from Arlington. She was on Highway 97 and had to cut across to get to Condon on 19. I'm hopeful, if it's a little out of the way road, she'll miss the onslaught of people. I wish there was more I could do, but with no cell service, I have to wait until she gets somewhere to read my message. I'm suddenly wishing she would've kept driving instead of stopping at such a remote location.

Malcolm asks if we should do the chores, and I agree we should. I pocket my phone so I have it if Mollie calls.

Chapter 17

Jake

About ten minutes into digging holes, I make an executive decision to call it good when we have two finished. I'll call Noah Hammer tomorrow and see if I can hire him to help dig. At sixteen, he's always looking for extra jobs to help bring in a little spending money. He's not driving yet, so getting a job too far from home hasn't worked out.

Close to having the second hole completed, we hear the roar of an engine. I briefly wonder if it's Morse driving by to flip me the bird again.

Nope. Alex MacIntyre, a friend. He slows his pickup, then stops and gets out. It's still running, so I suspect he just wants to say hello. Mollie and I give partial credit to the MacIntyres for us ending up in Bakerville.

Alex and his wife, Natalie, bought their place a couple years before we bought our place. They live in a different section of Bakerville, on the edge of the wilderness area. Their place was an old ranch, which stopped being worked a dozen years before when the owner died. The relatives tried, unsuccessfully, to sell it for many years. Then the market crashed. When things started to come back, they repriced it at a reasonable rate, and Alex and Natalie snatched it up. They moved here from Tennessee. He sold a very successful landscaping company, and she sold a real estate company with the dream of starting homesteading and permaculture classes.

Alex started learning about permaculture several years ago and implemented much of these design principals into his landscaping business. He eventually had two separate arms of the business: the regular lawn mowing and landscaping for businesses and individuals, and the permaculture design and maintenance. He started teaching permaculture classes, calling them edible landscaping classes, which sold quite well in his urban area. Permaculture led him to learn more about homesteading skills. Natalie became interested in this also, and the rest, as they say, is history.

They fully changed their lives, moved their seven children here, and now host students learning on-site in their immersion programs. The students show up on a Sunday evening and stay for a week or even longer. They've set up several off-grid places for lodging and some people pitch a tent. They open up their Saturday workshops to the public, in addition to their students.

We started learning about permaculture several years before moving up here. Mollie was surprised to find permaculture teachers in Wyoming. We signed up for one of their Saturday classes, taking advantage of my parents' guest room in nearby Prospect, and attended the daylong workshop. The workshop was great, and we loved the area. Afterward, Mollie started looking at property available in the area. The location, so close to my parents, was perfect, and it turned out to be just what we were looking for.

We've been good friends with the MacIntyres since the workshop. They really helped us figure out our plans for the place and how best to use our land and resources. When I think back on those early days of planning our place, it brings a smile to my face. Malcolm, a natural artist, was great at drawing out our ideas. We'd talk over what we were thinking, and he'd sketch it out and then color it in—blue ponds, green trees, purple grapes—it was all wonderfully done. Those drawings are very special to me. We even framed one and have it hanging in our rec room. Malcolm often says we should let him redo the picture since he was "too young" when he drew it and could do much better now. I think it's perfect.

Alex walks to the fence. Before he says anything, I remember his daughter is getting married tomorrow, and Mollie, Malcolm, and I are supposed to attend the wedding.

"Hey, Alex. How are you? Everything set for Annie's wedding?"

"Hello, Jake. Yep. I was just up at Noland's old place borrowing a few more folding tables and chairs, even though I'm sure we already have enough. It's a bit of a mess with all this trouble. The people who were flying in today for the wedding aren't coming, of course. And we've got students who were supposed to leave today, but it looks like they're going to stay on a few more days. Natalie invited them to the wedding.

"We're supposed to have new students arriving on Sunday. Heard from the ones flying in. But some were driving. Natalie's tried to reach them. She connected with one family who've turned around and headed home. Two more families are unaccounted for. We'll just have to see."

"You think they'll have any trouble getting here with the bridges out and the road troubles?"

"They might. I asked Natalie, but she doesn't know their exact routes, so it's certainly possible. I half expect they'll decide to turn around and go home, like the others. We might get us a week off. Probably be a good thing with the wedding."

"Annie getting excited?"

"She is. A little nervous too. Kaleb's family came in on Wednesday. That seems to have helped. Oh, hey, Mollie make it home? Wasn't she working out of town this week?"

"Not yet. After the planes were grounded, she decided to drive her rental car home. She's in Eastern Oregon right now."

"Away from the bridge problems? Wasn't Oregon hit pretty hard?"

"Portland was. She wasn't near there. She's pretty upset, though, since she lived in the Portland area most of her life and has many friends there."

"When you think she'll make it home?"

"I'm not sure. Last I heard from her, she was camped for the night. She left last night and slept a few hours in the car, so she was pretty wiped out. I think, if everything goes okay, she'll be home on Sunday. Sorry she'll miss Annie's wedding. Malcolm and I'd still like to come."

"Of course! We plan on you being there. And we totally understand about Mollie. Annie's being quite a trooper about the people not coming. She and Natalie briefly discussed canceling the wedding, but Kaleb convinced her they should go on with it. He's right about it. Even in the middle of a national tragedy, things have to continue on. I'd better get back home. We'll see you tomorrow, Jake."

"Goodbye, Alex. See you tomorrow. You need me to come over a little early to help finish setting up?"

"Nope. We've got it under control." He lifts his hand in something resembling a wave as he drives off.

Malcolm and I are walking back to the house when my text notification chimes. It's Mollie. I get an immediate smile on my face.

"It's Mom, right? What's she doing?"

"Hold on a minute, Buddy. Let me read it and then I'll tell you."

I fumble with my phone and almost drop it when trying to hit the button to open the text.

"Your mom says she got my message and decided to hit the road. She'll gas up in Condon and then decide where to go from there. She'll try to call me when the signal's better."

"That's good, right? She's driving again so she can get home."

"Yes, probably good. It's hard to know with everything happening." I decide not to say anything more.

Please, Lord, keep her safe . . .

Malcolm and I have an easy supper, then we check the computer again. I-84 out of Portland is still at a standstill, gas is scarce and hotel rooms are full, and restaurants are closed in many of the towns along the interstate. Some towns have set up emergency shelters in schools and community buildings. Food is an issue, with so many people using limited small-town resources. Even the larger towns, like Hood River and The Dalles, are stripped. Pendleton, while full of people, isn't quite as bad since it's so far away. Most people are simply stuck on the freeway with no way to move. It's getting close to bedtime when the phone finally rings.

"Honey! Are you in Condon?"

"Yes, I just fueled up and am getting ready to be on my way. I'm heading toward Lake Owyhee. You know, where we stayed that one time?"

"Uh, yeah. But you don't want to stay there. Remember how far it is off the main road? It took us forever to get to the campground."

"You're right. But it's nice, quiet roads that'll get me closer to home. My goal is Vale, which is near there. I'll go through John Day and Prairie City, so I'll have fueling options."

"I think that's a good plan. Did you look ahead on how to get home from Vale?"

"Not much. I'll be pretty close to Ontario. I think there's a highway running north from there I can take. I think it's the same one we took when we camped near there that time."

"Okay. I'm pretty sure the road goes up to Moscow, Idaho. You can probably find some small roads off it to continue east toward home. It's going to be a long, slow haul for you."

"For sure. I'm pretty happy to be off the interstate, though, if they're still parking lots. Are they? Or are things moving better?"

"Parking lots, last I checked. Many places with gas and hotel room shortages. Some towns are setting up emergency shelters in schools and such."

"What a mess."

"It's for sure a mess. I'm glad you're not caught up in it," I say, while letting out a breath of relief.

"Me too. The people ending up in those towns could be a lot like refugees. The little towns won't have the resources to sustain the sheer numbers."

"They don't. It's already to that point. You'd better get on the road so you can get somewhere and get some sleep. Do you want to say a quick hello to Malcolm?"

"Yes, I do. Can you put me on speaker phone?"

I flounder slightly looking for the speaker phone button, while speaking loudly so Mollie can hear me in the meantime. "Okay, I'm trying to switch to the speaker."

"Dad, the button is in the middle," Malcolm offers.

"Yep, there it is. Can you hear us, Mollie?"

"Perfectly. Hey, Malcolm. How are you?"

"I'm good, Mom. You driving okay?"

"I am! Everything is good. I took a little nap at a campground. You won't believe this, but there were antelope at the camping spot."

"Antelope in Oregon?" Malcolm asks with disbelief. "I thought all of the antelope lived here."

"Most do," Mollie says, "but there are some in Oregon, California, and remember we saw those ones up in Montana? They live in other places too."

"Neat. Did seeing the antelope make you miss home?"

"I missed home already. I can't wait to get there and hug the stuffing out of you."

Malcolm rolls his eyes but has a big smile on his face.

"Okay, Mom. I'll let you hug me when you get here."

"Well, thank you very much, Mr. Malcolm. I'm going to get going. I'll send you guys a text or call when I stop again. I love you both."

"I love you. Be safe," I say.

"Love you too, Mom."

We disconnect, and I'm suddenly exhausted. It's been a long, stress-filled day.

"Well, that's good, Malcolm. Your mom will get a hotel. She should get there in a couple hours. She'll get ahold of us when she does, but I suspect she'll be fine. She's far enough from the interstate she shouldn't have any trouble. I'm exhausted and would like to shut things down early. You ready for bed?"

"Uh . . . I guess. It's pretty early and the sun is still shining. Can I take the laptop and watch a movie on Netflix? Or play on my tablet?"

"Yeah, sure. The movie is fine for tonight. Let's go ahead and have you get in your pajamas and brush your teeth. You want to read some of your story before we hit the hay?"

"Yep. I do. I'll get ready and be back with the book."

I struggle with staying awake while reading tonight. Malcolm finally stops me and tells me to go to bed, saying we can finish the chapter tomorrow night.

He takes the laptop and heads to his room. I go to mine. I don't even bother to change or get under the covers.

I'm not quite sure what the ringing noise is, and by the time I realize it's the phone, it stops. Mollie. I call her back.

"Hey, Jake. I'm in a motel in John Day."

"Super, honey. How was the road there?"

"It was quiet. John Day seems quiet. I guess people aren't coming here or haven't thought to come here yet, anyway. I'm just logging on to my laptop to see what's up and have the news channel on TV."

"I went to bed a while ago but had the phone by the bed so I'd hear when you called. I haven't looked at anything on the computer for an hour or so. Anything new?"

"I'm looking at a Portland news channel. They are reporting a confirmed death toll of 358 but expect the number to rise considerably with so many bridges affected. People are being advised to stay in their homes and to not try to exit the city.

"There are shortages of gas in and around Portland, plus I-84 and I-5 South aren't moving at all. I-30 and I-26 West are also parking lots. All the little towns dotting the coast, including Alto, have been inundated. Alto, Jake. I guess I shouldn't be surprised, but I worry about Ben and Clarice.

"Have you talked to them?"

"Earlier today, to Ben, before the bridges. They are announcing no lodging available in these towns and none anywhere along I-5 or I-84 within the state, plus the gas shortages. Jeez, I suspect John Day will be hit soon by travelers if that's the case."

"Did you fill your tank when you got to John Day?"

"Yes, did that before finding a room. I want to be ready to jet out of here in the morning and not worry about fuel. With fuel shortages, people will start getting desperate. Depending on where I end up tomorrow night, I may have to worry about my gas being siphoned—you think?"

"Gosh. I guess so. Remember when gas prices were really high and I had a friend who did have his gas siphoned? Lots of people installed locking gas caps during that time. It makes sense, if stations are out of gas, people could start stealing gas from car tanks."

"I need to get home. This just gets crazier and crazier."

"You need to sleep," I admonish. "Then get back on the road early tomorrow. Did you bring your map in?"

"I did, but I'm going to look on MapQuest and see where to go from Vale. I'll spend a few minutes before bed figuring it out, then trace it on the paper map."

"Sounds like a good plan. Call me tomorrow once you're on the road?"

"I will. Sleep well, my love."

"You too, Mollie. Goodnight."

I'm thankful Mollie didn't have any trouble finding a room. Hopefully tomorrow will be a quiet trip for her and she'll be able to make it closer to home after a good night's rest. I settle back into bed, and as I'm drifting off, I wonder if there are any news updates on the food poisoning outbreaks. I should check in to that tomorrow and make sure to talk to the girls about those. I can't remember if I mentioned those when I spoke with each of them today.

Too much happening at one time for sure.

Chapter 18

Jake
Saturday, Day 3

Up at 4:30. Going to be another busy day. Alex and Natalie MacIntyre's daughter's wedding is at 2:00. Bubba is delivering the cabin I agreed to around noon. Before he shows up, I want to run into town and fill up all of the fuel cans I emptied to finish filling the transfer tanks purchased yesterday. I'll take the trailer and my wood cutting items so we can stop at a small swath of national forest on the way back. I'll give Noah a call later and see if he's interested in making a few bucks digging. Whew. So much going on. *Huh. And I'm okay with it.*

A few weeks ago, I would've balked at such a full day, lamenting on how I'd rather go fishing or hiking or just go anywhere. For a while, I started to think I was getting lazy. Mollie assured me many times I wasn't lazy, just not as motivated right now. And she agreed her motivation was also lacking. Still, not sure that's much different than lazy.

Now . . . I feel good.

Making coffee, I think of my wife. How's she doing? I could call her. What time is it on the West Coast? Too early. I'll let her sleep and call after chores. I'm glad she made it to John Day last night. That's usually a nice, quiet town.

Back in the house a little after 7:00. Chores went a little better than usual. The nasty goat wasn't quite as nasty today. As I'm finishing washing up, my phone rings. Mollie. She's probably just getting up and ready to hit the road.

"Hey, honey!"

"Hi, Jake! Guess what?"

"What's that?"

"I've crossed over to mountain time."

"Wow, you must have got an early start."

"I did. I think I left the hotel just after 3:30. I'm in Vale now and stopped to look over the map. My plan is to go from here up to Ontario and then head up Highway 95. Can you look on the computer and see if there's any reason not to do this? I could pull mine out and use my hotspot, but if you already have yours handy . . . "

"Yeah. Give me just a few minutes. We just came in from doing the chores."

"Thank you, Jake. What are your plans for today?"

"I have to dig some holes. I bought a few clearance vines the other night. Malcolm and I started digging the holes to plant them, but I'd forgotten just how rocky it is there—you know, along the front line? I'm going to see if Noah can come over and help dig."

"I suspect he will. He's often looking for ways to make a few bucks. You putting them in the sections that are a little bare? What are they?"

"Yeah, I'll fill them in where needed. That one spot where we lost the raspberries is where I started digging last night. I bought an assortment, ten total. Found a few gooseberries. Was surprised about that."

"That's great. I'm glad you found more gooseberries. The two we planted are doing well, and with their sharp spines, they really serve well as a deterrent."

"You want to talk with Malcolm for a minute while I finish getting the computer going?"

"Yes, I definitely do."

"Hey, Mom," Malcolm says. He sounds tired.

He pauses to listen to Mollie, then says, "Yeah, Dad says we have to go to a wedding today. Annie is getting married. At least I can play with her brother. What's his name? Tommy?"

I focus on getting the computer up and running. Even though I've turned this thing on many times and know how to get on the internet, I need to concentrate on what I'm doing. It's not like I'm a Luddite or anything, but technology isn't my greatest skillset.

I signal to Malcolm I'm ready. He says to Mollie, "That sounds good, Mom. Today would be better, but tomorrow will be okay. I think Dad's ready to talk to you again."

I take the phone back, tousle Malcolm's hair, and say, "Okay, honey. I'm checking I-84. It's still terrible to Pendleton, and even a little beyond, but clears up around La Grande. I think you'll be fine crossing I-84 at Ontario."

"All right. That's good. I'm going to go ahead and get on the road, then. I just had a yummy breakfast of a cheese and meat roll plus a granola bar."

"No coffee?"

"Two cups of gas station brew along the way."

"Ah . . . I know how you love gas station coffee."

"I was thinking it was better than nothing this morning."

"Stay in touch. I'm thinking these nuts aren't finished yet. I disconnected the solar system yesterday, just in case."

"Just in case? Oh . . . you mean in case of an EMP?"

"Right."

"Does that seem like something terrorists would do? It seems to me they'd want to continue to cause terror. Not do something so final. What could they hope to gain by an EMP? And where would they get a nuclear weapon?"

"I suspect they have connections. And we're assuming these are regular terrorists like Al-Qaeda or ISIS. What if this is North Korea doing these things?"

"North Korea? Wouldn't a country acting like terrorists be a little odd?"

"Yes, it would be. But the end result would weaken us so they could come in and take over," I answer, with a little more determination than I intended.

"They don't have near the people needed to come in and take over," Mollie retorts.

"Not on their own. But what if they aren't acting on their own?"

"Jake, you're sounding like you've been spending too much time on the internet."

I recognize her tone. I'm getting a slight scolding.

"I haven't. I've been thinking of these things on my own. I might do an internet search, though. Just to see if other people are thinking the same thing."

"I have no doubt you'll be able to find others thinking as you are. You can corroborate anything you want with the right searches. That doesn't make it true." The scolding is no longer slight; she's sounding a little hardheaded. I switch to my most patient voice.

"Honey, all I'm saying is it seems a little too organized. Too well planned. Could a terrorist cell plan and institute these things that have happened?"

"Why not? They've done things on a smaller scale. What if those were all practices leading up to this?"

"Hmm. Maybe. Whether it's terrorists or some country attacking us in an abnormal way, I think we should be ready. We've been storing food and materials and building our place just in case something like this happens. It'd be silly to stop thinking through the possibilities now. Speaking of, I thought I'd contact our solar guy and see if he has a used inverter and controller for sale that I could hook into our system."

"Jake, we've spent so much money the last few days. And you know how much those are. We decided not to buy a backup for the house because of the cost and operational security. The small system backups were expensive enough." She does not sound happy.

I take a deep breath before answering. "They were. And it seems you talked me into those. I trusted you knew best when we decided to buy them. And it's not just their cost, but the cost to put together the Faraday cages, while not super high, does add up. This is something I think is a good idea. You should trust me on this."

She lets out a small sigh. "You're right. I do trust you. It's smart to disconnect it. Go ahead and check with him. If he has something he's looking to move from his inventory, he may give us a good deal on it. Speaking of, you're still expecting Bubba today with the new cabin?"

What's this? She never gives in this easily. Victory for me! "Far as I know, Bubba should be here around noon. He said he'd call me from the pickup place if it's not what he expects. I'm kind of wishing I would've passed on it. Then the idea of a second solar system wouldn't be so bad."

"The second system is going to be more than the cabin by a long shot," she hurls back.

Oops. Should have skipped mentioning the solar system again. "Yes, it will. And I hope Bubba is on time. I completely forgot about Annie's wedding today."

"Me too, until Malcolm mentioned it. I'm glad you two are still going. Be sure to pass along my congratulations and regrets for not being there."

"Alex already knows. I saw him yesterday evening. He stopped by for a minute while Malcolm and I were trying to dig those holes. I let them know you weren't going to make it. Quite a few others not making it, too, with the flight cancellations."

"The gift I bought for Annie and Kaleb is in the gift closet. I wrapped it before I left. There's a card on it. You can't miss it."

"Great. I'll make sure I get it. You think Malcolm can just wear his black Wranglers and a button-up shirt? Me too?"

"Yes, that should be fine. It's an outdoor wedding during the afternoon. I think there will be cake and punch afterward. No dinner."

"Right. Maybe, when Katie gets married, we can do a nice afternoon one. Speaking of, she told me last night she loves Leo. I got the impression, once she finishes school, we'll be planning a wedding again."

"I've wondered," Mollie says with a small groan. "More because of what she doesn't say than what she does. I feel a little bad I made such a big deal about needing a break from weddings. That probably wasn't fair to her."

"We did need a break from weddings. Even though they were all wonderful and we're happy about them, three weddings in three years was a lot. But if Katie does want to get married, we'll help her with the wedding just like the others."

"Of course. I hope we can meet him before wedding plans are started."

"Yeah, me too. I'm going to take care of paying all of the bills. I only left a hundred in savings yesterday. I know you said you'd take more cash out of checking today, but how about I move additional to savings so you can withdraw from there also—you know, to beat the daily limits, just in case?"

"I think it's a good idea, but I'm not sure when I can get that out. There may be a rule I have to wait twenty-four hours from the last transaction. I'll keep an eye out for an ATM and try it. I didn't even think about it, but I suspect ATMs are out of money in the areas where the crowds are. Cash on hand is probably a good idea. And we can always put it back in the bank when I get home and this whole ordeal is over. Oh, Jake," Mollie says all excited. "I just remembered, I sent a bunch of books to yours and Malcolm's tablets and the spare eReader. Turn all three on and connect to the Wi-Fi so the books can download, okay?"

"Yes, sure. Good idea. I'd better let you get on the road. Call me later?"

"I will. I love you. Remind Malcolm I love him."

"Ah, honey, he knows. But I'll tell him anyway."

After disconnecting the call, I sit there for a few minutes gathering my thoughts.

"Hey, Malcolm. Run and get our tablets—mine's on my nightstand. You know where yours is?"

"Of course I do, Dad," he answers with a little cheekiness. I just give him a look. "Sorry. It's by my bed. I'll get both of them."

"Thanks, we also need the backup eReader. You know where we keep it? In the Faraday cage?"

"Yeah, I can get it. And I'll make sure to get the lid back on tight. I know the cage thing doesn't work until it's sealed up tight."

"Good man," I answer.

Malcolm gives me a nod and asks, "The eReader is in the trash can with the #2 marked on it?"

"Yes, that's the right one."

The eReader was Mollie's original electronic book I gave her for Christmas years ago . . . not long after they first came out. I was sure it was more of a novelty than anything. Guess I was wrong.

She's purchased a newer model, but we keep this one for the mass collection of information it has. She has categories for all sorts of subject matter: homesteading, cooking, camping, health, and more. Plus, lots of fiction books for either the joy of reading or because she's already read it and it had information she felt was worth saving.

We keep the device in the basement inside one of our garbage can Faraday cages. If there was ever an electromagnetic pulse or coronal mass ejection, we'd still have access to the mass amount of collected books.

Yes, our paranoia runs deep . . .

Chapter 19

Jake

Malcolm and I have a quick breakfast of eggs and toast. I take a minute to email our solar guy about a used system and pay all of the bills online. I briefly consider my trip to town. Should I get supplies in addition to fuel? I decide against it due to the time I have available today.

It's still early, so on the way back from town I'll call Noah about digging the holes.

I give Robert, my brother, a quick call. Even though he's on Pacific time, I have no doubt he's up and around. We tend to keep the same early schedules. He answers on the first ring.

"Hey, Jake. What a mess we have starting."

"Yeah. You get people from San Francisco area?"

"Not here. Not yet. Don't know if we will."

"Things look like they might get rough—all of the people leaving the cities with the bridges that were hit. Mollie's been working in Oregon this week. She's trying to drive home. She's in Eastern Oregon this morning and will come up through Idaho."

"I'm sorry to hear that, Jake. I know it must be hard having Mollie gone with everything happening. I'd probably be freaking out if Theresa was gone with all this happening."

"Yeah. Robert, I want to make sure you and Theresa know the four of you are all welcome at our place if things go bad at your place."

"Why would things go bad here? Oh, you mean if we get people from San Francisco?"

"Yeah, maybe, or if anything happens."

"Okay, Jake. But I can't imagine anything bad enough we'd need to leave. I really doubt people would come here. Everyone in California knows we haven't fully recovered from last year's fire season. We still have more people than our town can handle. And I certainly can't see Theresa leaving her mom.

"Theresa's mom is welcome too. At the very least, let me give you some directions on how to get here."

"If we decide to go there, I'll just give you a call then."

"What if the phones don't work? Remember the big storm when I lived in Oregon and our phones were down? And when the fire hit last fall, there were many people who couldn't get their phones to work. Things happen."

He gives a loud sigh. "Okay, Jake. You know, Mom and Dad said you and Mollie are kind of like survivalists now. Is that true?"

My parents told him this? *Survivalists?* I'm kind of surprised since we keep things very low-key around them. They haven't even had the grand tour of most of our stuff. They have an idea of some of the things we do, but that's about it.

Robert continues, "They said you have solar and stuff."

I laugh. "We do have solar and stuff. We're not survivalists, not that I really know what that means. The power goes out here sometimes when we have a storm, and the solar works great as a backup. Dad's been talking about getting a generator for the same reason."

"Go ahead and tell me where you live. I'll Google it and print out the directions."

The paranoid part of me doesn't like this—I envision a map floating around with a big *X* . . . something like marking a treasure, but I choose to say nothing. I suggest he may want to print a couple of different directions and avoid interstates with everything going on. He makes noises like he thinks I'm a wacko but reluctantly agrees. When we hang up, I half wonder if he'll even bother to pull up the directions.

We stop at the gas station on the very edge of Prospect, then, from there, we hit a swath of national forest fairly near our house. This is a well-picked-over area and isn't my favorite place to gather firewood, but it'll work for today's purposes. Besides, I don't have a ton of space, with the fuel cans taking up room.

Even though it's hot and sweaty work, Malcolm and I mostly enjoy our time cutting wood. Malcolm mentions he'd rather be doing something else, *anything else*, a few times. I suggest more work, less talk so we can get it done. With a sigh and a grumble under his breath, which I choose to ignore, he sets his jaw and turns away from me to gather up cut pieces.

We have the remaining space in the truck filled and are ready to head for home shortly after ten o'clock. Once we get back in cell service, I give Noah a call.

"Noah? Jake Caldwell. Feel like making a few dollars today?"

"Yes, sir. I'd be happy to."

"Great. I need some holes dug along the fence line. It's an even rockier section than usual. You up to it?"

"How many and how deep?"

"Ten total. Malcolm and I started on two last night—they need finished. Then eight more. Not too deep. It's for bare root bushes. You'll have to judge based on each of the roots. I can show you, so you'll know."

"Yes, sir. That's fine, sir. When should I start?"

"We're on our way back now. Should be there in about fifteen minutes. You know where the pick and shovel are in the tool shed?"

"Yes, sir."

"Feel free to start if you get there before us."

"Fine, sir."

And with that, he disconnects. Noah is always a man of few words. But he's a hard worker, and better him digging holes than me today.

I turn on the radio to see if there's any new information. Nothing new on the plane crashes or bridge explosions, and traffic is still at a standstill from people fleeing the affected cities. As they drone on, my attention fades and then I hear something that really catches my attention.

Sometime overnight, the FDA and CDC issued alerts to only drink bottled, boiled, or otherwise purified water. In conjunction with the water guidelines, all fresh produce is to be avoided. Both of these are a result of the continued increase in E. coli and typhoid throughout the US and even in Canada, now fully believed to be intentional.

These alerts are really causing troubles with the people who are on the road, having fled after yesterday's bridge attacks. There's already a shortage of bottled water in the hard-hit areas. Some municipalities have set up water boiling stations, and people are bringing containers to fill. I'm actually impressed these stations have been set up so early. The alerts to not drink the water only came out in the overnight hours, and most only heard about it when waking up this morning.

"There's been a new development in the bombs detonated at the airports on Thursday night and yesterday's bridge attacks. Originally

believed to be numerous suicide bombers in rescue vehicles, commercial vehicles, and even passenger cars and trucks, they are now thought to be remote-detonated explosions. There are surveillance videos from many locations providing evidence of the vehicles' drivers walking away before the explosions. The original assumption of suicide bombers was considered likely due to the nature of the attacks.

"In addition to the explosive devices mounted in vehicles, many of the bridges, like the airplanes brought down on Thursday, were hit by projectiles, believed to be guided missiles. In the next hour, we'll interview former Command Sergeant Major of White Sands Missile Range, Roger Martin, a career artilleryman, for his professional opinion on the bombings."

Huh? Maybe I was right! What everyone thought was suicide bombers may not have been? While these are definitely terrorist-style events, the remote detonations throw an interesting wrinkle into the plot. We expect terrorists to be suicide bombers. It's what they do in other countries. Why wouldn't they do it here?

As we're driving up our dirt road, my phone rings—Bubba, telling me he's a little earlier than expected and the cabin looks fine. Real fine. Can he head my way? I agree.

I'm still having a little buyer's remorse on this cabin, but I'll follow through with it.

Noah's dad drops him off about two minutes after we park in the driveway.

"Noah, thanks for doing this today."

"I'm glad to help, sir."

"I'll show you where we're digging. Malcolm, run and grab one of the raspberry bushes from the basement. I need it to show Noah how deep to make the holes. Mind the thorns. They'll poke you good."

"Okay, Dad. I remember from when we put them in the basement."

"Noah, I'll get you started, show you where each different type plant should go. Then Malcolm and I need to unload the wood. I have someone dropping off something I ordered and then we have a wedding to go to this afternoon. I'm not sure I'll be able to do any digging with you. You okay with that?"

"I'm fine, sir. I'm happy to work on it alone."

I grab a couple of shovels, a pickax, and a breaker bar, then we go out to the vine area. Last evening, I'd laid out where each bush should go. Malcolm is back with the sample specimen, and I confirm with Noah how deep each hole should be. He gets started while Malcolm and I tackle the wood pile.

As we finish emptying out the truck, the phone rings. Katie. Before I answer, I ask Malcolm to start taking the rest of the bushes from the basement out to Noah. He runs off to do my bidding.

"Hey, Katie."

"Hey, Jake," Katie says in a slow, low voice. "We're coming to your house. Manhattan got overrun with people leaving KC last night."

What? What does this mean? I'm instantly worried for Katie but do my best to respond calmly. "Oh, Katie. I'm sorry about this. I do think it's a good idea for you to leave, though. Drive straight through if you can. You heard about the water and food poisoning? You have enough stuff so you don't need to stop for food?"

"Yeah, I think we'll be fine."

"How about fuel? You know to stay off the interstates that have been overwhelmed?"

"We have a good amount of fuel. We're in Leo's truck. I rented a storage unit and parked my car there. I didn't want to leave it on the street, for fear it would be vandalized or stolen. I-80 in Nebraska looked okay last time we checked, but we'll check it again as we get closer. We'll have to avoid 80 closer to Cheyenne since lots of Denver people are there. And I-25's bad too. I talked to Angela this morning, and she says they have some people in Casper but not a whole lot yet."

I hadn't even thought about Casper being hit with people from Denver. "I hate to admit, I haven't talked to anyone but your mom this morning. I've been so busy. I have a guy coming to make a delivery in a few minutes, too, so I'll need to get off when he's heading up the road. This afternoon Malcolm and I are going to a wedding."

"A wedding? What a time to get married!"

"Yeah. But it also didn't make sense for them to cancel it. Many of the out-of-town guests arrived before the flights were shut down, so they're here until they can get out anyway. You remember the MacIntyres? They have the permaculture school up the road."

"Oh, sure. I met them. Met the one getting married too. I can't remember her name, but she and her guy were at the community rodeo last summer. Mom introduced us. She told me about the wedding a couple months ago, but I forgot."

"Yep. That's them. Sounds like a truck's on the road, getting ready to head up our hill. Probably my guy bringing my delivery. I need to go. But, seriously, Katie, don't stop if you two can take turns driving—just drive straight through. I have a bad feeling we haven't seen the end of these attacks. Especially with the new information coming out."

"New information?"

"Yeah. I heard on the radio driving home these don't look like suicide bombers. The bombs were remotely detonated. Strange thing for terrorists to do."

"That does sound strange. Every time I hear about terrorists on the news, they're driving a car into something and exploding it while they're still in it. But what about the guy who blew up the building in Oklahoma all those years ago? He's still called a terrorist, and he didn't blow himself up."

"That's true and a good point. I guess we'll know more as time goes on. Keep me posted on your progress. I look forward to meeting Leo, even though I wish it was a real vacation and visit you were on."

"Okay, Jake. I'll talk to you later."

Be safe, Katie, be safe . . .

Chapter 20

Malcolm

I deliver the last of the bushes to Noah and somehow manage to get three scratches from the raspberries. I'm trying to decide if I need a Band-Aid when there's a truck noise. One thing I really like about where we live is there isn't much traffic, so if someone's driving up, we hear them from a ways off. Mom says the sound travels a lot here, and she thinks it's a benefit. If we're outside, the car noise is really loud. When we're in the house, we don't hear it unless the windows are open. Sometimes people will get all the way to our driveway without us hearing them, especially in the wintertime. We have a little bell that goes off when they pull in the driveway. It's kind of like a doorbell only it's a road bell. Road bell . . . I think that's kind of funny.

A really big pickup pulling a trailer with a shed on it is cresting our hill.

"Whoa, looks great," Dad says.

"What's that, Dad? The pickup? You like it?"

"The pickup is fine, but the cabin looks fantastic. And check out the roof color. It's a little darker than what we have, but I think your mom will like it just fine."

"Oh yeah, and it has the curve to it like the cabin we already own has. The kind so we can have a bed up in the . . . uh, the loft."

"Yeah, it's a lofted barn-style roof. It gives extra head space."

"So you like it? You think Mom will like it?" I ask cautiously.

"Let's see the inside, but so far I'm very pleased."

Dad makes some motions to tell the guy in the truck where to park. I know I've met him before, when we got the bigger cabin last year, but I can't remember his name.

Dad has the trailer backed up near the bigger cabin. He sets it so the front of the cabin faces the big cabin.

"Why you putting it there, Dad? You don't want the door facing the road like the other cabin?"

"I think if we angle them this way— "

"They're perpendicular," I say.

"What?"

"The cabins, you've set them perpendicular. They could intersect at a ninety-degree angle. Right? That's perpendicular."

"Okay, yeah, sure. I think you're right. They're perpendicular. I think setting them this way, we could put a deck between them. Maybe make it kind of like one big cabin instead of two separate cabins. You remember the show we watched with your mom on Netflix where the people were buying vacation homes?"

"Which one?" We've watched several of those shows because Mom likes them so much.

"Good point. This one had lots of little homes—three or four—and they were all connected with decking."

"Oh . . . were they on a lake or ocean or something? Maybe I remember it."

"I think so. Anyway, a deck between the two might be nice if we use it as a cabin."

"What else would you use it for?"

"Storage. We'll just have to see what the inside looks like, which shouldn't be much longer. Looks like Bubba about has it lined up so we can get it off the trailer."

Bubba, that's his name. The truck stops moving, and he gets out, leaving it running. He's a big guy, not quite as big as I remember, but big. Taller than Dad—and my dad is tall; Mom says he's six feet tall—and Bubba's a lot heavier. It's not so much he's fat, he's just . . . big. His nose is big, his hands are big, his feet are big, even his ears are big.

Well, his belly is also big, so maybe he is a little fat. He's wearing blue jeans and a short-sleeved shirt with buttons and a pocket. I can see a pack of cigarettes in the pocket, but he's not smoking right now. He's wearing a hat, which says Carhartt. Hey, I have a coat that says that. I kind of like how we like the same things.

"Hey, Bubba. Good to see you again." Dad shakes his hand. "You remember my son, Malcolm?"

"Sure do, good to see you, sport." He holds his hand out for me to shake. I always get confused with handshaking. I know I'm supposed to shake with my right hand, but it feels wrong. Being left-handed isn't usually a problem for me, but my impulse is always to use my left, and I really have to think about it. I start to lift my left hand and then catch myself, quickly sticking out my right.

"Hello, Mr. Bubba. Good to see you again." I try to respond politely like Mom and Dad have taught me. For some reason, this makes Bubba laugh. He laughs so hard his stomach wobbles.

"Well there, sport, I suppose you can just call me Bubba and drop the mister. How about it?"

"Yes, sir, sure."

Bubba laughs again and shakes his head a little. "Jake, thanks for taking this off my hands. I really didn't have the space to put this back into inventory."

"Sure, Bubba. I wasn't really in the market for this, but it's hard to pass up a good deal. It looks pretty nice."

"You ain't kidding, wait until you see the inside. They did strip it some and sell things they could, which is what I expected. You want to crawl up on the trailer and look inside before I unload it? Just in case?"

"No, Bubba. I told you I'd take it based on your word and I will. I'd like to put it here so it'll make an *L* with the one we got from you last year. See any problem with that?"

"Nope. You're happy with the door facing the other cabin or you prefer the driveway?"

"The other cabin. I'm thinking we could put decking between the two."

"That's a fine idea. Looks like you got the other cabin all finished. You happy with how it turned out?"

"Sure am. Mollie modeled it after our bunkhouse, turning it into what's pretty much a small two bedroom with two sleeping lofts. Just has one bathroom, and we made it a semidry cabin with the water supplied by rain barrels. It turned out real nice. You want to take a quick look?"

"Let's get this one set up and then see how we are on time. One thing I noticed with this cabin here," he gestures to the one he's delivering, "it has a compost toilet. They left it in place. I think that was one of the things the wife hated about it."

"Yeah. I can imagine," Dad answers with a little laugh. "Mollie and I talked about doing compost toilets in our house when we were planning a much smaller, fully off-grid place and decided against it because of resale. It's not for everyone. So you think you can get it in place okay?"

"No problem at all."

"Super. Before I forget, let me pay you."

Dad takes out a big bunch of money and gives it to Bubba. Then Bubba pulls some blocks off of the trailer.

"Is the cabin going to be set on those?" I ask Dad.

"Yeah, he'll level up the area up with the blocks. We'll need to use some of those fence posts I bought yesterday to secure it so it doesn't shift in the wind. Then, when we get a little time, we'll make some cement anchors to secure it better. We don't want it moving."

"You think you'll want me to help with the cement like last time? I'm pretty good at it."

"You bet. I'll definitely need some help."

I get bored after a few minutes of watching Bubba, so I go and talk with Noah. The long row of bushes and berries isn't very far from the cabins. Noah's working at the far end, though, so I have to walk a little bit. I can still keep an eye on what Dad and Bubba are doing, so I can run back as soon as they need me.

Noah's older than me and taller. Not tall like Dad but almost as tall as Evan Snyder. But where Evan is normal weight, Noah is really skinny. He always wears blue jeans and a great big belt buckle that looks way too big for him. He wears cowboy boots and a cowboy hat and always has on a long-sleeved shirt, even in the summer. He's from Texas and talks kind of funny. It's hard for me to understand what he says sometimes. But most of the time, he doesn't talk much at all.

I need to be careful when helping Noah; most of the bushes have thorns on them. There's all kinds of stuff growing in this area. My favorite bushes are closer to the driveway. They're called seaberries. Dad said some people call them Siberian Pineapples; that's the name I like. I helped Mom make some fruit leather from them last year. They were pretty good that way, but I tried a raw one, and that wasn't good at all. Way too sour.

"Hi, Noah. You doing okay on the holes?"

He looks up at me and wipes the sweat from his face with the back of his hand, putting dirt on his cheek. "Howdy, Malcolm. Yeah, I guess so. Lots of rock, and it's pretty hot."

"You want some water? I can go get you some."

"Yep. Thanks."

I run as fast as I can to the house, which is very fast—Dad told me I'm one of the fastest ten-year-old runners he knows.

I know Noah is really thirsty, so I grab a water jug we use when we're going on car rides. It holds a lot. I get some ice out so he can have nice and cold water. It gets pretty hot in Wyoming during the summer. I like winter much better when we have to wear coats and gloves to go skiing. I don't really like sweating.

I don't run when I head back to Noah. The water jug is heavy, and the ice is clinking around. It's kind of hard to carry it in one hand and a glass in the other hand. Jeez, the water jug is really heavy. Maybe I shouldn't have put so much in it.

Dad sees me walking with the jug. "Thank you for getting water for Noah. I'm sure he'll appreciate it. Good thinking getting the gallon jug. Did you fill it up?"

"I did. I think it's a little too full. It's heavy," I answer, feeling a little out of breath.

"You're doing fine, Buddy," Dad says with a smile and a nod.

He seems proud of me. I straighten up a little, decide the jug isn't *that* heavy, and finish walking to Noah.

"Thanks, Malcolm," Noah says gratefully and pours himself a glass of water. He drinks it very fast and pours part of a second.

"You want me to help you?" I ask after he finishes drinking.

He shrugs. "Can if you want. You can start with the pickax on the next hole."

Using the pickax is a lot of work. I'm using the sharp part to break up the ground. I have to stop fairly often to remove rocks. I've done this work before, so I know what I'm doing, but I'm still careful not to hit my toe or something. Dad sometimes says, "An ounce of prevention . . . " hmm, I can't remember the rest. An ounce of prevention is better than something. Maybe it's better than cutting off my toe.

I'm starting to sweat when Dad calls me.

"Gotta go, Noah. See you later." I run over to Dad.

"Yeah, Dad? You need my help?"

"I think we're good at the moment. What I want you to do is run in and take a quick shower. We need to get ready for the wedding. I want you to wear your black Levi's and a button shirt."

"With my good cowboy boots?"

"Yeah, your new pair. And remember your belt. You don't want your pants sliding down and your bottom showing."

"Argh, Dad. I hate wearing my belt. It's not comfortable."

"Malcolm, you need to wear your belt."

"Okay." I'm not happy about it, but I'll wear it.

"Go ahead and make yourself a sandwich too."

"Okay."

"Um, Malcolm?"

"Yeah?"

"A good shower. Make sure you clean all of your parts."

"Dad! I know what to do in the shower." I can't believe he's reminding me. I'm almost eleven, after all. I know how to shower. I don't really like to shower, but I know how to do it.

Chapter 21

Jake

It takes the better part of an hour for Bubba to get the new cabin in place. I help as he needs me, but mostly spend my time monitoring his progress. I'm kind of useless and feeling restless. There's so much I should be doing right now. Malcolm is helping Noah with the holes. With the vigor of youth, Noah has two holes completed and is working on number three. Malcolm is starting on the fourth, wildly swinging the pickax. I decide it's a good time for him to head to the shower and get ready for the wedding.

Bubba finishes up a few minutes after one o'clock.

"There you be, Jake. She's good and level. You want to take a look inside?"

"Yeah, Bubba. I only have a few minutes. We're going to a wedding, but I'd like to take a quick look."

The front of this cabin, like the one we got from him last year, has a small four-foot porch. But where that one has bay-style windows across the front, this facade is flat with one window and a window in the door. A loft extends over each cabins' porch. Bubba tells me our first cabin has a front known as the Deluxe Playhouse. This one is just the Playhouse.

Inside, I'm very impressed. It's a whole lot nicer than the way I finished the other cabin, in what Mollie refers to as shabby chic and I think of as patched together. It's even nicer than the original bunkhouse we did. Shoot, it may be nicer than my house.

The walls, floor, loft, and ceiling are all in natural-stained tongue and groove pine. It's a very nice look. I notice the pine has quite a bit of blue, knots, and holes in it from being harvested as dead-standing beetle kill pine. The stain has brought this out. Mollie is going to love this, and I immediately know we won't be using this for storage. I have to admit, I'd stay here.

At 8 x 20 feet, I can get a pretty good view of the entire place standing by the door. The former owners removed all the light fixtures—likely they were easy to sell. The living room is completely devoid of any furniture, and it looks to take up about half of the twenty-foot length. The loft area is interesting. They added a loft above the kitchen and connected it with the loft above the porch. This gives a slightly lower ceiling throughout, but it doesn't feel claustrophobic.

The kitchen looks largely intact minus appliances. The cabinets, countertops, and sink are still in place, but there's a hole in the counter where the cooktop must have been.

"What do you think they did for heat, Bubba?"

"Think they used electric baseboard. The walls near the floor show evidence of it." He points to a spot where I can see something had been attached.

"Yeah, makes sense. Funny they'd plan for electric but not a toilet."

"Kind of is. Maybe they just hadn't got around to the toilet. The bathroom is less finished than the rest. Let's look."

The bathroom is off the kitchen, accessible by a pocket door. It's narrow, only the width of the small one-person shower stall, and not quite as long as the kitchen since the ladder going to the loft is attached on the end from the front door.

On the left side is a hinged bench with a toilet seat attached. I'm guessing, if I lift up the bench, a bucket will fit nicely underneath. There's a little cutout under the bench, likely to keep a small container of organic matter to add to the toilet for the composting function.

In the center, across from the door, is the sink spot, with no sink but piping still in place, and a window above. On the right is the shower stall, still in place.

The bathroom is unfinished, with only green board up. This moisture-resistant sheetrock is a good start, but I wonder what they planned for the future. The shower is a basic shower pan with glue-on, prefab walls, but the rest of the bathroom floor looks like nice tile.

"It's pretty nice, Bubba. They did a good job with the finishes. And, really, they left it largely intact, considering they turned it back to you. I'd think they could've got some money for the tongue and groove."

"They could have. But I suspect they just wanted out. You know, if the wife ain't happy . . . "

"Boy, do I! Definitely good to keep the wife happy. 'Course, I'd have a hard time wanting to live anywhere else, so I'm glad Mollie loves it here as much as I do. Thank you, Bubba."

We shake again and he heads out. 1:20. I need to hustle to get ready in time.

"Noah," I holler over, "I'm getting ready and we're taking off. You doing okay?"

He responds with a simple, "Yes, sir. I'm fine," and goes back to work.

Walking back to the house, I notice a text from Mollie. I must have missed hearing the indicator go off.

She's somewhere in Idaho. She's going to try to drive without a real stop, just for cat naps. She hopes to be home overnight or in the morning. I don't like the idea of her driving through without stops and hope she'll reconsider. I try to call her but only get her voicemail.

No problem, I'll text her later.

Within twenty minutes, Malcolm and I are driving down our hill. We'll make it on time, if I speed a little, but just. And we have the gift, thanks to Malcolm remembering it right as we were walking out the door. I'm glad Mollie had it wrapped and ready to go. I'm scarfing down a sandwich Malcolm made me and thinking how much I wish Mollie was here. She's so much better at these social events than I am. Alex and Natalie are good friends, so I'll go and enjoy the festivities.

The wedding is nice; not too long and Annie looks terrific. I try to pay attention to what she's wearing since I suspect Mollie will ask me.

After the wedding we move over to the reception area. I'm surprised to find appetizers on a table plus a couple of people walking around with food trays. There are several types of beverages available also. Malcolm has a red punch, and I take a glass of lemonade.

We head over to the yard games. People are visiting and playing horseshoes, bean bag toss, and a few other things. There are more snacks over here. Most of the conversation is about the recent attacks, but I'm not surprised by this. Malcolm asks if he can go play with some of the other kids. I caution him not to get his shirt grass stained.

He gives me a look I interpret as "duh" as he says, "I'll be careful."

I'm always impressed with Alex and Natalie's place. They have a great working homestead following permaculture principles, an agricultural design concept mimicking features observed in nature. We're in an area away from the animals, but I can still hear a cow every once in a while. They milk a couple of Jersey cows. As part of their homesteading classes, they teach how to care for the cows, chickens, horses, goats, and other animals. They also teach cheese and bread making and how to butcher the chickens, among other things.

After a week here, a person has a very good idea whether homesteading is for them or not. In many cases, it's not. And those people are very thankful not to have spent the money jumping into something they didn't enjoy for the week they were there.

Of course, in my case, a week wouldn't have been enough time to know if a homestead was for me. We lived and worked our farm for over three years before I started to think we'd made a mistake.

After about thirty minutes, the wedding party returns, and the bride and groom come in to cheers. They make their way around, visiting with people and thanking them for coming. The cake is cut, and the party begins to break up shortly thereafter. I decide this is a great wedding and hope Annie tells Katie how perfect it was.

It's not yet 4:30 and we're driving home. While there was much talk of the attacks, it was still nice to not be fully immersed in them. No radio or TV telling us what's going on. I didn't even see people on their phones, not that it would do them much good. The MacIntyre place is an old ranch on the edge of the forest, and cell service there is almost nonexistent. They have a repeater in the house, which helps, but it doesn't carry outside.

I turn on the radio for our drive home and quickly discover the couple of hours we were out of touch, big things were happening.

". . . affected banks are unable to offer any online services, which has shut down credit and debit cards, online banking, and ATM machines. While it is a Saturday and most bank branches are closed, people are prevented from withdrawing money directly from branches, since the computers cannot be accessed for these records. We're assured these attacks are being addressed and services should soon return to normal.

"In addition to financial institutions going down, social media giants Facebook and Twitter, along with YouTube, Google, and Yahoo, are unavailable due to what is believed to be a distributed denial-of-service taking these out.

"With so many people turning to social media and online searches to stay up to date on the latest news, this is causing extra panic. The affected sites hope to resolve these outages as soon as possible. 911 operators are being inundated with calls reporting downed status of websites. Please do not call 911 to report any websites being down.

Please reserve 911 for true emergencies only. We'll have more on this developing story as information becomes available."

Well, there's a new wrinkle. I couldn't care less about Facebook, and really have to wonder why anyone would call 911 about this, but credit cards not working is a huge problem with so few people, in today's world, carrying cash.

I'm glad Mollie took out money; hopefully she has enough. I only caught part of this report but think they are talking about a cyberattack. Mollie read stuff to me on these—I hope I was listening. I'm trying to think back.

"Sounds like a cyberattack, Dad. Mom and I did a lesson on these. Something like this happened to the Ukraine, I think it was, a couple of years ago. They took out the power grid. I don't think it lasted long, but one of the articles we read said they thought it was a test run just to see if they could. They use DDoS, which means *distributed denial-of-service*, to weaken the systems. Then they insert malware code to wipe it all out. It's actually pretty common, and usually they can fix it quick. If we're hearing about it, then it's probably bad. Real bad."

I suspect he's right. I remember Mollie telling me about these and that they happen, but there are many safeguards in place to stop them. I hope the safeguards work . . .

Chapter 22

Jake

As soon as we get home, I try to call Mollie. The phone disconnects without ringing. I try from the landline but don't even have a dial tone. I wonder if it's out because of the cyberattacks? Not good. I text but get a message saying the text failed. What is this, 1985 with no way to reach someone who isn't standing right next to me?

"Dad? Mom not answering?"

"The phone doesn't seem to be working right. Maybe from the— "

"Cyberattacks?"

"Yeah, maybe because of that. I'll try her again in a bit. For now, let's get changed and get on with what we need to do. I didn't see Noah out there, so let's see if he finished planting the vines."

I don't want Malcolm to know I'm kind of freaking out. I'm also mad at myself for not trying harder to get ahold of her earlier. I don't even know for sure where she is; her last text said she was in Idaho, an hour or so outside of the town of Grangeville. She'll continue with backroads and state highways, hoping to hit I-90 once the traffic on it lessens. I suddenly wish she would've told me her exact plans for getting home.

I attempt to stifle a sigh—and fail.

"You okay, Dad? Worried about Mom?"

"Yeah, Buddy. I'm okay. I'm not really worried. I'm just looking forward to her getting home."

"You think the cyberattacks will make it hard for her to get home?"

"Should be fine," I say, unconvincingly. The look he gives me tells me he's on to my lies.

We check the vines first; they're all planted and look good. I'll make a point of catching up with Noah to pay him in the next day or two.

Malcolm and I go into the new cabin. Malcolm hasn't seen the inside yet, and I want a closer look.

"Wow, Dad. This is nice. Like a real cabin on the inside."

"It is. They did a great job with it. The bathroom is still pretty rough. You want to help me come up with a plan to finish it out? I'd like to see if we have enough materials on hand. With the cyberattacks, on top of everything else, we might want to see what we can do without going into town again." As I say this, I realize I'm not dreading putting in the time to finish this cabin. A few months ago, just the thought would've overwhelmed me. I briefly wonder why—*what's changed?*

"You think we'll need to use this? Maybe for Katie's friend who's coming with her?"

"Maybe, we'll need to see."

"Have you looked upstairs, Dad?"

"Just from here. I haven't gone up yet. Let's check it out."

I follow Malcolm up the staircase on the left side of the room. It's an odd item. Like a ladder with a little too much lean. It's easy to climb, but I'm thankful it has slightly raised side rails so there's something to hold on to. Malcolm has no trouble, of course.

"Oh, hey. This is nice." Malcolm scoots around the room in a half crouch. I sit at the top of the stairs, which affords me a view of the loft area. It is nice.

With the loft covering the entire space except where the stairs come up, there's quite a bit of floor area. It's short on head room, but they've added some useful features. The main sleeping area is over the kitchen and bathroom. It has a platform and short headboard in place.

Each end of the loft has a small window, similar to the sleeping lofts in our bunkhouse and cabin. I'm surprised how similar this is to the sleeping lofts we've created. They must have found the same Pinterest pages Mollie did.

There are several functional features, like shelves and narrow dressers along the opposite wall from the stairs. Over the porch area they created, what I assume is, a guest room with a second smaller mattress platform. Or maybe they had a child? Bubba didn't say, but this makes sense.

The open area between the two rooms, with the cubby holes, drawers, and shelves, may have been a play area. There's even a cover to fold over the staircase and seal it off, even though a railing surrounds the space everywhere except where I'm sitting. With the covering in place, the entire upstairs would be sealed. No possibility of falling down the stairs. Smart. Yep, definitely a child lived here.

"Wow, Dad. This looks like a play area. Look at this." Echoing my thoughts, he pulls out a sliding table with something green on it. "It's a LEGO table. It has the baseplate built on to it, like the one you and Mom made me. It's a little smaller, though. I bet this was a little boy's play area."

"I think you're right. I was just looking at it, thinking the other end looked like it was a child's room, or child's section anyway."

"Wouldn't it be neat to live here?"

"It might be. But you'd have to get rid of some stuff to live in such a small space."

"Yeah. Maybe. But I could do it."

"Should we check out the main level?"

He lets a sigh escape. I can tell he's a little smitten with this space and will probably want to spend some time out here.

I hadn't noticed earlier, but there's enough space under the stairs for a desk. Nothing is there, so I'm guessing it was freestanding and not built in.

Malcolm sticks his head in the bathroom. "Looks like they didn't get to this. Except the floor. It looks okay."

"Right. I suspect they set it up to use but planned to go back and finish it. Their plans must have changed before they could."

"What are you thinking, Dad? We have those couple sinks Mom bought at the used store in Wesley when she couldn't decide what she wanted in the cabin. Can we use one of those? We'd need a toilet."

"I'm thinking we'll make this a fully dry cabin. Instead of a flush toilet, we'll stick with the compost toilet. One of the sinks will be great. Maybe we can build a cabinet to set it in."

"A compost toilet, like the emergency one you built? You think Mom will be happy with that?"

"Yeah. I think she'll be okay with it. What do you think about just finishing the tape job on the walls and painting it? We have assorted colors of leftover paint we could make work."

"I think that's good. Can I help you paint?"

"Sure. We'll try to get the wall color to go with the floor." I bend for a closer look. "Looks like it might be travertine tile. Nice stuff."

"When we going to work on it? After Mom gets home so she can help?"

"I think we might surprise her with this one. We'll go get a load of wood after morning chores tomorrow, then we'll get started on this."

I don't want to tell him, with these latest attacks, I'm suddenly happy to have this extra space. We may need it.

As we're walking back to the house, Evan and Doris pull into the driveway. They step out and wait for us.

"Hey, Evan, Doris. What are you two doing?"

"Hey, Jake. Hey, Malcolm. Nice cabin," Evan responds wearily. Doris gives a slight bend of her neck. She's obviously been crying. "There's a community meeting at the community center at seven o'clock. We were over visiting the Shermans when we heard about it. Dan Morse is going from house to house telling people."

"Why? What's the meeting about?"

"The attacks. With the cyberattacks and the power out, people are starting to worry."

"The power's out? Here?"

"Yeah. You didn't know?"

"Haven't spent much time in the house. We went to Annie MacIntyre's wedding this afternoon, came home and changed, and have been messing around out here. Didn't even try a light when we went in. I guess we're used to having them off during the daytime. You try a light, Malcolm?"

"No. Just changed and came out."

"Your solar should still be fine, right? It's independent, not connected to the power company?"

"Yes, correct. How long has it been out?"

"I think ours went out about 3:30," Evan says. "We left a few minutes after to go to Shermans' place. Didn't worry much about it. Their power was out when we got there. She had a battery-powered radio on. Pretty much sounds like all of Prospector County is out now, Park County and up into Montana also. No idea when it'll be back."

Evan is speaking very quickly as he continues with, "We were just listening on the car radio and heard most grids have been taken offline due to the attacks and some damage caused by the attacks. Elements of power grids have been taken down en masse, which has caused what is described as a 'cascading outage,' in which a power overload spills over from one region to another to another. Blackouts and brownouts are being reported throughout the US.

"And not just power outages—there's reports several power plants had what's being described as 'malware' attack their digital relay and backup generators. Seems this is causing some kind of power surge and destroying the generators—even causing a power surge and blowing up transformers."

"*One Second After*," Doris says, with a quick wipe of her eyes.

"Now, honey, it's not like that. An EMP would do different damage than a cyberattack," Evan says smoothly.

Malcolm chimes in, "Sort of. An EMP would definitely send the pulse out different and would damage electronic components very quickly. Faster than the blink of an eye. The cyberattack could do damage too. They've done tests where they enter a malware code and make things blow up. Blow up enough transformers and stuff, and it could be hard to fix. But at least our cars will still work. Of course, without electricity, I guess we can't get gas for them."

"See, Evan. I told you. Malcolm is ten and he knows this," Doris says with a big sigh. "How do you know this, Malcolm?"

"Oh, well . . . I asked my mom about how EMPs work, so we did a big study on it. We also watched a movie about a cyberattack, and I asked too many questions, so we studied that. Mom likes me to study things when I ask about them. And there's YouTube videos about these things. They're pretty interesting."

Malcolm's information doesn't seem to be helping Doris much. I have to admit, I'm surprised by her reaction. She's usually very stoic about things and keeps herself pulled together. Not that we've faced something like this before . . .

"You seem to know quite a bit about all sorts of different things, Malcolm," Evan says.

"Sure, if something interests me, I like to learn about it. Cyberattacks and EMPs are interesting. So are swords—I know lots about swords. You can ask me almost anything and I'll tell you. Mom sometimes says she wishes I'd spend as much time memorizing my multiplication tables as I do memorizing things about swords. Did you know my favorite sword is a— "

"I'm pretty sure Evan knows your favorite sword is a katana," I say. "You've told him before, and he's even used the practice swords with you, remember?"

"Oh, yeah. I guess."

"We can talk about your swords later," Evan says, "maybe even do the sword practice again. Sound good?"

"Sure! That'd be good."

"Uh, so, Evan, they're calling a meeting because the power's out?" I ask. "That doesn't make much sense. What do you think is really going on?"

"I think Dan Morse sees an opportunity to be the unofficial Mayor of Bakerville. I suspect he's an armchair survivalist and watched one too many prepper reality shows. Most likely, he thinks it has all hit the fan and he's going to be the one to save us all. 'Course, that's just my opinion since I think he's an imbecile who lacks a shred of common sense."

I think about the one-fingered greeting Dan gave me earlier today. "You might be right. Guess I'll skip the meeting."

"Don't think you should, Jake. Not only is he an imbecile, but he also thinks if you have two dollars, he should have one of those dollars just because. And he thinks you should give the other dollar to his wife. He pretty much wants what everyone else has but schemes and cheats to get it. You heard about him being arrested for writing bad checks?"

"Yeah, I heard it through the grapevine. Didn't know if it was a fact or not."

"It was in the paper . . . the arrest reports section. You need to be at the meeting. Dan knows too much about what you people have here. The grapevine is alive and well and often active."

Out of all of the people in our little community, Dan Morse is one I am most concerned about in any emergency situation. Mollie and I have discussed this a few times and both view him as a potential threat. He's not particularly a physical threat, at slightly taller than me and not really in shape. He's more of a wild card.

He proclaims himself to be a mountain man and tries to look the part in some ways. He wears his hair cropped and his graying beard long. His many tattoos seem to tell an angry story of anarchy and negativity. I've yet to see him without not only a wheel gun on his belt but a rifle strapped to his back. While open carry is no big deal here, the rifle on the back is not something we normally see. More than anything, his deceit and sneakiness are our main concerns.

"All right, guess I'll go. I'd better get ready since it's close to 6:00 now."

"Yep, probably best. We'll see you there. I was thinking of making a run to town after the meeting. You want to go? I'd like to get a few more things. Doris can keep Malcolm."

"Yes. Good idea. Let's do it." Evan and Doris give small waves as they drive off.

"Well, Malcolm, with the power out, let's consolidate the fridge items. Can you move everything from the upstairs fridge to the basement? Tonight we'll use one of the portable generators to run it for a while. Once things settle down, I'll rehook the solar system. Let's do the chores as quick as we can. You pass out hay and feed, and I'll take care of water. First, I'm going to connect the backup power to our water system."

Malcolm nods. "I do the fridge first? Then the feeding? You were talking kind of fast . . . "

"Yeah. You'll come with me to the meeting, but I'd like you to play on the ball field instead of being at the meeting. Okay?"

"Okay. It's good we're going. I don't much like Mr. Morse. When he used to come around, I tried to stick near Mom."

"Thank you for that, Malcolm."

We complete everything in near record time, put on clothes that aren't our barnyard clothes, and leave the house fifteen minutes before the meeting is to start.

Chapter 23

Malcolm

Dad and I are driving to the community center for a meeting. We go there quite a bit for different things like dinners and parties. Mom even does Zumba there sometimes, and I go along. I kind of like it. It's like dancing but also exercising. I only join in on the songs I like. The rest of the time, I hang out in the kid's corner where there's a chalkboard to draw on. There are toys there, too, but they're for little kids—not guys like me.

I think the electricity being out is a big deal. Usually, we don't worry about the power going out since we have the solar system and can always have electricity. But Dad disconnected the solar. I asked him why he did that, and he said he was just testing something. But I'm pretty sure it's because he's worried about the terrorists. I think he thinks if he disconnects the solar system, if they did something, like make an EMP, then the solar system will still work. I don't know if it will.

When Mom was teaching me about electromagnetic pulses, we looked at lots of stuff, and I looked up more stuff on my own. It's all pretty confusing, but one thing I noticed is, no one seems to really know what would happen if there was an EMP or a solar flare—something sort of like an EMP, but the sun sends it out and it has a different name. I can't remember what it's called, some initials other than EMP. With both, pretty much everyone agrees things would change.

The power would go out, phones probably wouldn't work, and maybe even cars wouldn't run. That's another place where different people think different things. Some people think only really old cars—like from when my parents were young—will work after an EMP. Others think only a few cars will be affected, so most cars will be just fine.

Not that I'm an expert or anything, but I think it was kind of silly for Dad to unhook the solar system. I think, even if it's unhooked and there's an EMP bomb, then it will still mess up the system. I'm pretty sure he hasn't watched the same videos I have, so he doesn't know. He's just doing what he thinks is best. I guess none of it really matters. We haven't been hit by an EMP; we're under cyberattack.

I'm trying to remember everything I learned about cyberattacks. I wonder if my friend Tony, who goes to regular school, learns about EMPs and cyberattacks. Maybe he'll be at the community center and I can ask him. I have to remember, though, if he doesn't know about them, I can't just tell him all I know. Mom told me a lot of kids my age don't learn about all of the things I learn and some of it's kind of scary. It doesn't scare me, but it might scare other guys my age.

I kind of like that I get to learn so many different things. Mom uses what she calls a curriculum, but we don't always stick to it—at least not every day. Dad says one of the reasons they homeschool me is so I can foster a love of learning and always want to discover more. He also wants me to be able to think for myself. He says it's becoming a lost art.

I know lost art means something people don't do anymore. But I don't understand how thinking can be a lost art. I mean, doesn't everybody have to think? How can you even get through anything without thinking?

"Hey, Dad?"

"Yes, Buddy?" He looks at me through the rearview mirror.

"You know how you say I should think for myself and it's a lost art? How can thinking be a lost art?"

"Ah, well, it's not so much thinking is a lost art. It's the thinking for *yourself* part that's becoming rare."

"What do you mean? Doesn't everyone think for themselves? It's not like someone else is in my brain doing the thinking for me."

"Maybe not really in your brain, but a lot of people just go with what others tell them. They might hear something their favorite actor says, and since they really like that actor, they decide whatever he said is true. Lots of times, though, the actor is just sharing an opinion."

"You mean like the cyberattack? I have my own opinion about this. My opinion is we are in trouble."

"Uh, yeah, sure, that could be an example. But is your opinion fact? Should you go telling everyone else they should believe the cyberattack is bad news and we're in trouble?"

"Yes! Yes, I definitely should. I've reached that opinion because Mom and I researched the history of cyberattacks and the possibilities of what they can do."

Dad lets out a big sigh, and just barely loud enough for me to hear, he says, "I wish we would've sheltered you a little bit more." Then louder he says, "Okay, so the cyberattack isn't such a great example. You've used critical thinking to reach your own conclusion. You didn't just decide the cyberattack was bad news because your mom told you it was bad.

"But, you see, lots of people don't do that. They let others tell them what to think. The media, movie stars, sports figures, they all play a big role. And not only do people not think for themselves, it's getting to the point where, if someone doesn't believe the same as everyone else or questions something, then they're labeled . . . well, they're sometimes made fun of or harassed."

"You mean like bullying?"

"Yeah, bullying is a good word for it."

"Wouldn't it be easier just not to tell people when you don't agree with them?"

"It is easier, but just because it's easier doesn't mean it's right. Sometimes we have to do things that are hard. That said, there's a time and place to express our opinions. Do you know the phrase, *choose your battles*?"

"No, I don't even know what you're saying."

"Choose your battles."

"*Nooooo*. I've never heard of that. What does it mean?"

"It's a phrase which means to save your breath or your strength for things that are important. Sometimes we feel strongly about something, and we know we have to say something, even if others won't like it. Other times, we may choose not to speak up or make a big deal about it. Does that make sense?"

"Not the choosing your battles stuff. But I guess I do understand how people don't really think for themselves. It's easier just to go along with other people. I mean, no one really wants to be different, right? I'm already a little different since I don't go to normal school. I'm glad I know a few others like me—you know, the ones from the wedding. They're homeschooled too."

"Yes, it's nice to have friends with whom you have things in common. You're already a great independent thinker. When you hear about something you aren't sure of or don't understand, you want to learn more. Your love of learning helps with this. That's something I hope you never lose. You're very fortunate, Malcolm. You have so many wonderful tools to help you learn and explore the world."

"Not if they don't get the cyberattacks stopped, Dad. One of my tools is the internet, and if it's not working then I can't learn as much. I learn a lot by watching videos."

Dad slows the truck as he pulls into the community center. He stops the truck, turns it off, and then turns to me. "You said they're very good at stopping the cyberattacks, right?"

"Nope. I said they *were* very good at it. And they happen all the time. If they were good at stopping *this one*, we wouldn't even know about it. I still think we're in trouble."

"Okay, but, hey, Buddy, I need you to do me a favor. I don't want you telling your friends what you know about this. That's something that should be up to their parents. Okay?"

"Sure, Dad. I know that. I know better than to spill the beans about something important."

Dad laughs and says, "You sound just like Katie. She used to say that all the time, 'spill the beans.'"

"Uh, yeah, Dad. I think she's who I learned it from. She still says it."

"It looks like the meeting's up on the ball field. I guess that makes sense, no windows in the community center and with no electricity . . . anyway, it's about time to start. There's a few of your friends over at the playground, why don't you go and join them?"

"All right, Dad. I'd rather go up with you, but I guess I can go and play."

We get out of the truck. "Thanks, Buddy. I'll see you in a bit."

I start to walk away, when he says, "Hey, I love you, Malcolm Caldwell."

I think, *Jeez, Dad. I'm pretty sure all of Bakerville heard you.* But I quietly say, "I love you too, Dad," and then race for the playground.

Chapter 24

Jake

As expected, the conversations floating through the group are all focused on the attacks, from Friday's plane crashes to the bridge explosions to the food poisonings to the newest threat from the cyberattacks.

Our community is a somewhat diverse group. It's comprised of a mix of farmers, ranchers, and retirees who, for the most part, live in Bakerville for the peaceful and relaxed atmosphere. We also have people who live here and commute to work in one of the surrounding towns—there are several within forty-five minutes in three different directions.

A few of the families are third or even fourth generation, whose ancestors where the original homesteaders. But most are like us. We've moved here at some point in the last several years for the lifestyle.

Mollie often says she can't believe she gets to live here. There's not a bad view anywhere, with the wilderness to the west, nearby mountains to the north and east, mountains in the distant south, and Prospector Peak—our county's namesake—in the southeast. Prospector Peak is a landmark for many. The way it rises up and can be seen from a distance always lets us know we're almost home when it comes into view. Scenery like this, anywhere else, would cost big bucks.

Of course, we do have Wyoming wind and winters, which keeps the costs and population low. And we like to be sure and play up those points when talking about Wyoming. Keeping the good points a secret helps. I do think people are on to us, though. We're seeing an increase in home and land sales, with property prices and values going up. This is a double-edged sword. It's always good to have property values increase but worrisome the population increase will change the area we love.

Even though we're a community, or a small unofficial town, we're spread out. Most people have at least thirty or forty acres. There's a handful of small five-acre lots, several twenty, and some folks with hundred—or even thousand—acre farms and ranches.

In this wide-open, fairly flat land on the edge of the wilderness, we can find a high hill and enjoy a view of the homes dotted about the vast countryside. The houses range from small, one-room cabins to palatial ranch homes, with even a small mansion on the very edge of the foothills before heading up to the trees. I've never met the owners of the mansion—rumor has it, they use it as a summer house. I wonder if they're here right now?

Our little unincorporated town on the edge of the wilderness has less than four hundred residents, with close to two-thirds being retirees. Of those, at least half are retired military, law enforcement, and government or state workers. Many put in their time and then got out, so they're not much older than Mollie and me, with a few our age or even younger.

Of those still working, many own a business, farm, or ranch, or work from home like Mollie does. The rest, like me, drive into one of the nearby towns for our jobs. We have people from a variety of professions living here—nurses, salespeople, oil workers, and more. There are probably less than fifty youth in our community, including Malcolm.

In addition to our full-time residents, we have a few dozen seasonal folks—like the mansion owners—spending summer here and wintering someplace with a warmer climate, plus several vacation cabins, which are rented out a week or more at a time. I'm a caretaker at one of these cabins near the national forest, and the place has been booked daily since before Memorial Day and is full up until after Labor Day.

Which reminds me, I should go and check on the cabin, to see if the people who were staying there this week are still there. I stopped by on Tuesday, before all of this started, and did the yard care. There was a family of four there this week. They were supposed to leave Friday morning. Hopefully they were able to get out and get home before things fell apart.

Wyoming is considered by many to be the most conservative state in the union. More Wyoming residents self-identify as conservative than in any other state per capita. While it's true, most of the people I know go with the idea of "live and let live," choosing to follow their own moral compass and let other people do as they wish, within reason. It's definitely a mix of people, and as I listen to the different conversations, I hear lots of politically motivated comments. Yep. This could be an interesting meeting.

The notice about tonight's meeting must have spread well. Looks like well over a hundred people are here. I recognize most of them. A few, like Dan Morse, could have interesting opinions. I don't see the MacIntyres or my friends Phil and Kelley Hudson. Their places border the wilderness area, several miles from here. Word of the meeting probably didn't get out to them. If anything interesting happens, I should drive out tomorrow and let them know. Of course, the MacIntyres are probably still busy with the after-wedding festivities.

Dan Morse—dressed in his usual armament of a sidearm on his right hip, large Bowie knife on his left, and a semi-automatic carbine worn crisscross-style across his back—stands up on a picnic table and asks for everyone's attention. It takes him a couple of tries before people begin to acknowledge him.

"Okay," Dan starts, "I'm glad so many of you are here tonight. I wasn't sure we'd be able to spread the message very well with the phones and internet not working as they should. Speaking of, by show of hands, how many of you had internet access last you checked?"

Three hands go up.

Dan asks who their provider is and when they last checked. Each had been able to get on the internet using their cell phones, but many websites were down.

"And how many of you've been able to make or receive phone calls in the last couple of hours?"

More people respond this worked for them.

"Those of you that have phone service, would you please let others use your phones to make calls they feel are important? We're all going to need to stick together right now and share the resources we have until these terrorists are finished with us."

I already don't like the sound of this. His words and his tone come off almost as bluster. I catch Evan's eye. A slight eye roll tells me he shares my thoughts.

"With the power out, we need to band together. I know many of you have generators or alternative power. I'm sure you're all more than willing to help those in the community who don't have these options."

Dan Morse looks directly at me when he says this. I hold his gaze and try to keep a neutral look on my face. I'm not the type of person who wants trouble. Just like I was telling Malcolm only minutes ago, I prefer to choose my battles.

I truly do believe in being a good and helpful neighbor. We've been fortunate in our neighborhood to have a great group, and I'd do anything I could to help these people who are my friends. And all of them have gone out of their way to help Mollie and me with many projects and tasks. I know I can count on them and hope they know they can count on me. But the way Dan Morse puts things does not sit right with me. Apparently, I'm not the only one who doesn't care for his bravado.

Terry Bosco jumps in. "So, Dan, you've called us together tonight, for what? To admonish us to do something we regularly do anyway? I know you haven't been in this community very long, but we tend to work together. You were here when we had the snow and wind a couple of winters ago, leaving people stuck in their houses, unable to get out. Do you remember people working together to dig each other out? In fact, I think Deputy Fred dug you out. Without even being asked, if I remember correctly. That right, Fred?"

Fred agrees it is, while Dan has an incredibly sour look on his face.

"Be that as it may," Dan continues, "I think we have some people in this community who need to be reminded the power is out and they should volunteer to help others. Jake Caldwell, is the power out at your place?"

I'm somewhat surprised he just called me out. While I don't care for Dan, we haven't had hostile interactions . . . well, maybe earlier today could've been construed as hostile. But that was only on his part; I didn't return the gesture. Up to now, I've simply made a point of not associating with him.

"Yes, Dan, it is. As far as I know, the electric company isn't providing power for anyone." The truth.

"Humph. I happen to know you aren't even hooked up to the electric company. You have those fancy solar panels. And I know they are working."

I feel the heat rising to my face. I try to keep my voice even with my answer. "Your information is incorrect. I *am* hooked up to the electric company. True, I have a solar system for backup."

No need to tell him I disconnected the system last night for fear of an EMP. That may just fuel the fire. I don't even mention I'm one of several in the community who has either solar, wind, or both as a backup; plus many, many people have generators. No sense putting others in the spotlight.

Terry Bosco says what I'm thinking, "Dan, you're calling Jake out because he has a small solar system? There's at least half a dozen other people with similar systems or wind systems. And most of us who have lived here any time at all, and choose not to be dependent on our neighbors, have a generator at the very least."

"But that's— "

"In fact, as I look around here," Terry booms over the top of Dan, "I see a group of people well prepared to weather a power outage, and I know this because I've been through it with them before. Of course, you may be the exception. I suspect the house you're currently residing in may not be well equipped, and I suspect you haven't purchased anything to change this.

"Unless you have another reason for this meeting or someone else has something to say, I think we should end this now and go on with the way our community usually bands together in things. Anyone who needs assistance, get with someone who lives near you. If you don't see a nearby neighbor here, come to me, and I'll help you out."

There are many other voices expressing the same offers of help. I'm kind of surprised to have support from Terry. While I know him enough to say hello, we don't live near each other and don't socialize. I do know Terry's father-in-law, Tom, fairly well, having visited with him at many community events. Tom's a semiretired hunting guide, and I love hearing his stories. Terry must have had some sort of run-in with Dan separately and is trying to make a point.

As I look around, many people are walking to others they think might need help and offering it up. Dan Morse is scurrying to his side-by-side UTV, looking none too happy. Terry, followed by Deputy Fred, walks over to me. Terry offers his hand.

"Jake, good to see you. What did you do to Dan to get him on your case like that?"

I shrug. "I have no idea. In fact, I'm not really sure what this is all about. Seems like he had some sort of agenda calling this meeting, but I can't figure out what it might be."

"Makes no sense. Definitely a waste of time coming here," Terry says, nodding.

Deputy Fred, not an actual sheriff deputy but a guard at the county jail, says, "Keep an eye open, Jake. He's a snake."

"Uh, folks, before you all leave, can we talk for a minute about what's happening?" I look to see who's speaking and am kind of surprised to see Doris. She's not on the picnic table Dan was on but is standing near it. Evan is next to her.

Everyone turns to look, and there are a few comments of "good idea" and "yes."

Doris takes a deep breath. "I think most of you know me. I'm Doris Snyder, and this is my husband, Evan." Doris gestures to Evan, and he gives a brief nod.

"Like all of you, we've been watching what's happening in our country the last couple of days, and we're . . . distraught. I guess that's the only word I can think of. At first, it didn't seem to affect us directly, not too much anyway, when the planes were crashed and the airports exploded. It was terrible, but it didn't happen here. The planes being grounded did strand some our friends and family, though." Doris and Evan both look at me, which causes many people to turn and see who they are looking at. I hold my gaze steady.

"Then, when they took out the bridges," Doris continues, "many more people lost their lives. Many of you know, my daughter lives in San Jose. She's fine, but both the Golden Gate and the Bay Bridge were taken out. That was a little too close for comfort and felt like it did directly affect my family."

I can't believe I forgot about her daughter living there. Been so wrapped up in Mollie being gone and worrying about my girls, I didn't even think to ask Doris about her daughter. It makes sense why Doris has been so upset. I can't even imagine the chaos in that area. And her daughter is a police officer. Things must be terrible for her.

"After the bridges collapsed," Doris continues, "people left the affected cities in droves, which has caused pandemonium on pretty much every interstate and highway. I've heard Billings is now being affected. The owner of the restaurant said he's seen an increase of people. Most of them want to know where they can get fuel.

"Then we started hearing about the foodborne illnesses and how they're likely targeted attacks on us, plus this latest attack on our cyber systems. My concern is, this is going to continue and possibly escalate.

While I don't think Dan was accurate in his assessment of . . . well, I'm not really sure what he was trying to point out."

This garners a few courtesy laughs along with several nods and voices of agreement.

"But I do think we need to continue to be the neighbors we've been in the past. Evan and I have always felt very welcome here. With our close neighbors, we all moved in about the same time and have a good group. We all know we can depend on each other. And as I understand from people in other neighborhoods, we're not unique.

"Those living on The Butte are always doing things together. As well as those living at Sugar Bend and many other small neighborhoods. If things don't improve, or if things get worse, our small neighborhoods will be vital, and our entire community banding together could mean the difference between . . . " Doris seems almost overcome with emotion and pauses for a moment.

Evan finishes for her, "It could mean the difference between surviving and not surviving. If the power doesn't come back, we're going to have trouble. I haven't been to town but doubt there are many gas stations pumping. If they are, you may not be able to use your credit card since the machines aren't working. You can't get cash out of the bank since the ATMs are down. Stores may or may not be open, but without power, they won't be able to stay open long. And, again, will they accept cards without the machines working, or is it cash only?"

As Evan speaks, he has to keep raising his voice because of the response from the crowd, most are expressing disbelief over things not being resolved in the next day or two, if not the next hour or two.

"I hear many of you saying things like, 'It'll be fixed soon,' or something similar. And you may be right. The cyberattacks have only been going on a few hours, so they could get a handle on them soon. I hope they do. I truly hope Doris and I are concerned over nothing. But looking at everything that has happened, it seems to me each attack has escalated.

"Maybe the cyberwar doesn't seem like a big deal, but if these terrorists have succeeded in taking out a good portion of the electric grid, eliminated our ability to use our credit cards, and have most of the internet affected, this is a big deal. Every one of us is affected by this.

"I found out earlier today, cyberattacks happen all the time, we just don't hear about them. For something to be happening of this magnitude is very concerning. I'd like to suggest, if the power is still out tomorrow evening, we meet here again at the same time. Not to complain about who has what and who doesn't, but to support and assist each other. That's the kind of community we are. One that works together."

Now there are nods and verbal agreement throughout the crowd. Even those thinking Evan was out of bounds before seem to agree now.

"Also," Evan continues, "I'm going to make a trip into town after we're done here. I highly doubt any of the service stations will be pumping fuel, but if they are and you'd like to send a gas can with me, I'll take it. I'd like to ask for cash to buy the fuel also, but if you don't have it, I'll cover you. I'll be leaving from here in half an hour to give you time to hustle home for your gas can and cash. Make sure your name is on your can, and if you give me cash, put it in an envelope with your name and the amount. I can only handle two cans per person, so don't go nuts on me." He smiles at this, and many people give a courtesy chuckle.

"Some of you may wish to head into town now, on your own. Get fuel, and even food if you can. With the way things are, it may be difficult for transport trucks to restock the grocery shelves. You may want to think about the amount of food in your house. I know many of us stock up well when winter is starting since it can sometimes be a challenge to get into town. But if you're like Doris and me, you let your stock deplete as the snow melts. Remember, you can always eat food, so no harm in buying it now, even if the power does come back on tomorrow and everything returns to normal."

There's a bit of an uproar as Evan finishes up and starts to walk to his pickup. A rumble through the crowd: *"This is nothing," "that Snyder is overreacting," "He's just a nutcase, like that idiot Dan Morse."* And several others: *"You know, he may be right," "Can't hurt to get a little fuel," "I'm not paranoid, but seems kind of smart to me."* He's stopped by several on the way, asking him to wait; they'll be right back with a gas can.

Like Evan, I doubt any stations will be pumping, but if they are, it could be a huge help for all of us. Of course, if they are, then Evan and I are going to have our hands full. Especially if there's a line of cars. It could get dicey.

Mollie and I have some supplies set aside for the neighbors. We haven't exactly prepped for them but have things for trade, knowing we'd be very generous with what we'd trade for. Now I realize we were shortsighted and should have included things for our whole community and not just nearby neighbors. Maybe I can remedy that somewhat on this trip to town.

I walk over to Doris. "Doris, I'm so sorry I forgot about your daughter being near San Francisco. How's everything going? I can't even imagine how crazy it must be for her."

"Oh, Jake. Please don't be sorry. I know, with Mollie trying to get home, you have a lot on your mind. And now, with Katie's town in such bad shape too— "

"What do you mean Katie's town is in bad shape?"

"The fire? You haven't heard?"

"No. Katie's on her way here. They left around noon. I didn't hear."

"I'm so glad she's on her way. I heard it on the radio on our way back here. A fire started in the college area, and it spread quickly. Then, when the power went out, they lost control of it. I guess they were housing people who fled Kansas City there. It's not good. With the phone problems, I haven't been able to reach my daughter in California, but I'm not hearing anything on the news about her town at least. Casper was on the news. They are being inundated with people from Denver now. Cheyenne, of course, was already overrun, being so nearby."

"Casper? I hadn't heard. I haven't heard from any of the girls since Katie called and told me she was on her way. I planned to call them all after we got home from the wedding, but then the cyberattack . . . my phone hasn't worked since."

"I think some of the cell service is hit or miss. I got through to my daughter in Germany after the cyberattacks started, but can't reach my youngest daughter in California. I spoke with her yesterday. She's having a tough time of it since they're seeing a lot of violence. I worry for her safety."

"I'm sorry, Doris. I know how you're feeling."

"I know you do," Doris touches my arm. "You should try to call them again, Mollie and your girls. You might reach them . . . at least one of them."

"Good suggestion. I haven't heard from Mollie since this morning. Funny how we've come to rely so much on being in constant contact."

"Definitely. We've become so used to it."

I turn to walk over near my truck when Doris stops me. "Jake, what's with you and Dan?"

"I have no idea. He used to come around a lot when we first bought our place. Pretty much every time we were here, he'd stop by. And when we first moved in, he would come over, but then it stopped. We were both glad it did. Mollie said he gave her the creeps. I don't know why he had so much animosity toward me today. It was strange."

"Be careful. I don't think he's quite right. Calling this meeting today and the way it went seems odd. Also, I hope you didn't feel blindsided about Evan offering to get fuel for people. We should've discussed it with you and didn't even think about it. We decided right before we came here. I saw your face when he mentioned it and knew then we should've cleared it with you. I can go with Evan to town if you don't want to now."

"Oh, no. It's fine. I was surprised, but it's a good idea. Don't know if anything will be open, but it'll definitely be good to get fuel for people if we can. I think some of those cars that tore out of here are probably going to town on their own after Evan suggested it, so there might not be too many people with fuel cans."

"True."

"Since we're leaving from here, do you want to take my truck home? It looks like Evan has your trailer hooked up and ready to go."

"Yes. We were thinking that'd be good. Do you have everything you need?"

"I do. I filled up my generators and threw in the empty fuel cans before leaving the house, thinking Evan might want to leave from here."

I slowly make my way to my truck. I want to make a list of things to buy, if possible. Several people stop me along the way, all asking but trying not to ask the same question. What's the deal with Dan? *I wish I knew.*

Chapter 25

Jake

Malcolm meets me at the truck. "Hey, Dad. We ready to go?"

"Evan and I are going to leave from here. I'm going to ride with Evan, and Doris will take our truck home. You'll stay with her until I get back."

"No problem, Dad. Can I go back over with the others for a while? Or do you think Miss Doris is ready to go?"

"I think she's still visiting, so you probably have some time. She knows to gather you up. Besides, I still have my keys, so she can't leave you." I give him a wink as he takes off to join his friends.

I write down the few things I'm thinking of, then try to call Mollie and each of the girls with no success. I decide to make my rounds a bit, visiting with people. As I think of something else, I put it on the paper. When the half hour is up, I walk over to Evan's truck. He's talking with one of the ladies in the community and taking her gas can. In the bed of his truck are over a dozen more cans. Most are red for gas, but a couple are yellow diesel cans.

Evan looks at me. "Ready to go, Jake?"

"Sure am. Many people need cash that can't cover it?

"A few."

"I'll help out. I'm still okay on cash."

"I appreciate it, Jake."

"Where's Doris?" I ask, looking around.

"Someone opened up the building. She's inside. I expect her back any moment. We've got quite a few cans. I think everyone's set." Doris is walking over. Malcolm sees her, too, waves goodbye to his friends, and runs to meet her. They walk to us together.

"Okay, Doris. We're going to go," Evan says, while reaching to her for a hug and kiss. I suddenly realize how it's been way too long since I've had a chance to hug and kiss Mollie.

I hand Doris my keys and tell Malcolm I'll be back soon. He gives me a wave as they walk to my truck.

"Well, Jake. That meeting started with a bang."

"Yeah . . . I'm glad it was only a figurative bang and not a literal bang. A couple of times, as Dan was caressing his sidearm, I wondered."

"Not sure why he does that. I ran into him at a craft show once, stopped to talk—you know, to be neighborly—and he couldn't keep his hand off his six-shooter. Always rubbing the butt or adjusting the holster, something. And if his right hand wasn't on his gun, his left hand was on his knife! He never brandished, but . . . "

"It was freaky, right? That's what he's done when I'm around him. Mollie suggested it might be a nervous habit."

"Yeah, well, that kind of nervous habit makes police officers jumpy. Never good to have a police officer jumpy. What's with this traffic?"

"Not sure. I don't think I've ever seen this road so congested. You?"

"Can't say I have. I mean, it's not congested based on most roads in the US, but . . . "

"But the two dozen cars in front and behind us is a traffic jam by Wyoming standards?"

"Exactly." Evan laughs. "Not sure I remember how to drive in this heavy of traffic. Wonder where they all came from?"

"And where they're going. Is Prospect going to have an influx of people like some of the small towns around the bridge disasters?"

"That wouldn't make much sense. We're nowhere near any bridge issues."

"Malcolm helped me look at the traffic issues so we could tell Mollie. Seems a lot of places nowhere near the destroyed bridges were still having people arrive from other places. Didn't make much sense. Maybe it's a grass is greener type thing?"

"Huh. Don't know about that. Sounds like a workshop I had to attend on our culture of fear and how the media blows things out of proportion. We're being taught to fear just about everything. Fear works and gets ratings, so why not play it up?"

"So you're saying the news told them to pack up and leave?"

"Not specifically. But they report and over-report on the situation. They emphasize how people are leaving and going to town X or state Y, because there weren't any planes crashed or bridges hit there. Maybe someone's saying, 'Hey, folks, Wyoming is safe. You should go there. We can't keep you safe here, but they can keep you safe.' Your average lackey says, 'Jeez, that's brilliant. Why didn't I think of that? It's only a day's drive to Wyoming, might as well pack up and go.' But he doesn't really think it through, and it ends up that he's not the only one going and then you have the mess that some of the towns are seeing."

I laugh at the absurdity of it. "You don't really think people in a town that was completely safe would pack up and leave, do you?"

"I don't know. But Thursday afternoon, we thought all of our towns were relatively safe. Now look where we are. And I do know that people like to follow the crowd. I watched that happen for thirty years."

"I guess so. Malcolm and I were just having a conversation about thinking for yourself. Guess I never imagined the power of suggestion could cause people to flee their homes."

"It's the world we live in."

~~~~~

NO GAS. The handwritten signs at the first two stations are extremely clear. The third station we reach has a small line, so we pull in. There are no less than eight signs declaring CASH ONLY.

Standing by the pumps is a rather large, overweight, sweaty gentleman of retirement age and a younger, just as heavy and sweaty guy. Father and son? Both are taking money and starting the pumps. A freckle-faced teen is talking to the car in front of us. A few seconds later, that car pulls out. He shakes his head and walks to us.

"Hey, there," he says quietly. "So it's cash only. If you don't have cash, you'll need to leave the line."

"We have cash," Evan says simply.

"Okay, good. So you wanting to fill your truck and all those cans in the back?" he asks as he gestures to the truck bed.

"We'd like to—will that be okay?"

"Should be. Paul will be the one making the final decision. We get too many people in line and you might have to stop and go to the back of the line."

"Sure. We're okay with that. We're trying to help out our friends and neighbors in Bakerville, brought along cans from many in the community."

"That's good," he says with much larger grin than I'd expect. "We've been seeing quite a few people helping each other out. Tell
~~~~~

Paul that. He's my grandpa, the older one, and should be the one taking care of you. It'll probably help you out."

Twenty minutes later, we finally reach Paul. Just in time for him to release a large stream of tobacco. "Howdy, folks," he says, wiping his mouth with the back of his hand. "How much you want?"

"Fill up the truck and all of the cans?" Evan asks.

"Yep, we can do that. My grandson said you folks are in from Bakerville, bringing cans for everyone."

"Well, not everyone, several though."

"You know Sally-Ann Hinkle? Dated her when I was in high school." He gives a small chuckle. "Seems like that was about a hundred years ago."

"Sure, she's a very nice lady. In fact, two of the cans in the back are hers."

"You don't say? Well, let's get this show on the road."

It doesn't take long to have the truck and all of the cans filled. After we pay, Paul says, "Say, if you don't mind, would you tell Sally-Ann hello for me? Paul Cameron. She might not remember, so tell her I'm the guy who took her to senior prom. You mind doing that?"

"Be happy too," Evan says with a wave.

With the fueling task completed, SuperMart is next. We both brought flashlights and cash in hopes of being able to shop in the dark with no power. I learned my lesson living in Alto all those years ago when a large storm knocked the power out. That grocery store let us shop a limited section of the store as long as we had a flashlight and cash. Turns out, our flashlights aren't needed since there's a big sign on the front: CLOSED DUE TO POWER OUTAGE.

"Well, nuts. I guess it was a crapshoot they'd be open anyway," Evan says. "Let's try the Albertsons. I think Rite Aid was open. Looked like it when we went by, anyway, so we can go there. And what about the little mom-and-pop store? We could try them."

"Yeah. They might be. Let's try them first, then Albertsons, and then Rite Aid on the way out. Sound good?"

The mom-and-pop store is open and lit up by assorted battery and fuel lanterns plus candles in jars with pictures of religious figures on them. Is that the Pope?

Surprisingly, we're the only ones in the store. On my list are things like beans, rice, easy-cook shelf-stable meals, toilet paper, and paper plates. Evan is buying pretty much the same things. We do our best to leave items behind for other shoppers who may find their way here. The refrigerator case is empty, but a freezer case has a sign on it saying all must go.

A lady dressed in jeans and a smock, with the name of the store stitched on the right, causes me to jump with her hearty, "Hello." She's a dozen years older than me and has a kind look about her but seems terribly frazzled.

"I need to move it all," she says in a tight voice, motioning to the freezer case. "My daughter took some of it home and is cooking it up, but we don't have the ability to keep it all cold."

I look it over, trying to estimate the amount and if my freezer space can accommodate it. There's quite a bit, at least a hundred pounds of beef, plus chicken and pork. If Mollie were here, she'd buy it and can it or jerky it. Shoot. I can jerky it. It's super easy to do in our dehydrator or smoker.

She must have thought I was taking too long to answer and says again, "I can make you a great deal. I really hate to just throw it all away."

"How much for all of it?"

"You want the regular freezer items also?" she asks eagerly.

In addition to the meat, there's a dozen pints of ice cream, about double that in individual TV dinners, a few bags of frozen veggies, a few small family meals, quite a few pizzas, and some breakfast foods. The TV dinners are mostly the larger man-sized ones I remember eating as a bachelor. I cooked them in the microwave then. We don't have a microwave—and I'm not sure we could run one on solar anyway—but they should cook just fine in the oven and likely taste better. Or at least a little less like chemically-laced cardboard.

"Sure. Why not?"

She's almost beaming. Her features soften, and her frazzled look seems to diminish as she looks over everything. She's calculating in her head. Evan is standing near me, listening in. She gives me a number, an incredibly low number of about 20 percent of retail. *Wow.*

"For the small case too." She motions to the end where there are hot dogs, sausage, cheese, and bacon. She has me with the bacon. I don't want to appear too anxious so hesitate a little.

"Hmmm. Power's been out a few hours already . . . I guess everything's still fine." I know it is. "I'll do it. I want to gather a few more things, then I'll start loading it up."

"Want me to grab you a cart?" Evan asks.

"No need," the lady responds with a small smile. "I have boxes. You can just load it in the boxes, then we don't have to mess with it. Let me get them."

When she's in the back, I look at Evan and mouth, "Lots of meat."

He mouths back, "Split it?"

I nod. They do have a couple freezers still full of wild game, but I was hoping he'd want some of this. And Doris knows how to can. She and Mollie have canned together before. I wonder if she'd be willing to help me with it. *I wish Mollie was home.* At least she should be back tomorrow, maybe even sometime overnight.

Jars. I need more jars. I find three boxes and buy all plus a few boxes of zipper bags.

I have everything in my cart as the lady returns with several boxes. "You want me to go ahead and pay, then I'll load up?" I ask.

"Sure. That's great. Oh, I see you found my jars. I have more in the back. You want them?"

"How many jars you have?"

"Not sure. At least a few boxes."

She goes to the back again and soon returns with a cart containing four boxes of jars and two more empty boxes. "This is it. No more regular mouth quarts but three large mouth and a box of half pints in the large mouth. Oh, and flats. Two boxes of regular and seven boxes of large. You want those too?"

"Yes, perfect." I take care of my bill. While Evan is paying, I start filling the boxes. It takes us several trips to get everything in the trailer.

"We'd best be quick getting this home. Think we should skip Albertsons? I got most of what I wanted here," Evan says.

"Yep. I'm good with skipping it. What about Rite Aid?"

"I'd like to give it a try. This store didn't have much in the way of first aid stuff, and more paper products wouldn't be bad. We'll make it quick."

Rite Aid is slightly busy, so we don't get through as quick as we'd like. We're surprised to see the cash registers working. When we get to the front, we find out they have battery backup. We both get more first aid stuff, toilet paper, paper towels, and assorted sundries. We also buy many soups, jerky, and snack foods. We would've liked to buy bottles of water, but with the food poisoning announcement to treat all water except bottled, there isn't any. Our bill is impressive, almost like a Costco trip.

"Let's try one more place," Evan says. "We'll make it quick so we can get the ice cream home before it turns to soup."

"Okay . . . " I say hesitantly.

He pulls into a pawn shop we both like. We're both a little surprised to see they're open. Even more surprised by the car skidding out of the lot and almost sideswiping us.

As we walk in, Evan says heartily, "Glad you were still open, Bill. I wondered if you'd be."

"Yep, barely. You just missed a near-event."

"Whatcha mean?" Evan asks.

"You see those guys tearing out of here? They're trouble."

"Saw them. They almost nailed us. My first inclination was to go after them, but I don't need trouble tonight."

"Yeah. They always show up after they've been overserved someplace, looking for a deal on something, and tend to be obnoxious. Usually, not so much I can't handle it, but tonight . . . it was close. When I told them I couldn't help them with anything, they said fine, they'd just take what they wanted and there was nothing I could do about it with the phones out. Well, that didn't go over too well with me. I'm sure you can imagine."

He pauses and looks to Evan and me for confirmation. I nod and Evan says, "Sure can."

Bill continues, "I let them know by racking my 12 gauge there was still something I could do about it. Pretty sure one of them wet himself. I would've hated to have to shoot them. They're not really bad guys, but tonight, they acted like they had nothing to lose. I guess, with the threat of calling 911 out of the equation, they were feeling brave."

"I suspect they won't be the only ones," Evan says with a shake of his head.

"Suppose you're right. Anyway. I'm shutting down—in fact, how about you turn the deadbolt for me. I'll help you and then that's it for tonight. I think I'll only open up during daylight hours as long as the power and phones are out. And, truthfully, probably won't be able to stay open too long until things get back to normal. I've done a booming business the last few days—people have been buying but not selling. Made a few trades but nothing of consequence. As you can see, I've already sold out of quite a bit of inventory."

I lock the door for Bill and glance around. Bill's place has always been rather cluttered and has a distinctly old and musty smell. There's a serious lack of organization in how he displays his wares. Mollie and I have shopped here a few times, at Evan's urging, when Bill had a new handgun or rifle worth looking at. We have yet to purchase a gun from Bill, but have found camping gear, items for outfitting our place, and several odds and ends.

"So what can I do you for tonight?" Bill asks.

"My buddy over in Red Lodge said he thought you recently took in a lever-action Marlin—a .45-70," Evan responds.

"Woo, wee. I did have one. She was a beauty. I had to take it home and try it out before I put it on the shelf. But darn, Evan, that bad boy didn't stick around too long. In fact, a guy from your neck of the woods bought it. Sorry, friend."

"Yeah, I figured it was a long shot it'd still be here. I should've made a point of getting in here as soon as he called."

"Anything else I can help you with?"

Evan glances at the rifles and shotguns displayed on the wall behind Bill, then he takes a quick look in the glass front case displaying the handguns.

"Nah, not in the firearm department, but we'll take a quick look around."

I find a few things to add to our camping gear. Evan picks up several miscellaneous items. Before he checks out, he gestures at a handgun in the case. "You know, let me take a look at that 9-millimeter. It's a Smith and Wesson?"

"Yep, sure is. Smith and Wesson M&P 2.0."

Evan spends a little time looking at it, then makes a deal to purchase.

"Mind if I walk out with you fellas?" Bill asks as we finish checking out. "I'm feeling a little skittish over those numbskulls." He gives a little laugh and shake of his head. "Silly, huh?"

"Nah, totally understandable. A thing like that will shake any man up."

"Thanks, Evan. Give me just a minute to shut everything down."

Bill flips a few switches and says, "That's it, except the overhead light by the door. You guys got your stuff?"

We each pick up our goods, and Evan steps out first, then I follow as Bill shuts of the light. He asks, "So you guys finished in town? Or you heading—*oomph*!"

I begin to turn to look at Bill when an arm goes around my neck and pulls me backwards, almost causing me to lose my balance. *What the . . . ?*

I drop my pawn shop purchases and quickly regain my footing, while reaching my arms up to pull down hard on the arm around my neck, pushing my chin into my chest and dropping myself into a lower base.

He pulls again, trying to drag me back. I step my right leg back behind his until I feel our calves connect. My slight move causes him to shift a little more, throwing him off balance.

Now's my opportunity.

I push off with my left leg, turning 180 degrees, twisting his arm and forcing his body to shift, allowing me to use a modified armbar and something like a hip wheel to toss him over and onto the ground.

My balance was slightly compromised, so I tuck into a right-arm forward roll, regain my footing, and turn to face him, ready for a front kick if needed. No need for the kick—he's on the ground.

None of it was pretty, and I'm sure our instructor would've had plenty of things to say about my technique. But I'm upright and he's still on the ground, having landed on my shopping bag, breathing hard. Even from this distance, the stink of his alcohol and . . . what is that, pee? Whatever it is, it's almost overpowering.

"Hey, man. No need to be hostile," he slurs.

"Stay down," I command between gritted teeth. The drunk gives a weak nod.

"Jake, you good?" Evan asks.

I don't take my eyes off the guy on the ground. "He's on the ground," I pant. "You okay?"

"Yep. My guy's neutralized."

Neutralized.

Does neutralized mean dead?

Chapter 26

Jake

"Stay there, buddy," Evan says.

Whew, not dead.

Evan then steps into my view. He quickly flips the guy on his stomach and secures his hands with zip ties.

"You carry zip ties on you?"

"Well . . . yeah. You never know when they'll come in handy."

I finally peel my eyes from my drunk and turn to look for Bill. He's leaning up against the building, holding his head. The guy Evan subdued is on his stomach, wriggling like a snake. I go to Bill.

"You all right?"

"Suppose I'm going to have a headache tomorrow. Those two . . . I told you they weren't too smart. Drunk as skunks and attacking the three of us."

"Want to go to the hospital?" Evan asks Bill.

"Nah. He didn't hit me that hard. Were they armed?"

I look to Evan, who shakes his head and says, "Not really. They each had a pocketknife, but that was all."

Bill nods. "What should we do with them? Take them behind the building and shoot them?"

"Hey, now, Bill. There's no call for that," the one I took down stutters. "You heard him. We weren't even armed. We were just messing around."

"Really, Glen? You and Carl came back here to do, what? Beat me up and rob me? Earlier you said there wasn't a law any longer. Well, I guess you're right. If we're going back to the old west, then let's do it. Ah, poor Glen. Did you just wet your pants again?"

The ground around Glen is noticeably wet. Carl makes a noise of disgust and says, "You idiot. He's not going to shoot you. He's just trying to scare you." With considerably less bluster, he says, "Right, Bill? You're just joshing. You know we didn't mean to hurt you."

Evan shakes his head, while Bill chortles and says, "Evan, you do me a favor and take these guys to the county lockup?"

"With pleasure. You okay to get home?"

"You betcha. Tell the sheriff I'll be in tomorrow to file a formal complaint. Glen, Carl, you two idiots should've left well enough alone."

We have to rearrange things in the truck to get them in. Evan has me drive. We put garbage bags on the front passenger seat, and stinky Glen rides there. Carl's in the back, with Evan guarding them both. I'm shaking slightly from the excitement and adrenalin, which makes putting the keys in the ignition a bit of a challenge.

Glen, eyeballing me, says, "Got you plenty rattled, didn't we?"

I meet his gaze and put on my best glare. "I'm not the one that wet myself."

Glen drops his gaze and quickly looks away, while both Evan and Carl laugh from the back seat.

I'm surprised at how quickly Evan's able to convince the deputy manning the desk to take Carl and Glen off our hands. I guess the fact Evan's retired law enforcement, and the deputy knows Bill, helped.

When we're finally rid of Glen and Carl, I start to get a hold of myself as we begin the drive. While I wasn't injured, I do have a bit of a blacktop burn along my forearm. It's dotted with gravel and starting to sting.

Both windows are down, trying to air out the stink Glen left behind. I take a deep breath, enjoying the fresh pee-free air.

When that arm first snaked around my neck, my instincts and limited training took over. But then, when I had Glen on the ground, my anger kicked in. I had to keep myself from continuing the attack, to make him hurt, to . . . neutralize him?

Yes, the thought of killing him crossed my mind.

Who am I?

The road home is as busy as our drive into town, with a steady stream of traffic heading toward us.

"Jake, you were great tonight. I'd say you've definitely got your money's worth from those martial arts classes."

"Uh . . . right. It helped the guy was pretty drunk and not too smart."

"No kidding. They were both dumb as a box of rocks. Not sure why they thought the two of them could get one over on three of us."

After a few minutes, he asks, "Want to drive in tomorrow morning? Maybe SuperMart will be open, and we can check Albertsons. The feed store too. I had hoped we'd make it in before it closed tonight. We could even drive over to Wesley. Of course, with tomorrow being Sunday, several places will be closed."

Do I want to go back to town tomorrow? After tonight, I'm not so sure. I hesitate before I say, "Yeah. It's not a bad idea to go in tomorrow. Start with SuperMart and make the loop ending up in Wesley. We'll miss out on some places, but many are still open on Sunday. I was feeling pretty good about our storage amounts and just filling in a few things. But with the meeting tonight . . . " I stifle a sigh. "I guess, I'm feeling compelled to do more, to make a point of finding things our community might need."

"Yep, agreed. I wanted to thank you—you know, for being so on top of things with this whole event."

"Okay, you're welcome. I'm not sure what you mean, though."

"Calling Doris the first night and letting me ride along with you. I might have gone into town for things the next day, but going with you then and getting a glimpse into your . . . I don't know, your thoughts on this whole thing made a difference. It's not like we don't know the things that could happen. I think it's more normalcy bias. It's too easy to underestimate the disaster and what could happen afterward. And it's not like we don't know the possibilites. Mollie and Doris are always talking about those disaster and end-of-the-world books they read. But to actually put things into play, to think something could be happening in real life. Nope."

"I know exactly what you mean. We've made some provisions and discussed multiple scenarios. But when it comes right down to it, it's hard to believe it's real."

"Precisely. Doris and I went to town on Friday and picked up a few more things. But most importantly, we took out all the cash we could. We mostly use our cards for purchasing, so cash on hand is usually limited. But we figured, why not get it while we could. We could always put it back in the bank."

"Yeah, that's what I figured too. I was kind of surprised when the banks gave me a hard time about taking the money out. It wasn't even that much."

"Yep, same here. Almost like they knew something we didn't."

"Or we weren't the only ones taking money out. Maybe there'd been others in before us and they were feeling the pressure? I don't think banks actually keep that much cash on hand. Mollie researched it once, but I can't remember what she said the average bank holds. And let's face it, lots of people around here tend to be on a similar wavelength as us. Either that or as paranoid as we are."

"No kidding." Evan laughs. "There's still a few more things I need, so I'm glad you're okay with making another run tomorrow. Say, you hear the talk going around suggesting these aren't terrorists, not in the usual sense? Maybe a country is behind this, like Russia or China or maybe North Korea? They're even tying the Grover school shooting to it. At least one blow-hard on the radio was suggesting it."

"I didn't hear much, but Mollie and I were discussing something similar this morning. I didn't hear anything about tying it to Grover, though. How are they figuring?"

"You know how they said they could only identify the one shooter and the other two had no ID? Now they're saying the two are European."

"Okay. So?"

"It's suggested it was staged to look like the kid did it alone, but the couple foiled it—what's their name?"

"Mitchell," I offer.

"Yeah, the Mitchells foiled it. It might have been a setup to enact more gun legislation."

"By our government? The current legislation doesn't seem to be quite so anti-gun."

"Not our government. Foreign. The less guns in our hands, the easier it would be to come in and take us over."

"They can't possibly think they could get rid of enough to make that happen. Oh. But if we're weakened because of the continued attacks and they wait long enough, then there could be a drastically reduced population too. Still, I could totally believe a country is behind these attacks instead of a group like ISIS, but I don't see the Grover shooting tying in. I agree it's totally fishy, especially with people dying and disappearing, but it doesn't fit for these attacks."

"Maybe not. That whole thing, what a mess. First the responding officers mistake Mitchell for one of the shooters and put the hurt on him. Surprised he didn't sue them for everything they had. 'Course, they were put on administrative leave pending investigation. Now, with our world falling apart, don't suppose they'll continue that process anytime soon. Then the teacher and the other staff member both dying sure sounded suspicious. And the Mitchells disappearing. Wonder when they'll find them. Or find their bodies. I can't imagine that will end well for them."

Evan said what I've often thought. "No. I can't imagine it will."

After a couple minutes of silence, Evan says, "Say, Jake, you carrying your handgun?"

"I'm not, Evan. I rarely do, really only if we're hunting or hiking."

Evan nods and says thoughtfully, "I can understand that. Always good to have some protection when in the wilderness with the bears and the cats. Of course, with a bear, you'll use your bear spray first, and if that doesn't stop him, you'd better plan on emptying your .357."

I say nothing for a couple of beats, then, "Probably be good to have some protection on a daily basis, especially after what happened tonight."

"I like the way you think," Evan says. "Probably would be a good idea. You didn't have any trouble subduing your guy tonight, but at some point, you could encounter someone with truly evil intentions since the law is no longer a phone call away."

I nod in agreement but say nothing. I'm not like Evan. He's a retired deputy sheriff and carried daily for thirty years. While I've shot rifles and shotguns since I was a kid, I've never really developed a fondness for handguns.

Sure, I've done some target practice over the years and a few years ago took a course so I could get my concealed carry permit. Wyoming very much respects citizens' rights to open or conceal carry. It's just not a habit I've developed.

Mollie, on the other hand, has embraced concealed carry and rarely leaves the house unarmed. When she's at home, protection is steps away in an easy-access lockbox.

"I know you're right. If he would've been armed or sober, I could've been in real trouble tonight. I don't have a conceal carry holster, unless I borrow one from Mollie's collection, but can carry open on my belt. You think that's okay? I know from the class you taught you prefer concealed."

"Yep. For everyday life, I think it's best just so it's not in plain sight. Here, open isn't that big of a deal. Shoot, people open carry in stores and churches. No problem. But concealed does let you be discreet about it. No one knows what you have. Can't freak out people and can surprise bad guys.

"With what we have going on now, I think open carry makes sense. And I'd rather have you open carry than nothing at all. That said, you could borrow an inside-the-waistband holster from Mollie. I know she has quite a collection, or I have one you could use. Whatever you're comfortable with."

Mollie does have quite a collection. She buys holsters like other women purchase jewelry. It's mildly amusing, considering she'd never even touched a handgun until after we moved here.

Evan and I continue the drive mostly in silence, making occasional small talk. As soon as we reach an area where I usually have good cell service, I try Mollie. It doesn't connect. I try each of the girls, starting with Katie. No good. Sarah is my last call; I'm surprised when the phone actually rings.

"Jake?! How'd you get the phone to work?"

"I don't know. I tried your mom and then your sisters but couldn't connect. It rang when I tried you."

"I'm glad. I've tried you several times over the last few hours. Can we come down there?"

"Of course. When?"

"Now? We're getting ready to leave. Power's out and things are getting weird here. We need to get out of Billings."

"Yes, sure. I'll try to wait up for you. Ring the bell in case I fall asleep and don't hear the driveway alert go off when you pull in."

"Thanks, Jake. I'm glad we reached you. Tate suggested it could be dangerous pulling in if you weren't expecting us, so we were trying to figure out what to do."

"Hmm. Good point. I wouldn't shoot first and ask questions later, but maybe we should think about some kind of code."

"You mean like *Alas, Babylon*?" There's a hint of a smile in her voice.

I laugh. Mollie had suggested we come up with code when we thought things were going bad. *Alas, Babylon*, a favorite book of Mollie's, was a likely code. We settled on only using *Plan A* if we thought it was necessary. Mollie and Sarah must have had a discussion about this.

"Yep. Your mom loves that book and thinks it's a great code. But it doesn't really work for someone pulling in the yard after dark. I was thinking more like honking the horn in a pattern."

"Oh, yeah. That makes sense. Tate is signaling me we're ready to pull out. Don't forget, his parents are with us. His sister too. She was able to get away last minute. They wanted to surprise us."

"It's fine."

"Okay. See you soon."

I put my phone away. I'm glad Sarah's heading this way. I didn't expect trouble in their neighborhood, at least not early on like this. I figured, if they had trouble, it wouldn't be for a few days. This makes me wonder how Angela and Calley are. Casper is half the size of Billings, but I suspect they have several more people out of Denver than Billings is getting from cities. Things could get bad there soon.

Angela and Tim will be ready to leave when needed. Out of all of the girls, Angela seems to have taken to our preparedness ways the most. Calley and Mike, not so much. I don't think they do much beyond the societal norm. And Calley has been adamant about staying at their home and banding together with Mike's parents next door. Not that she really thinks there could *ever* be this kind of need.

Evan interrupts my thoughts "Your oldest girl's coming down?"

"Yes. They're just leaving. And Tate's family is with them. They were visiting from out of state. Now I'm even happier we bought more supplies. We, uh, tend to store up quite a bit of stuff in case the girls have the need to stay here. But we weren't really planning on Tate's folks since they live so far away."

Even though Evan is a good friend, he doesn't really know the extent of our preparation measures. Over the years, we've amassed a considerable number of provisions.

Our goal was to have one year of food stored for each family member. As the size of our family increased through marriage and the birth of our grandson, we've added for each person. Living so close to my parents, they're also included in the numbers we prepare for.

When Mollie realized Calley and Mike wouldn't come up without Mike's folks, she extended an invitation to bring them along, and we started collecting for them also. In addition to food, we store any other goods we think might be needed, such as the clothes and miscellaneous supplies purchased during my recent shopping trips. We really want to offer a safe haven for our family members, should the need ever arise. I guess the need may be here now.

I realize Evan's still talking. "Must be a huge relief to have Sarah and Tate living so close. They timed that well, moving from Oregon."

"It certainly seems so. How's Doris holding up with her daughter where she is?"

"Not well. Our youngest is tough and she takes her duty as a police officer seriously, but she'll leave when it seems prudent. She and her husband have already said they'd hotfoot it here if they have to. Our oldest is more of a concern. No way for her to get here from Germany with the planes grounded, other than maybe finding a boat. Not that it would be easy anyway. She'd never leave her husband, and he has to apply for travel authorization before they can leave since his previous authorization is expired. He went ahead and put in his application on Friday. Once it's approved, it's good for two years, so not a biggie if they don't use it now.

"Of course, it's not looking good for air travel right now. Things are fine in Germany anyway, so maybe it's best they're there. Doris talked with all of them this morning on the FaceTime thing. Even the baby had things to say. He's cooing so much. Their five-year-old knew about the plane crashes. I guess it's big news there, and they were even playing it on the TV at his daycare. Seems young kids shouldn't be seeing quite so much."

I just nod, having nothing else to say. Doris and Evan have been married about the same time Mollie and I have. Doris's girls are Evan's stepdaughters, but he loves them like they were his own. And the grandbabies are his grandsons. It's no different than how I feel about our girls and Gavin. We may not have the same blood, but it doesn't change anything.

We stop at my house first. I'm surprised to see my truck in the yard and a light bobbing around inside the house. Doris and Malcolm must have chosen to stay here rather than up at Doris's place. Malcolm sticks his head out and waves. Then both Doris and he come outside, flashlights in hand. It's not full-on dark yet but getting close, so the lights are helpful.

Before we get out of the truck, I say, "Evan, can we keep tonight quiet? No need to scare Malcolm or anyone with it."

"Sure, no problem. I'll be telling Doris, but she won't say anything."

I nod and step out to meet Malcolm.

"Dad! I'm glad you got back so quick. Did you find gas?"

"We sure did, Buddy. There was a station open, and we were able to fill up everyone's cans."

"That's good. Should make people happy," he says.

Evan tells Doris about the great deal we got on meat. I can see she's not nearly as impressed with it as we were. Then she voices her concern. "Super, guys. But with the power out, we're in the same situation as the store. What are you planning to do with it?"

"We'll make jerky," Evan answers. "And I thought you could do some of that canned meat. It sure turns out good when you make it."

The look she gives him tells me she doesn't think much of the idea.

"Well, yes. I could. But we still have meat in the freezers from last year's hunt that I'll need to process if the power doesn't come back soon. We can keep it fine for now with the generator. And I'm not sure how many jars I have."

"I picked up some jars," I tell Doris. "You can have some of them."

She smiles weakly, but the look she gives me tells me I'm not helping the situation. "Thank you, Jake," she says frostily.

We unload the things going to my house. I put the ice cream and other frozen things immediately in the mudroom freezer. The edges around the ice cream are a little soupy, but it's fine. When Doris is inside, Evan asks me if I mind holding on to the meat for now until he can talk with her more. I let him know either way is fine. I planned to buy it all anyway, so if they decide to pass on it, I'm okay with it.

Once my things are unloaded, I offer to go up with Evan to empty his things out. He waves me off, telling me they've got it.

"What time do you finish chores in the morning?" Evan asks while walking to his truck.

"Around 7:00. I can start a little earlier if you'd like to leave before then."

"No need. Let's go at 7:30. I'll pick you up, and we'll take this trailer again? Doris can keep Malcolm."

"Sounds good. Let's do it. But with Sarah coming in tonight, Malcolm will be fine here."

Back in the house, Malcolm and I fill the mudroom freezer with as much as possible, then move on to the basement freezer, and then hook up both to small, portable generators. I'll rehook the solar system tomorrow.

We put the hot dogs, cheeses, and bacon in the upstairs fridge and add a couple of frozen water bottles to act as an old-fashioned icebox. While our solar system isn't large enough to run this full-sized fridge without a good dose of sunshine, it'll run our small dorm-sized beverage fridge all the time. After we work through what's in the basement and main-level fridge, we'll use only the small fridge. It'll take some getting used to, but we'll be better off than most people.

I suddenly remember Sarah's on her way and take care of a few things they'll need. After noticing the trailer Tate brought over on Friday is chock-full of stuff, I assume all five will stay in the bunkhouse, at least for tonight. Malcolm and I take a few minutes to set things up so they'll be comfortable.

I wonder, with Sarah here, can we start on the canning? Sarah canned with Mollie when she was visiting during harvest season. Maybe she can help with it and we can get this taken care of. Or, even better, maybe Mollie will make it home tomorrow. I do a quick calculation from where she was the last time I heard from her. I suppose it's unlikely she could make it home tonight, but tomorrow is highly possible. *Please, Lord, bring my wife home.*

Chapter 27

Jake

Once everything is put away and organized, Malcolm and I sit down to read. I'll leave the generators running at least until Sarah and her family arrive. That should give the freezer and fridge a good boost. Pretty soon, I can't keep my eyes open. Malcolm tells me to take a rest on the couch, and he'll keep watch for Sarah and Tate. I readily agree.

It's not long until Malcolm is shaking me awake.

"Dad. Dad. *Dad.* Wake up. I think they're here."

I wipe the drool from my cheek and the sleep from my eyes. With slightly blurred vision, I look out the window. Three cars in the driveway. *Beep, Beeeeep, Beep.* I guess Sarah decided on a pattern.

As Sarah pulls me into a hello hug, I notice she looks great, even at this late hour. Her makeup is done, and her shoulder-length brown hair is styled in gentle waves. She's wearing a sundress with a sweater over the top and flat shoes. At five foot seven inches, she's the tallest of our girls.

After we release, Tate comes in for his hug. While I'm not much of a hugger, Tate is, so I've learned to just go with it and not resist. He's almost an inch or two shorter than I am and about the same weight. Where Sarah is dressed up, he's dressed down, wearing sweatpants, a T-shirt with a rip in the sleeve, and athletic shoes that have seen better days. He's a few years older than Sarah and has the start of a receding hairline. He keeps it trimmed short so it's not super noticeable. His full beard is also clipped short and neat.

"Thanks, Jake. We appreciate this," he says, clapping me on the back.

"Jake, you remember Tate's dad, Keith; his mom, Lois; and his sister, Karen?" Sarah asks. I'm glad she reminded me of their names because, even though we met them at Sarah and Tate's wedding, I'd forgot the names of his mom and sister.

"Yes, of course." I shake hands with Keith, an older and slightly heavier version of Tate, fully bald with silver fringe and an untrimmed, slightly wild, silver beard. He looks tired and majorly stressed out. Lois gives me a hug, and Karen spares me a small wave. They share the tired and stressed look Keith has. Karen is older than Tate, never married. They own a duplex, and she lives in one section while the parents live in the other.

"Why are you using the lanterns?" Sarah asks. "Is your solar out?"

"I disconnected the solar."

"Really? Why's that?" Keith asks. His loud, booming voice causes Malcolm to jump.

"You scared me," Malcolm laughs.

"Oops. Sorry about that. I don't hear too well, so sometimes I talk too loud. Plus, all those years of telling the kids to sit down and be quiet on the school bus . . . guess I just don't know how loud I can be. We bus drivers really work at throwing our voice."

"Okay, it's fine. Dad, why'd you disconnect the solar? I know you said you were testing something, but . . . "

"Uh, yeah." I clear my throat, knowing I should've been honest with Malcolm from the beginning. "You see, with the terrorist attacks continuing and escalating, it seemed a possibility," I shrug and swallow hard, "a possibility we'd have an EMP, so I disconnected them last night. Now, with the cyberattacks, I'm not sure an EMP is quite as likely. They found another way to get to our grid."

"Hmm. I guess you could be right," he agrees, but doesn't sound convinced.

"Let's get you all settled. Are you wanting to stay in the trailer tonight, or can I put you all in the bunkhouse?"

"The bunkhouse would be good, Jake. I left a lot of supplies in the trailer, and it needs cleaned out," Tate answers.

Malcolm and I take everyone out to the bunkhouse. Even though we call this space "the bunkhouse," it's not the way I think of a bunkhouse—a big room with lots of bunk beds. This is more like a small two-bedroom apartment with a few bonus features.

In addition to being connected to regular electricity through the power company—which is no help with the cyberattack we're experiencing—it also has a small twelve-volt, independent solar system. I didn't bother with unhooking this small system, or any of the other small systems, when my paranoia led me to disconnect the house system. The small system runs a lamp in the main room and lights things up nicely.

"Oh! It's lovely," Lois gushes.

The main room, a 20 x 20 square, is the living room, dining room, and kitchen all in one. The kitchen, along the wall opposite the entry door, has all of the basics, plus a specialty range that runs on batteries instead of electricity and can be lit manually. We have the same range, only full-sized, in our house and have been very pleased with it.

The living room has two futons to provide extra sleeping space and a couple of small chairs along with a seating bench—actually, a rocket mass heater. This is a very efficient wood burning stove, which directs the fire through an insulated space and harvests the heat. These heaters work on the concept of warming people and not spaces by heating up mass—in this case, rock—and it holds the heat very well while using small amounts of wood.

The bench warms up and provides a cozy seating area while the heat is slowly released out of the rocks. It's really very ingenious. We use this heating system in the main house also, with a rocket mass heater in our bedroom and a second in the basement rec room. These work in conjunction with our large woodstove in the living room and whole-house propane furnace. Mollie is often stretched out on the long bench in our bedroom reading a book. She says it's her favorite winter spot.

"Are there bedrooms? Or just the couches?" Keith asks.

"Bedrooms. One on each end, plus a sleeping loft above each bedroom space. The ladders attached to the walls lead up to the loft. There's a full bath on this end," I motion to the right, "and a half bath on the other end."

"Mom, why don't you and Dad take the room on the right? Karen, do you want the loft above them or the bedroom on the other end?" Tate asks.

"The loft is fine." Karen's curt tone sounds like it's anything but fine.

"Okay, then," Tate says crisply.

"Uh, right," I stutter, "I've left a few things. The fridge is plugged into the solar, so it's working. There's milk, creamer, and eggs in there. Plus coffee, tea, sugar, bread, peanut butter, jelly, and a box of granola bars in the upper cabinet to the left of the stove. Sarah, I'm going to leave for town around 7:30 in the morning. You mind watching Malcolm?"

"Not at all. Send him over when you leave."

"Can I pick anything up for anyone?"

Tate flings his left arm, gesturing toward his dad, and says, "We're going to make a trip back to Billings for another load of stuff. We'll empty the trailer first and then go. Much to Sarah's dismay, we made a stop at the Laurel SuperMart on the way here, but it was closed. I thought we'd try it again tomorrow."

I'm slightly surprised they'd even try to stop at SuperMart. Sarah isn't a fan of SuperMart, and the store is on her list of places not to shop. I suspect stopping there wasn't her idea. "You have a list? I can pick up anything you need if the Prospect SuperMart or Albertsons is open. Doubles wouldn't hurt anything."

"Jake," Sarah says softly, "we used most of our disposable income to buy the trailer. We took out as much cash as we could, but we feel we should hold on to it. With the banks closed, it's going to have to last."

"True, Sarah," I say, "as long as the banks are closed, we'll only be able to use cash. My bigger concern is the stores may empty out before our cash does. The store you stopped at was closed and so was the SuperMart I stopped at tonight. I'd like to think the closed doors will keep people out, but if they get desperate, they may break in and empty the places out." I glance around in time to see Keith roll his eyes.

I shrug. "Or SuperMart may be open tomorrow, realizing they need to start moving things before they spoil, and there will be a buying frenzy. You all have seen pictures of stores before storms hit? It happened that way in Oregon some. Here, it doesn't as much. But in the south before a hurricane, many aisles are emptied. With so many interstates jammed and gas stations closed, it may be some time before trucks arrive to restock."

"Sarah, I think Jake's right," Tate gently says. "All our bills are paid for now and the things we want to buy are not frivolous, but things we can use. We can easily tighten our belts until our next paychecks. Plus, we'll have food to eat. What more do we need?"

"I suppose you're right. I'll make a second list of things for you to pick up, Jake. It'll be smaller than the list I send with Tate. His has things beyond essentials. Your list will be essentials. And perhaps you could try Albertsons and not just SuperMart?"

Now that sounds more like the Sarah I know and love.

"Do you mind if I go with you, Jake?" Karen surprises me by asking.

"No, not at all. Originally, I planned to ride with my neighbor, but I was thinking of taking our car also. I'd like to check in on my folks while in town. Be ready by 7:15? We'll be leaving no later than 7:30."

"Yes, sure. See you then."

"You think Prospect has fuel?" Tate asks.

"We found a station open tonight. You okay on gas?"

"We filled up the other night after your *Plan A* message and filled the couple of cans we had. I don't know if we can get fuel in Billings. Things were already getting weird at the gas stations before the power went out. You think you could try to fill up my cans?"

"Sure. They empty now?"

"No. But I'll put them in the truck. I should have enough to get to Billings and back. I'll be low, but if you can fill them up, we'll make it last."

"I have a full can or two, so we can get you a full tank. Then I'll take all the cans and see what we can do." I choose not to divulge just how much fuel we have on hand right now. The time will come for that information.

"Thanks, Jake," Sarah says warmly while wrapping me in a hug.

Tate nods, then comes in for his own hug once Sarah releases me. "I'd like to wait until morning when it's light before filling the tank."

"Absolutely. I agree. I'll leave two cans by the garage. Use what you need and leave the empties with me."

Barely above a whisper, Karen asks, "Do you think it's safe?"

"Going to Billings or Prospect?"

"Either," she says.

I want to say, *Yes, of course*, but that'd be a lie. With Malcolm intent on my answer, I simply attempt a smile and give a small shrug.

Chapter 28

Malcolm

I'm pretty excited Sarah's here. She's my oldest sister. She was twenty years old when I was born, and she lived at college. She's kind of a different kind of sister than Calley and Katie are, even different than Angela.

Calley and Katie used to live in the same house as us, so they were around a lot when I was a little kid. Angela didn't live with us but did live in the same town when we all lived in Casper, before Mom, Dad, and I moved to Bakerville.

Sarah used to live in Oregon. She'd visit us, or we'd visit her, but it was more like seeing a friend instead of my sister. Don't get me wrong, I love her and all, but don't get to be with her much. Now she and Tate live pretty close by. They only moved here a little while ago, but we've seen them almost every weekend. We even helped them move in. I know Mom's really happy Sarah lives so close now.

The community center meeting was kind of weird tonight. People were upset. Especially Dan Morse when he sped off in his side-by-side. He peeled out and gravel shot up from his tires. I was with some others on the playground, and we were all kind of surprised he'd drive like that—there were so many people around. Someone could get hurt.

My friend Tony wasn't there tonight, and neither were any of my other friends. Maybe they're still having the wedding party since their sister was married today. There were a few little kids at the playground, so I played with them.

Afterward, Dad went to town with Evan and I came back to my house with Doris. Doris and I played Crazy Eights while we were waiting. We had to set up a few lanterns so we could see since there isn't any electricity and the solar system isn't working. I'm glad I know where we keep the lanterns and flashlights.

Dad and I are getting ready for bed now. I brushed my teeth and have on my pajamas. The wind is starting to blow—nothing unusual in Bakerville. Dad says the wind here isn't too bad compared to Casper. I don't really remember the wind there. I was pretty young when we moved away. When we go back to visit, it doesn't seem much different than our wind. I don't mind the wind at nighttime. We're in the house and I can only hear it. But it's not too much fun during the day when we have to be outside. I've had the wind blow dirt and stuff in my mouth way too many times.

While I'm grabbing the book we're reading, I think about my mom. Where is she? Is it windy there too?

Dad said he had to go to three different gas stations to find gas tonight. I hope Mom can find gas so she can get home. Where is she sleeping tonight? Did she find a hotel room? Is she camping?

I hope she's not in the mountains where the bears are. I know she's a little scared of camping around the grizzly bears. I'm scared of camping where the bears are too. We do it sometimes, but Dad says we're smart about it. We don't cook anywhere near our camp, and we hang our food in a tree a long ways away from our tent. We also don't camp where there are signs of bears, like tracks or poo or things like that.

Thinking about Mom camping in the woods is really starting to make my stomach hurt. My breathing feels a little funny and my heart is beating too hard.

"Hey, Malcolm, you ready for bed?"

I wasn't expecting it, and Dad's voice scares me a little bit, causing me to jump. I take a deep breath. "Yeah, Dad. I was wondering . . . "

Dad waits for me to finish my sentence. When I don't say anything, he softly says, "You were wondering what?"

"You know, today has been kind of . . . scary. I was thinking, maybe we could read a little more of our story in your bed and I could, you know, just stay there tonight?"

Dad gives me a small smile. "Sure, Buddy. That's fine. Today has been kind of scary. The last few days have all been scary."

"You think tomorrow will be better, Dad? You think Mom will get home tomorrow?"

"I pray it will be better, and I pray your mom will be home."

"Me too." We head off to bed. I don't tell Dad I'm worried she'll be eaten by a grizzly bear. No reason to make his stomach hurt too.

Chapter 29

Jake
Sunday, Day 4

Even with getting to bed so late, I wake half an hour before my alarm goes off. Malcolm's sleep seemed very restless, with lots of tossing and turning and talking. He woke me up several times.

Starting the coffee, I think of Mollie. She loves French press coffee. *Where is she?*

While waiting for the water to boil, I rehook the solar system and whole-house generator, which is much easier than I expect, even by flashlight.

I make sure the mudroom freezer is plugged in. Once the sun is fully up, there should be enough power from the system to run both freezers for a little while. Right now, I start up the generator to charge up the downstairs freezer and fridge. I'll need to figure something else out later. Maybe I can put each freezer on a timer so they can rotate using the limited power provided by our small system.

It's still fairly dark out, so I take my time drinking coffee. On Sundays, I like to let Mollie and Malcolm sleep in and handle all of the chores on my own. We often leave the babies with the mamas overnight so we can even take the morning off from milking. Mollie's still usually up by 6:30, but Malcolm will often sleep until 8:00 or so.

Truthfully, I enjoy the quiet Sunday mornings on my own. While sleeping in is a treat for them, taking my time and enjoying the early morning solitude is a treat for me.

Last night, Malcolm asked if we could go ahead and milk this morning. He doesn't want to risk running out of his favorite beverage with the extra people here. I've decided I'll still let him sleep, and I'll take care of it on my own. While his smaller hands are better suited for the task, I can still do it. That one girl better not give me any trouble, though.

Before heading out, I check the calendar. We have two does who should be kidding soon. Mollie has one marked on the calendar for Tuesday. The second isn't until the following Saturday, almost two weeks away. There's also a mom with the singleton who'll be ready for milking on Wednesday. We give the mom and kid, or kids, two weeks alone, where she can nurse at will, before we expect her to share with us. The two-week time gives them good bonding and gets the babes off to a good start.

Two more pregnant does will kid late August or early September. Spacing out the kidding will allow us to have at least two goats producing year-round. We have a small barn with a propane heater, so winter milking isn't terrible.

I'm a few minutes away from starting with the goats when Malcolm comes out.

"Dad, you forgot to wake me up."

"Thought I'd let you sleep. We were up late last night. I can handle the milking."

"Thanks, Dad. I'm up now, so I'll help out."

"Thanks, Malcolm." I nod. "I appreciate it."

"You hear anything from Mom?"

"Nothing yet. I'm not sure the phones are working. There isn't a dial tone on the landline, and when I tried with my cell, it didn't ring or anything. Just dead air."

Malcolm looks so sad. I wish I would've delivered the news in a gentler manner. "I'm sure your mom is doing fine. She's probably working her way here. Hopefully, we'll see her soon."

"Yeah, Dad," Malcolm says but doesn't sound convinced.

After a few minutes, Malcolm asks, "You think we'll still have our Bible study meeting tonight?"

"I'm not sure. It's about the same time as the community meeting they planned again tonight. David and Betty weren't there last night, so . . . I just don't know. Maybe I can stop over there today and see what they think. I'd kind of like to go to the community meeting. Maybe we can talk to David about having Bible study another night this week."

"Yeah, I guess the community meeting is important. But I think having the Bible study and praying together might be more important," Malcolm says with finality.

I can't argue with his logic, so nod and say nothing.

We finish with chores a few minutes before 7:00 and grab a quick breakfast. Karen rings the doorbell as we're finishing up. She's wearing clip on sunglasses over her prescription lenses and reaches up to remove them. Without the sunglasses, the stress and tiredness from last night are still apparent. She's dressed casually in dark denim jeans and a black and white striped tank top. Her brown hair is pulled up, and a pink ball cap covers her locks. She and her mom, Lois, look very much alike, and their similarities are especially evident this morning. She looks ten years older than she should.

I plant a smile on my face. "C'mon in, Karen. I need to change and then I'll be ready. My neighbor should be here shortly, then we can go. You want some coffee?"

"Thanks, but no. I'm fine."

"Okay, give me just a minute."

I head to my bedroom to finish getting ready. Thinking about last night's conversation with Evan, I put my holster and speedloader pouch on my belt.

I remove one of my handguns, a Smith & Wesson .357 revolver with a transfer bar, from the gun safe in my nightstand. It's already loaded, and with the two full speedloaders in my pouch, I have eighteen shots. This is my usual armament for hiking and hunting. I can't imagine I'll even need one shot, but I'll go prepared.

I have a second handgun, a .45 caliber Glock 21, in the main gun safe downstairs. While I love shooting the Glock, I'm more comfortable carrying my revolver. Mollie is just the opposite. She also has a .357 revolver and .40 but prefers to carry the semi-auto. In fact, she likes the semi-auto so much she recently purchased a second—a compact Glock she's had her eye on.

I wear a plain blue T-shirt with a short-sleeved button-up shirt over it, leaving the top shirt untucked so it'll hang over my holster. It's one of my larger shirts and hangs well past the end of the holster. I check in the mirror and, even with turning, barely see any imprinting from the gun. I look completely dorky but accept that as necessary in this instance.

As I'm tying my shoes, Evan pulls in. I send Malcolm over to the bunkhouse and introduce Karen to Evan, then let him know I plan to take my car so I can check on my folks.

"Good idea, Jake. You should bring them out here with you."

"Yeah. I'd like to, but I'm not sure they'll be willing. They'll likely want to wait it out. I'll have to plant the seed today and let it grow."

"You have gas cans today?"

"Yes, a small can and Tate is emptying out a few. You mind if I put them in the bed of your truck? You bringing cans?"

"There were two cans on our porch last night. I emptied my cans into the Harvester and my old truck in hopes of refilling again today. Not sure we'll find anyplace but worth a shot. No problem putting yours in the truck."

There isn't near the traffic on the highway this morning as there was last night. Karen doesn't talk much, and I can't think of much to say either, so I keep quiet. We find a working radio station. They're on generator power and only sharing the top news stories at the top of the hour, then are off the air. Their sister station will give the news at the bottom of the hour.

"The cyberattacks have not let up. The damage from various malware has caused increasing issues, including transformer explosions nationwide. As far as is known, the power is now out in most areas with only small pockets still online, and any services relying on computers, of which there are many, are currently suspended. The stock market will be closed this week, and all banks will be closed. Even if they can somehow stop the attacks, with the damage already done, they'll need time to clean it up. There have been more food poisoning deaths. There's still no information on who is behind these attacks." The station signs off.

When we're just a few miles out of town, Karen says, "You seem to think this is going to get worse."

She's right. I do think it could get worse. I weigh my words carefully. "I'm not sure. With the things that have happened so far, it's possible."

"You think the terrorists are going to do more?"

"I don't know. Even if they don't do more, things could get worse for us."

"How do you figure?"

"Right now, the cyberattacks have taken out most of the power grid, closed the banks, and shut down many of the gas stations. No power, no money, and no gas are a recipe for disaster."

"Last night you said people could break into the grocery stores. You think they would?"

"I think most people keep a very small amount of food on hand. Here, in Wyoming, people likely keep more than average because of how our winters can be. But it's not winter now, so they may have let their stocks deplete a little. At some point, people will get hungry. If they think the store has food, it's likely to be broken in to. I half suspect this may already be happening in some places. You know there was looting with many of the protests over the past several years?"

"Yes, of course. But those were only a few people. Most people were peacefully protesting."

"Uh-huh. But many who were protesting joined in on the looting once they saw what was happening. I like to think Wyoming people are different, but people are people. And if people get hungry or their children are hungry, things could get dicey."

"But only if things continue. Surely the cyberattacks will stop."

"Maybe. But it's not just power outages. We just heard on the news several power plants had what was described as malware attacking their digital relay and backup generators. I think a lot of repair work will need completed to fully bring power back. I don't know how widespread this is and how many transformers were affected. Could be a few, could be many. It could take a few days or even many months to fix everything."

"Well, you're a cheery sort, aren't you?" There is—I hope—teasing in her voice. I glance at her and smile.

"Don't mean to be Mr. Negative. I think it's important to be aware of what's happening and what could happen. God gave me a responsibility to care for my family, and being aware of the possibilities helps me do this."

She doesn't respond, just looks out the window.

Chapter 30

Jake

Following Evan, we drive by the gas station where Paul helped us last night. Today it is closed. When we reach the SuperMart, there's a small line in front. Evan and I park, and I tell him I'll go see what's going on, to keep an eye on me and I'll signal if they should come over. I take a small battery-operated lantern with me and hand an identical one to Karen.

An employee is sitting at a table with a sign attached to it:

CASH ONLY
YOU WILL HAVE AN EXCOURT
BRING FLASHLIGHT
MAKE AN ORDRELY LINE

It takes me a moment to figure out EXCOURT must mean escort. And ORDRELY is likely orderly. Okay. That's cool. I signal Karen and Evan to join me.

We wait in line for only about twenty minutes. Karen asks if she can stay with me but push her own cart. When it's our turn, I ask if this is okay and if there's a limit to how much we can purchase. No limit. We can go together, but we need two employee helpers since they'll be marking the price as we go. And we're reminded it's cash only. A second employee appears as he finishes speaking, and we head on in, telling Evan we'll meet up at the vehicles.

Karen grabs one cart. I grab two, knowing I'll need them. We have our lanterns, and each of the employees—a young guy and gal—has a headlamp, a clipboard, and a portable radio on their belt. Each headlamp is on the red-light mode, which helps to not blind us.

"The meat case is empty," the guy helper tells us. "We couldn't sell it today, after the power outage, due to the health code. We're still selling things like cheese, bacon, and hot dogs until 11:00 am. They've been kept cool in the freezer. The actual freezer stuff has been pulled. You lead, we'll follow."

I defer to Karen. She stops briefly in produce and buys a few apples. I decide on several bags of apples since these will keep just fine in our root cellar. Our fruit trees, planted the year we moved in, may produce a little this year, but I'm not counting on much. We have some apples still in the root cellar we picked from a friend's place last year—they aren't looking too good—plus a couple bags I bought on Thursday night's shopping trip.

We wander through the outer aisles as Karen adds things here and there. When possible, I duplicate what she puts in her cart to increase the quantity. I figure, if she's putting it in her cart, someone in the family must like it. While I've met them all once before, I don't really *know* them. I definitely have no clue about their likes and dislikes as far as food is concerned.

Karen goes over to buy eggs.

"Karen, we're good on eggs, with our chickens and ducks."

"You sure? You don't mind if we eat your eggs?"

"Of course not. I assumed we'd be sharing food while you're here."

"Okay. Thank you. We didn't want to impose. Tate said they sent money and food so they'd have some stored at your house, but we weren't sure if it'd be okay for us also." I appreciate that she whispers this so the helpers don't hear. They're talking with each other and not paying much attention anyway.

"They did. And it's all fine."

Rice, beans, flour, oils . . . aisle by aisle we walk through the assorted sections. When we reach the candy aisle, I suggest Karen grab their favorite candies.

She stops midmove, eyes wide. "What is that? Glass breaking?"

"*You crazy . . .* "

"*Keep your hands off my stuff. I was here first . . .* "

The employee's radio squawks, then a panicked voice says, "*Condiments, ugh, aisle five. Emergency.*" The profanity and yelling continue between two women.

"Um, folks, let's just wait here a minute before moving out of this aisle. Let our people figure out what's going on over there," our male helper says.

"What *is* going on over there?" Karen nervously asks.

He shrugs, while the female says, "Probably just a little tiff. We're getting low on a few things, so— "

There's a new voice in the fight aisle, loud and firm. *"Stop. You ladies are done. Sam, escort them out. Bruce, take their carts to the front."*

"Fine. I'll just pay for my stuff and go," yells a female voice, full of indignity.

"No, ma'am. You'll just go. We have a zero-tolerance policy today. Your shopping privileges are revoked until this crisis is passed. Sam, I'll walk her out."

"No! Look what you've done, you . . . you . . ." the second woman screams. "*Please, please. I have to buy food for my family. I didn't start this, she did. I was here first.*"

More crying and screaming, which soon fades away. I guess they've been escorted out.

"Have you had much of that?" I ask.

"Second time. Our manager's the one who broke it up. He said we might have troubles, so he made some plans. He brought pretty much all of us in today, paying us double time, and even went to people's houses last night to round up employees. Official store policy is to remain closed during a power outage. I guess he thought it'd be better to make a few extra dollars and try to salvage things," the male helper says.

Hmm. The manager seems pretty on top of things to me. I have to wonder, is it about making a few dollars, or does he see the writing on the wall?

"We can go on now. What's next?" our female helper asks in a much too cheery voice.

Paper goods—toilet paper, paper towels, and paper plates—go in mine and Karen's cart. Just the amounts of these I've purchased since Friday are enough to last for several months, but can we really have too much toilet paper? We'll use it.

"How about clothes?" I ask Karen.

"No, we're probably fine. We'll just wash what we brought along." She gives me a quizzical look. "Oh. No power. I guess that means no washing machine."

We can run the washing machine using our solar on a sunshine day, but I choose not to go into this in the store. Instead, I quietly say, "Might be doing hand washing. But if this goes on for any length of time, your clothes might start to wear out. It may be a good idea to buy some basics at least—socks, underwear, and such—for you and your folks. We have a few things, but the sizes may not be right."

The look she gives me tells me she wants to argue. Then tears fill her eyes while she nods. "Maybe so."

"Would you like to meet me in the men's section? So you can get what you need from the women's? And how are you all set for shoes? Did you each bring good walking shoes?"

"I know my mother and I each brought one pair of shoes for walking, a pair of sandals, and a pair of dress shoes. My dad . . . I'm not sure. I've seen him in two different pairs. He doesn't walk long distances, so they're probably fine."

"Maybe we ought to get you each another pair?"

"Jake, I appreciate your suggestions, but I only have a limited amount of money. I brought half of the cash the three of us have. My dad took the rest. As it is, we'll have to use our credit cards to get home. And if they don't start working soon, I'm not sure how we'll manage. We can't stay here forever." Her tone is sharp, and her eyes no longer have tears but are shooting daggers.

I turn to our employee helpers. "Do you mind giving us just a moment?"

They step away. I turn back to Karen, whispering, "I completely understand. And I know what I'm suggesting sounds crazy. The truth is, you may have to stay here for a very long time. The reality is, while we have some extra things, it's unlikely we'll have everything you and your parents may need. What I need you to do is pick out the things you'll need. Think about what you'll need for clothes, shoes, personal items, and everything else you'll need to get you through at least the next year."

Karen starts to say something. I lift my hand slightly to ask her to hold on for a minute longer.

"If we can find winter stuff, which I kind of doubt since it's June, we'll want to buy those things too. And just so you know, this won't be a handout. If things go bad, we'll all have to work hard daily to get through this. And if things get better, not a big deal to have a few supplies." I give a slight lift of my shoulder. "Your folks talk about moving up here. If they did and we had a future problem, they'd already have some things here. Sound good?"

No longer angry, the tears have returned.

"Are you sure we can stay? Sarah said Katie is heading to your place. She thinks Angela may also. They were talking about it when the phones stopped working. Won't you have a full house?"

Angela is coming home? How does Karen know this and I don't? *What about Calley?*

"We'll have room," I say. "And Tate and Sarah bought the camp trailer specifically to provide a little more space. You don't know this, but we also got another cabin yesterday, completely by accident, but now I can see it was Providence. I didn't know about Angela coming up. That's super and I'm glad you told me."

"Oh. Sure. I don't think they were trying to surprise you. I think she couldn't reach you. Even before we knew about the cyberattacks, reception was off and on. I was talking to a friend back home and was disconnected several times. We finally decided to say our goodbyes. Now, I'm wondering if what you say could be true, and I'll never see my friend, any of my friends, again."

"Karen, I hope I'm wrong. I hope we're in this store, in the dark, buying a bunch of stuff for absolutely no reason. For now, though, it won't be possible for you to return home. We'll need to make the best of it. And we need to get this finished up." I smile to let her know I'm not angry, I just want to be done.

"Okay. I guess, if I'm going to get the stuff you want me to get, I need a second cart."

"Yes, you do," I answer, and then say to our employee helpers, "I need to grab the lady a second cart. I'll be right back." As I start to walk away, I ask, "Hey, is there someplace we can park the full carts? Since she needs a second one, I might as well grab myself an empty."

I'm pretty sure they both roll their eyes, but perhaps the darkness of the building is playing tricks on me. "Sure, sir. While you're gathering two additional carts, I'll park these for you, and we can get them when you're finished."

"Super. Let me do a little consolidating." I put as much as humanly possible in the cart he'll park for me.

When I return, I see Karen has added many clothing items and several pairs of shoes for her family. I add a few things to my cart, then we move to sporting goods.

I look for water filters but don't find any. There are packages of iodine tablets, so I grab four of those. I have Karen pick out backpacks for each of them. They aren't the kind we use for long distance hikes, but they'll be better than nothing. I also add three fanny packs.

I turn to Karen and ask, "What about bikes? You think your parents can ride bikes?"

She thinks a moment before responding, "My mother, for sure. I don't know about my dad."

"Should we get the three of you bikes? I'm going to get a bike for Calley and one for Mike, just in case."

A quiet groan comes from one of our employee helpers.

"For exercise?"

"Maybe, but I was more thinking along the lines of conserving gas."

"Oh, I guess it's a good idea."

"Pick out what you want, and I'll take the ones I want to the front." I turn to my employee helper. "Where'd you put the cart? I'll put the bikes with it."

"I'll take care of these, sir. You can help the lady pick out what she needs." He gives his counterpart a knowing look and walks off with both bikes I've chosen, guiding one bike in each hand. I'm impressed at how easily he handles them.

Karen takes only a few minutes to pick a bike for herself and her mom, then asks, "Which bike should I get for my dad? This one?" She points to a black mountain bike.

"Sure. Looks like a fine one." I'm not very knowledgeable on bikes, but it's one I'd ride. My helper shows back up.

"We've got the three we want," I tell him. "How about you and I take them up, and Karen can grab a few more things in sporting goods?"

"Fine, sir."

I give Karen instructions. "Can you grab four 2-packs of propane, plus they should have some warmer coats in sporting goods for hunting. Get the heaviest you can find. They'll be camo and may be all men's sizes, but it shouldn't matter—buy for all three of you. Gloves, too, if they have them. And anything else you see that makes sense. Be right back."

Walking to the front, my employee helper says, "You're buying like the power's never coming back on. Why's that?"

I want to make light of it, but this guy has been helpful to me. "Karen and her family are visiting from out of town and have only their suitcases. They have nothing if they're stuck here until winter.

The cyberattacks not only knocked out power, they destroyed important parts by inserting malware and exploding things like transformers. If enough was destroyed, it could be some time before the lights come back on, the credit cards work, and the gas stations are pumping fuel. And if the power does come back on, they'll have quite a story about their visit to Wyoming."

"Okay. Makes sense."

"And working here, I'm sure you know how fast the food can go off the shelves. Sometimes we'll come shopping and whole sections will be empty since you all are waiting on a truck."

"For sure. People get pretty upset about it. Especially if a truck is late. And, of course, today . . . well, you heard what happened over there. I guess we'll see more of that as the shelves empty out."

"You think there will be many trucks with the gas stations not working and the interstates jammed with people trying to escape the cities?"

He stops walking and looks at me. "No. No, sir. I don't think there will be many trucks. We don't expect to be open past today."

"You may want to buy some things." We start walking again.

"Yeah. In fact, I may buy things on my break. Our manager said he'll keep a few things in the back room for us so we can shop, but, yeah, I should buy things on my break."

When I'm back with Karen, she tells me how excited she is that her helper, Shelby, found winter gear.

I put more things in the cart: emergency blankets, disposable hand warmers, waterproof matches, flashlights, and a few odds and ends. I toss individually packaged dehydrated meals in the cart. We enjoy backpacking and have many of these on our trips. Some are definitely better than others. I pick the ones I know Mollie, Malcolm, or I like. These are a different brand and, in my opinion, slightly better than the family-sized meals in the emergency buckets we got. I'm thinking of the community again as I put these in.

My helper—I never noticed his name tag—pulls Shelby aside while I add additional choices to my cart. They whisper for a second, and she shrugs a few times.

Karen and I are ready to move on. "Where to now?" I ask her.

"Housewares? For blankets?"

"Yes, let's get a few. I know Mollie has some winter-weight blankets for the bunkhouse already. But now that you mention it, maybe we should get sleeping bags instead. They may be thicker and warmer considering the season." We walk up the aisle, and they do have zero-degree bags. I also pick out two small backpackers tents for them.

"Why are you buying tents? Planning a camping trip while we're here?" she says with a small smile.

I return the gesture and say, "You never know what you might need. If we had to leave our place for some reason, it may be good to have a tent to sleep in. These aren't very heavy duty, but if we put one of these tarps over them, it'll help." I put four brown tarps in the cart.

"Did you tell him the lights aren't coming back on?" Shelby's voice is full of steel and challenge.

"Shelby, he didn't say that. Not really. I asked and he said there's a lot of damage and it may take a while. I told you that," the male helper says.

Shelby ignores him and asks me, "Did you tell him we might run out of food?"

"Shelby, he didn't say that. He reminded me how empty the shelves get when a truck is late. You know they do too. We've talked about it before. And if the trucks can't get here because they can't get gas, because the power is out and the freeways are blocked, we will run out of food," he answers.

Shelby looks at him. "Grant, are you going to let him answer?"

They both look at me. "I told him pretty much what he says I told him. I don't know what's going to happen. I suggested Grant may want to buy a few things after he finishes his shift. Just in case. And with what happened over on . . . was it aisle five? Things might get a little dicey," I say hesitantly.

Grant looks at Shelby. Shelby continues to look at me.

"Well," Shelby starts, "let's get you two finished so we can take a break and buy things." Then she looks at Grant. "I have some cash, baby. You have some too?"

Huh. They're a couple? Looking at them, I never would've guessed. He's short, probably only five foot five, and weighs nothing. There's no meat on him at all. She's taller than he is, at least by four inches, and easily outweighs him. I'm not saying she's fat, but she's definitely bulky.

Grant nods and then asks me, "What do you suggest we buy?"

As we walk toward housewares, I point to Karen's cart. "Staples. Things like she has. If you don't have an easy supply of water, buy things that don't need water added for cooking, or need very little. If you need to find water in the river or a creek, be sure to purify it. We got these tablets." I pull the only package I found in sporting goods to show him. "This was the last one, but if you have more in back . . . or plain bleach would be better. That was gone from the shelf too, but if you can find it, use eight drops per gallon of water for clear water—double if the water isn't clear. It'll go a long way. You could even buy chlorine tablets, like the kind used for swimming pools."

"We have Brita filters in housewares. We could get one of those," Grant says.

"Not the Brita filters. They don't take out enough contaminants, and you could still get sick. You'd be better off boiling the water. FEMA says to boil the water for three minutes, but many people think five to ten is safer. You'll want to let the sediment settle first, then filter it through a cloth to remove the particles. Then boil it. Do that if you're using bleach too."

"I think there are some water filter things, like straws, in the back room. Should we get those? Do you guys want a couple of them?" Shelby asks.

"LifeStraws?"

"Uh, maybe. It seems like that's what they're called. They're blue. I can go grab a couple."

"If there are five, I'd like three. Be sure you can each get one."

"Sure, I'll be right back."

We're in housewares, and Karen and I add a few more things to our carts. Grant manages both of our lists while Shelby is finding the water filters. She returns after a few minutes with three LifeStraw brand filters and three Aqua Marine brand filters. I'm surprised these weren't brought out when the water purification guidelines were announced with the foodborne illnesses. Maybe the manager set these aside for the employees?

"We had two different kinds. I thought you might like to choose."

"Are there still a couple back there for you two?" I ask.

"Yes, there's several of each kind still."

"In that case, I'd like all six. Is that okay?"

"Sure." Shelby gives a slight shrug and puts all six in my cart.

We find more things in the toiletry and pharmacy sections, including three small first aid kits. These are for the bug-out bags I'm going to make Karen and her parents.

When we're finally near the front, I ask Karen to take a minute and think if there's anything else she can't imagine living without. She scrunches up her face, then says, "I'll be right back." Shelby tags along.

At the front, a checker is waiting for us. Grant hands over my list.

"We won't be bagging things. You can take some bags out with you. Shelby and I will help you to your car. But once we get there, we won't be able to help you load up, okay?"

"Yes, of course. Not bagging is smart."

"Right. The cashier will just total everything up and then you can pay."

Karen's back with an armload of art supplies. Adult coloring books, crayons, markers, acrylic paints, and I don't know what else, but she and Shelby are both carrying items.

"Smart, Karen. Always good to have things to do in downtime."

"You think? It's not silly?"

"Not at all." I turn to the cashier. "I'll cover Karen's also, so you can ring both sheets together."

"Jake, no. I can cover at least some of it."

"We'll talk about it later. It'll be easier this way."

Grant is pulling a cart and manipulating a bike. The ladies are each pushing a cart, while I have a cart in front and a cart pulling behind. I imagine it's quite a show. We park the carts as Shelby and Grant quickly return to the store for the other four bikes.

There's a paper stuck under the windshield of my car, a note from Evan. He went over to the feed store and will be back shortly. He put the time on it—about twenty minutes ago. I can see the store from where we are. His truck is in the parking lot.

Grant and Shelby are back with our bikes. They both say thank you and turn to leave. I call them back.

"Thank you both so much for your help. You made it much easier for us than trying to handle it on our own." I slip each two bills.

"Oh, no, sir. We can't take tips," Grant says.

"Grant, on a normal day you may not be able to take tips. Today is not a normal day."

Shelby grabs his arm and gestures toward her money. He looks at hers, then at his.

"Sir, this is . . . quite a lot of money. Are you sure?"

"What I told you in the store is what I believe. I think it may be a long time before the power comes back on and we get more food shipments. This should help you buy some food and supplies to get you through."

"I'm pregnant. About four months," Shelby blurts out.

"Congratulations," I say.

Then Karen says, "How wonderful. You'll want to make sure to buy foods that will nourish you and your baby. Protein is good—salmon, tuna, and sardines if you can stand them. Refried beans would probably do, especially if you eat the beans with rice or corn."

"The freeze-dried sausage and bean puree like I bought, get those," I say. "They're expensive. Here." I hand them another bill. "They have eggs, too, but they're a weird texture. Some people like them. You might, and your baby might."

Grant holds out his hand to shake mine. "Thank you, sir."

"Jake. I'm Jake. You're welcome. I hope to see you both again."

Karen hugs Shelby and slips her a little more money. Shelby hugs her again.

They turn and take a few steps toward the store. Grant turns back and says, "Looking at the line outside the store now, we'd better hurry. We've already brought most of the food out of the back. There's not much left for restocking."

I agree.

"I'll take my fifteen minutes as soon as we get back in," Shelby says. "Then you can go."

They wave to us and take off at a trot.

"You gave them five hundred dollars, Jake," Karen whispers.

I shrug without saying anything. I don't want to mention the money may not be any good for much longer, and I'd rather they use it today than have it wasted.

"Why would you do that?"

"They saw everything we were buying. He asked me why. I told him. You heard them in the back when she asked about their money. I didn't realize they were together until then."

"You didn't?"

"No. You did?"

"Yes. I knew from . . . I guess the produce department."

"Huh. Had no idea. They seem like a nice couple. Little young to be having a baby."

"They're probably the same age as Calley and Mike," she says, while giving me a goofy smile.

"You think? I thought they were just out of high school?"

"Nah. They're older than that. College age or a year or two beyond. Still young, I guess. If the power doesn't come back, she could have trouble giving birth."

I nod but think, *If the power doesn't come back on, we're all going to have troubles.*

Chapter 31

Jake

Evan pulls up next to us. "Good golly, folks. You bought even more than I did, and my assistant person said he'd never seen anyone buy so much," Evan says with a smile as he gets out of his truck. "I'm glad we brought the cargo trailer. Plenty of room for your stuff and much more. Let's get you loaded up."

While we're loading, we discuss our next plan.

"I pretty much found everything I wanted here," Evan says. "Don't think we need to go to Albertsons or over to Wesley. I'd like to go to a hardware store. Not sure if any are open today since it's Sunday and the power is out. And as crazy as the line is getting here, I suspect any open places will be about the same. There was even some shoving going on when I came out earlier. The guy manning the table called on a radio and got another guy out to help him break things up. Looked like they kicked the shovers out and wouldn't let them shop. Don't really want to be around if this powder keg gets ignited."

"Yeah, there was a problem in the store also. Two ladies got into it. The manager broke it up and told them there's a zero-tolerance policy. They can't shop until the crisis is passed . . . his exact words . . . 'Crisis is passed.'"

"Huh. Missed that. Sounds like things could get interesting."

"Yep," I agree. "Let's get this done and get home. We could try the hardware store on the hill. I think they're usually open on Sunday. And that's near my parents' place. You could get what you need there while I stop in and check on them."

"Sure. That works. Where else do you need to go?" Evan asks.

I look to Karen. "I'm not sure what else to get. You have any ideas?" she responds.

"Let's go to the hardware store. If it's open, we'll leave you there and decide where to meet up," I tell Evan.

The hardware store is open. "Evan, if you see a couple of decent rechargeable lights, can you get them for me? I'd also like a couple of programmable timers, the kind you hook up to an electrical cord to turn the power on and off. The really basic type, like an egg timer. Think they have those here?"

"Yeah. I think they probably do."

I give him money and say, "Oh, and batteries if they have them—especially rechargeable. I'd like to stop by the sporting goods and Rite Aid. You have any interest in those places?"

"Rite Aid? Since we went there last night, I'm not sure. What are you thinking of getting there today?"

"Karen bought art stuff. We have some things like that, but I thought I'd look for a few more. And a few more medications and pharmaceutical supplies."

"Huh. Not sure about that, but I could go to the sporting goods store. I can think of a few things I'd like to get there—especially after this latest event."

"Okay. We'll stop back here first. If you aren't here, we'll meet you there."

"Sounds good. See you soon," Evan says with a wave.

I reconsider. "Oh, Karen. Would you prefer to shop here with Evan, instead of going to my parents' house with me?" I ask.

"I think so. I thought of a few things they might have that'd be good."

"Super, then. C'mon, Karen. Let's get to shopping," Evan says.

~~~~~

My parents are both happy to see me. Not just happy—almost ecstatic.

"How are you doing with the power out?" I ask.

"We're okay," My dad, Alvin, answers. "Your mother's glad it's not winter and we don't have to worry about freezing to death."

I give a small laugh at this long running joke. Every winter my mom mentions she hopes they won't freeze to death this year. Before they moved to Wyoming, they envisioned bitter cold causing multiple deaths. While it certainly can be cold and people have died from exposure, it's pretty rare.

"Do you need anything?" I ask.

"I don't think so. We did our regular shopping on Friday. Have plenty of food for the week. But we were thinking . . . what we heard
~~~~~

on the news before the power went out didn't sound good. There was one guy saying the computer wars or whatever they call them were actually blowing up parts of the power stations. Might be a while before things can be fixed. You think that happened here?"

"I'm not sure if the power station here had damage. We're on a different system, but I didn't even know our power went out until the neighbors told me. I don't know if anyone knows the extent of what has happened, or is happening, here."

"When do you think we'll know?"

"I suppose when the power comes back on? Or doesn't? I don't really know, which makes it challenging."

"Mollie get home?" my dad asks.

"Not yet," I say with a sigh.

"Where is she?" my mom, Dodie, asks.

"She was in Idaho last I heard from her. She was going to try to drive pretty much straight through. I haven't been able to reach her since the cyberattacks started."

Mom and Dad exchange a look.

"What about your girls?" Mom asks.

"Sarah and Tate arrived last night. Tate's parents and sister were here for a visit, so they're at our place too. Katie's on her way home. She left around eleven yesterday morning. I expect to see her today. I think Angela is coming up but don't know for sure. I don't know about Calley."

"You're going to have a full house," my dad says.

"We have the room. Have room for you also." I say nothing further.

They exchange another look. My dad is a young seventy-five. With his daily walks and trying to watch what he eats, for the most part, his age doesn't show as much as it could. His full head of hair, while mostly gray, still has a few black streaks. His skin is slightly weathered from being outside most of his life. Bushy eyebrows frame gleaming brown eyes. He's still sharp as a tack and often keeps us on our toes with his conversations.

My mom has also aged quite well. She joins Dad in eating well and daily walks. While not skinny, she's also not overweight. Her waist-length hair is now fully gray and kept pulled up in a loose bun. I often wonder why she keeps it so long when she wears it up all the time. I think change is hard for her. My mom is on the shy side, always has been, but does offer friendly smiles to those she knows.

For as long as I can remember, she's made a point of avoiding the sun. She had a scare early in life she was sure was skin cancer. It wasn't, but since then, she's always done her best to keep covered up when outside. As a result, her skin still maintains much of its rosy glow from her youth.

I enjoy spending time with my parents. Growing up, we spent much time outside—hunting, fishing, hiking around looking for rocks or sheds. They really gave me a love of the outdoors. I'm doing my best to pass this love on to Malcolm.

"You know, Jake. Your mother and I were talking about going out to your place. With everything being electric here, it's not easy to cook. We used the barbecue last night. Just had cereal for breakfast—couldn't even have coffee. Thought about making it on the barbecue, but I don't even have our old camping pot anymore. Guess I could try to heat it in a pot and just throw the grounds in. We could strain it with our teeth." He makes a face while my mom shakes her head at him. Then he asks, "You have coffee this morning?"

"I did, Dad," I say simply.

"Told you, Dodie. I told you he'd have coffee," my dad says with a smug look.

"Alvin, nobody likes people who say, 'I told you so,'" my mom snaps back.

"You have anyone staying in the room off the garage yet, Jake?" Dad asks.

"No, it's empty." I know better than to offer the room to them.

"You think Mollie would mind if we stayed with you a few days, until the power comes back on?"

"Mollie won't mind at all. And you know Malcolm would love it. Plus, if Angela is coming up, Gavin will be there." My mom smiles at this. She has a definite soft spot for her great-grandson.

"Well, I suppose we'll put a few things in the truck and c'mon out then. What should we bring?"

Now I need to be careful. I want to tell them to bring everything. I want to tell them I don't know if they'll ever be able to come back here. But right now, they won't want to hear that. "Well . . . we don't really know how long the power will be out. The TV said it's bad in other places?"

"Very bad," my mom says.

"Now, Dodie," my dad adds, "we only saw those few people saying it was bad, and they were also talking about all of the—what'd they call them? Refugees?"

"I think they said displaced persons. The people who left the towns where the bridges were blown up. The towns they descended upon were already in bad shape. Oh, that reminds me, Katie's school was on fire. She left before then?" my mom asks.

"I don't know. I think so. She didn't mention it when she called me. I didn't know about it until last night."

"The news guy said some of those areas may take months to recover. Then, when the computer attacks started and the power started going out and things started exploding, he said they don't have enough of the parts to fix them. They'll need more parts made, which could take months, and they need power to make the parts or they have to get them from overseas. So it could be a while," my mom explains.

"I listened to the radio while driving in this morning," I offer. "One of the channels is on generator and sharing news only, then is off the air. The blackouts are across the US now. Everywhere. The stock market and banks are closed for the week. They haven't been able to stop the computer attacks yet, and the attacks inserted some code, which messed things up. Once they get the attacks stopped, they'll need to fix the problems before bringing things back online. I'd be surprised if they could get the power up very quickly."

"So it'll be on in a week?"

"I don't think so," I say cautiously. "They're closing the stock market and banks for this week, assuming they can stop the attacks and fix things. With the damage done, a week is very optimistic."

"How long do you think this is going to continue, Jake?" my dad asks.

"A long time," I say quietly.

Another look between them. Then my mom says, "Well, we really can't stay here without power. Maybe if we were younger we could do it, but at our age, we just can't. Jake, you'll tell us if we're imposing?"

"You won't be imposing, Mom. We want you to stay with us."

"We'll start packing. We'll be out to your house soon," my dad says decidedly.

"I'm running errands with my neighbor and Tate's sister. Let me finish our errands and I'll come back. We'll go out together. Pack more than you think you'll need. We can make room for it. Bring all of your clothes, even your winter things," I say, taking a chance.

"Why on earth would we do that?" Mom asks.

"Because of what happened in Katie's town," I say with a shrug. "If a fire started in your neighborhood, they wouldn't be able to get it out. You could lose everything."

"Oh. Good idea," my dad says, nodding vigorously. "Dodie, bring everything you don't want to lose. What about food, Jake? We just shopped—bring it?"

"Yes, probably smart. From the freezer too. You've left it shut?"

"Yes."

"Let me see if Evan can come back up here and we can get it in his truck. Maybe we can take the entire freezer. I'll be back soon."

"Okay, Jake," my dad says. "Do you think we should stop at the grocery store and get next week's food also? Is the grocery store open?"

"We went to SuperMart a bit ago. It's open, but I'm not sure for how long. I wouldn't want to go back there. It was getting kind of crazy. Albertsons didn't look bad when we drove by. I could pick up some things for you. I'm not sure what they'll have, though. For sure no meat and things from the refrigerator section."

"We have plenty of meat still from last year's hunting," Dad says.

"Could you go ahead and buy what you can?" my mom asks. "You know we eat most foods. I have a list started for next week's shopping. Just do the best you can on it, plus anything else you think is smart to buy." She gives me a grocery list with only a few items on it and two hundred in cash.

I'm not at all surprised she has cash to give. They've always followed a philosophy of paying their bills, then taking out cash for all other expenses. They don't use a credit card to make everyday purchases and rarely use one for big expenses, choosing to save up for things they need. They're from a time when cash was king and still follow that ideal.

As I step to the door, my dad stops me. "How do you think your brother's faring in this mess?"

I've wondered myself. They live in a college town of around 100,000 people. Robert is often telling us about the changes in the town since we've moved from there, including the increase in crime. Hopefully the power outage isn't bringing out the worst in people.

"He's well set up for the power being out," I say. "You know how much he loves to camp and has lots of great gear. Shoot, remember when they all went camping up in the Sierra's for two weeks? They'll be fine."

My dad sighs. "You're right. They can handle no power. But can the rest of the folks living around them handle it?"

With nothing else to add, I take my leave.

Robert and I had a wonderful childhood, the kind most boys can only dream of. Almost every weekend was spent camping and fishing or camping and hunting. Mom and Dad really strived to help us create lasting memories and share their love of the outdoors. I try to give Malcolm the same kind of childhood but often fall short. Now, with the way our world is rapidly changing . . . I shake my head. I'm still going to try and do my best for Malcolm.

Mollie and I made a pact, before Malcolm was even born, to strive for him to have a similar childhood to mine. When her girls were young, their life was very different. She and her first husband lived in the city. While Mollie did have a love of the outdoors and hiking, for the most part, they did city things. I don't think that's bad—not at all—just not what I wanted for Malcolm. Especially since we live in the wilds of Wyoming.

One thing Mollie made very clear, she wanted more for all of our children than she had in her childhood. At least how her childhood ended up.

Mollie was the older of two girls. Her dad was a salesman, often on the road, while her mom worked a variety of part-time and temporary jobs as needed. They had a small house outside of Portland. Mollie shared many fond memories of her early life, playing with her sister, Maggie, two years younger than her, and being fully loved by their parents.

This all changed when Mollie was in second grade. Maggie was in kindergarten and had half days of school. That day after school, she'd been playing outside in the fenced backyard. No one really knows why Maggie left the yard, or how she ended up a block away. The car didn't see her until it was too late, and she was killed on impact. Mollie's life was never the same.

Mollie's parents, Sam and Brenda, didn't deal well with losing Maggie. Their marriage became nothing more than a convenience, which ended the day after Mollie graduated from high school and Brenda left. Mollie has spoken with her on the phone a few times and exchanged a handful of letters, but she hasn't seen her mother since that day. We think she's living in Spain.

Mollie and Sam didn't keep up much of a relationship. Mollie moved out a few weeks after her mom left, sharing an apartment with Sharri while attending a vocational school and then working. When Mollie married her first husband, Sam didn't attend the wedding. When her husband died, Sam offered his condolences and visited a few times.

When we married, he attended our wedding. They still weren't father and daughter but were at least cordial. Malcolm was about a year old and we were living in Casper when Sam asked if he could come for a visit. It was then he told Mollie he had cancer and was unlikely to beat it. Sam ended up staying in Wyoming, renting a small house in town.

At first, they didn't have much of a relationship. Over time, they were able to get to know each other again. Mollie actually reached a point where she enjoyed spending time with him. Even though his cancer was considered terminal, Sam passed away peacefully in his sleep before the cancer became too painful. A blessing for sure.

While Sam's loss was hard on Mollie, it wasn't the same as when Sharri and Kenny died. Losing them so unexpectedly was a blow that cut both of us to the core.

We were incredibly close to divorce when Mollie finally suggested we start seeing a marriage counselor.

Seeing a counselor brought up more stuff. We were seriously discussing calling it quits. The counselor insisted she thought saving our marriage was worth a try. She said most of our issues were communication issues brought on by the grief and the mess our life had become. She suggested we spend more time playing and less time working around the farm, as a way to get to know each other again. We still just maintain what we were doing, but we haven't added any new ventures to our homestead in the last several months.

Spending so much time together over the past few months doing recreational activities—hiking, skiing, fishing, hunting, and so forth—

has really helped our marriage. Sure, we still have the occasional "thing," but for the most part, we're good.

Sure wish she'd hurry and get home . . .

Chapter 32

Jake

Taking a slightly different route back to the hardware store, I find a small gas station without a *CLOSED* or *NO GAS* sign.

As I pull in, a guy steps out from the side of the building—holding a shotgun. Not in a threatening way but cradled in his arms. He bellows, "Help you?"

"You have fuel?"

"Yep. $12.50 a gallon. Cash."

Yowza. Last night we paid regular prices. I guess capitalism is alive and well.

"Okay, sure. Can you fill it up?"

"Money first, friend. And I'm not giving out change."

"Uh, right. Then I guess I'll take four gallons."

"No problem. Fifty bucks."

I pay and he starts fueling. "How long you planning to stay open?" I ask.

"Oh . . . I don't know. I had a few people in earlier, but it's been pretty quiet lately. I'll be open awhile longer. Why?"

"I'm with some friends. I'm going to meet up with them and then we'll be back for more fuel. Just wanted to make sure you'd still be around."

"Yep, sure. I'll be open for a while. I'd be happy to take your money," he says with a smirk.

Evan and Karen are just coming out of the hardware store when I reach the spot I left them.

"Hey, Jake. How're your folks?"

"Scared. They couldn't have coffee this morning and realized things are serious."

"Coffee made them realize things are serious?" Evan asks with a shake of his head.

"Right? They're coming home with me. I'm shocked."

"Great. You'll rest easier if your family's with you." I can see he feels he said the wrong thing as he quickly adds, "You know, Mollie will be home soon."

"Yeah. She might be there now. She was hoping to drive without many stops."

"Great. Well, you need help getting your folks?"

"I do. You mind?"

"Nope. Let's go."

"My parents asked me to get them some groceries. I'd like to stop by Albertsons, give them a little time to pack while I shop. And I found an open gas station. Fuel is $12.50 a gallon."

"What? That's crazy," Karen says.

Evan just nods.

"I put four gallons in my car. I'd like to fill up the cans. Even at the cost, I think it's smart."

"For sure," Evan says. "Let's go there first."

"That's not right," Karen objects. "He can't gouge us. Isn't there a law against that? When there's an emergency, don't they have to leave prices the same?"

Evan and I both shrug. Evan says, "Yeah, there is, but we need the fuel, and I'm willing to pay the cost, so . . . " He gives an even bigger shrug in a "what are you going to do" type gesture.

Shotgun guy seems pleased to see me return to the gas station. "Good thing you got back here so quick. I had a few people in since you were here and was just getting ready to change my price. I guess you can have what you need at the same price per gallon as before. After you, it's fifteen dollars a gallon, so if you have any other friends, make sure you tell them the correct price and not the discount I'm giving you."

Karen looks like she wants to say something. I lightly touch her arm and slightly shake my head. She purses her lips and quickly looks away.

Evan fills his truck and the two cans that were left on his porch. I fill Tate's and my cans.

"Hope you don't mind our delay with getting my parents," I say to Karen.

"Not at all. I'm so glad I decided to come with my mom and dad. I wasn't going to but changed my mind a few days before. I'd be a wreck if I was there and they weren't when this happened. You must be freaking out about Mollie." She looks at me wide eyed. "I'm so sorry, Jake. I shouldn't have said that."

"It's fine," I answer tensely. Then I take a deep breath and admit, "I am freaking out. Sometimes more than other times. And with Katie on the road, too, and not knowing about Angela and Calley..." I shake my head. "It's not easy. But I can't do much about it. Doris, Evan's wife, is in a similar boat. She has a daughter in San Jose and another in Germany."

"Oh no. Germany should be fine, but her daughter doesn't know how her mom or sister might be getting along. That's terrible."

After the gas station, we make our way back to Albertsons. Evan, Karen, and I take our places at the end of the line. While Evan feels like he stocked up pretty good, he wants to take a look through here. He says he'll make sure to keep back enough money for the things he hopes to buy at the sporting goods store.

Karen has just over two hundred dollars left, plus eighty from the money Sarah gave her. I want to get the things for my folks, plus add more for our general storage. With my parents, Sarah, Tate, and Tate's family, we can't have too much food.

We quickly learn from others in line, as expected, it's cash only and they're allowing ten people in at a time at regular intervals. Unlike SuperMart, the cash registers here have a battery backup and are functioning. Our wait is only fifteen minutes or so, and the three of us go in at the same time, then separate for our individual shopping.

The store is lit with a variety of battery-powered lanterns. As I walk by, one blinks and goes out. This strikes a chord with me.

Mollie and I read a book around the time we started to get serious about farming. The book described living a completely off-grid life. Not relying on solar, like we do, but purposely returning to a time in history where electricity and modern conveniences were not available.

The author proclaimed in the early years of the US, people lived healthy, happy, and productive lives without the electrical grid. Even as a whole, society was better off before electrification than afterward. His theory was, there were very few rich people and very few poor people during the founding of America, with the bulk of the people equaling what would today be considered middle class—not the dark ages as we've been led to believe.

This book made a case for returning to the time before electrification and relying again on Agrarianism and the old paths. We thought it was an interesting concept and learned of small communities in the US living fully independent of electricity. We put a few of his ideas into play, such as our smokehouse, but mostly filed away the rest of the ideas for future use. While we have things like oil lanterns and such in storage, I realize additional items from time past would be a good idea.

There's an antique store on the outskirts of town Mollie and I have visited before. I think it's worth a stop to see if they have things we can use. After meeting up with Evan and Karen at the vehicles, they agree it's a good idea to check it out. We'll go there before gathering my parents, to give them a little more time to get things together.

Karen and I take the lead with Evan following. The few times I've been there, we were coming in from the north side of town. Instead of going around and coming in that way, I think about how I can get there from here.

Going through several neighborhoods will be quicker than going through the downtown area and around.

As we leave the parking lot, Karen says, "It's getting warm—not like Oklahoma warm, but warm."

"You want the windows down or the air on?" I ask, thinking windows would be the more conservative option.

"Windows are fine. It's not too warm," she says. "You seemed pretty surprised about your parents being willing to go to your place."

"Yeah. I wasn't expecting them to agree," I answer.

"Why is that?" Karen asks.

Hmmm. I think about how to answer quickly. Even at their age, they prefer to take care of everything on their own. My dad finally agreed a couple winters ago, when they got a foot of snow in twenty-four hours, to hire someone to help shovel the walk and driveway. When he told me about hiring out the work, he seemed almost embarrassed he couldn't do the job on his own. I think he hates to admit he might need help. And I know he hated spending money on something he used to be able to do on his own. They are incredibly frugal; they always have been. The frugality enabled my dad to retire from his bus mechanic job at age fifty-five, and while they certainly don't live lavishly, they are comfortable.

I decide to say, "They have a hard time giving up their independence."

"Understandable," Karen says with a nod. "My folks are the same way. Even though my mother has retired, I doubt my dad ever will. He says he'd feel totally useless. Mother is hoping he'll change his mind after this trip and decide retiring and traveling would be nice. Of course, the way things are right now . . . "

She doesn't need to finish her sentence. I know exactly what she's thinking and wonder if she may start crying again.

As I'm struggling for a new, safe subject of conversation, there's a flash across the hood of the car followed by the percussion of a gunshot.

What the—?

I slam on the brakes and swerve to the right, hitting the curb. What just happened? In my review mirror, Evan stops abruptly, then throws his truck and trailer in reverse. Reverse is the best choice for us also.

Trying to straighten out and get off the curb, I suddenly hear, "Hey, hey," in a raspy, weathered voice. I put my hand on the butt of my firearm. Is this the shooter? Should I draw?

It's an average guy wearing a gray Wyoming state flag trucker's cap, a black T-shirt with a pack of smokes in the pocket, blue jeans, and work boots.

"Looks like he nailed you," he loud whispers, gesturing toward the hood of my car. From my angle, I can just barely see a glint of silver across the hood. "Better back on up a bit and get out of the line of fire. He's probably reloading."

He doesn't need to tell me twice. I glance at Karen while straightening out and put the car in reverse. She's white as a sheet and breathing extremely fast.

I'm backing up, faster than I should. Evan's truck grill is grinning at me in the mirror. I slam on the brakes, barely stopping in time to keep from plowing into the truck. We've gone nearly a block from where the bullet grazed my car. I'm breathing heavy, like I just sprinted a mile.

Evan jumps out of his truck from the passenger's side and low walks over to Karen's side of the car. "Jeez, Jake. That was a close one. Another foot and the bullet would've— " He stops talking at the look on Karen's face. Then gently asks, "You two okay?"

I nod. Karen just shakes her head and bursts out in tears.

Another shot rings out and the three of us instinctively duck. A different guy, standing behind another truck, scurries over to us.

Evan's hand is resting on his holster as he remains behind the front of the car. This guy is also average looking, wearing jeans, a casual western-style button shirt, cowboy boots, and a NAPA trucker's cap.

"Hey, you seen any cops around?" the guy asks, cigarette dangling off his lip.

"Nope," Evan answers.

"Well, darn. Simon went after them over an hour ago. Hank's gone plumb nuts shooting things up. At least he let his wife and young 'uns out of the house before things got too bad."

I feel like we should offer to do something, but this is way out of my league. I look to Evan, who gives me a slight shake of his head, then says, "Well, okay then. Looks like there's plenty of you guys hiding behind vehicles. Good the family got out and you have help coming. We'll find a different way around."

"You sure? There are several of us around in case things get worse. Maybe you could help us by blocking traffic so no one else comes driving in?"

Evan looks at the guy with barely concealed anger. "Instead of standing behind vehicles waiting to shoot back, or whatever it is you're doing, the first thing you should've done was set up roadblocks to keep unsuspecting travelers from wandering into this nightmare. You know how close these two came to getting shot?"

Evan gestures toward Karen and me, which causes Karen to let out a wail, which the gunman must have heard since it was followed by another shot.

"That's it, we're out of here," I say loudly. "You schmucks need to— "

"Pull your heads out," Evan finishes for me, using his cop voice. "And get the road blocked off on each end. Do it now."

As Evan goes back to his truck, we see a police car sporting lights but no siren. Evan shakes his head and drops his shoulders. We've missed our opportunity to get out of here.

Evan gets back out of the truck and stands with his hands clearly visible. The car stops well back from Evan. Both officers exit their vehicle, remaining behind their car doors.

With my hands on the steering wheel, I quietly say, "Keep calm and visible, Karen. They look pretty on edge."

"What's going on here?" one of them asks.

“Not real sure,” Evan says. “My friends and I were driving through when a shot bounced off the hood of his car. There are several locals hiding behind vehicles, and one of them said someone’s taking shots at them. He said he didn’t think there were hostages involved. My friends and I are just trying to leave since this doesn’t concern us.”

About that time, another shot rings out, causing the officers to both duck. Evan says, “Shooter’s a good block up. Mind if we take off and let you handle this?”

The same officer says, “Give me your names, numbers, and addresses so we can follow up as needed.” Evan gives his info, then mine for me, telling them Karen is stuck here and staying at my place. The police car parks along the side of the curb behind Evan. We can go; they’ll be in touch if they need us.

Evan backs up to where he can turn left at an intersection, and I follow until he stops several blocks away. Karen is still crying. Evan walks back to us and says, “Well, that was a close one. As much as I’d like to go to your antique store, at this point, I think we should get your folks, visit the sporting goods store, and get home lickety-split.”

Karen takes a deep breath and hiccups while nodding in agreement.

“Absolutely. I’ll take the lead to my folks’ place. Umm . . . maybe we can *not* mention this to them right away? I’ll tell them after we’re back to my place.”

“Agreed,” Evan says, and Karen nods.

Chapter 33

Malcolm

Dad and Tate's sister, Karen, went into town with Evan. A little while after they left, Tate and his dad also left. Tate's going back up to his house in Billings to get the rest of their stuff and do some grocery shopping.

I had to stay home with Sarah and Tate's mom. I've met Tate's mom before, when Sarah and Tate got married. She's pretty nice, but I don't know her very well. She does seem to like me.

"Malcolm, I made some breakfast for you. Sarah tells me you like scrambled eggs and toast with peanut butter and jam. How does that sound?" she asks me shortly after everyone leaves.

"Sure, I like that. Dad gave me some cereal before he left, but second breakfast is always good."

"What are you, a hobbit?" Sarah asks.

"Yes! And next we'll have elevenses, then lunch, then teatime, then— "

"Okay, okay. I'm sorry I asked," Sarah laughs.

After I have my second breakfast, Tate's mom, who said to call her Lois, asks if I want to hear a story.

"Sure. You want me to get a book from my house?"

"No, that's fine. I have books on my phone. Did you know, until last month, I was a teacher?"

"A teacher? No, I didn't know. How come you aren't a teacher now?"

"I retired. You know that word, retired?"

"Sure. My grandpa's retired. It means you work for a long time and then you don't have to work anymore. But even though my grandpa's retired, he stays pretty busy. Do you want to stay busy?"

"I certainly do. It's important to stay busy. Now, let's see if we can find a book to read. Then, if you'd like, we could work on a few other things, like handwriting and some math."

No, I really wouldn't like to, since Mom said I don't have to do school until she gets back. But instead of saying this, I mind my manners and say, "I can, if you'd like to." I figure, maybe she's a little sad about being retired and wants to be a teacher again for today.

She gives me a big smile and says, "Let's do it. We'll have fun."

Miss Lois is a good teacher and does make it kind of fun. Of course, I would've rather just played outside. Sarah wouldn't give me a real "elevenses" meal, but I did have a snack. A little later she makes me a sandwich for lunch.

Shortly after, Sarah asks me to run outside and play. She seems really upset, and Lois is crying. Uh-oh. I hope everything's okay. I want to ask and find out what's wrong but decide to wait a bit. Maybe, once Lois stops crying, they'll tell me.

Chapter 34

Jake

At my parents' house, I'm impressed with what they've accomplished. Suitcases and boxes are stacked in the front room. They've met Evan before when visiting our place. Since they were unable to attend Sarah and Tate's wedding in Oregon, they don't know Karen or any of her family. Karen has pulled herself together and declined my suggestion she could wait in the car if she preferred. She still looks a mess but isn't actively crying.

I make the introductions. "It's nice to meet you," my mom says to Karen. "I'm sorry it's under such . . . rough . . . circumstances."

Karen's face begins to crumble. She bites her bottom lip and shakes her head. I think she's going to start crying again, when she visibly straightens and then sighs. "It is rough. I'm sorry, but I don't seem to be handling things well and seem to burst into tears over . . . well, anything."

"It's okay, I understand," my mom says with a weak smile. "We're all in the same boat."

We load the freezer first. They still have a considerable amount of game from last year in it. We quickly empty it to make it as light as possible, get it in Evan's trailer, and reload it. Karen brings everything from the freezer above the fridge out to it also, and my mom puts a few things she's able to salvage from the fridge into a cooler. She fills the trash can with the rest and we take it out to the city-provided garbage can. My dad says he'll move it to the pickup spot in case their regular Monday garbage collection occurs. Doubtful.

Pretty much every useable item is packed up to go. My dad asks about their recliners. Evan does some rearranging and we get one in the trailer; the second goes in the back of Evan's truck. My mom takes another look around the house. I ask Evan if he thinks we could put the mattress from the guest bed in his trailer. The trailer is already very full.

Evan looks it over and says, "Sure, why not. I think we can maybe stuff it along the top. Give me a minute to move things around. Should be fine."

"Mom, you think we could bring the mattress off the guest bed? I bought another cabin yesterday. It has a loft, and it would be great to have a mattress up there. I'll buy you a new one after this is all over."

"Sure, Jake. Go ahead. We have a camping cot too."

"I think we've already packed the camping gear you had left. Dad?"

"Yep. We don't have much gear anymore, but it's already in my truck, along with the fishing gear."

My mom looks around. "I guess that's it, then. Jake, do you think we're being a little bit ridiculous here?"

"I hope so, Mom."

She gives me an odd look but says nothing.

"Next stop, sporting goods store?" Evan asks.

"I'd like to, if you think . . . uh . . . we have the time." I almost said, *If you think it's safe*, which would've not been the best thing for my folks.

I think Evan knows what I was thinking as he says, "Sure. Let's do it."

"How are you on gas?" I ask my dad.

"Filled up when we did our Friday shopping. Haven't drove it since then. I have a two-gallon can, also full, in the bed of the truck."

"You have any empty gas cans?" Evan asks.

"Nope."

I tell my parents the plan. My dad would like to go in the sporting goods store. Mom wants to wait in the truck. I look at Evan to see what he thinks about that; he gives a shrug. We can only assume a store parking lot is safe, and if it doesn't seem to be when we get there, we won't stop.

Karen rides with me.

"Hey, Karen. How about going into Rite Aid to see about more games, art supplies, journals, card games . . . you know, stuff like that? Things you think people may enjoy in the downtime. You up to it?"

She hesitates before saying, "I suppose I can do it. Probably be better than just sitting around thinking about getting shot at."

"Uh, right. Maybe see if there's any movies that look good? Mollie and I have a pretty good collection but haven't bought anything new in a long time. With the solar system, we can probably have the occasional movie time."

"Yeah, okay. Maybe books and magazines too?"

"Sounds good. Whatever you think. How are you set on cash?"

"Umm. Looks like fifty from my money and twenty from what Sarah gave me."

"Okay, I'll give you some additional. I want to make sure you can buy anything you think we can use. Look at every aisle. Don't just limit yourself to the free time stuff we're discussing."

"Sure, Jake. You paid for my stuff at SuperMart, and now you're going to give me more money. Aren't you worried about spending all of your money?"

I hesitate to answer. I'm not sure I want her to know what I really think, then decide to give her a slightly watered-down version. "If the power doesn't come back on and new shipments of food and supplies can't be brought to us, money isn't going to be worth much. You can't purchase things that aren't available. I'd rather we buy what we can now. When things get back to normal, we can make more money." I hope the last part is true. I don't tell her I still have money at home, and I'm wondering if it will make better fire starter or toilet paper.

"Hmmm. I guess that's a good point."

While the two stores don't share a parking lot, they're right next to each other. Rite Aid and the sporting goods store both look open and both seem to be on the busy side. I give Karen the lantern. Last night Rite Aid had several lanterns out, which was helpful. The store should be lighter since it's daylight and they have skylights, but it still might be on the dark side.

"You want anything from the sporting goods store?" I ask her.

"I can't really think of anything." Karen walks to Rite Aid.

Evan and my dad walk into the sporting goods store with me. I give my mom a small wave. She has her little dog sitting on her lap. Butterball is a ten-year-old Yorkie. They've been talking about getting a second Yorkie pup after their older dog died this past winter, but they've not yet found what they're looking for. I should've bought more dog food.

The three of us separate in the store. I find several pairs of wool socks to add to our stock. There are also a few pairs of snow boots I don't remember seeing the other day on the clearance table. The clerk sees me putting the boots in my cart and walks over.

"We have a couple more pairs in back, I think. You want me to grab them?"

"Same sizes?" I ask.

"Not sure. Give me a minute and I'll bring them out so you can look."

I mill around, finding a few small things for my cart, including more winter gloves. My dad walks over to me. "Jake, Evan's buying some of those camping meals. You think I should get some?"

"We have some of those, Dad. But if there's a type you like, get them."

"Don't know. Haven't really eaten those. I'm getting some ammo for my guns. Evan said he thinks this is a good idea."

"I agree, Dad."

He looks at my cart. "Why are you buying snow boots?"

"They're on clearance," I answer with a shrug. He shakes his head and goes back to his shopping.

I check out the tents. I know my parents have limited camping gear since they no longer camp. They have a very old, very large tent. I want to set them up, similar to how I set up Karen's family, with makeshift bug-out bags, so a backpacker's tent is a good idea. There's an A-frame style one for only twenty-five dollars. That should work. I especially like the green color. I put two in my cart. I've made sure the tents I bought for Karen and all we have in our stock at home are a neutral color. We don't want bright orange tents if we can help it.

The tarps I've purchased are all brown or camo for the same reason—no bright blue. The trekking backpacks here are too expensive, so I skip them. We have a couple of utility carts and sleds, which will work for hauling my parents' gear. Probably a better choice for them than big backpacks anyway. Maybe I should buy another? I look around. No sleds—wrong time of year probably. There's a utility cart, which costs almost as much as my first car. I skip it.

The clerk returns with a couple pairs of boots—ten dollars each. They'll work, especially for the price.

"We have some more winter stuff in the back. Coats and snowsuits. You interested?"

"Yeah. Sure. I'll take a look. You want me to follow you back?"

"That'd be okay. Then I don't have to pull it out. We had it out to sell but couldn't, so we moved everything to the back to make room for other things. We'll do a sidewalk sale over Fourth of July to try to clear it. Well . . . maybe we will." He gives me a knowing look.

On the way to the back, I overhear Evan talking to another employee by the gun counter. "Yeah. Even though our verification is down, I can sell to you since you have your LEOSA. We're selling to people with concealed carry permits too. We don't need to do a background check since you already have those."

Evan sees me walking by. "Jake, you need anything here? With your permit, you can purchase."

"Maybe. I'm going to check out something else and then I'll stop by."

Evan knows I don't really feel the need for any more guns. I bought the .22 for Malcolm the other day. We have assorted rifles and shotguns for hunting plus our handguns. I can't really think of anything else we need but will take a look.

Evan might have something in mind. As a tactical training instructor and retired police officer, I defer to him for knowledge of weapons. It's a given he'll be the one in charge of self-defense if our neighborhood has a need.

I suddenly find myself wishing we would've formed an official Mutual Assistance Group. Mollie and I talked about approaching Evan, Doris, and a few of the other neighbors about this, but the time never seemed right. Now, a MAG would be helpful. The interesting thing is, while it's never an open conversation, there's a large contingency of preparedness-minded individuals in our community. Not getting together with them was certainly a lost opportunity.

The store's winter gear is impressive, especially for June. There are several heavy coats in sizes which will work for Tate's family and insulated bibs, all in Carhartt or Wahl, at okay prices. I decide to get a few extras for others in the family.

"You have any toddler or kid's sizes?"

"Hmmm. I think so." He walks around the rack and pulls out a few. Toddler size four and kid's size eight in bibs. A different brand but still okay. "Oh, and here's a size six and a size twelve. You want these too?"

"Yes. Sure. You happen to have any game sleds that don't cost an arm and a leg hanging around back here?"

"Got some of those roll-up ones for around twenty bucks."

"Roll-up ones? Not sure I've seen those."

"Yep. Not quite as sturdy as the toboggan type, but they sure are easy to store. I've been using the same one for the last three seasons. No holes yet. Got a super nice game cart out front. Suppose you saw it."

"I did—not interested in spending that much today. Are the roll-up ones easy to get to?"

"Sure 'nuff. How many you want?"

"Uh . . . I don't know. Maybe three? Can I look at them first?"

"Yep. I'll grab three. You don't have to buy any if you don't like them."

He returns a few minutes later.

"We only have the magnum size, perfect for elk. They're a little more. Twenty-seven dollars, I think. And you didn't ask for the harness, but I brought them out anyway. They're ten bucks each.

"Huh. So it's just a big piece of black plastic?

"Nah. It's some kind of polymer. It's thick, though. Stretch it out and then plop your animal on it. Pull the sides closed and use bungee cords, rope, or something to tie it shut. Works pretty slick. Keeps the meat fairly clean also."

"All right. You've sold me. I'll take three of them and the harnesses."

Evan has several items picked out, laid carefully across the counter on protective pads to avoid scratching the glass, including a couple of semi-auto rifles.

"Jake, you don't have anything like these?" He motions to the rifles.

"I don't, but I've shot them at your place and at the Smyth's house."

"I think the one they have is an AR-15, like the tan one and these three black ones. It's a 5.56mm or .223. Easy to shoot for sure, fairly light, and is a good rifle for hitting what you point it at and doing it over and over again, without breaking the bank. This one here— " Evan motions to a black, slightly larger one near him "—is an AR-10 7.62x51millimeter, or a .308 equivalent, and has more muzzle energy than the AR-15, accuracy and power at long distances, plus more stopping power in general. Both serve a purpose.

"It'd be great if you could get both—the 10 to use as a perimeter rifle, you know, if we needed someone acting as sniper or in open country on longer engagements. The AR-15 is the better choice for building entries—plus you can carry a ton of ammo and engage targets accurately out to three hundred yards. If you can only choose one, then choosing the AR-15 for the weight and ease of handling would be what I'd recommend." Evan then whispers to me, "Get the 15 for Mollie too. Then you can use your hunting rifles for perimeter control, plus I do have a couple of the 10s at home, along with a few 15s—you know, for my gun school."

"We've talked about getting one of these but didn't feel we could justify the expense. Rifles and shotguns for hunting, and handguns and a shotgun for self-defense . . . sure. Those make sense. But this? I'm not really sure we have a true need for one."

Evan turns and looks at me full on. "Maybe not," he says. "Your hunting weapons are great. Good firepower if you need long distance shots for taking down deer and elk or . . . other possible threats. And you have the skill and accuracy to take those shots.

"You have shotguns and handguns also. But if we had a need for self-defense, the semi-auto could make a huge difference. I've seen how fast you shoot that bolt-action 7 Mag of yours, and it's impressive. But this could give you a bit more of an edge when microseconds count, plus the larger capacity magazines are a benefit in a firefight. We both hope we'd never be in a situation to 'need' one of these, but if we were . . . be good to have it and not look back on today wishing."

"Yeah, I know you're right. How much money are we talking about?"

"Probably around seven or eight hundred for each, after adding a midlevel scope and at least one additional magazine. More for the 10. These are fine rifles but on the less expensive side—what I'd call an entry-level brand. It's an okay label for getting into an AR. This one— " he gestures to one "—is even on sale. It seems no one wants the tan. It's an AR-15. I asked if we could get a discount on our purchase. He offered 10 percent off. I can try for 15 percent. I'm buying one for Doris and one to have for the neighborhood."

After getting two rifles, along with what I have in my cart, my on-hand money will be close to gone. I still have a good amount of cash stashed at home in case we decide to do another crazy shopping trip, provided it's even possible.

I'm feeling a little skittish after being shot at earlier today. Which, if I'm being truthful, is leaving me feeling vulnerable. Karen and I were sitting ducks. We're going to have to start being a whole lot more careful and aware. While a semi-auto rifle wouldn't have made a lick of difference in today's situation, I can suddenly envision a time when it would make sense. Not just sense—the difference between life and death.

I nod. "Let's do it."

I buy the discounted tan model and a black AR-15 plus three magazines for each. Evan gets a 15 and a 10. He manages to finagle us a 15 percent discount on the guns, optics, a few boxes of ammo, and extra magazines. My dad walks over while we're gathering everything up to move to the checkout. He pulls me aside.

"Jake, you think we're going to need guns like that? I brought all my rifles and shotguns. I have my 7 Mag, you have your hunting rifles, and Mollie has . . . whatever it is she hunts with. Shouldn't that be enough?"

"Maybe. Evan suggested we could be attacked and we might need something more."

"Should I buy one?"

I look at my dad. He's an excellent shot and was my teacher. We used to do a lot of target practice for fun. We did archery competitions, which he is also very good at, so I know how well he stays calm. After the incident of being shot at, I want to immediately say, yes, he definitely needs one. But does he? I don't know. I don't even know if Mollie and I need these. I take the easy way out and defer to Evan.

"Maybe. Evan? What do you think?"

Evan gives me a look I interpret as, *Thanks, friend.* He says, "You might want one. It's a very versatile weapon. You can use it for predators and self-defense. I know you hunt. You shoot a 7 Mag like Jake?"

"7 Mag Ultra," my dad says proudly. "I also brought my other rifles and bows. Didn't want to leave anything behind. Jake, you have your bows, too, right?"

"Yep. Mollie and I each have a cross and a compound. And Malcolm has the nice compound you bought him for Christmas."

Dad gives me a startled look at my mention of Malcolm using his bow. I'm also kind of surprised I mentioned it. What am I thinking? Malcolm will need to use it for . . . for what? It's barely large enough for hunting since the draw maxes at forty pounds. Legally, he could use it for deer and antelope, but not elk. Of course, it'd still take down a man . . .

"Nice," Evan says, bringing me back to the conversation. "You have a handgun?"

"Nope. Gave my revolver to Jake a few years back. Oh, wait. I forgot, I have a single-shot .22 that was my dad's. It's ancient. Never used it. It's in the closet in a box. I wonder if Dodie thought to grab it when she was packing up."

"Might be best to get yourself a new handgun before going for a semi-auto rifle. I think it'd be smart for all of us to carry while this is going on," Evan says.

"Hmm. You think? Jake, you going to carry?"

"Already am, Dad," I say quietly and lift my shirt up slightly, just so he can see the bottom of my holster.

"Huh," my dad says. "I wondered why you had your shirt hanging out. Not like you to look so sloppy."

Thanks, Dad. "It's the .357 you gave me. I could give it back to you if you'd like."

"Nah . . . I never really liked that gun. I'd rather choose something else. Evan, you think I could get a decent handgun and a rifle? I'd like a semi-auto for each."

"Think we should check out Bill's pawn shop for a pistol?" I ask.

"It's Sunday. Bill's not usually open. I think we'll be fine with what they offer here," Evan answers.

My dad and Evan spend some time looking over the available options, finally deciding on a 9mm Taurus. My dad balked over the Taurus, knowing their reputation isn't great. Evan said he completely understood, but he knows several people who own a Taurus and love them, including Doris. And for the two-hundred-dollar cost, it's hard to beat. He chooses an AR-15 for the cost and ease of shooting, figuring for long shots, he too would use his hunting rifle.

Evan manages to get our discount up to 18 percent with the additional items. My dad is still a little short on cash and says, "I'll need to go out and get some more money from Dodie. I can't imagine she's going to be happy about this."

I can't either.

"How short are you? I might have enough to make up the difference, which might be better than asking Mom for money to buy guns."

"You're right about that, Jake! I can hear it now, 'Alvin, what do you need *that* for?' Maybe it would be best to get it without asking her for more money."

"Well, let's see what we can do," I tell my dad.

Evan says, "I still owe you for the meat, so I can give you it now if needed."

"We'll see."

The clerk lets me ring my purchases at one register, which includes my dad's choices, while Evan rings at the other. With my dad's money, I'm thirty dollars short, which Evan covers. The clerks have to walk us and our guns to the door. I ask if they can hold mine for a few minutes while I load up the rest of my purchases. Evan asks the same, and the three of us walk out.

Karen's standing by my parents' truck talking with my mom, giving Butterball pets through the window. Some of my purchases go in the back of my car, which is already well filled with the things Karen found.

Our car is a hatchback with a split folding rear seat and cargo area floor. It's great for hauling bulky items. It's claimed to be modeled after the 1949 Suburban. We've had it for years and originally bought it for the great gas mileage. It still does well in that category. We hold on to it for this and its usefulness. Mollie even hauls goats in the back of it when needed. It's terrible in the snow, so it's limited to fair-weather use.

Every fall we talk about buying a nice, new car which will be good in snow, but we keep putting it off. We have my pickup truck, which is still in good shape, and a 1977 Jeep CJ5. The CJ5 can be a chilly ride. Bought mainly for off-road driving and hunting, it can get us to town in a pinch.

The things I can't fit in our car I put in the small rear seat of my parents' Toyota Tacoma. Once Evan and I have our stuff loaded, we go back for the guns. After securing the guns in the back seat of Evan's truck, Evan asks, "Anyone need to stop anyplace else?"

I look at Karen and ask, "You in good shape?" I hope she says yes since I'm out of money.

"Yes. Oh, I have a little of your money left." She hands me a twenty, a five, three ones, and a few coins.

"I have a little money left too," Evan says. "I think we should buy more food with what we have left. Is there much food in Rite Aid, Karen?"

"Maybe some things like chips and other snacks. The shelves are getting pretty bare."

"There's still those camping meals in the sporting goods store," my dad adds.

Evan nods. "Jake, what do you think?"

"I think we'd get a little more bang for our buck in Rite Aid. They may have some canned goods still. They still had quite a bit last night."

"You all mind if Jake and I see what we can get? We'll only be a few minutes."

"I'll join you boys," my dad announces. "Dodie, I'll need some money."

"Now, Alvin. We already had Jake buy us some things at Albertsons, and you spent more than enough money in the sporting goods store. You think I didn't see the rifle you put in the back seat?"

"Dodie, Evan says I need one of those!"

I can see Evan looking a little concerned about being thrown in the middle of my parents' business. They are quite the couple. They've been married for fifty-six years and are still very much in love. They're definitely the cliché of "bicker like an old married couple" and have done this as long as I can remember. It's best to not say anything and just let them work through this on their own.

"Well, Alvin. I guess if Evan thinks you need it, you probably do. Thank you, Evan, for thinking of us."

"Uh, you're welcome, ma'am," Evan says with uncertainty.

"And, Jake, do you think your dad should join you in Rite Aid?"

Now that she's including me in the conversation, I do need to offer my opinion.

"I think so, Mom. Doesn't sound like there's much left, but this may be the last chance we get to buy food for a while."

"If you think so, Jake. Alvin, here's some more money for you to get what we need."

We each find odds and ends throughout the store, including a small bag of dog food. My dad comments as we move through the aisles, "Your mother loves these," or, "Haven't had this in a while, looks good." When I have what I think will use up my twenty-eight bucks, I head to the front.

My total is $28.72, which I'm able to scrounge up. I have a dime and two pennies left.

Evan rings out, his total is $52.23. He gives her fifty-three.

My dad's total shocks him. He gives the clerk all of the cash from my mom, digs for change, and is still short. I offer my twelve cents and Evan puts in a little change to make up the difference.

As we walk out of the store, my dad says, "Thank you, you two, for helping me pay. Guess I didn't keep track of the costs too well. Should've had Dodie give me more than she did."

"I can't believe I spent all the cash I brought in," Evan says. "I have a dollar or two in change left. That's it. You think we're nuts, Jake? Doris told me to spend it all. You know, we read a lot of those end-of-the-world books, and people end up with cash not good for anything except toilet paper, but they don't have any food. Have we read too many of those books?"

"We might have. It's the same for us. Mollie reads a lot of that genre. I read them, too, but not as fast as she does, so not nearly as many. Malcolm and I read a *Little House* book not long ago, *The Long Winter*, which scared the dickens out of me. Everything could be just fine tomorrow, and we'd be sitting on enough food and supplies so we never have to shop again. I have to admit, that sounds pretty good right about now. I never liked shopping before, and as much as I've done these last few days, I really don't like it now."

We share a small laugh over this.

Heading out of town toward home, I try the radio station broadcasting on the half hour. It's on, and the update isn't good.

Chapter 35

Jake

Within the past hour, there have been new explosions on US soil. These have targeted the oil refineries on the Gulf of Mexico and a few others scattered throughout the US. While the loss of lives from these explosions is minimal compared to the airport and bridge explosions, the long-term results could be devastating. The announcer makes a point of saying this will ensure a severe fuel shortage. The announcer also says the president will speak this evening at 9:00 pm eastern time. He'll share the latest updates on the cyberwar, the food poisonings, and all of the explosions.

Karen is crying softly. I stay silent while she composes herself. While I'm upset, my reaction is different. When the planes crashed, I experienced very real emotions. Sadness, anger, fear, all at the same time, and my body reacted to these with my mouth going dry and difficulty breathing. But now . . . I hear the news, and I absorb it, but I'm not reacting. What does this mean? Have I become desensitized to the violence and death we're now experiencing?

"I guess it's a good thing we got so much stuff today," she says between sniffles. "Now it really sounds like we might be stuck here for a while. I just can't imagine . . . "

I have nothing to say to this so simply remain quiet. Maybe I'm not desensitized. Maybe I'm just being realistic.

We're in a mess. It has definitely hit the fan, and all we can do now is . . . what? Keep doing what we're doing? Keep finding supplies and keep our heads down? Just get by until things return to normal? Normal . . . what will the United States look like after the terrorists, or whoever they are, are done with us? I don't know. What I do know is, I'm tasked with providing for and protecting those in my family—and my extended family, like Karen and her parents. I pray I'm up to the task.

Please, Lord, protect and bless my family. Give me the wisdom to lead them, the ability to protect and guide them. Help me grow more like You, become the strong leader You need me to be. Watch my steps and carry me through the difficult days ahead. Help me remember, it's Your strength I need. Oh . . . and if the need arises, help me to shoot straight and true. But please, Lord, if You could keep that need from arising, I'd sure appreciate it.

When we reach our gravel road, Karen says, "It's so hard to think about all of these disasters, to think people are purposefully causing so much destruction. At least nothing's happening back home. I'd really be a mess if I thought my friends, or my students, were in danger."

Her students . . . ?I wrack my brain.

"You're a teacher?"

"Yes, third grade."

"Oh, I knew your mom was. Didn't realize you were a teacher also."

"Yeah," she shrugs. "I enjoy it."

When our driveway comes into view, I frantically search for an extra car—where's Mollie? Disappointed there isn't a spare car in the yard, I do my best to choke back a sob. Where could she be?

Once we're all parked in our driveway, Malcolm runs over.

"Grandma! Grandpa! You came for a visit?"

"Thought we'd stay with you a few days," my mom answers.

"That's great. You haven't ever stayed the night before. Are you staying in the guest room?"

"Your grandparents are going to stay in the studio," I answer.

"Yay! You'll like the studio. It's really nice. Can I help you move your stuff into the apartment and get it ready?"

"Why not?" my dad says.

"That'd be very nice of you, Malcolm. I'm sure we can use the help," my mom answers.

Sarah and Lois both walk over. Sarah introduces Lois to my parents and to Evan.

"When did Tate and Keith leave?" I ask.

"Around 8:00. He said he'd try to be back by 2:00. I was starting to get worried—you were gone so long."

"Helped my folks pack up. And we did a lot of shopping." Again, I choose not to mention the shooting incident.

"We sure did," Karen says, seeming to sense my reluctance to mention the shooting. "Did you hear about the refineries?"

"Yes. Sarah's been using the radio in the bunkhouse. They're only broadcasting every hour. We couldn't get the half hour one to come in, and we listened at 1:00. It's so bad. Karen, honey, I'm concerned about what this means for us," Lois declares.

"I know, Mother. Jake and I talked about it. We planned for the worst. You'll be surprised when you see all we bought."

"Oh, I can imagine," Sarah adds with a chuckle.

"What refineries?" Malcolm asks.

I take a deep breath and say, "There were some explosions at the oil refineries on the Gulf of Mexico and a few other places."

Malcolm nods. "That's bad, right? Refineries are where they make gas and stuff? Like the one we drive by on our way to Sarah's house? Does that mean they can't make more gas?"

"Yes, like the one in Laurel. But I don't think that one was affected. We don't really know yet. We don't know how bad the damage was or exactly how many places were affected. The president's speaking tonight, so maybe we'll know more then." I try to be as nonchalant as possible. Malcolm doesn't need something else to worry about. He gives me a look which makes me think he's not buying my explanation.

"Here comes Doris," Malcolm says. "She must have seen you guys pull in."

She stops her SUV and gets out. She's, again, looking a bit of a mess. I know how hard this is on her with her daughters so far away. Evan goes over to her, hugs her tight, they talk for a minute, he nods, and they walk over.

"Well, friends," Evan says, "the refineries being blown to smithereens makes me feel not quite so foolish with our 'crazy shopping trips,' as Jake referred to them. We have ourselves a real crap-sandwich. Mr. and Mrs. Caldwell, I think you did a good thing coming out here today. It could be a long haul before things are back to normal.

"Karen, Mrs. Garrett, I can already tell you're going to be a welcome addition to our community. Oh, Sarah, you too. I meant the other Mrs. Garrett. You and Tate already felt like part of our family." Everyone laughs a little with Evan over this. "Should we start unloading?"

"Yes, I think the stuff from my parents' place can go in the shop. I plan on putting the freezer in there anyway and plugging into the shop's solar system. Everything else can go into the shop as a holding area while we do some rearranging. We'll have it in good shape soon." I direct the last part toward my parents.

"I'm helping Grandma with her house. Don't forget, Dad," Malcolm says excitedly.

"We'll need your help, Malcolm," my mom tells him.

"Hey, Jake," Doris calls out, gesturing at my hood, "what in the world happened to your car?"

The jig is up. While I would've told everyone eventually, it would've been better to wait until Tate was back. Sarah's probably going to freak out.

"Just a small incident we stumbled into," Evan says. "Seems some guy was unhappy with . . . well, the world, I guess, and was taking pot shots. One scraped across the hood of the car. I don't think anyone had been hurt. Sheriff showed up and we got out of there."

I'm thankful for Evan making light of it, but just the mention is a little much for Karen. She tears up. Everyone speaks at once, exclaiming their dismay over the event. Lois and Sarah each have their arms around Karen. Malcolm is looking at me with fear in his eyes.

"It's okay, Buddy. We didn't get hurt. It was pretty scary at the time, but we were able to get away without anything but a scratch on the car." I give his hair a ruffle.

Malcolm nods at me in understanding, but the fear is still there. My mom notices and says, "Malcolm, I can't tell you how glad I am you're going to help us get our place put together. It's a lot of work for your grandpa and me on our own."

Emptying Evan's trailer goes quickly since we're offloading but not putting away. He was smart and put in a barrier, so it's easy to see where his SuperMart and feed store stuff starts. Everything forward of there goes to his place. We unload the bed of his truck next.

"Hey, gang, I'm going to go up and help Evan unload. Then we'll unload the car and the Toyota."

"Need some help?" Sarah asks, while Malcolm says, "Can I go too?"

"Malcolm, why don't you take Grandma and Grandpa into the house? They'd love a cup of coffee. Show them where everything is? You've watched me use the coffee press, so you can instruct them?"

"Yeah, I can do it, Dad. And a snack? I could use a snack. I'm sure Grandma and Grandpa could too. And Butterball. She looks hungry."

"Yes. A snack. Remember the wild game sausage I pulled out of the freezer? I think it's in the small fridge. There's cheese also. And grab some crackers. Lois and Karen, please also go in and make yourselves at home. Sarah and I won't be long."

We take my truck up to the Snyders' place so they won't need to drive us back. Evan pulls around to his shop and positions the trailer near one of the bay doors. Last night's crazy shopping made its home in their shop.

The gas cans for the community are lined up along the outside edge.

"A few people came up and got theirs today," Doris says. "The president's speaking at the same time as the meeting we arranged for tonight. Should we still go?"

"Yes," I answer. "I think we should have it on a portable radio, and everyone can gather around to listen. I have a radio—do you have speakers we can hook into it?"

"I have speakers. And I have a radio that'll work perfect for this. I'll take care of it."

We quickly unload the trailer and the few items still in the truck.

"You want help putting things away?" Sarah asks.

"No need," Doris says. "We're not really sure where to put things yet. I'm taking the food in the house so it doesn't get too hot, but the other things . . . I don't know. I'm glad to see the shelves, those will help."

Evan purchased several freestanding shelving units, and also precut lumber to put together additional shelves.

"Say, Evan, Doris, there's something I need to talk with you about," I say. "It's confidential, so I'd appreciate your discretion on it."

"Of course," Doris says.

"What is it?" Evan asks.

Sarah just looks at me with curiosity.

"With everything happening, I'm concerned what may happen next."

"Yes, so are we," Evan says. "Anything's possible."

I nod. "We all kind of hem and haw around about our preparedness stuff. You guys have your stuff and we have ours."

Doris interrupts me. "Well, we don't really do too much. I try to keep a full pantry and we have the freezers full of game—and you know Evan's big on keeping us stocked up on wood. This year he even ordered those uncut logs. I'm so grateful the truckload arrived before all of this started."

"Yep, me too," Evan says. "I figure we have ten cords of cut wood, and the truckload will add about fourteen cords once it's all said and done. And with the four freezers pretty much full of deer, elk, and antelope, we can eat some meat. 'Course, my sweetie here is working her fingers to the bone getting it all processed, so it's either going into jars or jerky. But the other stuff, we have—what do you think, Doris? Six weeks or two months' worth of canned and dry goods?"

"More now, with the shopping you and Jake have done. It was smart for you two to make those trips. But, after today, I question whether you should go after any more supplies."

Evan and I share a look, then he says, "I think we're still okay. Today was one guy freaking out over who knows what. I don't think things are in the toilet yet."

Doris shakes her head. I decide to continue with my original thoughts. "It's good you have so many things in place. Mollie and I have often thought about talking to you to develop a full-on Mutual Assistance Group but never felt the time was right. And now, the time seems to have passed because we're in the thick of it. I really appreciate your help with the guns today. That would've been something a MAG would likely do, have weapon standards and education."

"You bet. We did sort of do that on the fly today, with the three of us purchasing weapons with interchangeable magazines. But with a little planning, we could've ensured more uniformity. Speaking of, we need to get your rifles set up and sighted in. Tomorrow, maybe?"

"Yeah. Tomorrow would be good. Another thing a MAG often focuses on is shelter. Most of them, from what I know, will buy a retreat and then have people buy in to a shelter. Here, we don't really have a need like that. I can't imagine finding a retreat any better than where we live every day."

Both Doris and Evan agree.

"Of course, many die-hard preppers would say Wyoming is a terrible place for a retreat with the Yellowstone Caldera—but I'd rather take my chances with Yellowstone blowing than live in the city or somewhere with a high population. I figure it's a choice of the lesser of two evils."

"No doubt," Evan says passionately.

“So, the shelter part. We chose to live here for several reasons. It’s beautiful, my folks are nearby, the sparsity of the population, and . . . well . . . this one’s going to be a doozy,” I hesitate a bit. What I share next will really blow it wide open and show just how fully invested we are in preparedness. Will they think we’re mentally ill?

Chapter 36

Jake

Take a deep breath and just blurt it out, Jake. "Another reason we chose Bakerville is our research leads us to believe this area would receive little to no fallout in case of a nuclear attack."

I wait for their reaction. Sarah, who's already aware of the scope of our measures, says nothing.

"Okay?" Evan says. "That's a pretty good reason. We didn't think about checking into that, but it seems like good info to have with everything going on."

"Yeah, I think so. Mollie did lots of research on nuclear attacks. She spent hours looking at FEMA, CDC, and other websites, some government sponsored and some from the tinfoil-hat crowd."

"Mollie's a good researcher," Doris says.

"She is. And she's good at determining the fact from the fluff. When she thought she had a good handle on it, she told me about the nukes and how the radiation works. I had a general understanding before but learned a lot more. We grew up at the end of the Cold War—well, the official Cold War, anyway—and remember the drills of hiding under our desks and covering our heads. You two probably had a little more of those than we did."

"Sure," Evan says. "I remember Civil Defense and community fallout shelters. Plus, people digging out their backyards or setting up their basements."

"Me too. And when I was in the Navy, we were still officially in the Cold War and had assorted nuclear attack drills and training," Doris says.

"Yep, we had threat responses on nuclear attacks when I was with the sheriff department. But from what I took away from the classes, I'm not sure the fallout shelters would be much help. The dangerous radiation will pretty much kill you, so why bother?" Evan asks with a shrug.

"That's what I thought too," I say. "I was pretty sure a nuclear attack was not a survivable event. And even if we did survive, wouldn't we just be living in a nuclear wasteland? Like Chernobyl?"

Doris and Evan both nod. Sarah gives me an odd look.

"One thing I was surprised to discover from Mollie's research is a widespread nuclear event is survivable with certain caveats: the size or yield of the device, distance from detonation, and surface or ground burst. Living here, we have the advantage of not being a likely target in case of attack. There aren't any military bases or large cities nearby. Billings, at only a smidge over 100,000 people, is our only metropolis and pretty small as far as cities go."

"So, then, we have nothing to worry about," Evan says with finality.

"Right, I don't think we need to worry about a direct hit. Unless, of course, the missile went off target. Not sure how likely that'd be. But we should think about fallout. If the nuke hits the ground, fallout would be created. This fallout consists of weapon debris, fission products, and radiated soil. For a burst near the ground, large amounts of dirt and debris are drawn into the forming mushroom cloud. A nuclear explosion emits several kinds of radiation—gamma, neutron, and ionizing—that are emitted not only at the time of detonation, the initial radiation, but also for long periods of time afterward, known as residual radiation.

"People close to the blast—you know, ground zero—may receive lethal doses of radiation immediately but are usually killed by the blast and thermal pulse. Only a small amount of people die from initial radiation near ground zero."

Evan interrupts to say, "Yep, that's what I remember. The radiation is lethal, so why bother?"

"Wait," Doris says. "I think what Jake's saying is only the people near ground zero receive the lethal radiation, but they're killed by the blast before the radiation can kill them?"

"Sort of," I answer. "The blast is definitely an issue close to the detonation site, but the lethal radiation can travel farther than the blast site. And we need to consider the residual radiation. This is mainly from radioactive fallout. The larger particles of fallout will fall within a short distance of ground zero. Smaller particles can be carried hundreds of miles in the wind, resulting in serious contamination far from the point of detonation. These radioactive particles have differing half-lives. Some are very short, lasting only seconds. Others can be a hazard for months or years.

"Fallout particles collect on the ground, roofs of buildings, bushes, and other surfaces. As fallout accumulates, the exposure rate will increase until most of the particles have fallen. After it's reached maximum accumulation, the exposure rate will begin to fall. The decrease is rapid at first, then gets slower and slower. The exposure rates decrease according to the rate of radioactive decay." I can see I'm starting to lose them, so I wrap it up.

"Mollie has a book, *Nuclear War Survival Skills*, which goes into detail on how healthy people can receive small doses of radiation and survive. The key is finding shelter, and staying sheltered as long as there's fallout. So . . . that's what we have. A shelter."

"You have a bomb shelter?" Doris asks.

"Not a bomb shelter, and not really a full-on fallout shelter. We have a decent basement which attaches to the root cellar and has a few extra features you've probably not noticed."

"I knew you have a partial basement. I've seen the windows at the back of the house. Your root cellar connects to your house? I've been in your root cellar. I had no idea," Doris says with disbelief.

I laugh a little. "It does. The root cellar is nothing fancy but would provide more protection than just the basement if there was some sort of a need. It'd for sure be cozy, but I'm not sure how much it would matter. And with it connecting to the basement, that adds a little more space. The basement is a full basement, but we only have windows in the one section. We added a cement roof to the basement, which provides a little protection, and the windowless section is even more fortified than the rest to be better shelter space. You want to stop by before we go to the community center for a quick tour? I want to show my parents and the Garretts also. Not Sarah, she's seen it. The other Garretts," I say with a nervous chuckle.

"Okay, yeah. Sure," Evan says. "So you've planned for a fallout shelter?"

"Wasn't that expensive?" Doris asks at the same time.

"The cement ceiling added some costs to the construction, but it was still within what we could finance. Always nice to be able to get a mortgage," I say with a rueful laugh.

"For sure," Doris says. "We've got our own extensive financing for our compound."

I nod. "When Mollie's dad died a few years back, we were able to pay off all our debt from what he left her. We still had a little left over—that's how we bought the land and started on the trees and dirt work."

"Plus mom's money," Sarah says. "You know, from her job. You used her commission income for extra stuff, right?"

"Right. And to answer your question, Evan, we have something resembling a fallout shelter. Like I said, we're not really in an area where we expect to get fallout from a nuke, but it could happen. We made some minor provisions just in case. So stop by about a quarter to six?"

"Yeah, Jake. We will. See you then," Evan says.

As Sarah and I start toward our house, Tate's truck is cresting the hill where our property starts. I do love our wide-open spaces and being able to see so far. Sarah lets out a yelp of happiness and encourages me to speed up a bit.

Tate and his dad are out of the truck when we pull in. Sarah rushes to Tate for a hug.

"Tate. Keith. Good to see you back. How'd it go?" I ask.

Tate shakes his head. "We made it to the house and filled the utility trailer up. Everything was fine in the immediate neighborhood but getting in was questionable. We noticed lots of broken store windows and a generally bad vibe."

Keith interrupts, "It was nothing like the town we left last night. I couldn't believe the change in just a few hours."

Tate agrees and then continues with his story, "After we finished at the house, we decided to see if we could find any stores to shop at. We ended up going to a neighborhood market and several mini-marts. The ones away from the interstate weren't bad. We tried the Billings SuperMart. It seemed okay but crazy busy. But we thought we heard a shot— "

"Yep. Pretty sure it was a shot," Keith interrupts. "We got out of there right quick after hearing it."

"We bought lots of canned goods," Tate says. "Some mini-marts had better selections than others. We also went to a used clothing store—the one you don't like, Sarah." Sarah makes a face at this, but Tate continues, "It was open, and Dad wanted to get more things for himself, Mom, and Karen. We think they might be here awhile."

"Yeah. I think we might be," Keith says. "I was especially glad we bought the clothes after hearing about the refineries blowing up. You all heard about that?"

Sarah and I both say we did.

"If I'd known about it while we were still in the used store, I would've bought some things I passed on. But I don't think going back to Billings for anything would be a good idea. We'll just make do."

"Karen and I picked up a few things for you all also. Between us, we might have most of what you need."

"Where are Karen and Lois?" Keith asks.

"In the house. My parents are here. They're going to stay while the power is out in town. We were helping Evan and Doris unload, and they're having a coffee break."

"Your parents came to stay?" Tate sounds surprised, as well he should be.

"They did. They'd heard enough before the power went out yesterday to realize this could be a big deal. They couldn't make coffee this morning, and that sealed it for them. Said they are too old to not have electricity."

"Boy, I hear that," Keith says. Keith is only ten years younger than my parents. "We sure appreciate you letting us stay here. At first, I wished we would've not been on the road when this all started. Being at home for this seemed best. Now, I'm not sure. I imagine Tulsa is going to get ugly quick."

"Dad, Tulsa can be ugly every day."

I laugh a little at this. I've been to Tulsa before and didn't think it was too bad.

"You speak the truth, son. And we've been wanting to move. Just not this way, with leaving everything we own there. And poor Karen, not having her dog. I know she's upset about this."

I didn't realize Karen had a dog back home. Missing her friends and her dog is probably a big part of why she was upset. Oh, and the fact we were shot at and terrorists keep trying to kill everyone.

"You think we can get a cup of coffee? I could sure use one after our trip," Keith says.

"Definitely. First, I should tell you about a small incident from earlier. Karen's a little upset about it."

"Okay . . . " Keith says cautiously.

"When we were in town, we came across a guy taking pot shots. One scraped across the hood of my car." I gesture toward the car.

"Uh-oh," Tate says. "Was that the only shot? You two weren't hurt?"

"The only shot when we were in range. He shot a few other times after we were out of range. There were a bunch of neighborhood people around and then the police came. We got out of there."

"I imagine Karen was pretty startled," Keith says. "She's not much of a gun fan. Thinks they're fine for people who live out in the country but doesn't think town or city people should have them. She's never liked the fact I have a few weapons at home. Kind of wishing I'd have thought to bring one along. With the way Billings was today and you two getting shot at . . . seems it might be smart to be prepared to defend my family." He shakes his head sadly.

"Dad, I've brought all of my guns. Even though my collection isn't large, we'll get you set up. Of course, I can't imagine we'll need weapons for anything around here . . . other than maybe shooting a coyote or something."

I pray Tate is right.

Chapter 37

Jake

The rich aroma of coffee hits my nose. I take a deep breath, savoring the aroma. I've tried to quit coffee a few times, but the fragrance is part of the allure and helps feed my addiction. It's similar with chewing tobacco. Cracking open a fresh can and inhaling the first whiff is always a treat.

Over the years, I've quit many times. Quitting is easy; not starting again is what's hard. My tobacco habit has been a bone of contention in my marriage. When things were really bad between us, Mollie would harp on my chewing. She's sure I'm going to get mouth or throat cancer and lose all of my teeth. Sure, it's a valid concern. So I quit . . . at least I told her I quit.

What I was really doing was not chewing around her and sneaking it. Big mistake. She caught me one day, and the blow up was worse than anything we'd ever experienced. While the argument was terrible, it was also a turning point for us. She lightened up on me, and I stopped sneaking. Now, while I openly chew, I still try to be discreet about it. I hate to rub it in her face, especially since her concerns about my health haven't changed.

Mollie . . . where is she?

In the house, I introduce Keith to my parents. Tate, having met them before, shakes my dad's hand and hugs my mom. My mom is not a hugger and she immediately stiffens up. Tate doesn't even notice.

I pour coffee and put out more snacks. I think again about the sausage I took out of the freezer. We made several snack-sized rolls last fall. Every once in a while, I'll pull a roll out for an easy snack. I took this out on Thursday, before everything started, so we'd have it to take hiking on Saturday. Mollie and I planned to celebrate her return with a short loop up in the Big Horns.

Thursday, during the day, life was normal.

Thursday night is when the airplane crashes happened and everything started falling apart.

It hasn't even been seventy-two hours yet, but things feel very different. Our hike would've been yesterday. Instead, I'm spending our days stocking up as best we can and fretting over my missing wife. A wave of despair washes over me. Is Mollie safe? Is she in a ditch somewhere? Is she dead? I excuse myself and retreat to my bedroom. Nobody needs to see me lose it.

Sitting on the bench, I take several deep breaths. My Bible is resting at the end, opened from the last time I was reading. Mollie continually reminds me not to leave books face down and open, for fear of damaging the spine. Picking it up, I glance over the page then quickly flip to Isaiah. I know what I want to read . . . where is it?

Ah, here.

Fear not, for I am with you; be not dismayed, for I am your God. I will strengthen you; yes, I will help you; I will uphold you with My righteous right hand.

One of the suggestions the counselor made early in our sessions was to start reading our Bible together. Over the last few years, we'd stopped attending church. At first it was because of the move. We were so busy we felt we didn't have time to take Sunday mornings off. Then it became a habit compounded by our grief and, oh . . . we had many excuses: we didn't want to drive into town, the church wasn't quite right, we didn't need to go to church to be Christians, we could have our own services at home, and so on.

While it's true we can be believers without attending church, the fellowship of others is important, and we found we didn't have our own services at home. Reading the Bible together was a good suggestion. The counselor had us start with Song of Songs, reading it alone in our bedroom.

I'd never read that book of the Bible and had no idea what to expect. Mollie seemed to know.

The first night, she lit candles and wore a nightgown I hadn't seen her in for years, which showed off her toned arms and strong legs.

She'd done something with her short brown hair. It's cut in what she calls a Pixie and usually lays flat and somewhat smooth. That night, though, it had stuff it in making it spiked in places, with a touch of glitter on the ends. Glitter!

Mollie, a natural beauty, doesn't wear much makeup, but she looked like a fashion model ready for the catwalk. A petite version of a Victoria's Secret Angel, maybe. Her lips were a deep berry color, and her makeup played up all the right features.

There was more glitter on her cheekbones. I had no doubt I'd soon have glitter all over me.

Imagine my surprise to discover this book of the Bible is all about a couple anticipating their love making. Song of Songs was a definite turning point in our bedroom life.

It also spurred us to start reading the Bible with Malcolm, which led us to join David Hammer's neighborhood Bible study.

A friend once told me *Christians are just a bunch of hypocrites.* I suppose that's true. At least it is for me. I'm human. Very human . . . and while I'd love to be perfect and Christlike, my human side tends to win out.

I argue with my wife, use profanity every now and then, occasionally drink too much, can't seem to quit my tobacco habit, and so on, and so on. But I still lean on God for strength, comfort, and wisdom. I'm leaning on him right now, after the tragic events we're experiencing, to bring my wife home to me.

Almost as an afterthought, I think about the thousands of people being affected by these disasters. Those from the original plane crashes, the bridge explosions, the cyberattacks, and now the refineries. So many deaths, so many people hurting.

After coffee, snacks, and visiting for a short while, we get to work unloading. Tate has brought quite a bit of their furniture. I'm surprised how much he was able to fit in the small utility trailer and bed of his truck.

"Jake, we brought several things last night also. I unloaded stuff into the bunkhouse. I need to empty out the camp trailer and then we can get stuff moved into there, but we're going to have a space issue. We brought things we didn't want to lose in case something happened to our rental."

"Okay. Did you and Sarah want to move into the trailer?" I ask.

"We thought the five of us would stay in there," Sarah says.

"Be a bit crowded, don't you think? I haven't been inside, but it seems a little small for five adults. I think we have plenty of space for Keith, Lois, and Karen to stay in the bunkhouse. The only thing is, Katie is bringing her . . . boyfriend. I'm not sure where to put him yet."

"Where will Katie be?" Sarah asks.

I blurt out, "Wherever Leo isn't." End of subject.

"Lois and I thought the bunkhouse was great," Keith says. "Our room is comfortable and plenty big."

"Karen, we could move you to the other bedroom so you don't have to climb up to the loft," I say.

"I like the loft just fine. It isn't a problem to climb the ladder, and with the storage areas, I can tuck my stuff away. Plus, with the window open last night, I could hear the creek. That was great. And, with all of us on one end, it leaves the other end open for someone else." Lois pulls Karen into a side hug.

"Okay, then. Let's set the three of you up in there. If we run out of space, we may have to give you roommates at the other end, like Karen suggested. We'll try not to do that. I'm just not sure who all might show up. Katie and Leo should be here anytime. Karen said she thinks Angela and Tim are coming?"

"Oh, Jake. I thought you knew," Sarah says quickly. "I think they're coming. We were talking yesterday but the phone kept going out. I don't have a for-sure answer but believe they are."

"And Calley?" I ask.

"Not as far as I know." She sighs and shakes her head. "I texted her yesterday and tried to call. I didn't hear back."

I'm disappointed in this but try not to let it show. We all know how Calley can be. "Okay. I bought this new cabin yesterday." I gesture toward it. "It was completely by accident, but I'm happy I did. I think it'll be nice for Angela, Tim, and Gavin."

"Ah, man. I wanted to live there," Malcolm says. Everyone laughs.

"Tate, can you take a few minutes to help me move things into the little cabin—not now, but in a bit?" I ask.

"Sure, happy to help."

"We'll leave the larger cabin empty for now. Katie and Leo can stay in the house. I think we can unload things to where I usually park my truck in the shop. I'd like to park it in there again someday, so this will just be temporary. I want to get Mom and Dad's freezer plugged in and get everyone situated for sleeping tonight.

"Tate, Sarah, right now the trailer is next to the garage. I think we ought to find a better, long-term spot for it. We can leave it there for now, but let's think on where to get you set up with a little more privacy."

“I was thinking of that,” Sarah says. “I’ve spied a few spots I like but can’t commit. We’re fine where we are right now. Oh, unless it’ll bother Grandpa Alvin or Grandma Dodie with us being so close to their apartment.”

“Not at all,” my dad says, while my mom answers, “It’s no bother.”

“Okay, then we’ll leave the trailer there for now,” I say. “I’d like to think this will only be for a few days, but with the newest trouble . . . ” I shake my head but don’t continue my thought. No reason to scare Malcolm, who’s hanging on my every word, any more than needed. Sure wish Mollie was here.

Chapter 38

Malcolm

I'm pretty happy my grandpa and grandma are here. The studio will make a nice house for them. Kind of small, compared to their real house, but I really like it. And the best part is, they'll be right here. I can see them all of the time instead of only when we go to Prospect.

I think they'll be here for a while. I know Dad doesn't want to scare me so he isn't saying too much. But I can see the way all of the adults are looking at each other. They're all sad, for sure, but they're scared too. Maybe I can do what Dad does and try to pretend things are okay.

"You've been in the apartment before, right, Grandma? Do you want me to show it to you again?"

"Sure, Malcolm, that's fine."

"We go in the door here. It's kind of nice with this little porch, and there's a bench you can sit on and look out over the cow field."

Grandma laughs a little. "That's a nice feature. Always good to have a cow pasture nearby."

"Yeah, we can hear them sometimes, but they're not much trouble. They don't smell or anything since it's a nice big field . . . uh, pasture. So here we are. C'mon in the door. Just walk in a few feet and the bathroom is on the right. I like this door. It slides instead of swinging. Dad said it's because the bathroom is kind of small, and the door sliding into the wall takes up less space than a swinging door. It has a special name . . . "

"Pocket door?" Grandma asks.

"Yeah, sounds right. There's a shower but not a tub. Is that okay? If you want to take a bath in a tub, you can use my bathroom in the house. Or you can use Mom's bathtub. It's a claw foot. I'm sure she won't mind."

"Shower is fine. That's what your grandpa and I prefer."

"Okay, good. But if you ever change your mind, you can use my tub. I don't care. The closet is in the bathroom too. Well, not really in the bathroom. There's another one of those pocket doors. You like it?"

"Sure, it looks like a nice closet. With having the coat closet too, we'll have plenty of space for our things."

"Good. Let's go back to the main part. Mom says this is a studio apartment, which means it's really just one big room. The kitchen has most of the stuff you need for cooking, but there's only a stovetop. Mom said we didn't need an oven in here because people can just use the one in our house."

"That's fine, Malcolm. If there's anything we want to bake, we'll come in the house and you can help me with it. Maybe we'll make a cake or some cookies after we get all moved in."

"Sure, that's good. I can help with those things. Your bed is right here. Mom had Dad put a window up the wall, above the headboard. She said it would bring in light but keep the privacy."

"It does bring in light. I like it very much. And the full wall of windows on the far side is very nice."

"Yep. That's your TV watching area. Are you going to move the chairs you brought in here? I don't think they'll fit very well with the chairs over there already."

"I think your dad and grandpa will move these chairs out and move our chairs in. I suspect your dad already has a plan."

"Grandpa can watch TV. It's not a very big one, but since it's such a small room, it should be okay, right? Oh . . . I mean, if the power comes back on. I don't know if the TV's working right now. I guess we can try it."

"We'll try it later. The TV is fine. The whole room is fine."

"And over here, where you said there are windows, those are really glass doors going out to a patio."

"Oh, I see. They're French doors. Very nice. And a little sitting area on the patio."

"You can have your coffee out there in the mornings, Grandma. When Sarah and Tate stayed here, they had coffee and breakfast out there. Sarah said it was a little chilly to be eating outside, but it's June and warm now."

"Hmm. I guess it would make a nice breakfast spot. Good thinking."

"Do you like it?" She seems really happy with it, but I want to make sure.

"Yes, I do, Malcolm. It's very nice."

My grandpa's in the studio now also, standing by the small sink in the kitchen. Dad is right behind him.

"You like it, Grandpa?"

"Yep. It's good. Took a peek in the bathroom. I like the shower. Nice and roomy."

"Malcolm, we're going to move the small chairs out and move the recliners in," Dad says. "You want to scoot on out of here so we have a little room to work? Maybe take your grandma out and show her the view from the patio?"

"Sure. Grandma, let's go outside. You can see the mountain range and the trees in the forest. You can see the house Pete and Amanda live in, and the Snyders' house too."

"Okay. I don't know who Pete and Amanda are, but I'll look at their house."

"Look over there," I say, once we're outside on the patio. "See that house up there that looks a little bit like our shop? That's Pete and Amanda's house. Sometimes Amanda watches me if Mom has to go somewhere and can't take me along. During the summer Pete works for a rancher we know, but during the winter his job is trapping animals, like foxes and coyotes."

"Oh, yes. I think your dad's mentioned them. And where do the Snyders live?"

"Up there at the very top of the hill. Oh, and I forgot about Noah's old house. That little house by the creek is where Noah used to live, but they moved to another house. We can't quite see it from the patio, but if we were in the front yard, we could see it. The little house is still theirs, too, but it's just for guests now. They have a big house and a second, small cabin. Noah's brother is living in the small cabin. Did you know the cabin is really old and even has bullet holes in it from a long time ago?"

"No . . . I don't think I know about the old cabin."

"Yep, there was probably a shoot-out or something. Lots of cowboys used to live around here, and I bet there was bank robbers or something hiding out in the cabin and then the police found them. You think so, Grandma?"

"Hmmm. I suppose that could explain the bullet holes. And how about the tan house over there?"

"I don't know. There are some people who live there, but I can't remember their names. They usually only live there in the summer, but they aren't here right now. At least, I don't think they are. I think Miss Doris said they were visiting their children somewhere. I guess their children are probably happy they were visiting when this all happened," I say, thinking of my mom and how I wish she were here.

"I suspect they are. And I suspect you're missing your mom quite a bit?"

I look at my feet so Grandma doesn't see the tears in my eyes. I quietly answer, "Yeah, I wish she'd hurry up and get home."

The next thing I know, Grandma is hugging me. That's not something she does very often, so it surprises me. Sometimes I'll ask her for a hug, and she'll give me one, but I know it's not her favorite thing. I still know she loves me a lot . . . she just doesn't like to hug. I kind of wish she wouldn't have hugged me because now I can't stop my tears.

Grandma doesn't let go of me until I start to pull away. I wipe my tears before looking up at her.

"I think they have things moved around," she says. "Should we go back in and see how it looks?"

Back inside, Grandma pulls the curtains open so she can look out the glass doors from inside.

"Hmmm, your chairs look good, but they seem kind of big."

"They do seem a little on the large side, but I think they'll work fine. We'll be nice and comfortable in our recliners. The whole room seems very cozy."

My dad and grandpa come back in, each carrying a suitcase.

"Well, Dodie, what do you think?"

"It's just fine, Alvin. Malcolm has done an excellent job showing me everything. It'll be perfect. Jake, is there room for you to put our things in the garage for now, and I'll have your dad bring them in one at a time for me to empty?"

"Sure, Mom. You want the suitcases in the garage also?"

"No, leave them and I'll start to empty those out. There should be another large suitcase and a small overnight bag. I'll take those too. Everything else can go to the garage. Oh, and bring the cooler and boxes from the pantry too. I can probably get those all put away pretty quickly. Can they just sit right outside the door? Maybe on the bench?"

"I'll put them there," my dad says. "Malcolm, can you go to the basement and bring up a solar desk lamp, solar hanging lamp, and two battery-operated lanterns? Do you know where we keep them and what you're looking for?"

"Sure, Dad. I know where they are. I think I know what you want."

"Good, bring one of the NOAA radios also for your grandpa and grandma to have out here."

"Are you going to turn the solar system on for them?" I ask.

"It's already on, Buddy. The lights I'm having you grab are extra." He turns to my grandpa and says, "Dad, the apartment was hooked into grid power, but we also have it connected to the garage solar system. It's not a huge system, but it's large enough to power the fridge and a few outlets. The solar-system-powered outlets have an elk head sticker on them." Dad shows them one of the outlets with the silhouette of an elk on it.

"These outlets will still work. We'll need to figure out lighting for the bathroom. There's an elk outlet in there, so maybe we can do a hanging lamp or something. For now, the battery-operated lights should work in the bathroom and closet."

"I'll go and get those for you," I say.

One of the shelves in the basement holds extra lights. We have lots of different kinds of lights. Mom sees something interesting and buys one to try it out. If she likes it, she buys more.

I find the lights Dad asked for—the ones that charge from the sun—and two battery-operated lanterns like we use for camping. Then I find a little round light which can hang on the wall. This one also uses batteries, and it has a switch to turn it on and off. I think this might be a good light for their closet, so I grab it too. I pick up a package of batteries and take a NOAA radio. I realize I'm carrying quite a bit. To make things easier, I find a box to put everything in.

Dad's still talking with Grandma and Grandpa when I get back to their apartment. The front door is open, with only the screen shut, so I say, "I'm back," then walk in.

I help Dad take the lights out. We put the solar lights by the window to charge. Dad's pretty impressed I brought the small light to use in the closet. He says it was good thinking. After we get everything set up, Grandma starts unpacking.

"Jake, what's the plan?" my grandpa asks my dad.

"What do you mean?" Dad says.

"Mollie's not home yet. You going after her?"

Dad sighs. "I'd sure like to, but I don't even know where she is. She was taking small roads to avoid the interstates and the mass amounts of people on them. I haven't heard from her since yesterday. I wouldn't even know where to start looking."

"Terrible thing. Funny how much we rely on phones now. Can't even find a pay phone if you wanted to. I guess those probably don't work either."

"I don't know. I tried our home phone last night, and there was no dial tone. Maybe I'll try it again. I haven't tried my cell for a while either. I'll give it a shot."

My dad looks at me and gives a small smile.

"So I was thinking," he says to my grandpa, "you should set this up as your own place. I know you two like your privacy. Malcolm will try not to bug you too much." Dad winks at me.

"I'll try."

Dad continues, "We got all of your food, so set up your cabinets and things. You have a cooktop in here. I'm sorry there isn't an oven. We have one in our house, of course, and the bunkhouse has one. I'm sure Lois won't mind if you use it, and it's never a problem to use ours. I'll give you a key to our house, and I have the keys to this place over in the drawer. I have one on my keyring, but I won't use it unless there's an emergency."

"Malcolm already talked to me about the oven," Grandma says. "We're going to make something later, isn't that right, Malcolm?"

"Yes, maybe a cake or cookies or something. Okay, Dad?"

"Sure, that's fine."

"Can I take a shower?" Grandma asks.

"Shouldn't be a problem," Dad says. "The water pump is solar powered, and the on-demand water heater runs on batteries. Let's run the water in the sink to make sure everything works as it should," Dad says, as he turns on the kitchen water.

After fifteen seconds or so, he says, "Yep. It's working fine, so any time you're ready, Mom."

"I won't want to shower until bedtime, so that's fine."

"Okay. Last night we scheduled a meeting at the community center. It's for the same time the president is speaking. Do you want to go to the meeting or stay here?" Dad asks them.

Grandpa doesn't even look at Grandma before saying, "We'd like to stay here." Dad nods and says, "You mind if Malcolm stays with you? Last night's meeting became a little heated. I'd prefer he not be there."

I sigh, wishing I could go along, but then think, maybe we can make the cookies while they are gone.

"No problem at all. Don't suppose the TV works?" Grandpa asks.

Dad smiles and says, "Not sure, it might. We have power from the solar, but I don't know if stations are broadcasting. If there isn't much sunshine, you'll need to monitor your power use. Let me show you where the solar system guts are located in the garage and how to keep track of it."

I follow my dad and grandpa to the garage while Grandma stays in the apartment, putting things away.

After Dad finishes explaining the solar system, he says, "Dad, I'll have Malcolm grab a regular radio for you. In case the TV doesn't work, the radio should pick up the president this evening. The NOAA might also, but I'm not sure how they're doing this right now. It's usually reserved for emergency broadcasts, like storms, but who knows right now. Malcolm, why don't you get the radio we keep in my bathroom and bring it over for your grandparents. It's all set up and ready to go."

"Sure, I'll grab it," I answer before running off to get it. I decide to practice my fast running from the apartment to the house. It's not very far, so I'm pretty quick.

When I get back to the garage, Dad and Grandpa are still standing where I left them. I'm panting from my running.

"Before we go to the meeting tonight," Dad says, "there's something I want to talk with everyone about. Okay?"

"Sure. No problem," Grandpa answers.

"Here you go, Grandpa," I say, handing him the radio between pants.

"Thanks, Malcolm. That'll come in handy if the TV isn't working. Be good to keep up on what's going on. Guess I'll go in and see if I can help put things away. What time you want to have your little talk?" Grandpa asks my dad.

"The Snyders should be here at 5:45."

"Okay, we'll be ready," Grandpa says as he walks to the apartment.

Dad pulls me into a hug. "I really appreciate you helping your grandma and grandpa so much, Buddy. Remember, the apartment is their private space. I don't want you over there bothering them all of the time."

"But, *Daaadd*, they love me. I'm not bothering them when they love me."

"True. But sometimes people need their space."

"Okay," I answer but am not sure I really agree. I don't think Grandma or Grandpa will mind me visiting them.

"Thank you, Malcolm. Now, I have a few things to do. Why don't you give me a hand? First thing is, check and see if we plugged your grandparents' freezer in—I can't remember if we did. Be sure it's plugged into one of the elk outlets."

"The elk outlets—I think it's funny you call them that. Why don't you say 'outlet with the elk sticker on it'?" I ask.

Dad gives me a look, which tells me he knows I know what he means so I should just do as he asks.

"Okay," I say quietly. Then he messes up my hair, making me laugh.

Chapter 39

Jake

With my parents squared away, I check in on Tate and Sarah. Malcolm follows me as we step over to the trailer. It's only a few feet from the garage to my parents' attached apartment, and to the trailer immediately to the right of the apartment.

Sarah and Tate have moved everything out of the trailer and into a pile outside.

"We'll start getting things put in and organized once Sarah gives everything a wipe down. Anything I can help you with in the meantime?" Tate asks.

"Glad you asked. I want to get the new cabin together in case Angela and Tim show up. I'm going to check on the basement room. I think I'll set it up for Katie and put Leo in the guest room in the house. Give me a few minutes to take care of those rooms, then we'll work on the new cabin. At least until Sarah needs you again. Malcolm, why don't you give me a hand?"

As we head for the house, I check my watch. I took my old windup watch out of Mollie's jewelry box. It no longer has a strap, so I'm carrying it in my pocket. Even though my phone still seems to be keeping time, I wasn't sure if it'd continue to work as a timepiece with the cyberwar going on.

It's after 3:30. I'll hustle at getting things put together. It'll be chore time soon, then the Snyders arrive, and then the meeting this evening. Part of me wants to skip the meeting since I expect it may be similar to last night. Just thinking about Dan Morse calling me out gets my blood boiling.

Talk about a storyteller. Some of the things I've heard from Dan were something. At first, they sounded believable. But as time went on, the stories would get more outlandish. Then he'd tell us things, and later we'd hear something else from him. There were many times we caught him in outright lies. He used to ride by our place on his side-by-side regularly, with his AR strapped to his back and his dog in the passenger's seat. When he'd stop to visit, he'd often leave the rifle strapped on and make a point of showing off the "Dirty Harry" gun in his shoulder holster and the Bowie knife on his belt.

Both open and concealed carry are legal, and encouraged, in Wyoming and are truly no big deal. But there's something about the way Dan does it that just doesn't sit right. Instead of carrying, it almost seems to be brandishing in his case. And the way he's always fiddling with his rifle, handgun, or knife . . . maybe it's a nervous habit, or maybe it's his form of intimidation. I don't know, but I don't like it.

~~~~~

Malcolm and I double check the basement room to make sure it's set up for Katie. It's nice and cool, plus the basement bathroom will give her some privacy. We could even turn the rec room into more of an apartment for her. With the bar sink, cabinets, countertop, and small beverage fridge, there's already a kitchenette.

"Katie should like it down here, Dad," Malcolm says, as we quickly spruce up the bathroom. It's not super bad, but things are a little dusty. Same with the bedroom."

"I think she will. Can you take this paper towel and go wipe things down in the bedroom? Once I'm finished here, meet me in the storage section."

"Sure, Dad."

I quickly finish up the bathroom and move into the storage part of the basement. Malcolm is there in just a few minutes.

"Whoa, Dad! Why'd you open up the tunnel? And the safe room too? You have everything wide open!"

"Yeah, I wanted to air things out a bit."

"Did you open up both ends of the tunnel?"

"Sure did."

"Oh . . . I would've helped," Malcolm says, voice dripping with disappointment.

"Sorry, Buddy. I didn't think of it."

"It's fine. Do you need my help with something?"

"Yeah, why don't you do me a favor. I didn't really check the tunnel to make sure there isn't any . . . uh, stuff on the floor. Can you just quickly walk through it and check it out?"

"You bet I can," he exclaims and hurries off.
~~~~~

I take a few minutes to make sure things are situated on the shelves in this open section of the basement. I'm not worried about checking the grocery section or the gun room. I won't be opening those up tonight.

After a few minutes, Malcolm returns. "The tunnel was good. I checked everything out, and it all looks fine."

"Super. Thanks, Buddy. I'm going to leave things opened up and we'll head upstairs. I want to make sure the guest room is good for Leo."

"Oh . . . well, maybe I should go first. There might be some LEGO blocks in there."

"Good idea, I'll be right there."

I take another look around. Everything looks okay, nice and neatly organized, thanks to Mollie. Mollie . . .

Where is she? Why isn't she home? I'm suddenly filled with anger. She should've just driven through Portland on Thursday night. She would've been past there before the bridges were taken out, and she would've been beyond the trouble with the traffic and should've been home by now. But no . . . she let her paranoia take over and she had to get all fancy, trying to take backroads home. And now where is she? I have no idea. I don't even know if she's still alive. I stifle a gasp. Could she be dead?

Of course not. She texted me yesterday. She was fine, somewhere in Idaho. It's absurd to think she's not okay. Kenny, my good friend . . . could it be the same? He and Sharri had called us in the morning. They were on a family road trip and we were to be one of their stops. They called to ask if they could arrive a day early. Sure, no problem, we said. Can't wait to see you. But we didn't see them. They were dead a couple hours later.

Not Mollie.

"Please, God, not Mollie," I cry out. "Bring her home to me. Give us another chance. We're better now; we're working it out. I want to be with her. Don't take her away from me now. Malcolm needs her. I need her. Please, Lord, oh please . . . " I dissolve into tears. For many minutes I continue my prayer, my petition, *Please bring my wife home to me.*

It's several minutes before I pull myself together and head upstairs to the guest room where Malcolm has picked up the toys off the floor and is sweeping.

"Looks great, Malcolm."

"I smoothed out the covers also. The top one was a little wrinkly. I'm pretty sure Mom puts clean sheets on before . . . "

"Yeah," I quickly answer. "The sheets are fine. Go ahead and pick up the debris on the floor, then we're going to head over to the new little cabin."

"You okay, Dad?"

"Sure. Of course."

"You sure? Your eyes look . . . " His voice fades away and he looks at his feet.

"Hey, I'm okay. I was feeling a little sad, but I'm okay now. We're okay, Malcolm. You know that, right? You know that whatever happens, we're okay?"

"You really think so?"

"I really do."

Chapter 40

Jake

Outside, Sarah has Tate and Keith moving things into their trailer. "You ready to set up the place for Tim and Angela?" Tate asks.

"Yep, whenever you are."

"Jake, we brought our couch with us since it's new," Sarah says. "I didn't want to risk losing it or our chairs. You think we could put them in the bunkhouse and move the futons around?"

I think for a second about the new cabin, completely empty of furniture. "Let's see if we can move one of the futons to the new cabin and fit in one of the chairs from the apartment. You want to come look at it and help decide? Tate, we might as well carry the mattress over with us."

A decent-quality mattress is wonderful to sleep on, but terrible to move around. This mattress is no exception. The queen-size makes it plenty awkward.

We only move the mattress a few feet when Tate says, "Could we load it in the truck to get it over there? It's pretty far to be carrying this beast."

A serious duh moment for me. "Great idea. I should've thought of that."

We load it in the truck and drive the mattress to the front door. Getting it inside and up into the loft isn't much fun either, but we get it done. Sarah looks around while we take care of wrestling the mattress.

"Wow, Jake. This place is great. The bathroom's a little rough, but . . . wow. Very nice."

"Yeah, I'm happy with it. Bought it sight unseen from the same guy we got the other cabin from. It's a repo he wanted to unload. Funny thing is, he repo'd it sight-unseen and had no idea it was this nice either. I'm sure he would've priced it considerably higher had he known. He's a good guy, though, and stuck to our original deal. As you probably noticed, the previous owners took out the stuff they could easily sell. It should be fine."

Sarah looks up in the loft and remarks, "It'll be perfect. It looks like a little boy lived up here before. Gavin will love it."

"I think the futon will fit, you agree?" I ask Sarah and Tate.

"Yes, it should fit fine," Sarah says. "Do you have a mattress for Gavin? Looks like a full-size platform on that end."

I shake my head. "No. I'll have to figure something out."

"The mattresses come off the futons in the bunkhouse, right?"

"I don't know. Maybe. I think they sit on the frame. Yes. They do because Mollie put some kind of anti-slide stuff between the frame and the mattress."

"We could bring both futons over here. Put the mattress only upstairs for Gavin to sleep on and set the other up as a couch. One chair from the apartment should fit also and make a fine sitting area. You'll need to stash the frame to the second futon somewhere, since we'll only use the mattress."

"I like the idea. Should be able to store the futon frame in the storage room of the bunkhouse."

"Should we get those moved, Jake?"

"Yeah. Also, Tate, I don't think I told you. There's a meeting tonight at the community center. We'll listen to the speech from the president together, then meet afterward. You're all welcome to come along. You two, and your parents and sister, are part of the community. I don't think the meeting will amount to much, but you should be involved. My parents don't want to go, so they'll stay here. Malcolm's staying with them. It got a little heated last night."

"Sarah told me about the meeting. She also said the Snyders are coming by beforehand for the 'grand tour,'" Tate makes the little air marks to quote grand tour, "and to see all your secrets."

"Ha. Well, I don't know about all my secrets. But, yes, they're coming for the full tour. With the refineries being the latest targets, nothing much would surprise me now. The Snyders are good friends, and I know they'd do anything they could for us—all of us. We'd like to do the same for them. Mollie and I had talked about forming more of a preparedness group with them and a few others, we just hadn't moved forward with it. Wish we would have."

This time, thinking ahead, we drive the truck to the bunkhouse. Tate and Malcolm ride along with me while Sarah returns to working on the trailer setup. We also pick up one of the chairs moved out of the studio apartment. After we arrange the furniture, Tate returns to helping Sarah. Malcolm asks if he can go back to the house—he wants to clean up his room before Katie gets here.

"Really? You're going to clean your room?" I ask with a laugh.

"Well, sure. And I thought I'd maybe draw a picture for Katie. She likes my pictures."

"She does, for sure. Go ahead. I'll be in shortly. I just have a few things I want to do to get this place ready."

I head back toward the new cabin to take some measurements and figure out what I'll need. The hole in the countertop, I want to fill it in. Maybe with a length of 12" x 1" pine? I can piece it together to make a slab, then stain it. We have several leftover stains from various projects. I'll cut it a little longer than the hole and it can sit on top, secured underneath. I'll plop the little one-burner alcohol stove on top of it.

While there's quite a bit to be done to this little cabin, today I'm just doing the basics so they can sleep comfortably tonight, provided they show up. It's 4:18 now, and going to be tight to get things done. Stepping off the porch toward my tool shed, I hear the sound of an engine. Doesn't sound very big, more like four-wheeler size.

I'm about halfway to the shed when the UTV crests the hill. Is that Morse? Great. Maybe he'll give me another drive-by bird.

Don't even look at him, Jake. Just ignore him as he drives by.

Ah, jeez. Is he slowing down? Yep. And turning in the driveway.

Malcolm, from the front porch, hollers, "Dad? What's going on?"

"Go back inside. It's fine."

"Dad?"

"Now, Malcolm."

He nods. I wait until I see the door close before I turn and start slowly walking toward Dan Morse, as he quiets the motor and instructs his dog to stay put.

Tate and Sarah are both standing beside their trailer. I make a motion, which I hope they interpret as stay put, and quietly say, "Let me see what this is about."

My mind's racing. What could he want? I take a deep breath and speak loudly but, I hope, kindly, "Dan. Something I can help you with?"

"Uh, yeah, Jake," he says, stepping out of his side-by-side. "I, uh, my wife she suggested I come and see you. Said maybe I didn't handle things as well as I should've last night. I'm planning to go and see Terry Bosco next."

So, he's here to apologize for being a jerk? Cool. I can handle that. "Okay, I guess we're all a little on edge with the things that have been happening."

"Yes, that's exactly it," his fingers drop to his gun holster. I tense slightly, until I see him rubbing the holster before taking his hand away. Weird. I take note that, while he's wearing his sidearm and Bowie knife, the carbine usually strapped on his back is missing.

"So, I figured, if I came by and talked with you in private, we could come to a suitable agreement."

"Suitable agreement?"

"Yes, for how you can help the community."

"For how I can help the community?"

"Right. I can now see I was wrong to call you out last night. I figure we can reach an agreement, and we can announce it at tonight's meeting."

"Dan, I think I must have missed part of the conversation. What is it we're agreeing to?"

"You know, how you can help the community. Didn't I already say that?"

"You did . . . " What is going on here?

"Okay, this is what we'll do. Since you have power, you need to offer up your fridge and freezer. I brought a few things over with me to tuck in, then tonight, we'll let others know."

What the . . .

"I also need to charge my cell phone. We don't have any clocks, and my battery's about dead. I'll leave it and my portable battery. You can bring them to the meeting tonight."

I'm slightly dumbfounded as I blurt out, "Can't you just charge it in your car?"

"Nope. Car charger broke. So, where's your freezer?"

"You're kidding, right?"

He doesn't answer, simply stares.

A few years ago, I'd be stumbling over my words trying to make a point. But Mollie taught me a few negotiating skills, and especially "he who speaks first loses," so I say nothing, waiting him out.

"Kidding about what?" he finally spouts.

"All of this. You want me to keep your food for you and charge your electronics? And you want me to do the same for everyone else in Bakerville?"

"Well, not everyone. I'm sure there are a few people who won't need it. But, yes. I think it's the neighborly thing for you to do. Don't you?"

"Go home, Dan. I can't help you."

Anger fills his eyes. "Can't or won't?" he barks, as his left index finger caresses his Bowie knife.

"Take your pick. There are things I'm willing to do, *to be a good neighbor*, but I can't help with the things you're asking. I do have an extra charger that will work in your vehicle. I also have a frozen pop bottle you can use to keep your food cool for now. I'd suggest you cook and use your fresh food first. Let me grab those things for you."

"I knew I was right about you. My wife said you were a good guy, that you had a good *heart*. But I knew all along you could care less about your neighbors. You care only for yourself. You made this little . . . compound . . . and outfitted it with everything you'd need—everything our community needs—but you're going to hoard it. Selfish. That's what you are. Selfish."

"It's time for you to go, Dan." Anger's welling up inside me, threatening to brim over. It's like with Glen, his arm snaking around my neck . . . and my desire to neutralize him. *Neutralize means dead, Jake.*

"Fine." His right hand caresses his holster. "I'll take the charger and ice block, then be on my way. Don't think for a minute this is over. I'll make sure everyone knows you're out for yourself and that's all. People like you and Terry, acting like you're so . . . so . . . "

"Jake," Tate says quietly, causing me to jump. "I grabbed a frozen soda bottle and a dual port car charger."

"Oh, who's this, Jake? Company?" Morse sneers.

"Go ahead and hand them to him, Tate," I say, nodding in Dan's direction.

Tate thrusts the ice block toward him, which seems to fluster Dan and throw him slightly off balance.

"Be careful, you jerk," Dan snaps. "This isn't over, Caldwell. You had a chance to do the right thing, to show your commitment to our community. You think I'm here only of my own volition? There are several of us who see you and your ilk trying to take over. We won't be cowed into silence by loudmouthed slobs like you, Bosco, and Snyder, spouting off and assuming you can squelch any opinions not complying with your brain-dead teabilly sensibilities."

Between clenched teeth, I hiss, "Goodbye, Morse."

Part of me wants to turn my back on him, shun him, as I walk away. But the idea of turning my back on this weasel . . . not happening.

He tosses the frozen soda bottle and charger onto the passenger seat, barely missing the dog. "Did you see what you made me do? Almost hurt my dog. You better be glad he's okay or else I'd be . . . " The engine roars, drowning out whatever he was saying. He throws the engine into reverse, almost killing it, then spins around, shooting gravel everywhere. His middle finger flies a salute as he reaches the road.

"What just happened?" Tate asks, completely bewildered.

"Not completely sure, but Dan Morse . . . I don't think he's quite right."

"I'll agree with that."

A noise causes me to look over near Tate and Sarah's trailer. There's my dad, iron-sight rifle in hand, walking around the corner. Guess I wasn't the only one thinking we might need to do some neutralizing.

Neutralize means dead, Jake.

Chapter 41

Jake

"What was that all about, Jake?" my dad asks, cradling his old open sight .30-30.

"I'm not really sure. You heard him, about using our freezer and charging his phone?"

"I heard him. At first, I thought, 'Okay, that's kind of odd, but would be neighborly.' Have to say, I was kind of surprised when you told him to leave. At least you did offer him alternatives. I got a little concerned with the way he was rubbing his knife and gun, which is why I grabbed my rifle. Would've hated to have to shoot him, but who rubs their gun like that? Seemed like a threat."

"He does that. Kind of a nervous habit. Glad you didn't shoot him for it, but also glad you had my back."

"Yep. So, what was that about?"

"I don't know any more than what he said. Last night, at our community meeting, he called me out. But this—this was just peculiar."

"Why didn't you just let him use the freezer?"

I let out a big sigh. Should I have? "I don't know, Dad. Maybe I should've. But if I did, where would it end? Would he be happy to just keep a few things here and come up and get his food as needed? Or would he start needing more and more? I have no problem with helping out the community—Mollie and I have even planned for it—but helping out is going to be on my terms. I'm not going to be bullied into— " I realize I'm yelling.

My dad, mom, Sarah, Tate and even Malcolm, who's no longer in the house but now standing with the group, are all staring at me. Over near the garage, a safe distance away, Keith, Lois, and Karen look wide eyed.

I'm shaking and need to wipe spit from my chin. Have I ever been this angry before? I take a deep breath. "Malcolm, I thought I asked you to stay in the house?"

He shakes his head and starts to cry. "Sorry, Dad," he sputters. "I saw him leave and thought it was okay to come out. I didn't know you were so— " He breaks down in tears.

I open my arms to pull Malcolm in; he hesitates for a moment before launching himself toward me. I can feel my face, no longer hot with anger but now red with embarrassment. My outburst is quelled and replaced by shame. I wish Malcolm wouldn't have seen me like this.

Is my dad right? Should I have just let Morse use our freezer? I have a small portable freezer in my processing room. We could plug it and open it up to the neighborhood.

"You were right to turn him away, Jake," Sarah says firmly.

What's this? Sarah, particularly compassionate and concerned about people who face disadvantages, should be the last person to agree with me. She feels everyone's pain. I lift Malcolm's chin and give him a nod and a wink. "Sorry, Buddy."

"Sarah's right, Jake," Tate says. "You don't want someone like him around. 'Give a mouse a cookie, he'll want a glass of milk.' A slippery slope for sure. If you want to help people, which I know you and Mollie have planned to do, it should be on your terms. You've spent your time and money to put this place together. And Sarah and I—my family also—are very grateful. Maybe . . . maybe I'm saying this partly out of my own selfishness, but you let a guy like that come around, and none of us will be provided for. He'll take more and more, leaving us less and less."

"Well, Jake. When he puts it that way," my dad proclaims, "I have to agree. You've got your other kids to think about too. Katie's going to be here shortly, sounds like Angela also. I don't want my grandkids and my great-grandson going without. Wishing Dodie and I would've done more to plan for something like this. Have to admit, we knew a little of what you were doing and kind of thought you and Mollie were . . . " He puts his index finger to his temple and twirls it. *Thanks, Dad.* "But now, I guess you were right."

Keith, now standing with our group, says, "We only caught the tail end of what was happening, but I agree with my son and your dad. There's always people like that, people who take, take, take. Nip it in the bud now. 'Course, I guess the fact that you opened up your home to us, maybe people might think we fall under the same category. I'm telling you now—Lois, Karen, and me—we'll be pulling our weight.

I might be old and fat, but I'm not dead. And as long as I'm not dead, I'll be at your service."

He gives a deep bow and flourish of his right hand, mimicking removing his hat. He may have even clicked his heels together. His overtly exaggerated gesture breaks the tension, even giving Malcolm a laugh.

"Thank you, Keith." I reach my hand out to him. He grabs it and pulls me in for a hug. I guess this is where Tate gets his hugging from.

"Something you probably know," my dad says, "guys like him, they don't give up easily. I'd expect him to be back."

We spend only a few additional minutes discussing the issue. Then I return to what I was working on before Dan showed up. Getting my mind back on the projects isn't easy. Dan Morse is nuts. While I've often thought him a little off, it's clear he's gone beyond being just a little off. Way beyond. And my dad's probably right. He'll be back. And he'll probably make a stink at the meeting tonight. Great.

I take a deep breath and think of Mollie. Where is she?

I can't help but think things didn't go as planned. If they had, she'd be home by now. Even if she stopped somewhere last night, she'd be home. I'm concerned. Even though it's against our agreement, I'd go looking for her if I had any idea where to look.

When I last heard from her yesterday via text, she was somewhere in Idaho. Originally, she was going to try to catch I-90 away from where it was backed up. Did she? Or is she still on some backroads somewhere? Is she coming down from Montana? Did she come through Yellowstone? Or did she have to circle back and will be coming home from the south? Too many options. It'd be like looking for a needle in a haystack. *Stop. You don't need to start bawling your eyes out again, Jake.*

Jeez, I seem to be waffling between sadness over Mollie and anger over Dan.

Focus on the task at hand.

I find the stuff I need for the hole in the counter and to anchor the cabin, so in case a strong wind comes up, it doesn't blow away. Strong wind . . . I pay pretty close attention to the weather reports. When winds are predicted, I'll often batten down the hatches. With our location, close to the mountains, we can get some doozies. Mountain waves. We pay attention when those high wind warnings are issued. I guess those warnings are now a thing of the past.

Better set up the bathroom facilities. A five-gallon bucket and a smaller two-gallon bucket will work for putting the compost toilet into service. They'll need a wash bin and some sort of bathing options. The small shower can hold one of our solar showers. Need a hook from the ceiling to hang it from. Ha. Angela isn't going to like a compost toilet and camp shower. She'll be fine with the rest of the cabin, but not those features.

What else? The beds need bedding. Should have thought of this in town today; I could've bought things then. Mollie has a collection of extra sheets and blankets in one of the cabinets in the house. I'll see what I can find.

Also need to bring over drinking and washing water. I'll fill a gallon-size water cooler with boiling water for washing. No sink in the bathroom, but they can use the sink in the kitchen with a bucket underneath since the outgoing plumbing isn't in place. I'll leave a couple gallons of water from our storage for drinking. I have the supplies to put together a DIY filter system using five-gallon buckets, a faucet, and Berkey filter elements.

The Berkey system is our chosen water filtration method. We have a large system in the kitchen and smaller systems in the rec room kitchenette, our bathroom, and each of the guest quarters. Yeah, we're big Berkey fans. The DIY kits aren't nearly as attractive as an actual Berkey, which looks something like a commercial-sized coffee maker, but it'll do the job. Now that I think about it, I wonder if we might not have another system in storage. I'll have to take a look.

This is taking me forever. I found the stuff I wanted okay, but with the low ceiling of the loft space, getting the beds made and ready is a chore. I should've had Malcolm help. I went ahead and closed off the access to the root cellar and shut up the safe room while I was in the basement looking for stuff. I even grabbed a replacement NOAA alert radio for the kitchen.

Now that the cabin is done, what about dinner? Frozen pizzas? We have way too many. It'd be good to use those up since they won't hold up as well to my freezer manipulation tactics. Eight ought to be enough for tonight, and we should even have leftovers. No need to preheat the oven. Just add an extra five minutes to the timer for the quickest-baking pizza. Seriously, it just needs to be hot and bubbly, right? The pizzas will be done before the Snyders get here, so they can enjoy a slice with us.

"Hey, Malcolm," I holler up the stairs.

"Yeah, Dad?"

"Let's get started on the chores. I've got pizza in the oven. We've got twenty-five minutes before the first ones are done."

Penny and Scooter are suddenly barking their heads off. Too early for the Snyders—only five minutes before 5:00.

Maybe Mollie is home!

Chapter 42

Jake

I look out the window, no . . . not Mollie in a small rental car, but a red truck pulling a long trailer. Tim! Angela is following in her Jeep.

"It's Tim and Angela!" Malcolm exclaims from the upstairs window. He's in such a hurry he almost falls down the stairs.

We're out the door. "Wait until they park before you go running out," I caution him, right on his heels.

Malcolm is super excited and stands on the apron of the garage, jumping up and down waiting.

Another car crests the hill. Is that . . . ?

Yes! *Calley!* Her SUV, followed by her husband Mike's truck.

Calley, my second to youngest daughter and definitely the most stubborn of the bunch, was always so adamant there'd be no reason for them to leave their home to come up here. What happened for them to change their mind? Three more vehicles. Don't recognize them. A dark blue Chevy pickup, a black Yukon, and a silver Dodge Ram; both pickups are pulling trailers.

Calley's out of her Tahoe and running over to me for a hug.

"Jake! I'm so glad we're here. I'm sorry I didn't call. I couldn't get through. You don't mind, right?"

I hug her tight. "I don't mind at all, Calley. I'm very happy you decided to come here. With everything going on and the phones not working, it's a relief."

Mike is at her side. He looks terrible. Both eyes are black, and his nose is swollen and misshapen.

We're not huggers, so I reach out my hand to him. "Mike, I'm glad you're here." I choose not to mention how he looks. I look over his shoulder; there's Mike's dad, mom, and sister. Mollie was right to invite them, and likely the only reason Calley is here.

"Jake, glad to be here," Mike says. "I had a run-in with someone at the gas station yesterday. He thought I cut in front of him. Caught me off guard and whopped me a few good ones. I was on the ground when people started pulling him off of me. Lots of things like that happening around Casper. So, we decided to head up here until things calm down. Hope you don't mind my folks came along? We're all off work for now, until the trouble is over, and we were all a little jumpy."

"It's perfectly fine. Things won't be a problem here like they were in Casper." I think about the shooter from earlier and the recent confrontation with Dan. At least, I hope there won't be problems. "Who else is with you guys?" I ask, glancing around.

Katie.

She jumps out of the Dodge and sprints my way. Pandemonium reigns.

We're all crushed together. Malcolm has wrapped himself around Calley. Angela hands Gavin to Sarah so we can hug. *Thank you, Lord, for bringing them here safely.* Angela's father-in-law is also with them—oops, didn't even think about him coming. Art is an interesting sort. Where can he stay? We'll figure it out.

Tate's hugging anyone holding still. My parents are even in the fray. Katie pushes her way through the craziness. Angela grabs her and pulls her toward us, making a three-way hug.

"Jake, I thought we'd never get here," Katie cries.

"You made it. You're here. It's all good now. Heard about the trouble your town's having. I'm so glad you left before it started."

"Yes. Leo was the one who said we should. Come over and meet him."

"Not sure I can," I say with a laugh. She signals him to move closer, as I untangle myself from the crowd.

"Leo, this is Jake. Jake, Leo," Katie says by way of introductions.

Leo offers his hand. "Leo Burnett, sir. I'm pleased to meet you."

"Hi, Leo. Jake Caldwell. Thanks for helping Katie get home."

"Yes, sir. Thank you for allowing me to join Katie and all of you here. I appreciate it."

"You're welcome." I'm not sure what else to say. So far, he seems nice enough, but I'll wait to reserve my judgement until I get to know him a little better. It's not that I don't trust Katie's judgement, but I sincerely doubt he's anywhere near good enough for her.

Of course, I thought something along those lines for each of the girls' spouses before they were married. So far so good. I've gained three fine sons through marriage.

"Mom's not here yet?" Katie asks, looking around.

"Not yet. Hopefully soon."

She nods sadly. "We brought lots of stuff, Jake."

I'd noticed all of the vehicles seem fully loaded.

Katie continues, "Leo and I brought things from home, and we all stopped and shopped in Wesley when we heard about the latest attacks on the refineries. I can't believe how bad this is."

"I know. The refinery attacks will really be a challenge to overcome. It sounds like they hit all the big ones. Maybe we'll know a little bit more when the president speaks tonight. Oh, by the way, we're having a community meeting tonight. We set it up last night for the same time the president is now scheduled to speak. We'll put it on the radio there. Not sure what the turnout will be, but you can join us."

"Okay. We should probably try to unload some things tonight. Maybe we should start before we go. You think, Leo?"

"Actually," I say, "why don't we hold off? The Snyders are going to be down here in a few minutes. I invited them for the grand tour."

"The *full* grand tour?" Katie asks.

"Yes. Thought it might be a good idea. Good idea for all of you."

Leo, to his credit, says nothing. Katie's quiet for a moment and then says, "You think so?"

"I don't know. Maybe. With everything that has happened, I'm not sure what to think."

"And Mom's not here. What are we going to do? We need to get her home."

"I'm not sure how we could, Katie. I don't know where she is. I haven't heard from her since yesterday, and there's too many routes she could've taken. We just have to wait."

Katie starts to cry. I pull her into a hug. Like her, I wish there was something we could do. Something to get Mollie home.

"Things seem grim right now. But I know your mom. As much as we want her here, she wants to be here and is doing everything she can to get home. She'll make it home. I *know* she will."

The adventure continues in
Katie's Journey: Havoc in Wyoming, Part 2.

Thank you for spending your time with the people of Bakerville, Wyoming.

If you have five minutes, you'd make this writer very happy if you could write a short Amazon review. I appreciate you!

Join my reader's club!
Receive a complimentary copy of *Wyoming Refuge: A Havoc in Wyoming Prequel.* As part of my reader's club, you'll be the first to know about new releases and specials. I also share info on books I'm reading, preparedness tips, and more.

Please sign up on my website:
MillieCopper.com

Now Available

Havoc in Wyoming

Part 2: Katie's Journey

Katie loves living on her own while finishing up her college degree, working her part-time jobs, and building a relationship with her boyfriend, Leo. When disaster strikes, being away from family isn't quite so nice, and home is over a thousand miles away. Will she make it home before the United States falls apart?

Part 3: Mollie's Quest

Two or three times a year, Mollie Caldwell travels for business. Being away from her Wyoming homestead is both a fun time and a challenge. The farm—started to help provide for an uncertain future for their family, friends, and community—keeps the family busy, meaning extra work for her husband while she's away. This time while on her business trip, disaster strikes. Mollie is determined to make her way home. Will she be successful?

Part 4: Shields and Ramparts

The United States, and the community of Bakerville, face a new threat… a threat that could change America forever. As the neighbors band together, all worry about friends and family members. Have they found safety from this latest danger?

Part 5: Fowler's Snare

Welcome to Bakerville, the sleepy Wyoming community Mollie and Jake Caldwell have chosen as their family retreat. At the edge of the wilderness, far away from the big city, they were so sure nothing bad could ever happen in such a protected place. They were wrong. Now, with the entire nation in peril, coming together as a community is the only way they can survive. But not everyone in the community has the people of Bakerville's best interest at heart.

Part 6: Pestilence in the Darkness

Surrounded by danger, they band together with the community of Bakerville to move to a new defensible location. But they weren't prepared to have to give up so much for the security they so desperately need. And they quickly learn trust must be earned, not freely given.

Part 7: My Refuge and Fortress

When Jake and a group of hunters return to Bakerville and find their former neighbors slaughtered, they realize there is a new, even more deadly threat. Will their reinforced location be secure enough? And what about the radio announcement from the president? Will his promise of help arrive in time?

Find these titles on Amazon:
www.amazon.com/author/milliecopper

Acknowledgments

Thanks to:

Ameryn Tucker my editor, beta reader, and daughter wrapped in one. I had a story I wanted to tell, and Ameryn encouraged me and helped me bring it to life.

My youngest daughter, Kes, graphic artist extraordinaire, who pulled out the vision in my head and brought it to life to create an amazing cover.

My husband who gave me the time and space I needed to complete this dream and was very patient as I'd tell him the same plot ideas over and over and over. Two more daughters and a young son who willingly listened to me drone on and on about story lines and ideas while encouraging me to "keep going."

Wayne Stinnett, author (WayneStinnett.com). A few years ago, I was looking for tips on moving my nonfiction PDF books to a new platform. I read Mr. Stinnett's book *Blue Collar to No Collar*, and while there were useful tips for nonfiction, what I really discovered was, I had a story I wanted to tell. As long as I can remember, I'd start creating narratives in my head and, occasionally, moving them to paper. *Blue Collar to No Collar*, and specifically Wayne's personal story, inspired me to move forward. Imagine my thrill and surprise when an email to him received a response and tips on how to proceed in my own publishing. Thank you, Mr. Stinnett! I'm also a fan of his fiction works, *Jesse McDermitt Caribbean Adventure Series* and *Charity Styles Novel Caribbean Thriller Series*—very fun reads!

My amazing Beta Readers! Thank you, Jennifer B., Julie B., Janet K., and Barbara P. An extra special thanks to GS who gave me valuable feedback on an earlier edition to help produce the copy you just read, Tim M. for his expertise in firearms and all things that go boom, Joe I. for reminding me to keep it simple, and Judy S. for always saying, "I can't wait to find out what happens next!"

And to you, my readers, for spending your time with the people of Bakerville, Wyoming. If you liked this book, please take a moment to leave a review on Amazon, Goodreads, or your favorite book site. I appreciate you!

Notes on Caldwell's Homestead

For the fictional Caldwells, preparedness is a lifestyle. Many times, a book like this will result in a wake-up to the need to become prepared. Or for those who are already preparedness-minded, the need to move on to the next level.

To help you with your "prepper" research, I've developed a Pinterest page full of information shared in Caldwell's Homestead. Go to: https://www.pinterest.com/MillieCopper33/havoc-in-wyoming-part-1-caldwells-homestead/

About the Author

Millie Copper, writer of Cozy Apocalyptic Fiction, was born in Nebraska but never lived there. Her parents fully embraced wanderlust and moved regularly, giving her an advantage of being from nowhere and everywhere.

As an adult, Millie is fully rooted in a solar-powered home in the wilds of Wyoming with her husband and young son, milking ornery goats and tending chickens on their small homestead. In their free time, they escape to the mountains for a hike or laze along the bank of the river to catch their dinner. Four adult daughters, three sons-in-law, and three grandchildren round out the family.

Since 2009, Millie has authored articles on traditional foods, alternative health, homesteading, and preparedness-many times all within the same piece. Millie has penned five nonfiction, traditional food focused books, sharing how, with a little creativity, anyone can transition to a real foods diet without overwhelming their food budget.

The twelve-installment *Havoc in Wyoming* Christian Post-Apocalyptic fiction series uses her homesteading, off-the-grid, and preparedness lifestyle as a guide. The adventure continues with the *Montana Mayhem* series, scheduled for release in the summer of 2021.

Find Millie at www.MillieCopper.com
Facebook: www.facebook.com/MillieCopperAuthor/
Amazon: www.amazon.com/author/milliecopper
BookBub: https://www.bookbub.com/authors/millie-copper